BOOK BOYFRIENDS

MELISSA WHITNEY

AI RESTRICTIONS

ABOUT THE BOOK

Who needs real men when you have book boyfriends?
Romance author Georgia Lane wishes to find the kind of love
she writes in her books. But as they say, be careful what you
wish for.
After yet another terrible first date— in a series of bad dates—
Georgia fears she'll never get her happy ever after. After a
devastating heartbreak and an unbreakable case of writer's
block, she may not even be able to write one.
Until a "lucky" penny changes everything and Georgia comes
face-to-face with three ideal book boyfriends—a dashing
duke, an adorable boy next door baker, and a sexy werewolf
alpha. They are everything she wants, which is why she
wrote their stories to begin with.
These three men are not just carbon copies of the characters
from one of Georgia's books, but the actual men. Transported
from their books to the real world, each believes they may be
her happy ending. Now, Georgia is in a literary version of The
Bachelorette. They're perfect, but are they perfect for her?
All she needs to do is date them to find out. Except, what
happens to the other two once she picks one? To the leading
ladies they left behind in their books? Not to mention Geor-

gia's growing feelings for Davis Mackenzie, a blind date gone wrong that is now going very right.

Can a woman whose business is writing happy endings find one for herself in this *The Bachelorette* meets *Lost in Austen* sexy romcom?

NOTE FROM THE AUTHOR/CONTENT WARNING

Dear Reader,

Is this really the sixth time I am writing an author's note? It seems like just yesterday when I sat down to write my first book, and here I am publishing my sixth one.

Like Georgia, storytelling has long been part of my life. As a disabled kid growing up in a less-than-ideal home situation, stories gave me refuge. They provided comfort and hope for my own HEA. Fast forward, I'm in the middle of my HEA with a life I am so grateful for. Amazing friends. A career I love. Writing. A pug. Married to my real life book boyfriend.

Book Boyfriends started as an idea I mulled over during a writers' retreat as I listened and discussed the way stories shape our lives. I kept thinking about what it would be like for an author to unspool the threads of her stories with her actual life. Before I knew it, the story took flight, and here we are.

While *Book Boyfriends* is a fantastical and sexy romcom with a guaranteed happy ending, there may be some things that are difficult for some readers. Your mental health is important, so please take care of yourself while reading. The following is discussed and/or depicted in the book: consensual sex (on page), gaslighting (not between the FMC/MMC), false labor (not the FMC), ableism (discussed), impact of autistic burnout (discussed), impact of chronic illness (discussed), cheating (discussed and not by the FMC/MMC), parental death (discussed), parental substance abuse (discussed), parental divorce (discussed), and consumption of alcohol (on page).

Your mental health is more important than my book. If any of these topics are too much for you, please do what you need to do to take care of yourself.

Book Boyfriends is a work of fiction. While there are some real places mentioned, details may have been fictionalized for the sake of the story. Any resemblance to a real person or place is purely a coincidence.

Thank you,
  Melissa

I *wish I were on a date with Captain Wentworth.* Davis Mackenzie is *no* Captain Wentworth. In fairness, none of my dates ever hold a candle to my dream book boyfriend. They don't have to be top-tier Austen male romantic leads, but at least in the ballpark of the book boyfriends that cause my pulse to race. In the pages of my favorite romances are the perfect men. Men who do battle, traverse distant lands, and say all the pretty words while still ensuring their lady is well-sexed.

In real life, I'm sitting across from Davis. He's thirty-six, single, and breathing. Just my type. At least, that's what my younger brother Jackson must think.

"It's fascinating, Georgia. It all happened on Bainbridge Island," Davis says, his focus fixed on his phone.

"The island off Seattle? What happened there?" I cock an eyebrow, which he'll not notice since his vision appears permanently fused to his phone.

We're twenty minutes into this meet/cute orchestrated by my younger brother, and the only connection here is between him and his phone. Even my breasts, served up on a platter thanks to this gravity-defying pushup bra, aren't dragging his attention.

"Joel Pichard and Bill Bell founded pickleball in 1965 on Bainbridge Island," Davis goes on about the one topic that's dominated this blind date: pickleball.

I'm not anti-pickleball, even if I am not a sporty girl. It would just be nice to talk about anything else or for him to ask about me. Right now, it would be nice if he'd look at me.

Note to self: never again accept a date with someone Jackson has raved is 'just my type'. I bite the inside of my cheek, attempting to force my face into a serene expression.

My younger brother means well. Everyone means well. Our soon-to-be-a-dad, older brother, Rem. My best friend, Hope. Colleagues from work. They all want me to have a relationship that lasts beyond the first date.

This isn't the best first date but it isn't the worst. It's not like the guy who robbed me after I went to the bathroom or the one who asked for the server's number in front of me.

At least Davis is attractive. If you're into neat, dark stubble brushed across a strong jawline, thick raven hair, and ashen eyes rimmed in gold which peek out from behind trendy black-framed glasses. With his height, which I clocked at just over six foot, and the lean physique visible beneath a blue short-sleeved button-up, he has the "hot nerd" look that sends a tingle to my lady bits. It's almost enough to wash away the simmering annoyance at the tick of checking his phone every three minutes. *Almost.*

"You've never played pickleball?" Right eyebrow arched, he looks up.

Well, that got his attention. Grinning, I lean against the chair's cushioned back. "Nope."

"How is that possible?"

"I'm more of an indoor kind of girl." I sip my pineapple cider. Its crispness explodes on my tastebuds. At least, for this blasé date, I'm at Fisher's Landing, my favorite—and the only

—local gluten-free brewery with their unrestricted menu of tidbits and ciders for my consumption.

"There are indoor courts," he says, his stare—again—drags back to his phone.

Seriously, dude? "Do they now?" My tone skews flippant.

I could be flirty and bat my lashes. The only promise I made to Jackson was to go on this date, and here I am. I don't have to feign flirtation for someone whose focus is elsewhere. I may be single, but I'm not desperate. It's far better to be lonely than unhappy. It took a devastating heartbreak and the last five years to drill that lesson into my head.

He leans against the chair's high back. "Maybe on date two, I can introduce you to the sport. On an indoor court, of course."

Second date? I almost choke on my drink. Beyond our shared basket of steak fries, there's no commitment. Drinks are all I promised my brother. This happy hour meeting is for Jackson's sake, not mine. An evening in with a good book and takeout is far superior to the squeeze of these Spanks, and this black mini-dress Hope talked me into.

But I promised… At least, I get french fries. Bad dates—really anything—are always better with french fries. I rarely get a chance to indulge in the salty treat while I'm out, due to my celiac disease. Most places lack a dedicated fryer or kitchen to ensure gluten-free options. That oversight often results in stomach cramps, migraines, and too much bonding time with the toilet for me.

"Have you been here before?" I pluck a fry from the basket.

"Nope." His long fingers tap against his phone screen.

"It's a favorite spot for my best friend, Hope, and me."

He simply nods.

"Do you have a best friend?"

"Yep." His focus remains tethered to his phone.

With a tap of my kitten heel against the chair's leg, I force my mouth into an almost painful smile. "Besides pickleball, what kinds of things do you enjoy doing?"

A vee forms front and center on his brow. "Hike."

"Guess you're an *outdoorsy* guy."

"Sure." With a shrug, his attention moves back to his phone.

I bite back an annoyed breath. "My older brother, Rem, is a big hiker. He loves Chino Hills. Which trails do you like?"

"Lots of them."

Seriously! The fries here are good but not worth this. Blind dates aren't my thing either, but at least I'm present. Davis appears more décor than an engaged partner. Granted, what hiking trails do you like isn't going to whip me into a verbal frenzy, but I'm at least trying.

I brush my long brown hair behind my ears. "If you need to be doing something else, it's okay. If you need to leave—"

"What?" Confusion twists his features when he looks up.

I wave between us. "You've been looking at your phone a lot."

"I… I didn't realize… Sorry." He places the phone on the table.

"If you need to go, it's okay."

He rubs the back of his neck. "No. I'm here, Georgia."

My nose crinkles. "Are you sure? Because we can call this if you want…"

"Yes—" His face scrunches "—I mean, no. I don't…. We don't need to call it. Let's do this. I promised your brother, and I hate breaking my promises."

Promised my brother? Great! Did Jackson call in a favor for this blind date? My dating history is less than stellar, but I had no idea it was *younger brother calls in a favor* bad. When Jackson told me there was a guy he wanted me to meet, I assumed it was because he thought we'd get on. However, Davis's engagement screams uninterested.

Is this how my younger brother sees me? Desperate? Shifting in my seat, mortification blazes my cheeks.

For several beats, we stare at each other. The clank of dishes, chatter from other patrons, and muffled music from the bar's speakers spin around us. It's the trademark awkward first date pause, where neither of the participants knows what to say. In a book, my *actual* love interest would rescue me from this awkwardness. My real-life book boyfriend isn't in sight. No dashing duke, cinnamon roll baker, or devoted werewolf alpha is coming to my rescue.

"You're not athletic like your brothers."

My spine stiffens at the *statement of fact* aspect of his question. True, I'm not cut out of marble like the pickleball champion of Southern California across from me. With my round hips, thicker thighs, and squishy belly, I'm built for comfort. I detest running, love pastry, and adore my soft curves. Still, I bristle at the undertone of his accusation about my lack of athletic prowess.

"Why do you say that?"

"You're an indoor girl, remember?" He smirks.

"I can think of some *very* athletic indoor activities." I skate my fingertip around the glass's rim.

Interest sparks in his eyes.

"Yoga," I say with a *dream on, buddy* lilt.

Davis may have this whole hot nerd aesthetic thing going on, but I don't plan to engage in *indoorsy* activities with him. I've been fooled by a handsome face before. Though fooled seems a poor choice of words for what Will did and its impact on my heart. *But we're not going to think about that.*

"Yoga?" Davis huffs a breathy chuckle. "Can't imagine someone from Jackson's gene pool not being into competitive sports. They call him Beast at the pickleball courts."

"It's a deep genetic pool… Lots of options." My gaze flicks around the crowded bar.

This isn't the first time someone's noted the difference

between me and my siblings. Rem and Jackson are your poster children for Type A personalities. Sports. Grades. Careers. It's all a competition for them.

Then there's me, Georgia Lane. Sometimes, it's as if the only thing we have in common, besides a shared last name, is each being named after one of Dad's favorite artists.

"Jackson says you write." He dips a fry into the ketchup.

"He did?" Queasiness swirls in my stomach at the idea that Jackson is telling people about my writing.

"He says it's a hobby of yours."

And there it is, the reason for that churn in my belly. Hobby may be the kindest term my brothers used to describe my writing.

I clear my throat. "It's not exactly a hobby. I've published three novels."

"Really?" His head tilts. "Impressive. Jackson didn't mention that. Who's your publisher?"

"I am."

After years of scribbled story ideas and starts/stops with manuscripts, I completed my first novel four years ago. Instead of the traditional path of querying agents even to have a chance at a publisher, I took a different route. Not waiting, I got a freelance editor and cover artist and did all the things to independently publish. And honestly, that's a big deal, all businessy and stuff.

"Did you self-publish because you couldn't get an agent?"

"No." I narrow my gaze. "I prefer to have control over my career."

He nods. "And you make a living at it?"

"Not yet."

It's *the* dream, though. Even if my bank account sometimes reflects my older brother's concern that this is just an expensive hobby, just like Jackson's many intramural teams. Somehow, our younger brother's pickleball, flag football, and basketball leagues don't seem to drum up the same level of disapproval.

Still, I do okay enough... Enough to keep me going. To reach for the dream of days spent crafting my stories and seeing my book on the shelves of all bookstores instead of just a few indie ones in Southern California.

"In the meantime, I'm a hospice social worker. Not sure I'd want to give that up. It's a tough job, but I love it."

His smile dips. "All that death must be hard."

"It's not a giggle-fest, but it fills me up. The end is just the beginning for so many, and I get to help those left behind find their way." I slosh out a breath at Davis, whose gaze is fixed to his phone. "What do you do again?"

"I work with your brother at No Boundaries, remember?"

That's right, Mr. Glued To His Phone works at the new startup where Jackson is deputy chief financial officer. My love for my younger brother is unquestioned, but he's a finance bro.

Forbes and spreadsheets are my brother's porn. No doubt Davis shares that same predilection. I've interacted enough with Jackson's finance bros to know the type. In every romance novel, Davis is the man the main character drops for the grumpy mechanic with a heart of gold.

"You must enjoy writing if you're paying to do it." He takes a long drag from his habanero strawberry cider.

"I do," I say, determination tightens my expression. "Everyone needs a heart to live. Writing is mine."

It's something my dad says. Nolan Lane isn't the sitcom dad with pretty speeches and sage advice outside the belief that a life without passion is not worth living. This truth is rooted so deep inside me that it's almost the steady beat pulsing me toward my passion. No matter how many times the voices, both inside and outside, try to steer me away, I always come back to writing.

"I get it," he murmurs.

"You do?" I say softly, my gaze linking with his.

Something akin to understanding glints in his dark pupils. So few people in my life seem to get this, let alone understand my passion for writing.

Davis blinks out of our tethered gazes. "Surprised you'd keep doing it, even though you don't make a living at it." He dips a fry he's already bitten into the ketchup.

Eww… Double-dipper. My stomach twists at both his action and question. "Most authors don't make enough to support themselves. A lot of us keep our day jobs to supplement."

"You're not George R. R. Martin or J.R.R. Tolkien level yet."

Not a single woman or marginalized author. Perhaps shared french fries were too hopeful for this date. Rem lectures that my standards are too high, which is why I'm single, but there is a bare minimum. A man who doesn't double-dip into the joint condiment before we've even had our first kiss and whose writer references aren't only white, heterosexual, cis, non-disabled men isn't too much to ask.

He juts his chin at me. "What do you write?"

"Romance."

"Really?" He snorts.

Brows knitted, my smile flattens. "What's wrong with romance?"

"It's all hitched breath and happy endings."

"It's about people. What drives us—"

"Into bed," he guffaws with a dismissive wave of his french fry.

"If you're doing it right." I lift a brow.

"There's more to life than sex."

"Said no man ever," I retort with a huffed laugh.

Challenge flashes in his eyes, and his mouth flexes into a teasing grin. "Someone's judgmental."

"Says the man that judges an entire genre of novels that he's *never* read."

His forehead creases. "What makes you think I've never read a romance novel?"

"Have you?"

He leans back. "Well…"

"Just as I thought." I pick up my drink.

He grabs another fry from the basket. "Romance has just never appealed to me. I prefer to read things with more substance."

A scowl forms on my face. "But you've never read a romance."

"I know what I like. I don't need to try something to confirm that." He dips his fry and then bites it in half.

"But we're not talking about you liking it, we're talking about you *not* liking it… About you denigrating an entire genre, one that makes billions annually, without having read a single romance novel. You don't need to try peanut butter to confirm you like Nutella, but you do need to try it to confirm you don't like it." I motion wildly between us.

The corners of his mouth quirk. "Your brother says you're choosy."

"Excuse me?" Face scrunched, I tilt my head.

"Do you go on a date with every man who shows interest?" He dips his half-eaten fry back into the ketchup.

"Of course not. What does that have to do with anything?"

"If we follow your logic, how do you know you wouldn't like to date them if you don't go on a date with them?" He gestures with his fry before tossing it into his mouth.

My jaw slackens. *Is he serious?* These are two different things. Not to mention, staring longingly at his phone for most of this date and only asking me questions about myself to dismiss or insult me doesn't scream *I'm interested.*

"You may be missing out on someone who gives you hitched breath and the happy ending you crave."

"Who says I crave those things?" I purse my lips. "What has my brother been telling you?"

"A few things… Also, you write romance, and I'm sure you have an entire bookshelf filled with swoony page-turners."

My mouth opens and then closes. He's not wrong. But he doesn't get to paint me as the lonely spinster—the patriarchy's word, not mine—who writes happy endings and dreams of the day she gets hers. Even if he's sort of right. *Emphasis on sort of.*

"There's nothing wrong with wanting a happy ending."

"Our happiness shouldn't be contingent on another person, especially when most people fail you or won't always be there." He leans back and his lopsided smile flattens into a firm line. A wisp of sadness shades his expression.

I bite back the urge to say, "Who hurt you?" The wounded male main character whose heart just needs a plucky love interest to heal him may cause a flutter in my belly in a book, but in real life, it's a red flag. We'll add this to the many reasons there will be no second date with Davis. Skeptical men with emotional baggage are for my books, not my heart. It's already been tattered by one commitment-phobic man. It doesn't need another.

"It's unrealistic to wrap one's happiness up in a single person. Romance just feeds us the delusion that it is." Forehead pinched, he waves another half-eaten fry between us.

"The happy ending in a romance isn't just about the couple. Yes, that's part of it. We root for them, but it's about their individual journeys. It's also about their relationships with others, not just each other or themselves. The best romances show that."

"Again, that's not real life. Most people are on their own."

"It's some people's lives."

"Not everyone is lucky enough to live in a fairy tale, Georgia," he says, his voice a little gruff.

Indignation simmers in my bloodstream. What Davis knows about me wouldn't fill a page's footnote. My life is hardly a fairy tale. If it were, I'd be here with someone else—the someone else who, despite my hope and heartbreak, is now someone else's Prince Charming. Instead, I'm here with Davis.

"I'm well aware." I meet his stare.

"Are you?"

"Very much so." I hiss through a tight smile.

So predictable. It's as if it's in one of my books. He's the jaded finance bro, and I'm the hurt but still hopeful romance author. The girl who believes so much in happy endings that she spends hours crafting them. Happy endings may be my business, but none of my characters get them without getting a little scrappy.

Scrappiness isn't something I'm known for, at least with my friends and family. But Davis is neither. *He's* just a bad date, and I'm done with bad dates.

My mouth curves into a sardonic grin. "You're right, though. Life isn't a romance novel. In one of my books, a handsome stranger who turns out to be *my* love interest would have rescued me already from this *terrible* date. From a date with a man who spent the first twenty minutes checking his phone and the next twenty insulting me." I drain my drink and slam the glass onto the table with a *thwack*.

"I didn't insult you—"

"Nothing makes me swoon like someone referring to what I write as *lacking substance*." Expression tight, I scoot from my chair and grab my purse from where it's hooked on the back. "But since this isn't one of my books and it's real life, I'll rescue me."

"Wait, Georgia… Are you leaving?"

"Yes. Whatever favor you did for my brother, please consider it paid." I pull out fifteen dollars from my wallet and toss it onto the table. "For my drink. You can pay for the fries since your double-dipping ensured I wasn't touching them. Manners dictate that you forgo double-dipping of a shared condiment until after the first kiss. Everyone knows that."

"Wait? Kiss?" Befuddlement laces his words.

"*Never* happening." I sling my purse over my shoulder. "Though, maybe you're right about that too... I've never kissed you, but I can say for certain I would not enjoy it... I like a man with more substance."

And with that, I turn and march out.

CHAPTER TWO

MAKE A WISH

Warm air kisses my skin with each step, easing the post-bad date tension. In the fifteen minutes since I left a gaping Davis, the interaction has played on repeat. Moving down the front entrance walkway trimmed in leafy succulents, Davis's words hiss inside me. A whoosh of cool air mixed with the scent of disinfectant and lavender greets me as I step through St. Philip Neri's front doors.

At the front desk, Kerry, the receptionist, peers over a copy of *The Duke's Darling*. "Lord James better not die in this duel, Georgia. Someone promised me a happy ending," she titters.

Kerry is as obsessed with romance novels as I am. She and a few other staff have read my books. Mortification may twinge when they mention my books' saucy parts, but their support makes the blush worth it. If only everyone in my life was as supportive of my writing.

"Have I ever let you down?" I tease.

"No, but you cut it close when Selena left Owen back in Sugarville."

"But she came back." I wink.

"And that epilogue!" She fans herself with the paperback.

"Only thing better is that scene in the pond from *Shifted Heart*."

I crinkle my nose. "That's not even between the main characters. That was between Lars and his second in command… All they were doing was sparring."

"The sexual tension." She mock-swoons.

"His mate was Ivy, not Victor."

"Why not both?" She waggles her blonde eyebrows.

With a laugh, I make my way past reception toward the stairs. Most people wouldn't think popping back into work could be a pick-me-up after a bad date, but it is. The renovated hacienda-style estate turned sub-acute facility has been my happy place for the last five years,.

Not only does the brick building offer a magical whimsy with its courtyard's *Secret Garden* aesthetic, but here I am Georgia the Capable. Besides a few staff, volunteers, and even some patients that try to set me up with single sons, brothers, and someone's accountant, there's no arched eyebrow at the decisions I make. Unlike Davis, with his mouth's dismissive firm line, or my brothers.

With each step closer to the hospice unit's main door, the annoyance that wound tight in my body dissolves. Plucking a mask from the dispenser, I place it on and then squirt sanitizer on my hands before I swipe my badge to enter. It's after seven, so the unit is locked down for the night, other than staff and a few stray family members camped out beside loved ones' beds. Unlike the rehab unit in the east wing, visitor's hours here are loosely enforced to allow friends and family ample time to say goodbye.

"Georgia!" Pilar looks up from the computer, amusement sparkles in her amber-colored eyes. "Didn't think we'd see you tonight."

Tossing my purse onto the desk at the nurses' station, I lean against the counter. "Wouldn't miss it for anything."

"Even for a date?" Pilar's head tilts.

"Of course." I bat my long lashes.

"Liar!" Head shaking, she taps at the keyboard. "You're dedicated, but *not* that dedicated. Must have been a bad date."

There's no getting anything by Pilar Ramirez-Gellar. St. Philip Neri's chief physician isn't just an astute doctor, but she can also read people with a single glance. Not to mention, over the last five years of working together she's heard plenty of my bad date stories.

"I hope this one didn't get your credit cards."

"Only my social security card. Is that bad?" I clutch my chest in mock dismay.

"Ha!" She pushes her glasses atop her head. "What was wrong with this one?"

"He spent half the date on his phone and the other half insulting me."

"He didn't!" she says, her eyes wide.

"He did." I cross my arms.

"What did he say?"

I puff out a long breath, the sound reminiscent of spinning helicopter blades. "He belittled my writing. Well, not *my* writing exactly, but romance as a genre."

I don't expect my partner to share my fondness for romance. However, I do expect them to respect it, and by extension, me.

"Was he at least attractive?"

"He's your typical white boy finance bro—even if he skews undercover hot nerd." I wave my hands dismissively.

"You do like a hot nerd."

Heat crawls up my spine. Hot nerds are my thing, at least in real life. My book boyfriends bounce between sexy shapeshifters, boy next doors with filthy mouths in bed, and the dashing Mr. Darcy-types.

But Davis with his glasses. The hint of a muscular body from beneath a short-sleeved button-up shirt. Hair neat, but not overly styled. A soft, minty eucalyptus scent. The *Star Trek* phone case—Next Generation, not the original. From the superficial assessment of first impressions, a flutter had bloomed in my belly at the sight of Davis. I'm adult enough to admit that, but the wrapping didn't match the interior.

"Did you miss the finance bro part?" I motion at her.

"Not every man in finance is a bro. They're not all Will."

Gut punch. I almost rear back at the mention of my ex. It's been five years and countless bad dates between present day and a time when I wasn't just me, but one half of Georgia and Will. Five years since the now fogged-up idea of a happy ending with someone seemed so crystal clear that I could reach out and almost grab it.

"I'm aware they're not all like Will." A hard lump chokes my words.

Pilar reaches out and squeezes my forearm. "Sorry I mentioned Will."

"It's okay."

Concern knits her brow. "Is it? With the—"

"It will be," I interrupt and force a tight smile.

Like an amulet warding away bad spirits, I cling to that mantra. It's how I've always got through life's murky waters with my gaze tethered to the shore. *Mom is sick.* It will be okay. *Dad's not coming.* It will be okay. *This isn't what I want.* It will be okay.

I clear my throat. "Davis may be attractive, but he's a jerk, and someone wise once told me not to waste my time on jerks." I pull a hair tie out of my purse and fingercomb my long hair into a messy bun.

"They sound very wise and extremely beautiful." She waves her hands and strikes several sassy poses.

"Their intellect and beauty know no boundaries," I say cheekily.

She crinkles her forehead. "Besides him fitting your hot nerd type—minus the finance bro faux pas—why do you think Jackson selected him for you? Your brother isn't so vain to use looks as the sole criteria to set you up on a blind date."

That question had rattled inside me for the entire drive here. What was it about Davis that Jackson thought was a good fit for me? Not to mention, the date with me was a promise. My younger brother thinks I'm so pathetic that he needs to get his coworkers to do him a solid and take me out.

It's humiliating.

I rub the center of my forehead. "I think he played musical chairs with the single men at work, and Davis lost."

"Davis is a loser, but that didn't happen until he showed up for your date and acted a fool." She taps her shoe against my bare calf. "Don't forget that, Georgia Lane. You're the prize."

A prize nobody wants. I don't let the negative thought breech my lips. I won't allow one man's rejection to toss me back into that deep well of insecurity. A well I so recently climbed out of. Even if I'm the one who walked out on Davis, the sting of rejection still twinges inside me. I had been attracted to him from the start, but his lack of interest was apparent.

"You're right." I offer a small smile beneath my mask.

"At least this one didn't give your dog chocolate."

"How do these men keep finding me?" I almost whine.

"You gotta kiss a lot of frogs." Pilar leans back, stretching her slender arms over her head.

"Says the woman that met her wife at sleep-away camp in the tenth grade." I roll my eyes.

"Perhaps we should explore an adult sleep away camp for you," she deadpans.

"Sleep away camp wouldn't be necessary if she'd take me up on my offer," Henry teases, striding toward us.

"To run off with you," I sass.

He pats his chest. "My ticker couldn't handle you, Peach."

The nickname akin to the perfect cup of tea. Most of St.

Philip Nerri's—or SPN—volunteers drift in-and-out. They tend to be students in need of extra credit or resumé padding. Henry Lincon; however, is part of the facility's foundation. This former SPN chief physician retired on a Friday fifteen years ago only to return the following Wednesday as a volunteer, saying his wife told him to get out of her hair.

For thirty-five years, Dr. Lincoln, or Doc as most people call him, hasn't just been part of SPN's fabric but the thread that holds it together. Besides me and Kerry, most of the staff have worked here for ten-plus years. Within a single shift, ever the bloodhound, he sniffs out who is SPN material. If, by the end of your first day, Doc bestows a nickname on you, you're in. It's not scientific, but there have been several nurses, one psychologist, and a handful of physical therapists with no nicknames after day one. They only lasted a few months.

"Doc, are you still trying to betroth her to your grandson?" Pilar shakes her head.

"Kenny and Peach would be perfect for each other," he says, assuredness almost glints in his dark brown pupils.

"You mean the mythical grandson from Canada nobody has ever met." I bump his shoulder.

Doc, a Black man in his early eighties, has the sturdiness of a strong oak with his tall, broad physique. Unlike my grandparents, who seemed to wither into wisps of their once healthy selves after retirement, Doc, and his wife, Estelle, maintained an active lifestyle of travel, volunteering, and morning park tai chi classes. They may be in better shape than me.

"Seattle, not Canada, Peach." His lips pucker. "Well, not anymore. He's in Irvine now."

It's almost a dare. For the last three years, Doc and Estelle have dangled their grandson like he was a piece of candy for me to take.

"It must be nice to have him so close." I don't take the bait.

I may want a relationship and be open to finding it, but blind dates are the worst. Tonight reinforces that. First, there's the pressure of the blind date. Second, there's the potential to disappoint the person who set you up. No doubt, Jackson will be unhappy with tonight's outcome. Even though I'm hurt that my younger brother had to call in a favor to get me said bad date, my stomach churns at Jackson's impending disappointment. I can already hear his "Another one, Georgia?" admonishment.

Affection brightens Doc's features. "We hated having him so far away, but he was making his way in the world. You know how it is… One must follow one's passion. A life without it is just empty."

My heart squeezes at that. After Hope, Doc is the second person I'd shown my first completed manuscript to. A voracious reader, he'd devoured it in three days and returned it with so many notes.

Once the mortification of an octogenarian's notes on the sexier scenes in my book dissolved, Doc became my go-to alpha reader for all my books. *Shifted Heart*, my werewolf/vampire, opposites attract paranormal romance. *Twice Baked Love*, my small-town second chance romance. *The Duke's Darling*, my regency romance. He's read them all, multiple times.

"Speaking of passion, I believe someone's late on their latest manuscript." He wags a thick finger at me.

"It's coming. Just polishing up." The lie sours in my throat.

For the last six months, I've started, stopped, deleted, and restarted three different projects. The way the words just came with the first three books meant I'd never considered what would happen if they stopped. Ideas aren't my issue, it's the execution. Each book's ending is clear, but there's no map to get me to it.

"It's just a first draft. Nobody expects perfection." He places a palm on my shoulder, and the weight soothes the worry slinking through me.

"I know," I murmur.

That's a lie, because I have no idea. Is it the fear of making mistakes? Is it that my talent has dried up? Is it the fear of disappointing readers like Doc? Whatever the reason, the stories inside me aren't talking to me. *What if they never talk to me again?*

"Doc, it's almost time." Pilar tips her head toward him.

"My public awaits!" He bows and turns.

It's the best part of the week. Each Friday night, available employees and volunteers escort patients from the rehab and hospice units to the outdoor courtyard at the center of the building. This little courtyard is my favorite place at SPN. Despite the sadness that often tiptoes through this place, the courtyard is an oasis for patients, loved ones, and staff. Where death and worry may live outside the four walls surrounding the courtyard, hope resides here.

Patio tables and chairs, some shaded by umbrellas and others under leafy palm plants, fill the area. The solar lights at the edge of the cobblestone path that loops through the garden and overhead strings of lanterns cloak the courtyard in a magically romantic glow, as if fairies would appear at any moment.

Pilar and I grab a spot against the west wing's wall. Despite the coolness of the bricks seeping through the thin fabric of my dress, warmth twines around me every time I'm here. Unlike most hacienda structures built in California during colonization, this former residence, constructed in 1908, is an ode to the style. Still, I can't help but feel transported to a different time and place. The way every crevice shimmers in both sunshine and moonlight. How the sweet smell of jasmine drifts around the space. The quiet hum of the water fountain at the heart of everything.

"Where is my fairy queen?" Doc steps in front of the fountain, his right hand above his bushy black eyebrows as if searching.

"I'm right here, you old goat!" Estelle hands a patient a cup of water before she shuffles toward her husband.

"Well, come on, baaaby…" he says, mimicking a sheep. "Curtain call is promptly at eight."

"I said goat, not sheep," she teases. Where Doc is tall and broad, his wife is a short Black woman with a plump pear-shaped figure.

Laughter wafts around the courtyard. Their playful banter is just one part of this weekly spectacle. Even before Doc retired, they'd pick a different Shakespeare play, mostly the comedies, and do a dramatic reading for staff and patients. Outside of *Romeo and Juliet*, they never perform the tragedies. Despite death's presence within these walls, hope and joy remain the mission. Goodbyes are sad enough; there's no need to add to it.

"Tonight's offering is *A Midsummer Night's Dream*." Pilar leans in and whispers.

"I figured as much." I point at the fairy queen crown that Doc bestows on his wife, the pink flowers pop against her short white curls.

The sweetness of this moment surrounds me. Scripts in hand, Doc and Estelle laugh through lines and overact in terrible, fake British accents. They weave through the clusters of seated patients in wheelchairs or in patio chairs, asking those who are able to read different parts. Despite the ache of my feet in my high heels, I remain pressed against the wall with a smile stretched across my face.

This is my happy place. For the ninety minutes that it takes Doc and Estelle to read through the play, that worry that knotted in my belly unspools. There's no thought of the bad date, Jackson's forthcoming disappointment, or the uncompleted manuscript. There is only joy. Joy in the happiness of this courtyard full of people, some who don't have long left in this world. Joy for the love that radiates at its center.

"I want that," I whisper to myself. Hollowness twinges in my chest from the unfulfilled want within me.

"What's that?" Pilar leans close.

"Nothing…" I murmur, emotion thick in my throat. "Just hope I'm like them when I'm older."

"Don't we all."

After the applause subsides, the courtyard empties except for a few people. Pilar sits beside Estelle at a patio table. Their heads bent over Pilar's cell phone, watching a video of her twins' dance recital. Doc and I flutter around the space, picking up discarded cups and snacks.

"Another stellar performance," I say, scooping up an empty bag of chips and tossing them into the small trash bag he holds.

"I just ride Estelle's coattails." His tender stare drops to his wife, her head tossed back in laughter. "She's the sun, I just orbit her."

"That makes you the Earth."

"Or Uranus," he deadpans.

I snort. "Even in their eighties, men act like teenage boys."

A deep chuckle vibrates from him. "That may be the trick to sixty years together." He gestures toward his wife, who flashes him a sweet smile from across the courtyard. "Never lose that tenacious youthfulness. That belief that no matter what happens, you can find a way. Every hardship. Every fight. We never lost that."

"That's all it takes?"

"And a lot of luck." He bends down, picking up a coin someone had dropped on the stone path. "And I've been a very lucky man. I met the one at the right time, and, luckiest of all, she felt the same way."

A frown drags down my mouth. The wear and tear of the last five years erodes my once steady belief that the future I want will happen. It's a fear I barely admit to myself, let alone anyone else.

"It sometimes seems like the only luck I have is bad." My admission is quiet.

"You've had a string of it, but you've also had some good."

"I know." I shift foot-to-foot. "I'm just feeling sorry for myself right now. It will pass. Just the hangover from a bad date."

He frowns. "He's the one with the bad luck. He's missing out on you, Peach."

Which one? Two names flash in my mind's eye: Davis or Will.

He holds up the coin. "But just in case, take this. Maybe some of my luck will rub off."

Blinking back threatening tears, I take the coin. "My older brother says luck is what you make of it."

"He's not wrong, but you still need some to make something of it. If anyone can, it's you, Peach. Your writing shows me that. You were gifted the talent, and look what you've done with that."

Despite my nod of agreement, queasiness sloshes in my belly. *What if that talent is gone?*

"I know whatever else luck has in store for you, you'll not waste." He squeezes my shoulder. "Hopefully, that lucky penny brings you what you're looking for."

As Doc says goodbye and collects Estelle, Pilar sneaks off for one last check in with the charge nurses before heading home to her family. Perched on the stone edge of the small fountain, the garden's decadent perfume fills my nostrils, and the crickets' melody plays in my ears. I skate my left hand along the water's cool surface, the penny clutched in my right.

Luck isn't something the Lane family subscribes to. It might be the one commonality between my brothers and father. Nolan Lane doesn't believe in luck. He subscribes to a stubborn belief that if he just keeps painting, keeps doing show after show, his effort will pay off. Jackson is as determined in business, and Rem in law. Even me. With my writing and dating. If I keep doing both, it must hit, right?

I want a happy ending, but I don't know what it looks like or how to get it. It could be like Doc and Estelle, a love that lasts a lifetime. It could be like my brother Jackson, single but fulfilled in his career. It could be something different. Something that is just mine.

"I just need a little luck to find it." With a soft kiss to the coin, I toss it into the fountain. The coin's splash joins the fountain's constant flow of ripples. Sighing, I whisper my wish, "Show me what my happy ending is and how to get it."

CHAPTER THREE

HE WANTS ME GONE

Each blink of the cursor mocks me from the laptop balanced on my lap. Wentworth, my six-year-old chocolate lab, is curled into a ball beside me. His quiet snores are almost in cadence with the flashing *blink blink* on the screen.

Weekend mornings are my peak writing time. I wake early, walk Wentworth, brew a pot of Lady Grey tea, and write. At least, that's how it's supposed to be.

Today, however, I sit, the last sips of tea cold in my *Who Needs Real Men When You Can Write Them* mug, a gift from Hope, with no torrent of words in sight. Thanks to my bestie's Etsy addiction, I have an entire cabinet full of mugs to put a humorously optimistic spin on my disastrous dating life. The mug's whimsical promise fades with the realization that I may not even be able to write a book boyfriend anymore.

As if my mojo is submerged in quick-drying cement, I'm stuck. It's not the lack of creative ideas. The notebook beside me, pages filled with my sloppy handwriting, is proof there is no shortage of ideas. Something happens between the idea and its execution. Like my love life, it's stalled out.

"I give up." Frowning, I close my laptop, set it to the side, and fall back against the couch. I let the plush softness soothe the annoyance that ripples inside me.

The movement causes Wentworth to stir. He crawls on top of me, his heavy body nuzzling in as I stroke his silky coat.

Four years ago, Wentworth showed up, ribs sticking out and his coat matted, behind SPN. My office window overlooks the back parking lot, and I spotted him there, lying beneath one of the small trees at the sidewalk's edge. He just slept and periodically poked his head up to watch staff or visitors come and go.

Each time I snuggle with this now chunky love nugget, I'm reminded of how the facility's director worried this little sweetheart was dangerous. After animal services picked him up, I called daily to check on him. No chip. No collar. Nobody else claimed him, so I did.

"Who needs a boyfriend, in a book or in real life, when I have you?" I massage his floppy ears, which elicits a flurry of kisses.

Bad dates I can deal with. It's become the norm. While I have hope that my story will come with great love—like the kind in my books—I can live without it. I have so far. But the idea that it won't include writing is almost too much to bear. For every start and stop of a story in the past, the words always came. Now, they remain tucked inside somewhere deep, in a place I don't know, and I don't have a map to find it.

Forget wallowing. I choose pastries. The gluten-free blueberry scone drizzled with lemon glaze that awaits me may not coax the words out of me, but it will console me until they come.

"Let's go see Aunt Hope." I motion for Wentworth to jump off me so I can change and head out.

Hope and I have been best friends since her family moved next door to mine when we were ten. Her physician parents met while working for an international healthcare organization. After they married, they first settled in Boston until Hope's mother, Emmie, took a position at UC Irvine's Medical School. Lucky for me, they settled in Tustin, buying the red-roofed, tan Spanish-style house next to my parents' grey Victorian. From the moment she appeared with pink glittered barrettes in her thick red curls, I fell in insta-love with my bestie.

Twenty-two years later, my affection for Hope is only stronger. We still meet each Saturday in my childhood backyard. Only now, it's Rem's backyard, and instead of choreographing dances to our favorite pop songs, we drink bottomless mimosas. Thanks to my catering business mogul best friend, the many freshly baked, gluten-free pastries she serves help soak up the booze.

"Let me help," I say, striding toward the patio, Wentworth in tow.

Hope is shuffling through the glass doors that spill onto the red brick patio, a large tray of baked goods and fruit in her hands. "I've got it." She shakes her head. "You're as bad as your brother. I'm not infirm; I'm just knocked up."

The other difference from the good old days is that my beautiful best friend is not just married to Rem, but seven-and-a-half-months-along with the Lane Family's next generation. There was nothing on my life bingo card that had my often grumpy, always tucks in his shirts—even T-shirts—attorney older brother marrying my bestie.

Seven years older, Rem is the quintessential big brother. At eighteen, he'd gone off to college in San Francisco but transferred a year later to a school closer to home after our mother's multiple sclerosis—MS—diagnosis. Our parents had divorced six months prior and dad had split for a gig as an instructor at an art school in Paris. Rem came home to help care for me and Jackson. Despite mom's protest, he insisted.

Twenty-one years later, and he's still here. As am I. My brother took over Mom's house after she moved into an adaptive apartment seven years ago. It was only my first year after getting my masters in social work, and finances were tight, so I was still at home. Rem had lived in the carriage house apartment at the back of the property, so we swapped after he took ownership of the house.

"You'd think I was made of porcelain," she says, placing the tray on the patio table.

Plopping into a chair, I pour orange juice into champagne flutes while Wentworth settles at my feet. "Maybe he'll bubble wrap you."

She rolls her eyes. "Don't give him any ideas." She adds Prosecco to my glass. "Drink up, you're drinking for two these days since I'm abstaining for two."

I take my glass and salute her. "Is he being more overprotective than normal?"

Rem is the classic older brother. There's an almost always present annoyance with me, *especially me,* and Jackson below the surface, but that aggravation came with fierce protectiveness. That vigilance extends to Hope. Though, what appeared as mere affection for his younger sister's best friend morphed into the type of love I write about in my books. The firm line usually glued to Rem's face melts in Hope's presence, especially after she'd moved back home to start her catering business six years ago.

After culinary school, Hope moved to Los Angeles to work her way up in some of the finest restaurants. Tiring of the sexist assholes with their micro and full-on aggressions tossed at a young female chef, she broke out on her own. Hope used her savings, got a small business loan, and moved back in with her parents to start Good Girls Grub, a food truck-based catering company. Fresh out of business school, Jackson offered financial advice, I gave moral support, and Rem lent legal counsel for contracts.

Those legal conversations got lengthier, and Jackson swore they were eye-fucking each other each time they were in the same room. I'd told him that he thinks everyone is eye-fucking. Jackson, of course, was extra smug after they told us they were going to start dating each other. Fast forward a year, and Hope went from best friend to sister-in-law/bestie.

Hand placed on her round belly, she takes a chair across from me. "He's just a little more tightly wound than normal. It's first-time daddy anxiety. All the books talk about this."

"I'm sure he'll be fine once Boudica comes along." I break off a piece of scone, pop it into my mouth, and moan as its sweetness hits my tastebuds.

A furrow dips her brow. "We're *not* naming her Boudica."

"It's a perfect name. She was a warrior queen, just like my niece." Winking, I motion to Hope's belly. At her unconvinced facial expression, I let out an annoyed puff of breath. "I wouldn't have to keep guessing if you'd just tell me the name."

The agony of not knowing Hope's baby's name is killing me. Yes, the baby will be my niece, but *she'll* also be Hope's baby. It's like Christmas on a Saturday. Both are individually amazing, but together, they are perfection. For the lifetime of our friendship, Hope has never kept a secret from me. The night Rem kissed her, and they decided to date, the first thing she did was tell me.

"It's killing me!" Head tossed back, I whine with the conviction of a bratty child melting down with a temper tantrum.

"We don't know yet." She laughs, spearing a piece of melon with her fork.

"There's no way that's true. We're talking about the man who hangs his suits in the order he plans to wear them through the week and never deviates. Rem likely has a twenty-year plan for little Helga." I swat at the air as if the notion is a pesky mosquito here to suck away the reality of my older brother.

"Helga? Absolutely not!" She purses her lips and then

continues, "As hyper-fixated on this pregnancy as he's been, he hasn't been able to settle on a name. Every time we have a contender, he changes his mind."

"Rem?"

The idea that my brother is waffling back and forth about baby names almost knocks me out of my chair. He never leaves things to chance. Hell, after his first date with Hope, he'd told Jackson, "In a year, I'll be her husband."

Jackson, of course, immediately told me.

A year later, they were married in this very backyard.

"Names are important. Especially in this family," Hope teases.

She's not wrong. Like my artist dad's predilection for meaningful names, I named Wentworth after my first book boyfriend; Captain Wentworth from *Persuasion*. Not to mention, Jackson has an aquarium full of fish named after his favorite basketball players.

"He just wants to make sure he gets it right," she says, a warm smile covers her face.

"You know, if you just told him what name you wanted, he'd just go with that."

She fiddles with the pink sapphire ring on her finger. "Yes, but I want this to be our decision. For him to trust himself as a dad."

"He'll get there." I reach across the table and squeeze her forearm. "Like you said, it's part of first-time daddy anxiety."

If anyone can daddy up, it's Rem. Even before my parents divorced, Nolan Lane wasn't exactly father-of-the-year material. There's a lot about my dad to like. With his passion for his work and big personality, he's the life of every party. Dad's great at the fun stuff. Unique outings, like when he took us to an art exhibit where we smashed pieces of furniture and then glued them back together into art pieces. At nine and seven, Jackson and I thought it was the coolest, while Rem tutted it wasn't appropriate for children.

"Plus, he's had years of practice fathering. Even when it's not solicited or necessary." The statement is meant to reassure me, but a bitter lilt punctuates my words. I try to hide it with an extra-large smile.

Hope's sigh telegraphs that she's not buying my fake smile. "It comes from a good place."

I motion with a piece of scone at her. "Bestie Card."

As much as I adore Rem's good sense in marrying Hope, there are boundaries. The bestie card reminds us of when we need the other to just be a friend. Not Rem's younger sister. Not his wife. Just Hope and Georgia.

"Fiiiiine." She puffs out a long breath. "How was the date? I saw your car pull in after ten. That's a *long* happy hour." She waggles her brows.

"It wasn't eyebrow waggle-worthy. I left before I finished the first drink and went to SPN for Doc and Estelle's weekly reading."

"That bad? What happened?" Her red-painted lips tick down.

Grabbing a second scone, I share the details. It's not the worst Georgia Lane date disaster. No theft. No emergency trips to the vet for Wentworth. No finding a date making out with the bartender after learning that I was only there to make his ex jealous.

"I wonder if I can find a *No Double Dipper* mug on Etsy." Hope taps her manicured finger against her chin.

"Bitch!" I laugh, tossing my napkin at her.

She catches it. "Language in front of your niece," she says cheekily, rubbing her belly. "You and Jackson may swear like drunken sailors, but this little peanut will have manners."

I arch a brow. "Says the woman with the *Fuck the Patri-archy* keychain."

She wags her finger. "There's a protest clause to my no swearing rule for—"

"Saffron?"

Her head tilts. "Now, that one I kind of like."

"Please don't name my niece after a spice." My brow pinches. "Though, it's on brand for this family. Consider combining your love of cooking and Rem's obsession with the law. Saffren Sotomayor Lane," I say, making jazz hands.

Laughter vibrates through her. "Oh god, no!" She swipes at her eyes. "Perhaps we keep the over-the-top book character names away from my baby girl."

"Sure," I sigh, breaking off a piece of scone.

"Still blocked?"

"I'm not blocked—" I sit up a little straighter. "I'm just…"

The half-hearted protest is the crumbling realization that this isn't just a mere blip. For months, the words haven't come. No matter the writing exercise. No matter the suggestions from fellow authors. It's like the words are walled away from me.

With a head shake, I meet Hope's eyes. "It's just temporary. It will all be alright."

Rem asks, "What will be alright?" Worry deepens the firm lines of his mouth as he emerges from the house with a large white sun hat in his hand.

"If I have a third scone!" I flick my wrist and then pluck another pastry off the tray.

The last thing I want to discuss in the presence of my older brother is my writing. He'll have lots of opinions. Many that he's already shared.

"That doesn't go with your athletic leisure wear getup." Hope gestures at the sun hat in his hand, a wry grin across her lovely face.

Bless my bestie. No words needed. She may champion that he just wants what's best for me, but she's witnessed enough brotherly *I know best, Georgia* lectures through the years.

Smirking, he looks down at his Anaheim Ducks T-shirt tucked into mesh shorts, his standard weekend attire. "I leave the fashion expertise to you, sweetheart. It's for you." he bends and presses a peck to her cheek. "The marine layer is almost burnt off."

"If only our little ole' female brains thought of some sort of sun shielding contraption," I sass, waving at the large green umbrella that shades the table.

"Your little ole' female brain I worry about"—he juts his chin toward me and then back at his wife—"Not hers."

"Thanks, baby." Hope takes the hat.

He sits beside her. "If you're carb-loading, I take it last night's blind date didn't go well?"

I bite into my scone and say nothing.

"That well?" He chuckles.

"He double-dipped," Hope offers as an explanation.

His nose wrinkles. "Please, tell me you were at least at Fisher's Landing where cross-contamination wasn't an issue." His brown eyes, the same as mine, fix on me. "Are you feeling okay this morning? Should—"

"Easy, Nagging Ned." I raise my hand, palm up. "I know to always have my blind dates in food-safe venues."

It's a habit I started two years ago after a terrible date ended with me in bed the next day with the Niagara Falls of migraines. Thanks to my celiacs, any trace of gluten can cause a reaction. My body doesn't process it, but revolts against it. While I experience my share of stomach cramping and nausea, migraines seem to be my body's choice response.

As a kid, I was sick all the time. Rem often volunteered to stay home with me, so my parents, and then just mom after the divorce, didn't have to take time off work. He'd sit by my bed, the curtains shrouding the room in darkness, and press a cold compress to my head or rub soothing circles on my back.

It wasn't until I was twelve that doctors diagnosed me with celiac disease. Knowing helped me to manage things. There's no pill to cure the condition, just an adherence to a gluten-free diet. As mindful as I am, sometimes that pesky gluten finds its way through kitchen cross-contamination or food mislabeling.

"This is the guy that Jackson set you up with?" he asks, tipping his head toward me.

More like the guy he bribed or blackmailed. Nodding, I take another bite, hiding my annoyed expression.

He shifts in his chair. "What'd he do? Do I need to—"

"Would you leash your husband?" I groan, my gaze meeting Hope's, her mouth drawn into a patient smile. "No big brother talking to needed. We just aren't a good fit."

"What does that mean?"

"He's a pickleball-playing finance bro."

Even if Davis hadn't spent half the date locked in on his phone nor the second half insulting me, we're not an ideal match. Opposites attract may work in some cases. Like with Hope and Rem. She softens his edges, bringing out his sweeter side. He dotes on her. Rem may be overprotective, but he supports Hope with everything she does. The start of her business and now its expansion with their recent acquisition of a fourth truck.

"I told Jackson this wouldn't work," he mumbles.

"Excuse me?" I narrow my eyes.

"You never make it past the first date."

Hope reaches over and squeezes his hand. "Baby, some of them aren't second date material. Georgia has had some less-than-ideal candidates for her Mr. Right."

"True. But, for some of them, we'll never know they weren't her Mr. Right because she finds the most ridiculous of reasons to eliminate them."

"I do not!"

Ignoring my protest, he goes on, "The guy that wore flip flops to their first date."

"Flip flops aren't appropriate date attire unless you're at the beach," I interject.

"The guy who said his favorite ice cream was vanilla. The

one who wore tapered jeans. The one who had too much product in his hair. The one who said *Free Willy* was their favorite movie." He counts each reason I'd nixed past dates on his fingers.

At the time, each appeared to be a perfectly logical reason to chuck the Mr. Not-So Rights. With each tick of Rem's fingers, the foundation for my previous excuses wobbles.

"Maybe he's not the right one for you, but you'll never know if you don't give anyone a chance beyond a first date." His tone softens. "They're not all going to be Will."

Breath *whooshes* out of me. It's been five years, but the mention of Will still has the power to make me speechless. It used to be the happy speechlessness of his big romantic gestures or swoony words. But those experiences belong to someone else now. All I get is the dull ache of lingering heartbreak that snatches away the words that want to come out. *Will has nothing to do with this. I don't use ridiculous standards to protect myself. Fuck you and your self-help paperback psychoanalysis.*

"Georgia…" He closes his eyes, lets out a hard breath, and then opens them. "I just want to see you settled. You're thirty-two. Single. You—"

"I don't need a relationship to be settled," I snap back.

While I hope for the clichéd happy endings from one of my books, I already have so much. A career I love. Friends. Wentworth. Family. Even if one brother thinks I'm so desperate he had to get someone from work to do him a favor, and the other one's factory mode is constant disappointment in me, I love them.

"I know you don't need a relationship. I wouldn't worry about you being alone if you had more direction. If you were more established in your life. You still live at home."

"You still live at home, too," I scoff.

"But I *own* this house. It's my home. With my wife. You live in a one-bedroom apartment above the garage. All your money goes towards your books instead of building something."

Anger boils in my bloodstream. "I'm building a career."

It always comes back to this with him. After winning a national short story contest my senior year of high school, I'd said I wanted to write. Rem went into full big brother lecture mode with facts and figures about financial security and the likelihood of success. So, I put the dream on hold. After high school graduation, I got my Bachelor's and then my Master's. I went to work establishing my career as a social worker, but the passion wasn't gone. It just slumbered quietly until it roared awake five years ago. Even now, the words may be hidden from me, but the desire burns like wildfire to keep going.

"You're just like Dad." He shakes his head.

The barb pierces straight into my gut, and the disappointment that shadows his stare as he looks at me twists it. There it is. The real reason Rem's judgment always finds fault with my choices. Of the three Lane siblings, I may be most like our dad. Rem has inherited Dad's strong jawline and height, but he's more practical, like our mother. Although, Rem's practicality is on steroids compared to her. I may look like my mother with a rounder figure and long brown hair, but my thirst for creative fulfillment is one hundred percent Nolan Lane.

"Rem." Hope places her palm atop his hand, her voice featherlight.

He pinches the bridge of his nose. "Georgia, I'm sorry. I just want to see you settled. To know that you'll be okay. Things are going to change after the baby comes."

I blink. "Are you saying you want me to move out?"

"No," Hope says quickly, her fierce gaze shoots to her husband. "We're not saying that."

"We're not, but..."

"You're thinking that?" I sit up straight.

This is only the second time that the idea of me moving out has come up. The first time was five years ago, and that had been my idea. Well, mine and Will's. He had his own place. A place we discussed becoming *our* place. At least, that was the plan until two days before I was supposed to move in when a *This isn't what I want* text arrived.

Rem clears his throat. "Maybe if you're on your own, it will help you get your priorities straight. To focus on what's important."

"We haven't discussed this." Hope glares at him.

"I know, but—"

"No buts." She raises her left hand, points at her ring, and then at his on his left hand. "These rings mean we're a team. *We* discuss things like this. Like asking my best friend, your sister, and the only aunt to *our* daughter to move out."

Hope may be the human embodiment of a Care Bear, but bears have claws. There have only been a few times throughout our decades-long friendship that I've seen feisty Hope come out. The time she verbally castrated a bully who shouted homophobic slurs at Jackson at a high school base-ball game. The time Will showed up to pick up his things after our breakup and she turned the garden hose on full blast and sprayed him as he walked, box in hand, to his car.

Rem rubs the back of his head. "Sweetheart, I'm—"

"Don't sweetheart me." She gestures wildly.

Affection may bubble inside me at my friend's ire directed on my behalf, but it curdles in my stomach to see them argue. The hurt that cascades within me aside, I don't want to see this. The anger isn't good for Hope's blood pressure. I know it's something their OB-GYN has mentioned they should keep an eye on.

"It's fine," I blurt, drawing both their attention. "I have been thinking that it may be time to move out."

"You have?" they say in unison, Hope's eyes wide and Rem's forehead wrinkled.

Shifting in my seat, I nod. "Yeah."

It's a total lie. Since unpacking my packed boxes for a move that never happened, the idea never crossed my mind. In all my daydreams of future relationships or selling enough books to write full time, I never imagined a future that isn't the carriage house apartment. Maybe I am in my own version of Peter Pan syndrome, where I just live at home the rest of my life.

"Pregnancy Card!" Hope tosses her hands into the air.

"The doctor said you shouldn't have fried foods, but..." Rem says, the conflicting emotions that wrestle inside him are visible in his pinched expression. His desire to always keep his wife happy is at war with that to keep her safe.

"No, *not* a mozzarella sticks run," she tuts. "Georgia moving. Can we put a pause on it until after the baby comes?" She rubs her stomach and the action drags both Rem and my attention to her pregnant belly.

Oh, she's good. There's no doubt that my bestie is emotional about this. The baby hormones have gotten the best of her at times but she's playing both of us.

A silent laugh tugs up my lips. "Sure."

Rem places his hand over hers, tenderness making his eyes bright. "Of course, sweetheart. I'm so sorry I brought it up. I didn't mean to upset you."

"And your sister?" She almost pouts.

She's ruthless. God, I love her. I bite back a snicker.

"Of course." He meets my gaze. "I'm sorry, Georgia. I know how I can be, but please know it's just me wanting what's best."

I try not to fixate on Rem not telling me he doesn't want me to leave. The attempt isn't valiant. It's a flat-out submission to the truth that my brother wants me gone.

CHAPTER FOUR

THERE'S A MAN... NO WAIT THERE'RE THREE

My brother wants me gone. That truth nips at me as I take the stairs to my apartment, Wentworth trotting behind me. Outside of the dorms in undergrad, this has always been my home.

Opening the door, I step inside. This is my safe space. It's where I picked up the pieces after Will. It's where I write my stories.

The smell of cinnamon and vanilla greets me. "Did I leave a candle burning?" A crease forms on my brow.

Wentworth pushes past me, his tail wagging furiously. I step fully into the apartment and shut the door behind me. The ding of the timer pulls my attention to the kitchen, where a man stands in a *Cinnamon Rolls Aren't Just Pastries* apron.

"Just in time!" He opens the oven and pulls out a tray. "Vanilla chai muffins from scratch. I had to improvise some of the ingredients. You really do need to restock your spice cabinet."

"Who are..." Eyes wide, my pulse quickens. "Wentworth, come," I hiss, motioning for him to come back to my side so we can make a quick escape.

Ignoring me, he scampers up to the unidentified assailant

who has broken into my apartment to… *Bake me muffins*? The stranger bends, offering ear scratches with his free hand.

"Wentworth." Hissing, I inch backwards, hitting something hard.

Not something, but *someone*. I whirl, my hands raised in a defensive posture, the thud of my heart choking off my ability to speak.

Another man stands there. Similar to the one in my kitchen, he's tall. But where chef burglar is lean with closely cropped blond hair, this man is broad-chested with thick chestnut hair and a suit that is straight out of a Jane Austen retelling.

"Dreadfully sorry," he says in a buttery, smooth English accent.

"I…" Fear licks up my spine, and I lurch back.

I snap my fingers for Wentworth, but the lab ignores me and sits on his haunches in front of Kitchen Guy.

Worst guard dog. I peer around the room, looking for an exit. The Mr. Darcy look-a-like stands between me and the door.

"Lord James, you're scaring her," Kitchen Guy scolds warmly.

"Lord James?" I say, my breath ragged. Confusion and fear fight for purchase inside me.

He places his hand on his chest, indignation flashes in his green eyes. "I'm doing nothing of the sort, Mr. Baker."

"You're definitely scaring her." Another low and growly voice filters into the room.

Spinning, I turn to find a beast of a man stalking toward me. His eyes are almost violet. A neat black beard accentuates his strong jawline. Something primal radiates from him, as if he'd put me over his shoulder and carry me away to have his way with me.

He sniffs the air, something wicked darkens his eyes. "I can smell it all over her. She's like a scared rabbit."

Oh god, is he going to eat me?! I lunge for the coffee table and grab the first thing I see. Lifting the remote control, I hold it in the air and swing it at them. "Don't come any closer, or I'll—"

The bearded man smirks. "Mute us to death."

"What do you want with me? Who are you? Are there more of you? Are you going to hurt me?" Each question is breathless.

Hands raised, Kitchen Guy rounds the counter. "Georgia, we're not going to hurt you."

"How do you know my name?" I aim the remote at him as if it's a loaded pistol.

"Because we were sent here for you."

"What?"

Lord James clears his throat. "Perhaps introductions are in order. I'm Lord James Everly, First Duke of Chamberlin." He gestures to Kitchen Guy. "This is Mr. Baker."

"You can call me Owen," he says, a slight twang in his accent.

"And you can call me, Alpha," bearded guy says, leaning against the kitchen island.

"Nobody is calling you that, Lars," Lord James says, one thick eyebrow curved up.

"Oh, he's Mr. Baker and I'm Lars."

"Lars? Owen? Lord James?" I drop the remote, my chest heaving and vision spotty. "But those are the names of my..." Head shaking, I take two steps and...

My eyes flutter open. An achy twinge pulses between my brows. I lay in my bed, my head propped on a pillow and Wentworth's heavy body draped over my legs like a furry blanket. Sunlight breaks into the room through half-open blinds.

"How did I get here?" Groaning, I rub the center of my forehead.

The last thing I remember is being in my living room with three men, their gazes fixed on me. Then pitch black. Did I faint? Had I really tried to fend them off with a remote control?

Other than the dull throb in my head, I appear to be unhurt. Squinting, I lift my head to scan the room. There's no sign of my uninvited guests. Not Mr. Kitchen, the Mr. Darcy doppelganger, or the sexy wolfman. Correction; Owen, Lord James, and Lars.

But that can't be.

Those are characters from my books, people I made up, not real people. Although, they are carbon copies of the three book boyfriends I'd spent months crafting. It's as if they'd been pulled directly from my imagination.

Owen Baker is the owner of a small town bakery. Granted the last name and occupation weren't my most clever idea.

Lars Hunt, the grumbly-voiced wolf pack alpha.

Lord James, the suave, slightly snooty, but very dashing duke.

"It's not real. None of it," I murmur to myself, taking in the quiet.

No muffled voices from the other room. No lingering scent of Lars' woodsy aroma, sensation of Lord James's firm chest against my back, or image of Owen's sweet smile.

"It can't be real. This has to be the booze." My face scrunches, and I wince at the sharp twinge. How much Prosecco had Hope poured into my orange juice? The way I felt, the answer was way too much. "Stop drooling over fictional men."

Whether it's a hallucination or real-life stalkers impersonating my characters, my stomach shouldn't swoop at the thought of these three men. *Maybe I have been single too long.* Well-adjusted adults don't fixate on real versions of book boyfriends who break into their houses and bake muffins.

Those muffins did smell good, though. "Stop it," I chide myself.

Scooting from beneath a snoring Wentworth, I sneak off the bed. His undisturbed slumber lulls me into a sense of safety. I'd like to think if I truly were in danger and this wasn't just a tipsy delusion from too many mimosas, he'd be at the ready. The way he obediently sat in front of Owen, begging for treats, gives me pause.

"Maybe I should call Rem, just in case."

The anxiety that prickles beneath my skin overpowers any hesitancy to call my older brother. No doubt this would feed into his narrative about me being unsettled. Settled people don't imagine book characters coming to life and being in their apartments. *Still…*

I tip my head toward the bedstand, finding it empty besides one of my moleskin notebooks, a Captain Picard bobblehead, and a small replica Tiffany lamb. My phone, which normally sits there, is nowhere in sight.

With quiet footsteps, I move to the door and place my ear against it. Just to confirm this is only a booze-fueled dream and not the start of my very own episode of a True Crime or Why-Choose Dark Romance. Ignoring the clench in my core at the idea of the latter, I lean into option A. The thump between my eyes tips the scale to thinking this is all booze-induced.

The door creaks open and I tentatively poke my head out. My nose wrinkles at the faint aroma of vanilla and cinnamon. A plate of muffins rests on the coffee table. James sits, his muscular frame properly straight, on the couch, a *Real Men Read Romance* mug in his hand. Lars leans against the windowsill, his gaze fixed outside as if standing guard. And Owen is folding my laundry.

"What *the*..." I mutter, eyes blinking.

"Our lady has awakened." Lord James rises and offers a bow.

Lars faces me, and Owen raises his head. All three men's gazes are trained on my face.

Lars sniffs. "Still a rabbit."

"You're real," I yelp, heart racing. Jumping back, I slam the door.

Crap! There isn't a lock on the door. I press my body against it, praying they don't break it down. My gaze jumps around the room for something–*anything*–to use as a weapon or a barricade. All I see is a sleeping Wentworth sprawled atop my bed. *Terrible guard dog!*

My focus drops to the pink ruffled bed skirt. "Justice's Arm," I let out a shaky breath.

Thanks to Rem's overprotectiveness, a baseball bat is tucked beneath the bed. He'd given it to me the day we swapped living spaces. "I'm just a backyard away, but use Justice's Arm until I get there," he'd directed, handing me the battered wooden bat. How funny that a man who worried about my safety on the other side of the backyard is the same man who wants me to move out.

"Focus, Georgia. You're either having a breakdown or are about to be murdered by sexy book boyfriend look-a-likes."

Jaw clenched, I reach for the bed, trying to remain against the door. There might as well be an entire backyard between me and it. In the time it may take me to get the bat, they could breach the flimsy door standing between me and them. The bat may help me fight them off, but I don't want to risk hand-to-hand combat with three men.

A gentle rap sounds at the door. "Georgia, it's Owen."

"This isn't happening. This isn't happening." Head shaking, I close my eyes. Somehow, I'm six again believing that if I close my eyes the nightmare will vanish. Only, instead of a monster, I want three very attractive men to disappear.

"My lady, I assure you we mean no harm," Lord James coaxes, an air of command in his smooth timbre.

"She's still scared," Lars says. "It's all over her."

A loud smack reverberates through the door. "Stop smelling her. It's ungentlemanly," Lord James scolds. "Dogs are for the hunt, not for wooing ladies."

Wooing ladies?

"Want to find out what dogs like me can do, Lord Fancy Pants?" Lars grits.

"Beyond chewing my boots, I doubt you can do much harm," he says haughtily.

"I'll shove that boot up your—"

"Stop! This isn't helping," Owen interjects. "Georgia, I promise that you're safe with us."

"Who *are* you?" I press tighter against the door.

"We told you."

"*Oh yeah*, you're my fictional characters come to life." An unhinged laugh falls out of me.

"Fictional characters?" Lord James's protest is filled with disdain as if holding up a smelly sock. "I assure you, my lady, we are indeed real."

"I don't believe you!" As the words leave my mouth, there's a nip of uncertainty.

The resemblance is uncanny. The boyishly sweet curve of Owen's smile. The seductive haughtiness of Lord James's voice. The primal sexuality that radiates from Lars. Even their mannerisms. It's not just things in my book but from inside me. So much about the characters I create live off the page. Little tics or parts of their backstory help me craft them but readers never see. Things only me and the characters would know.

"Georgia, how can we help you feel safe?" Sincerity braids around every syllable of Owen's question.

The fear coiled tight within me unspools just a bit. While

still scared, something inside me recognizes these men. Not as perfect replicas but as…

"Prove it," I breathe, not believing the request that falls from my lips.

"Prove what?"

"That you're…well, you."

There's a beat of silence. I'm sure they are standing there, silently wondering how they can meet my request. For a moment, I wonder the same thing. How does someone prove not just who they are but they are real and not merely a vivid delusion?

Worrying my lower lip, I scan the room searching for an answer. My vision snags on the bookshelf in the corner. In the colorful spines of some of my favorite books sits a proof copy of each of my novels. I'd kept them like a trophy celebrating each book's publication. At this moment the little trophies give me an idea.

"Lord James, what was the name of your first horse?"

In the first draft of *The Duke's Darling*, Lord James tells Lady Cecily about his first horse. The scene, while sweet, did nothing to help move the narrative along, so I cut it after my first round of self-edits. Nobody saw it but me. I didn't even save it for a special deleted scene bonus feature for my newsletter.

"Shakespeare," he says.

I swallow thickly, not letting the correct answer smooth away the lingering doubt that this is real. "Owen, what was your favorite subject in school?"

After a short pause, he answers, "Chemistry. It's just like baking."

That's only in my character analysis for Owen Baker. It's based on something Hope always says, "Baking is chemistry, and cooking is mad science." She'd provided consultation to add authenticity to my small-town baker. There's no way anyone else would know that.

"Her scent is less scared. More confused." Lars's whisper is gravelly.

"Stop smelling me, Lars!" I huff an annoyed breath.

"Ladies do not enjoy being smelled," Lord James tuts.

"Your mother had no complaints," Lars snarks back.

Oh, Lars. I let out a strangled laugh. There's no need to test Lars. Those violet eyes. The way he can smell every emotion. That gruff timbre. His sarcastic quips. Most authors make the werewolf alpha all broody grumpster, but I made mine a protective snarkster.

I rub at my temples. "This isn't happening. This isn't real."

"Did Pretty Boy and Lord Fancy Trousers convince you?" Lars asks.

"I beg your pardon," Lord James scoffs.

"*Aw*, thanks for calling me pretty, man," Owen says.

"You can't smell it on me?" A disturbed laugh accompanies my words. Am I really sitting on my floor talking to fictional men? As authors, we talk about our characters speaking to us, but this... *Does writer's block cause delusions?*

"You told me not to smell you anymore," he grunts. "IF you'd like—"

"Don't smell me!" I shout, causing Wentworth to jump off the bed and lumber toward me. Closing my eyes, I lean my head against the door. "Why are you here? What do you want with me?"

"To help you," Owen says, his sweet smile audible in his voice.

"With what?"

"To find your happy ending."

"And ours, my lady," Lord James adds.

I blink. "But you already had your happy endings. Lady Cecily. Selena. Ivy."

Like any good romance, my books came with a happy ending but included a cherry on top in the epilogue. Lord James and Lady Cecily welcome their first child. Ivy proposes to Lars after a demon hunt. Owen opens a second bakery with his now wife Selena, who'd left her corporate job to live in Sugarville. *God, that really was a terrible book.*

"Selena went back to the big city," Owen says, befuddlement punctuates his statement.

Big city? Did I write that? I cringe, remembering the very clichéd Hallmarky plot points of that book.

"Lady Cecily is engaged to the Marquis," Lord James adds.

My eyes widen. "And Ivy?"

"She's halfway back to the vampire territory," Lars says dismissively.

I shake my head. Somehow, each man is here just after their third act breakup. Before the twist that unites them with their lady love. Lord James's realization that his vendetta against her father isn't as great as his love for Lady Cecily. Lars giving up his role as pact leader to join Ivy and the human/supernatural alliance to fight rogue demons. Selena quitting her job for a simpler life with Owen.

Seriously, who let me write that book? Clearly, I was working out some inner misogyny there. I close my eyes.

The clichéd and un-feminist small-town romance aside, the certainty that this isn't real is reduced to a mere wisp. Each stroke of truth paints a picture that may appear surreal, but its reality seeps through me. Not wanting to believe something doesn't make it not real. I know that better than anyone. Didn't I sit on this very floor among packed boxes, wishing my breakup with Will wasn't true? Only to lie in my bed a month later, tearfully begging that the reason he'd ended things wasn't real?

Opening my eyes, I meet Wentworth's curious stare. Not a trace of hesitation or fear is evident in his dark pupils.

None of this makes sense. I may lose myself in a story from time-to-time, but not like this. Not where the pages of a book blur with the reality of my life.

Wentworth moves closer, his wet nose meeting mine. I inhale his oatmeal perfume and stroke my fingers along his silken coat. He's real. He's here. That means…

Nodding, I suck in a breath. "Okay, boy." After counting to three, I stand up and turn. My hand grasps the doorknob, but I stop. "Just in case," I whisper. I spin and pull Justice's Arm out from beneath the bed.

Fingers gripped tightly around the bat, I inch the door open and come face-to-face with my three book boyfriends. Bewilderment twists their handsome features.

"What do you mean you're here to help me get my happy ending?"

CHAPTER FIVE

WE'RE YOUR HAPPY ENDING

My expression tight, I step fully into the room. Wentworth rushes past me to sit before Owen, who bends and scratches his floppy ears. Despite my defensive stance with the bat, my dog is undisturbed by the three strange men standing in the middle of my living room.

Each man looks at me with a different expression. Owen's is warm. Lord James is bored, as if he's already tired of this. Lars doesn't smile as much as smirk, like this is just a game.

"What do you mean you're here to help me get my happy ending?" I repeat, curling my fingers a little tighter around the bat's base as I rest the barrel on my shoulder, prepared to swing fast and hard, if needed. While something inside me recognizes these men, I still don't trust *it*, or them.

"Just that…" Owen raises his palms, taking a hesitant step toward me. "We've been sent here to help you."

"Who sent you?" I motion at him with the bat.

His blond eyebrows knit, and he steps back. "I don't know."

"What do you mean you don't know? How are you here? How do you even know who I am? How do you *know* you're here to help me if you don't know who sent you?" Each question sprints out of me more high-pitched than the last.

"We just know," Lord James offers.

I scoff. "You just know?"

He shrugs.

I wave the bat. "How? And how are you so calm?"

Somehow, these three men poofed into existence, and they're chill about this. If I found myself in an unfamiliar world, I wouldn't be all like, *Oh, let's hang out and bake muffins until this woman we've never met and are on a mission to help comes home.* I'd be freaking out. Hell, that's what I'm doing now.

They look between each other as if trying to decide what to say or who should say it. With a head tilt, Lars gestures to Owen. He appears to be their unofficial spokesperson, which is wise. Not only is Owen Sugarville's de facto statesman, but he's also the least intimidating of the three men. He's the cinnamon roll book boyfriend, after all.

He shifts foot-to-foot before meeting my stare. "I was in my bakery's kitchen. Selena left last night, and I was going to bake away my feelings with some pumpkin tarts. Then suddenly, this image popped into my head of a woman with big brown eyes, the color of warm caramel. She sat in a black dress, her long dark hair in a messy bun, on the edge of a stone fountain."

Realization jolts through me. The description melds with the memory of me perched on the edge of the SPN fountain. I was alone. How did they…

My wish.

It couldn't be.

Could it?

My pulse ticks up, and the splash of the penny after I'd tossed it into the fountain flashes in my mind's eye.

"Sadness swam in those beautiful—yet dulled—eyes as if the flames of hope flickered to mere embers about to be extinguished," Lord James adds, his timbre reminiscent of a gentling breeze.

"It was you, rabbit. The vision of the woman we saw was you," Lars juts his chin at me.

"You all had the same vision?"

"Yeah," they say in unison.

Eyes blinking, I loosen my grip on the bat. "How did you know it was me?"

One dark brow quirked, Lars waves at me. "Besides that *exact* woman's photographs on these walls, and then *she*–AKA *you*–waltzes into this apartment, you mean?"

"Yes, smartass."

A lazy grin kicks across his face. "Look at that; my little rabbit has given me a pet name."

Lord James *tsks*. "Now is not the appropriate time for flirtation."

"The pink crawling up her neck says otherwise, Lord Fancy Pants," Lars's deep voice is filled with playful seductiveness.

"Focus, gentlemen." I clear my throat, hoping to tamp down the flush that is apparently visible and not just inching up my internal temp.

It's foolish to pretend that the impact these three men have on me doesn't exist. The flutter in my chest with each of their different gazes locked on me reinforces their seductive power. Owen's icy-blue gaze is filled with sweet sincerity. Lord James's green eyes are as lush as a clover field with a glint of wicked promise. Lars's violet eyes are somehow playful but steady. Each man's gaze offers something a little different but tantalizing.

"Help her. Help Georgia find her happy ending," Lord James says. "It was almost a prayer that one would chant in church. Something inside me commanded me to come to you. To find you. To help you."

"Who sent you? And how? And why?" I practically whine

my questions.

"We don't know." He motions between himself and the other men.

"How are you not freaking out about that?"

"I don't know." Owen rubs his nape. "Being here, being near you feels like..."

"Like coming back to home base after a hunt," Lars adds.

Somehow, I get what he's saying. I created these three men, so it makes sense they'd feel a connection. As surreal as this is, something tugs inside me; I'm tied to these men. Whether it's because I'm the author of their stories, or for another reason, I don't know.

"So, you hear a mystery voice telling you to come to me, and you just listen?" I arch one eyebrow.

"Yes," Lars says.

"Just like that?" I scoff.

"I'd never ignore a cry for help," he murmurs.

A cry for help? It was less a cry and more a plea, but wasn't that what I wished for? I wished for my happy ending, and less than twenty-four hours later, these three...*poof*...just magically appear.

His earnest smile turns wolfish. "It's like *Field of Dreams*, only we get you instead of a baseball field." His voice drops almost unnaturally deeper, causing a tingle to pulse between my legs. "If your happy ending requires a homerun, then I'm ready to play—"

"Bad dog." Lord James swats the back of Lars's head.

"I warned you!" He whirls, his large fists balled and teeth bared.

Lord James steps up, his mouth curled into a sardonic grin. "It may be time to put the dog outside."

Stepping between them, Owen pushes them apart. "Enough, you two."

I wag my finger. "Let's set some rules. No smelling me.

No flirting. No sexually propositioning me. No fighting. No derogatory anti-werewolf comments. Agreed?"

"Agreed. Right, *fellas*?" Brow puckered, Owen looks between Lars and Lord James, scowls painted across both their faces.

"Of course, my lady." His expression softens and Lord James places his hand on his chest then offers a quick dip of his head.

"Fine." Lars crosses his arms over his broad chest, his thick black eyebrows almost kiss in frustration.

Note to self; no more alpha male characters. Sighing, I rub my temples. While I hope there isn't an influx of more book characters appearing in my apartment, I should do future Georgia a solid. My unshakable case of writer's block may save me from that worry. There's no reason to fear fictional characters coming to life if I'm unable to write them.

"*Something* told you to come help me. How'd you end up here? You were in Sugarville, the Pacific Northwest, and the English countryside." I point the bat at each man.

Owen rakes his fingers into his short hair. "I'm not sure. I closed my eyes, said your name, and suddenly I was in your kitchen."

Lars nods. "Same. One minute I was looking out my window, and the next I'm leaning against *your* windowsill."

"I was sitting on the settee in my library and then on yours." Lord James tips his head toward the pink sofa in the living room.

"We all appeared simultaneously and put what we knew together. After seeing the pictures of you on the walls"—Owen points to the photos of me with my brothers, mom, and Hope that cover the living room walls—"we knew that you'd brought us here."

His words cause me to stiffen. "I didn't bring…"

But hadn't I? The thought steals my protest. The vision that pulled them out of their story and into mine was of me immediately after I'd tossed that penny into the fountain.

"My wish." I lower the bat to my sides, my lips trembling. "I didn't mean to..."

These men were mere pages away from *their* happy endings, and, somehow, I yanked it away from them. All so I could have my own. Doing to them what was done to me.

Guilt causes tears to prick, but I push them back. "I am so sorry," I whisper, my eyes dropping to my feet.

Lord James steps close, cupping my chin and guiding my gaze to meet his emerald eyes. "None of that, my lady. You did nothing to be remorseful for," he murmurs, moving his hands to my upper arms, their warmth soothing me.

"I wished for my happy ending and stole yours. You'd said it. You're here to help me find my happy ending and yours."

"The two may not be mutually exclusive." His thumbs knead my biceps, uncoiling the tension-filled muscles.

"Perhaps we should add no touching while staring longingly into Georgia's eyes to the rules," Lars snarks.

"Good idea." With a stuttered breath, I step out of Lord James's arms, a chill slinking down my spine at the loss of his body heat. I move to face the window. And away from the way his decadent scent envelopes me with the sense that no matter how unreal this is, it will all be okay as long as I'm in his arms.

That's how I wrote him... wrote all three of them. Lord James with his steadying energy below a snobbish exterior. Lars's blend of flirty, rough charm folding you into the knowledge that he'll make you laugh but always protect you. Then there's Owen. Just like the pastry his character type is named after he's sweet and pure comfort no matter what life throws at you.

They're not real. Even if they stand in front of me, even if I can touch them. They aren't flesh and blood. *But they are,* the thought almost taunts with the promise of three perfect men. *Perfect for someone else.* Three someone else's whose stories are already written. I won't have my heart broken by a man in love with someone else... *Not again.*

"You already have your happy ending. I wrote it." I spin, facing the three of them.

Face pinched, Owen tilts his head. "You wrote it?"

"Your stories." I gesture wildly, swinging the bat in front of me. "Selena. Ivy. Lady Cecily."

Lars grabs the bat from my hand. "Easy, slugger. I think we've established you don't need this." He tosses the bat onto the sofa and steps back, giving me a little space.

"What do you mean you wrote it?" Lord James lifts an eyebrow.

"I..." My eyes widen.

The confused expressions etched onto each man's features telegraphs that they have no idea they are merely characters in stories. While they may only be stories to me, it's these three men's lives. How would I feel if someone swooped in to tell me that the world I know isn't real? That the people I love aren't real? That *I'm* not real?

"Nothing... I'm just... This is a lot." Even I hear the lie in my tone, but I push on. "Don't you love your ladies? What about them?"

It serves no purpose to pop their realities' truth bubble. Being magically teleported into this world, away from everyone they know, to help a woman they've never met find her happy ending is scary enough. I can't imagine what it would be like to discover *that* woman is the writer of their stories.

Lars shrugs. "Ivy made her choice, and I made mine."

"I enjoyed Lady Cecily's company, but she's promised to the Marquis," Lord James says nonchalantly.

"I just want Selena to be happy." Gray clouds shadow Owen's features.

My mouth drags down into a frown. "What about your happiness?"

"I'm happy."

It's almost like looking in a mirror. How often had I said that to Hope after Will broke up with me? Each time she assessed me, I'd turn away and insist that I was happy, even though my heart had shattered into so many pieces I never thought I could glue it back together.

I gnaw on my lower lip. "How are you supposed to help me?"

Lord James unnecessarily smooths down his jacket. "Our theory is that one of us is your happy ending."

"Wh...wh...what?" I choke out.

"You're unmated," Lars says.

"Rude." Hands on hips, I shoot him the most indignant glower I can manage.

Being called single is one thing, but unmated conjures images of a single shoe discarded by the door without its other half in sight. As much as I say I'm okay if my life comes with me not finding that one person, the idea that they may not exist at all snatches that last bit of hope from me.

A lopsided grin curls his lips. "Am I wrong?"

I open and then close my mouth.

"It's not a judgment... Not on you, at least," Owen offers.

"It is a judgment of the fools who don't see the diamond in front of them," Lord James adds, his caramel-smooth voice dropping low.

"How do you know I'm single?" I mutter, fiddling with the hem of my blouse.

"The only scents here when we arrived were you and him." Lars points at me and then at Wentworth, who sprawls in his bed in the corner, asleep. "If you were mated, they'd be all over you. Even if it's been days, their scent infuses itself to you. The mated smell different, two distinct aromas that meld into one... And you are not mated."

"Again, rude." Lips pursed, I flick a wrist at him. "And what makes you think you're here because of that?"

"We're all drawn to you. Like a siren's song, the vision of you called us. That irresistible song is powerless compared to the thrall of your beauty. Never had I known beauty until my eyes clamped upon you." Lord James saunters closer with jungle-cat grace, ready to pounce on its meal.

And I'm dinner. I almost gulp. Every muscle in my body spools tight with conflicting emotions. They're not real, but the attraction that pulses through me is more real than anything I've felt in a very long time. Not since Will or the momentary attraction to Davis. *Eww, why am I thinking about him at this moment?*

"They really were fools," he murmurs, brushing a tendril of my hair behind my ear, the heat of his stare almost having its way with me.

"Who?" The question is breathy.

"Every man who has been in the same vicinity of you for more than a moment without falling to their knees to worship you."

"Oh dear," I squeak.

"No flirting," Lars yanks Lord James away by his collar.

"This is not flirtation. This is seduction. Quite different, I assure you. I am certain that you do not know the difference. No doubt your idea of seduction is hoisting someone over your shoulder and taking them back to your lair." Lord James jams a finger into Lars's chest.

"Your mother didn't seem to mind. Also, you're confusing her." He crowds Lord James, causing him to take two steps back. "This is overwhelming her."

"You are not supposed to be smelling her."

"I'm not. Just look at Georgia's face."

Lord James peeks around Lars and studies me for a beat. His features squint with concern at whatever he sees there.

"Alright. Let's add no seduction to the rules." He steps away from Lars. "At least, until my lady says otherwise."

"*Our* lady," Lars growls.

"Our?" I guffaw.

The absurdity of this situation slams into me with the blunt force of a train. I'm standing in my living room with two men I dreamed up and brought to fictional life from my books fighting over me while a third one stands by half-concerned and half-confused. Belly-deep laughs rack through me. The intensity of my laughter causes my knees to buckle, and I fall to the carpet, plopping onto my ass, with loud gulping laughs. Wentworth trots over, nuzzling into my arms.

"Georgia?"

"My lady?"

"Rabbit?"

Raising my hands in the air, I shake my head. The laughter steals my ability to speak. As unreal as this entire situation is, what breaks me is that these three men that I wrote believe they are here to date me. That, after all the bad dates, my Mr. Right may have just been in one of my books.

"Someone approaches." Lars grits out, his spine straight.

The doorknob turns, and then a loud bang at my door silences my laughter. My three would-be suitors meet my wide eyes.

Lars prowls to the door and sniffs. "Not a threat. They smell related to you, Georgia." He tosses a 'not sorry' expression at me over his shoulder. "You didn't say anything about me not smelling anyone else."

"Georgia? Why's the door locked?" Jackson's muffled voice filters through my front door.

CHAPTER SIX

YOU MADE HER CRY, FUCKER!

"Crap! Jackson," I yelp, jumping to my feet.

"Who's Jackson? Uncle? Cousin? No..." Head shaking, Lars sniffs the air. "Brother."

"Yes." Pulse ticked up, my gaze jumps between them and the door.

How am I going to explain the appearance of these three men? If I tell him the truth, he'll think I've truly lost the plot this time. Jackson may be the more understanding of my brothers, but he leans more into Camp Rem territory at times. Unlike Rem, he's actually read my books, even if he worries about my financial investment in my writing.

Lying is always an option. Merely smile and say, "These are old friends that you've never met nor heard about" or "Hey, you're super worried about me having a date for our cousin's wedding, well here are three contenders," but neglect to mention they are fictional characters.

Ugh. I rub my brows at the realization that none of this will work. Jackson is a bloodhound. He may play finance bro meathead at times, but he's the most perceptive of the Lane siblings.

"Georgia, are you okay?" Jackson knocks again.

"Totally." I cringe at my high-pitched tone. "Hide!" I whisper-shout, making a shooing motion toward the bedroom.

"I'm not hiding like a scared pup." An incredulous expression twists Lars's features.

"For once, I agree with the mongrel," Lord James drawls.

"Mongrel? I am pure red wolf," Lars spats out, moving toward Lord James.

"Not the time." Owen jumps between them. "We also agreed no fighting and no wolf slurs."

"Yeah. Stop being speciesist, Lord Fuckwad." Lars flicks Lord James's nose, who slaps him away.

"Who are those voices? Are you okay? Do you need help? Can you open the door? I don't have my spare key?" Concern coats Jackson's words.

"Audiobook!" I yell and shoot a *please help me* look at Owen.

Shaking his head, he grabs both men's shoulders. "We're here to help, so let's help."

"Let me just turn off my audiobook," I shout, my eyes flicking to where Owen ushers my annoyed duke and now-grumpy werewolf into the bedroom.

"Keep them quiet, and… don't let them kill each other," I hiss.

Once the bedroom door shuts, I stand for just a moment. With a deep inhale, I smooth down my hair and move to the door. On the other side, stands my younger brother. Despite the bill of the OC Soccer Club cap shading his eyes, the annoyance in his gaze is evident in the firm line that anchors his jawline.

"You *never* lock the door." It comes out as more of an accusation than a statement of fact. "You even sometimes forget to lock it when you leave. Rem checks most mornings before he heads to the office."

A furrow lines my brow. In my defense, a six-foot-tall

stone wall encircles the property, including my carriage house apartment.

"Was the door locked because you were listening to a smutty audiobook?" The corners of his mouth flex into a lascivious grin.

"If I were, that's none of *your* business. Why are you here?" I sigh, moving so he can enter. "Shouldn't you be at your intramural fight club or whatever you do on a Saturday afternoon?"

"Fight club is on Tuesdays," he jests and strides to the sofa, picking up the baseball bat and holding it up. "Why's Justice's Arm out?"

"I'm rearranging things." I stride over and yank the bat out of his hand.

His lips twitch into a cheeky grin. "What kind of audiobook are you listening to?"

Mouth tight, I just glare.

He chuckles and plops down. "I just came from pickleball with Davis."

"Oh," I say, ignoring the sudden queasiness in my belly, and propping the bat against the bookshelf.

No doubt Davis regaled him with me leaving mid-way through our first drink. Even if there's a good reason why I pulled the plug on the date, Jackson may see it as Rem does. That this is just another example of me being picky or still being hung up on Will. That I sabotage every potential relationship before it's even left the ground.

"How'd it go last night?" Jackson tosses his cap onto the cushion beside him, his strawberry blond hair tousled and a little damp. From the almost dry sweat dotting his gray T-shirt, the damp hair is no doubt also part of the afterglow from his pickleball match.

"He didn't say?"

He plucks up a muffin from the plate that rests on the coffee table beside the mug Lord James had been drinking from. Heart racing, I scan the room for any signs that I'm not the only one here. Anything that would catch the attention of my nosy younger brother. Outside of the bat, it's all textbook for my place; a laundry basket full of now folded clothes, a single mug of tea, and carbs.

"This is good," he moans with his first bite of muffin. "Did Hope bake this?"

"New bakery."

"And it's gluten free? It's too good to be." He flashes an apologetic expression. "Sorry."

"Back to Davis." I gesture impatiently.

Curiosity almost pulses inside me to know what he'd told Jackson about our date. Though could the forty-ish minutes we spent together even be considered a date?

"He said you were lovely."

"What?" I gape. "He did not."

Lovely? None of this makes sense. Had Davis had a second date after us that he's confusing me with? In what world would the appropriate response to last night be "she was lovely"?

He shrugs. "He did."

Head cocked to the right, I nibble on the corner of my mouth. "What specifically did he say?"

"Other than you were lovely, nothing. The guy's a vault—"

"Ha!" I bark a dismissive laugh. "Surprised you'd set me up with somebody you couldn't get all the details from."

"Trust me, I'm as shocked." He smirks. "Was the smutty audiobook you claim you weren't listening to in aid of some pent-up tension after your date with Davis?"

"Gross!" My nose crinkles. "You're my brother."

He rolls his eyes. "Says the older sister who gave me condoms before I took Mark Soto to the prom."

"In fairness, they were the ones you'd gifted me for my birthday."

"We are a safety-first family." He chuckles.

With an eyeroll, I shuffle to the kitchen and open the fridge to grab a bottle of iced tea. "Why don't I grab us some drinks and we go sit outside?"

It's best to get Jackson out of here. I'm not sure how long Owen can keep Lars and Lord James quiet. Not to mention, my brother's spidey sense may go off at any point. Just like Lars, Jackson also seems to sense things others don't.

His head tilts. "You trying to get rid of me?"

"No!" Guilt is evident in my laughing reply. "It's just such a beautiful day."

He arches an eyebrow.

"Why did you set me up with Davis?" I ask, hoping to deflect his curiosity and satisfy my own.

"Besides him being a snack, I thought you'd be perfect for each other," he says through a mouthful of muffin.

"Because he's single and breathing?" I grumble.

"It helps."

I shoot him a death glare.

"You have things in common. He's a big reader—"

"Of heterosexual, white, cis, non-disabled men," I mutter.

"Georgia..." He shakes his head.

The way my name tumbles out of him telegraphs his assessment that things didn't work out between me and Davis. No doubt, that's why he's here. Davis may be a vault, but my brother is smart enough to figure out that our date hadn't gone well. No giddy texts were sent post-date. Not like with past Mr. Potentials. Back before Will, and since then, the seemingly unending train of bad luck dates.

"We're not a good fit," I say, my spine straight.

"Did you even give him a chance?" Brows lifted, he rises and places his hands on his hips. "Of course you didn't. I should have listened to my gut."

Hurt radiates in my chest. "You and Rem and this narrative." I slam the iced tea bottle onto the counter.

"What narrative?"

"The one where Georgia is a disappointment, still hung up on Will."

He blanches. "That's not—"

"You just said you should have listened to your gut about Davis!" I toss my hands into the air. "Why'd you even bother if you knew I was going to fuck it up?"

"I thought you two would be a good fit."

"Suuuure!" I let out an incredulous laugh. "I'm a perfect fit for one of your finance bros."

"Judgy much? Also, he's not a finance bro. He's..." He shakes his head. "It doesn't matter. He could be one of your perfect book boyfriends, and you'd still find an excuse to not date him."

"Maybe focus on your *own* love life and leave mine alone. You don't have a date for the wedding either." Exasperation burns within me, its flames boiling my blood.

It's not like I'm the only Lane sibling who will be single at our cousin Lena's wedding. Jackson is just as single, but nobody worries about him. We just smile at his string of short-term relationships and friends with benefits situationships.

"It's not *my* ex marrying *our* cousin." His gaze meets mine, pity swimming in those brown pupils.

I know his words aren't meant to hurt, but they are almost a kill shot. It's been months since my cousin Lena's wedding invitation arrived. An invitation for every member of the Lane family, including me, the cousin whose ex she's marrying. We'd always been close as we are the same age. Sleepovers. Parties. Double dates. We shared everything, including, apparently, my boyfriend.

One month after the breakup with Will, I learned the truth that when he'd said, "I don't want this," what he'd meant was "I don't want this with *you*." He'd wanted it with her, and she was good with that.

"Thanks for the reminder," I croak.

"Georgia." He tips his head back and lets out a heavy sigh. "I'm sorry."

"For what? For the bad blind date? For thinking I'm a fuck up? For telling me I should have listened to your warning about Will?" I swallow back the hard lump in my throat, the sting of unshed tears building.

With his thumb always on the pulse of who people are, Jackson had raised concerns. Concerns I brushed off. *They spend a lot of time together.* They're just friends. *I don't like the way they look at each other.* You read too much into things. *I don't know if moving in with Will is wise.* You're acting like Rem, be my fun brother.

I swipe at my face. The battle with my tears is lost. It's all too much to hold in. Will. Lena. My brothers. My writer's block. The three men currently hiding in my bedroom.

He takes two steps closer, but stops, his expression weary but soft. "Georgia—"

"Don't you dare, fucker!"

I spin to find Lars storming from the bedroom. Despite Owen's attempt to pull him back, he breaks free and stalks toward Jackson.

"What the…" Eyes wide, Jackson points at the beast of a man charging toward him.

"I won't stay hidden while you hurt her. I don't care who *you* are."

"Who are you?" Jackson shouts.

"You're worst nightmare."

"Lars! No!" Chest heaving, I look to Owen and Lord James for help.

"Sorry, Georgia! I tried to hold them back, but…" Owen stands in the open bedroom door, his features twisted with regret.

"We're here, my lady," Lord James soothes, pushing past

Owen and striding to me. He pulls me into his firm chest. "Lars shall dispense with that emotional ruffian."

"At least you're calling him Lars, now." Owen sighs.

"My lady? What—" Jackson's question is cut short by Lars's large hands curled into his shirt, a menacing scowl covers his face.

"Ours," he growls.

"Georgia, what's happening?"

CHAPTER SEVEN

YOU WROTE YOUR OWN BOYFRIENDS?

"Let go of me." Jackson squirms in Lars's clenched fists, the pale white of the alpha's knuckles a sharp contrast against his olive-toned skin.

"Not until you apologize for hurting your sister," Lars grits.

Wentworth shoots up, barking loudly. It's the first time he's shown any protectiveness. Though I can't tell if he barks to defend Lars or Jackson. Owen scoops him up, despite his chunky seventy pounds, and soothes his barks.

"I didn't hurt her," Jackson spits out.

Is this really happening? My breath catches at the ominous fixation of Lars's eyes on my brother.

"It will be alright, my lady," Lord James assures, pressing a tender kiss to my temple, his masculine scent overwhelming my senses.

Like a stray kitten, I lean into the sturdiness of his arms as if it's my new home. This is where I live now… In the arms of a fictional duke while a fictional werewolf threatens my brother and a fictional baker stands by, exasperation twisting his expression.

"You made her cry," Lars sneers, baring his large teeth.

Jackson's eyes jump to mine, remorse swimming in the brown pupils. "Georgia, I didn't mean to make you cry."

"Do better." Lightning flashes in Lars's eyes. "That's not an apology."

Despite my body's protest, I pull from Lord James's embrace and round the kitchen counter. "Lars, it's alright, I—"

My protest is cut off by Jackson slipping out of Lars's grip. In a swift motion, he maneuvers the burly werewolf into a headlock.

"I repeat, who are you?" he snarls.

"Pretty boy has moves." An amused chuckle slips from Lars.

"Wrestled in high school." Jaw clenched, he tightens his hold. "Even went to the state tournament."

"Impressive."

Hands on hips, I huff out an annoyed breath. "Would you please let Lars go and—"

"But high school was a long time ago." A dark laugh vibrates from Lars. Hitching forward, he moves to break out of Jackson's hold, then launches my brother into the air.

"Jackson!" I lunge forward as if to catch him.

"My lady!" Lord James's arms loop around my waist, pulling me back against his front and ensuring I don't crash into my brother's flailing body.

Jackson drops to the carpet with a loud thud. "Oof," he groans, his face pinched with pain.

"State champion, huh? Must not be a *big* state." He places his boot atop Jackson's chest.

"Your...mom...never   complained   about...the   size," Jackson gasps out his retort.

"Ha!" Lars's violet eyes almost twinkle with admiration. "Nice one, pretty boy."

"You...wish...you were as pretty as me."

He leans over, his face hovering mere inches from Jackson's. "Says the man who's flat on his back for me."

"You wish. You're cute… But not *my* type."

He smirks. "I'm *everyone's* type."

"If you're into the wolfman lumberjack thing," he scoffs playfully.

If Lars didn't appear straight out of central casting as sexy werewolf number one from a paranormal TV show, Jackson's comment would give me pause, as if he knew who these three men were. With his flannel shirt that molds over a 'carved out of stone' physique, ripped fitted jeans, black boots, and dark beard and hair, he's the epitome of the pack alpha from an episode of *True Blood*.

Lars howls with laughter. "I think I'm going to like you." A furrow notches his brow. "Well, I will once you apologize to Georgia."

"The feeling may be mutual, once you take your boot off my chest."

"Wonderful, there are two of them," Lord James mutters.

Oh, god. I pinch the bridge of my nose. Did I accidentally base elements of my snarky werewolf character on my brother? If one of these three men is, indeed, whom I'm supposed to end up with, this assures Lars is no longer a contender. My brothers may think I'm picky, but this one I'm sure they'll bless. Romantic entanglements with fictional men are one thing, but those having shared personality traits with my brothers are deal-breakers.

Good lord, am I seriously considering dating one of these men? Also, are they even real live men if I made them up? I rub the erratic pulse beating in my temples, the twinge of a coming headache forming.

"Jackson, are you okay?" I ask.

"I will be once Wolverine lets me up." He juts his chin up at Lars, who merely grins.

"Lars, would you please let Jackson up?" I sigh.

"Once he apologizes."

"Lars?"

Ignoring my brother, I go on, "He did. He said he didn't mean to upset me."

"That's not an apology."

"He's right." Jackson turns his head on the floor to look toward me. "I am sorry, Georgia. My *not* intending to hurt you doesn't change the fact that I did… And I'm so sorry. You've had enough happening without me pushing or lecturing you."

"What's been happening, Georgia?" Owen places a calm Wentworth down.

"Nothing," I lie.

There's enough going on here. The last thing we need to add to this ridiculous scenario is the melodrama that is my life.

Sighing, I motion at Lars. "Please let him up."

With a nod, he removes his boot and extends his hand to help Jackson up.

"And you should apologize for attacking Jackson." One eyebrow lifted, I take in Lars's now sheepish face.

"Sorry. As alpha, I get a little overprotective. Not to mention, in my pack, we tussle a bit." He pats Jackson's back.

"Alpha? Pack?" Jackson looks between the three men, then jerks his gaze back to me. "Who are these guys?"

"Uh…" I worry my lower lip.

The lies form so easily inside me, but none breach my lips. How to explain who these men are. Telling falsehoods, even for the sake of keeping the peace, isn't my strong suit. Not to mention, Jackson always sees through them.

"I'm Lars. We've met." His mouth quirks.

Relinquishing his hold on me, Lord James strides to my brother. "And I'm Lord James Everly, First Duke of Chamberlin. Your sister is my future intended."

"She's what?" Jackson's eyebrows shoot into his hairline.

"Excuse me!" Marching up to Lord James, I jab a finger into his way-too-sculpted chest. "I am nothing of the sort."

"My lady, it's only a matter of time. After all, this is why we're here."

"That may be true, but we only just met." I toss my arms into the air, my voice hitting an almost shrill octave.

"Why *they're* here?" Jackson's head tilts.

"What makes you think it will be you?" Lars says, incredulous.

"You're after my sister, too?"

Ignoring them, Lord James moves closer, raising his hand and cradling my cheek. "My lady, you must feel what is between us. Not only have I been utterly enraptured by you since you appeared in that vision, but there is a pull between us. I know you feel it too."

The flutter in my chest doesn't disagree. Like a gravitational pull, something unseen attracts me to Lord James. My body reacts to each of these men, but it comes alive with *his* attention.

"From the moment I caught you when you fainted, I knew you were meant to always be in my arms." He leans in, his lips scant inches from mine, his breath a ghost of a kiss.

"You caught me? You put me to bed?" I breathe.

"I'll always catch you, my lady," he murmurs, swiping the smooth pads of his fingers against my skin.

A drunken buzz bubbles in my bloodstream with his pretty promises. How easy it would be to allow him to sweep me off my feet, replacing Lady Cecily in his story. But that's not my story. It's hers.

"Alright, Lord No Boundaries—" Lars grabs Lord James by the arm and tugs him away "—rules, remember. No seduction until she asks for it."

"It is only a matter of time before she asks for it. From me." He yanks himself from Lars's grip, wickedness blazes in his green eyes.

"Careful; that's my sister." Jackson shoots a warning glare. "Rules? What's happening?"

"Your sister somehow summoned us from her books to help find her happy ending." Owen emerges from the bedroom with copies of each of my books in hand.

In the chaos of the last few moments, I didn't realize he'd slipped away into the bedroom. To where one of the three bookshelves throughout my small apartment sits. The one with each of the proof copies of my novels.

"We have a lot to discuss." He tosses all three books onto the coffee table.

All our gazes are drawn to the three discreet cartoon covers popular with romance novels. The kind that hides the sexy nature of what you're reading from fellow passengers at airport terminals. Nobody would suspect behind those covers lies a small town baker that drizzles icing all over his lady love before licking her clean, a werewolf that bends his vampire rival over the hood of his pickup as he fucks her, or a Duke that uses his cravat to muzzle his lady's moans as he falls to his knees and feasts on her in her father's study.

My brother's wide eyes illustrate his understanding. There's an uncanny–almost identical–resemblance of each man that stands in my living room to their cartoon versions on the book covers.

"Georgia." My name is almost an accusation from my brother.

"I didn't mean for this to happen," I croak.

"I know." Owen places a hand on my shoulder, its warmth forcing my focus to him. "Let's have tea and muffins, and we'll talk."

"Are they gluten free, because my sister has celiacs, and—"

I shoot him a sharp look and lift my hand a little. Clearly, my brother is unable to turn off his ability to interfere in my life. I know he and Rem both mean well. My mother's soft voice almost whispers inside me, *"That's what brothers do for sisters,"* but it would be nice if they meant well just a little less.

"Of course they are. I would never do anything to put Georgia at risk." Owens' forehead pinches.

"How'd you know?" I clear my throat.

"After we appeared"—he makes air quotes with his fingers—"I decided to do some stress-relieving baking as we put things together. You only had gluten free ingredients in your cabinets, which I used for the muffins. But thank you for letting me know it's a dietary restriction versus a preference." He juts his chin toward Jackson. "Now, there's a lot to process, so let's get to it."

And that's what we do. I sit, my fingers curled tight around my *Book Men v. Real Men* mug—the irony not lost on me—and peer between each man that claims a different part of the apartment. Owen sits beside me, his expression warm, offering periodic reassuring pats on my thigh. Lars leans against the windowsill, his arms crossed and his gaze moving between Jackson and me. Jackson almost mirrors Lars's position but leans against the kitchen island facing into the living room. Lord James sits, posture upright and rigid, expression flat, at my small dining room table.

"You tossed a penny into a fountain, and this happened?" Jackson scrubs his palms down his face.

"It appears so," I say with a slight tremor in my voice. After laying it all out for my brother and my trio of suitors, it makes even less sense. There's no logical explanation for any of this. I didn't wish for this. *All I want is to know what my happy ending is and how to get it.* I lean my head against the sofa cushions. "What have I done?"

"How do we fix this?" Jackson waves his hand in front of him.

Lord James's right eyebrow ticks up. "Fix what?"

"You all. Getting you back to your books."

"There's nothing to fix," Lars says dismissively. "We're here for a purpose—"

"But you're *not* real."

"Was I not real when I knocked you on your ass."

"Rematch?" Jackson's mouth quirks.

Lars mirrors Jackson's smirk. "Anytime."

"Enough with the dick swinging." I place my mug on the coffee table and stand up. "I don't know what is happening, but they are here for a reason."

As farcical as this is, there's a reason for this. I want to know what my happy ending is and how to get it. Whether fate, my happy ending-riddled brain, or the lucky penny Doc gave me that conjured these men, there's a reason they are here.

"Fine." Jackson straightens. "If you're going to do this, we might as well do it properly."

"What does that mean?" I face him.

"Let's figure out which one of these bachelors is the future Mr. Georgia Lane."

"Wait? You believe that one of them is meant to be with me?" I shoot him a disbelieving look.

Jackson may be my fun brother, but he's still the logical one. He's Mr. Finance with his quarterly projections and love of spreadsheets.

"It's about as far-fetched as the idea of three fictional men coming to life. No offense, guys." He flashes an apologetic smirk. "Somehow they're here and they believe their purpose is to date you."

"It's ridiculous." I toss my hands.

"Now who's rude?" Lars snarks.

"Sorry." I frown. "It's just… This is a lot to process. And how are you so accepting of this?" I ask Jackson.

"Because in business, you sometimes have to trust your gut, and mine says this is real. They appeared after you made a wish for your happy ending. If they're real, then so is their purpose."

I shake my head. "You can't be serious."

"I am."

"So are we," Lars adds.

"You just *believe* that one of you may be meant for me?" I gesture to them.

It's too much to process that they believe they're here to date me. Maybe it's the residue of the last five years, but the idea that one of these men would actually want me is more far-fetched than their origins.

"It is not belief, it is certainty," Lord James says, his gaze locked on me. "Just as I know the sun will rise, I know that I am here because of you."

"For you." Lars clears his throat. "*We* are here for you."

"It doesn't make sense to us either, Georgia, but we know it. It's like how I just know how much salt to sprinkle in without measuring," Owen says.

I take in their words. This whole situation is like something out of a silly rom-com, but it's happening. It's my reality.

Jackson crosses over and places his hands on my shoulders. "Like you said, they're here for a reason. They're here for you. Give it a chance." He grins. "At least, for the next eight days."

"Why the next eight days?"

"That way, you can make a choice before the wedding." A wry smile bursts across his face like a sunbeam. "Although, if you took all three that would be the best fuck you to Will and Lena."

"Who are Will and Lena?" Owen asks.

"And why do we want to give them a fuck you?" Lord James's head tilts.

"Do I have to end someone?" Lars growls.

"Will is Georgia's asshole ex, who'd strung her along for

five years, asked her to move in, and days before she did, broke up with her via text message. Fuckhat. Turns out he'd been pining for our cousin Lena, who'd broken up with her boyfriend, so he dropped Georgia to seize his chance with her. They're getting married in a week," Jackson lays out the whole sordid story, minus some of the more heartbreaking bits and pieces.

Like the fact that, despite the story they spun that it didn't start until after we broke up, they'd had several "moments" during the tenure of our relationship. Lena, who'd at least had the kindness—if you can call it that—told me in person. A month after the breakup, she sat on my sofa, tears in her eyes, and admitted everything. Their mutual attraction. How they fought it. Their loss of that fight several times in the final three years of Will and my relationship.

"So, I do have to end someone." Lars's features grow menacing.

"Jackson!" I narrow my eyes at my brother.

"If you're going to date them, you'll need to share these things with them. Relationships are about honest communication. I believe someone uses them as story arcs in her smutty books." Jackson wags a finger.

"Our stories aren't that..." Owen closes his mouth, no doubt thinking about the icing scene that occurred well before my wish snatched him from his story to mine.

For teleporting to the real world and learning that the woman in their vision is the author of their stories, all three appear to be handling this situation well. Though I'm known for writing steady male main characters. Lars's quick temper aside, all three of my fictional suitors are steadfast captains amid choppy waters. They meet every gust of wind and slap of a wave, no matter how it batters their boat around. Thank god, I don't write explosive, morally gray mafia dons or knife-wielding stalkers.

"Gentlemen, you're coming with me." Jackson pushes away from the counter.

"What?" I blink.

"I'm not leaving these three men alone with you. First, your place is too small to accommodate all of you. Two, I'm sure you wouldn't like to explain them to our older brother."

Rem. He wouldn't be as cool about this as Jackson. It may just fuel his desire for me to move out. Not to mention how this may stress Hope.

"Three, pretty sure Lord Tight Trousers over there plans to practice the art of not-so-subtle seduction and find his way into your bed in the middle of the night." Jackson glares at Lord James.

"Excuse me? My trousers are the appropriate fit." Lord James says, aghast.

"And you're not in the right mind to deal with second-rate Mr. Darcy," he goes on.

"You don't see us as a threat?" Smirking, Lars points to himself and then to Owen.

"That's right, True Blood, I'm not worried about you and small-town British Bake Off over there. You're not all insta-lovey like that one." He tips his head toward a scowling Lord James. "Four, if we're going to do this, we're going to do it right to figure out which of these three is your perfect fit."

Am I really agreeing to a literary version of *The Bachelorette*? Despite the anxiety that buzzes just below my skin's surface, something pulls me on. All I keep thinking is about Doc saying that we first need a little luck in order to make something of it. Maybe these three men are that luck, and I just need to make something of it. Do what my brothers have been pushing me to do since Will: Give someone a chance.

"Alright," I breathe.

CHAPTER EIGHT

IT WILL BE OKAY

Did I write my soulmate? The thought taunts me as I pack up what muffins the guys didn't eat yesterday, before Jackson took them to his place, to take to my mom. With the crazy topsy-turvy spin my life took this weekend, all I want is to soak up some of Mom's calming presence. She may be the practical parent, but she's as warm and soothing as apple cinnamon tea.

"Muffin delivery," I sing, holding up the plastic-wrapped plate and stepping fully into her apartment.

Seven years ago, Mom moved here. The senior community is more accessible than her house and offers her both independence and socialization. There are several book clubs, water aerobics, and a rather intense cornhole league that my mom dominates with Allen, her boyfriend who lives across the courtyard.

She chews her first bite, moaning quietly, then swallows and asks, "Did Hope make these?"

"No… Another friend." I shift in the chair.

We sit at the small dining room table, a pot of green tea and the plate of muffins between us. Everyone points out how much I look like her with my large brown eyes, fair complexion, curvy figure, and long dark hair. Strands of gray may wave through my mom's now short hair, and wrinkles kiss the edges of her eyes, but it's easy to see the mother/daughter resemblance.

The same people who talk about how much I look like my mother point out how I am *nothing* like her. With a career in corporate finance —before she retired last year – she's logic and data-oriented.

"A male friend?" She waggles her thin eyebrows.

"Yeah," I let out a hard breath.

"Not second date material?" She picks up her teacup, assessment winking in her eyes.

"I don't know." I fiddle with the placemat's lacy edge. "We haven't gone on an actual first date. In fact…" Gnawing my lip, I mull over what exactly to tell her.

Normally, this would be a conversation with Hope, and the jury's still out on *when* I'll tell her. Let's face it, I'll tell my bestie about this. I can't lie to her, but I need to wait. This situation is too stressful to put on her, especially with the doctor's concern about her blood pressure.

She smiles. "But there's someone else?"

"Two other potential guys, in fact."

"I see you've entered your *why choose romance* era." Her pink lips tip up into a teasing grin.

I snort out a laugh. "And you're supposed to be the practical parent."

"Having only one person meet all your needs is impractical." She sips her tea.

"I don't think I'm built for multiple boyfriends. One is hard enough."

"Polyamory or monogamy—" she bats at the air with her hand "—as long as whoever you're in a relationship with treats you well and doesn't smoke." Her nose scrunches. "No smokers, Georgia."

I chuckle.

"I just don't want you to put all your hope for happiness in *a* relationship."

"Tell your sons that. They're obsessed with my romantic viability."

She shakes her head. "Your brothers just want to see you settled. They worry."

"Do you worry?" I swallow thickly.

"I worry about all my children."

"Nice dodge of my question." Smirking, I sip my tea.

"I've had practice." She winks and grabs her teacup. "Relationship or not, happiness shouldn't be contingent on any *one* thing. Career. Romance. Family. If the twists and turns of my life have taught me anything, it's that true happiness is about being well-rounded." She waves to herself. "It's always the sum of those pieces that brings me joy. Never forget that our lives aren't just *a* single picture, but the entire collage."

What does my collage look like? I know what I'd like it to look like. The career. The family. The passion for my writing. Someone to share it all with. The knot that winds tighter in my stomach steels me against the truth; there are too many missing pieces to complete the picture of my hopes for my life.

I clear my throat, pushing out the emotion that clusters there. "Jackson wants me to date all three of these men like my own personal dating show."

"Of course he does." Her laugh-filled expression sobers. "Is this about the wedding? You don't need to go."

"But I do," I say, my spine straight. "We're family."

It's not the familiar relationship with Lena that pushes me to attend. It's my mother. Lena is the daughter of my mom's only sister, Maggie. Twenty-nine years ago, Aunt Maggie died unexpectedly of a blood clot, leaving Lena and her dad behind. My mom stepped in to help Uncle Hans raise my cousin. In so many ways, my mom is the only mother Lena has known. All the mother-daughter things were always done for both of us by my mom. Makeup tutorials. Prom dress shopping. The sex talk.

Thanks to Jackson, I know that Mom helped Lena pick out her wedding dress. Something we'd dreamed about doing as girls together. Not just as girls, but as women. Only now, I realize that at times we daydreamed about the same groom to complete our wedding fantasies.

This whole situation is messy enough. The last thing it needs is for me to make my mom choose between me and Lena. Mom will choose me, which means losing the last tether to her sister, and Lena would lose the sole maternal figure she has. It's why I've never told her or my brothers that Lena and Will's relationship actually started before we broke up. Though I suspect Jackson's put the pieces together. That knowledge may solidify this betrayal in their books, snapping any already tenuous relationship.

My heart may never forgive Lena, but I can eat over-cooked steak, make small talk with extended relatives, and fake smile, at least for a few hours.

"It's totally fine." I tighten my smile.

"You don't have to do this." Mom reaches her hand across the small table, threading our fingers together. "If this is too much for you—"

"It will be okay." I force an extra sprinkle of sweetness into my voice, hoping it hides the shake in my resolve. "After all, I may have a sexy date and, if that doesn't work out there's an open bar."

The conversation with my mom weighs heavily on me as I walk through the SPN doors. The moment that distinctive disinfectant and lavender aroma fills my nostrils, my muscles relax. It's Sunday, so the facility's hustle and bustle is a mere murmur. Most staff, outside of each unit's nurses and some support staff, don't work on the weekends, and visitors tend to trickle in later in the day. The serenity I find at SPN isn't the only reason I'm here.

"Doc." With a wave, I stride into the courtyard.

"Peach!" He beams, looking up from the stack of board games in front of him.

Each Sunday, Doc hosts a lunchtime board game party for patients. With a lone pair of two men squaring off over checkers at one of the tables and other patients departing, it appears they've just wrapped up.

"Here for some chess or, perhaps"—he shakes a small rectangular box—"dominoes?"

"Nah." I make a dismissive gesture. "I actually have a question for you."

"If it's to be the date to that wedding, done. Although my grandson Kenny looks better in a tux." He winks.

The offer, while sweet, stiffens my spine. Doc's cupid antics are always done with his good-natured focus on help-ing, but right now, it pokes at the gaping wound that reopened yesterday.

"I've got it covered." My smile flattens.

He arches one bushy eyebrow, seeming to assess me. Just like Pilar and Jackson, he's perceptive, and I'm not doing a good job of hiding my emotions. The mask I wear in moments like this is cracking.

"What can I do for you, Peach?" He takes pity on me rather than asking the questions visible in his expression.

"You've been here the longest of any of the staff." I fiddle with the end of my long ponytail, trying to figure out how to ask this question. "Um… Have you ever heard of anything strange happening here?"

He tilts his head. "Strange? What do you mean?"

I shift foot-to-foot. "Like supernatural?"

He taps his fingers against the stack of board games. "Like ghosts? We always open the windows after someone passes, and there are some nurses that burn sage from time to time after a particularly pain-in-the-ass guest checks out, in hopes that they don't linger—"

"Not ghosts, but magic. Maybe things associated with the fountain? Like wishes coming true…" I trail off, realizing how ridiculous this all sounds. If the book boyfriend-shaped proof weren't currently at my brother's place, I wouldn't believe it myself.

He twists towards the fountain, and then back at me. "There's folklore about fountains, like the Trevi in Italy, granting wishes.

"You toss a coin in to make the wish."

"The coin isn't to make the wish, but to pay for the wish being made. All wishes have prices that someone must pay," Doc says.

Like three men ripped from their stories with guaranteed happy endings. They're paying the price for my wish. Guilt sloshes inside me. Even if one of them turns out to be my happy ending, what happens to the other two? To the three women they've left behind? Real or not, their happy endings are gone. *Because of me.*

"Peach, are you okay?" Concern furrows his brow.

"Yeah," I breathe, stepping back. "Just being silly."

"You know what cures silly?" He rises. "Cookies. I believe I know where there are some gluten free Oreos around here."

"Yeah. My office." I chuckle. "Doesn't Estelle have you on a no-sugar diet?"

He grabs the stack of boxes. "What she doesn't know."

"Let me take those, at least." I reach for them.

But he backs away, chuckling. "I've got this. You're as bad as my Kenny thinking he's got to come over a few times a week to do chores. See what kind of man you're passing up?" he teases, continuing to move backwards until he hits a discarded chair. Jolting, he lurches forward, letting go of the boxes, his body tumbling forward and crashing into the table. The boxes skitter to the hard stone ground just as his body slams into it.

"Doc!" I fall to my knees beside him.

He landed on his side. A pained expression pinches his face, and a groan falls from his lips.

"Oh, my god!" One of the men at the table shoots up. "Is he okay?"

"I think he's hurt." With a shaky breath, I take in the agonizing twist of Doc's features.

"I'll get help," the other man says, standing and shuffling out of the courtyard.

Groaning, he tips his head up, eyes glossy and face pinched. "Peach…"

"Don't move," I order, stopping his attempted movement. "It's going to be alright." I'm not sure who I'm assuring: Him or myself.

CHAPTER NINE

YOU'RE PEACH?

My joints are stiff and achy from spending the last several hours in hard plastic chairs. After SPN's nurses rushed to help Doc, an ambulance was called. Since Estelle wasn't there, I rode with him, then posed as his granddaughter to sit beside his gurney in the ER until she arrived.

Now, we sit in the surgical waiting room. Doc's tumble resulted in a fractured hip. Thankfully, the orthopedic surgeon said he'd only need a simple surgery to repair it and took him to the OR a few hours ago. Despite Doc's eighty-fifth birthday next month, he and Estelle are in good health. Besides the head cold he had two years ago, this is the first medical scare I've witnessed for him or Estelle.

Still, worry blends with the guilt swirling inside me. Its acidic mix causes a burn in my stomach. This is all my fault. If only I hadn't reached for the games. Doc and Estelle would be at home enjoying Sunday dinner, instead of here. One in surgery for the last two hours and the other in the waiting room, a tense expression on her face.

"Do you want food? I could go to the cafeteria," I ask, nibbling on my lip, wanting to do something—anything—to help.

A wilted hospital cafeteria salad would not absolve me from this. Moments before Doc fell, he talked about wishes needing to be paid for. Is this the price? As if the three happy endings I stole weren't enough, I'd somehow caused Doc's injury.

"I'm okay." Despite the hint of a smile flexing the corners of Estelle's mouth, concern swims in her expression.

"It will be okay. He's so strong. He may be in better shape than me," I say.

I'm not sure if the statement is to assure her or myself. Doc and Estelle are like no octogenarians I've met. Outside of Jackson, they aren't like most people of any age that I know. An exuberance radiates from both, causing me to almost forget that they are just as vulnerable to breaking as anyone else.

"He knows better than to die on me," she says.

I let out a soft snort of laughter.

"I know he'll be okay. I just worry how he'll handle being laid up for a bit. Henry's not one to slow down. Always doing something. It's why I sent him back to work after he retired. Three days into retirement, he'd fixed every squeaky door and replaced all the light fixtures in our house. The moment he started talking about renovating the kitchen, I shooed him away." A soft chuckle smooths her worried features. "Some souls are at peace with stillness, and others die because of it. Our Kenny's the same way. They both are in constant motion."

"Your grandson is just like Doc?"

"Always doing something. His brain never stops. It's what makes him brilliant at his work. Just like his grandfather." Affection curls her lips into a broad smile. "They're so close. They even play in a weekly cornhole league at a local bar…" she sighs. "But Henry will be out of commission for a bit."

"We'll figure out how to keep those things, even if they may need to be done a little differently during his recovery."

While this is a simple surgery, the recovery will take several months. As long as there aren't any complications, he'll spend a few days at the hospital before he's transferred to SPN. Both the admissions coordinator and Pilar are already aware that Doc will start his rehabilitation with us before transferring to outpatient therapy after a few days.

"Thank you for coordinating that." She threads our fingers and squeezes. "Knowing Henry, he'll not let this stop him from our Friday night readings or his Sunday board game tournaments."

"Probably not."

"Thank you for staying with me, even though you don't need to."

"I didn't want you to be alone." I shift in my seat.

Doc and Estelle's daughter, Deanna, and her wife, Mimi, live in Boston. Their grandson Kenny is the only family in the area, but he'd gotten on a plane this morning to fly to the Bay Area for work. Despite her assurance that it was okay, he booked a new flight to come home today.

If I am honest, even if Doc and Estelle's family were here, I may have still stuck around. The gnarled knot in my stomach may not unspool until I know he's okay. The truth that Doc is strong may pulse inside me, but so does the worry that I could be wrong. It wouldn't be the first time my gut instinct failed me.

She arches a sculpted eyebrow. "*Plus,* you feel guilty."

"I am *so* sorry."

"As I said in the E.R., you have nothing to apologize for." She shakes her head, a silent laugh lights her face. "You're just like our Kenny… Always taking responsibility for things that aren't your fault. Henry's accident was brought on because he is a stubborn old goat who refuses to accept help, even though *he's* the first to give it."

Nodding, I just swallow thickly.

"If you feel like you need to atone, maybe you can go find

us something to munch on after all. It's been hours since either of us ate."

It had been closer to nine a.m. when I'd shared a muffin with my mom. Slipping my cell phone out, I check the time. It's just seven in the evening. Somehow, the knowledge that it's been ten hours since I last ate wakes up my stomach, forcing out a low growl of hunger.

"I'll go grab something." I stand up and head to the cafeteria.

Just like SPN, the hospital is quiet on Sundays. Outside of a few staff, the halls are deserted. This isn't unheard of for most hospitals. This also means that the cafeteria offers limited hours or the weekends. By the time I reach it, the doors are shut. Thankfully, there's a small alcove down the hall with vending machines full of to-go premade meals.

"Naturally," I almost whine, perusing the mix of premade salads and sandwiches lining the machine's shelves

None of which are gluten free. Even if they are, they aren't trustworthy. I've been burned before by these grab-and-go situations. At least, I'm smart enough to have some nuts in my purse that I can snack on until I can grab something on the way home. It may be a few hours still. I'm not sure how much longer Doc will be in surgery or what Estelle plans once he's out. What I do know is that I won't be leaving until I know both are okay.

"My car," I groan, remembering that my car is still at SPN. Those nuts may have to tide me over longer than I thought. A frown pulls down my lips as my stomach unleashes a gurgling hunger pang.

Sighing, I grab a salad and a sandwich for Estelle and two bottles of water for us. I slip both bottles into my purse and head back to the waiting room with the plastic containers balanced in my left hand. Rounding the corner, I enter the long corridor that leads to the surgical waiting area. A loud *beep* snags my attention, causing me to look up just as an old man on a scooter speeds towards me.

"Look out!" someone shouts, grabbing me and spinning me into a firm chest, the plastic containers of food flying out of my hands and skittering to the ground.

"Crap," I draw out the word with a long breath, my face buried against my rescuer's chest, a minty fresh scent wafting off him.

"Sorry!" The old man calls, whizzing past us.

"Are you okay?" my rescuer asks, gripping my biceps. His touch soothes the frazzled nerves buzzing inside me.

"Yes." I nod, my head still pressed against him, the cadence of his heartbeat hums like a lullaby.

This is the second time in twenty-four hours that I find myself in someone's strong arms. Tension drains from my body with the warmth of this stranger's embrace. Not just the rigidity from almost being run down by a scooter, but from everything that's transpired since Friday night. The bad date. The argument with Rem. My book boyfriends. Doc.

"Are you sure?" His hands move from my arms to my back, offering calming strokes along my spine.

"Yes. Thank you..." Tipping my head up, my breath catches.

Ashen eyes rimmed in gold peek out through a pair of black frame glasses. Dark stubble dusts a strong jawline, and surprise seizes his expression.

"Davis," I murmur.

His mouth quirks. "Georgia."

"You think I'm lovely," I breathe.

His smile gets just a little bigger.

"I mean... You told Jackson I'm lovely." I wince. "That our date was lovely..."

Stop speaking! Stepping out of his embrace, I clamp my mouth shut. Mortification blazes heat up my neck and into my cheeks.

An awkward silence stretches between us. His gaze flicks from me to the beige walls to the off-white floor and then back to me. Confusion plays in the irises of those beautiful eyes. The same confusion that filled them Friday night.

Though *it* doesn't fill my narrowed gaze. I know exactly why I walked out on him. Despite the way my traitorous body just melted into him, Davis Mackenzie is an ass.

"What are you doing here?" I smooth down my blouse, scanning the empty hall to locate the salad and sandwich that flew out of my hand as Davis rescued me.

"Visiting someone," he says, turning to scoop up the containers, both still sealed, and holding them out. "I did."

Brows knitted, I take them. "Did what?"

"Tell Jackson it was lovely—" He rubs at his nape. "It was… until it wasn't."

"Until it wasn't," I repeat.

"But Jackson didn't need to know that."

"Because you promised him and you didn't want to disappoint him." I cross my arms over my chest. The action holds back the memory that Davis only went on the date as a favor to my brother.

"Isn't that also why you were there? You promised your brother?" He arches one dark eyebrow.

"Excuse me?"

He motions between us. "You promised Jackson you'd go on a blind date with me, so we both made promises."

"It's not the same," I scoff.

"It's exactly the same." A crease lines his forehead.

"I wasn't doing Jackson *a* favor. I was just saying yes to a blind date," I say, lips pursed.

"Favor?"

I motion wildly with the plastic containers. "To take out his relationship-challenged sister."

"Our date wasn't a favor."

"What was it? It was clear you didn't want to be there from the start."

"I wanted to be there." He takes a step forward.

"Suuuure… Being glued to your phone for the majority of our date screams interest."

He opens his mouth, closes it, and then lets out a harsh breath. "Stimming."

"What?" Face scrunched, my head tilts.

"I'm autistic. Stimming is part of it. I don't even realize I'm doing it half the time. It's a tic I can't control. I also click my tongue. Did I do that?"

"The phone, yes. The tongue clicking, no."

He nods.

"Do you also get fixated on topics?" I ask, cataloging some of the things I know about autism.

While my experience with neurodivergence may be limited, I know that autism isn't cookie-cutter for any person on the spectrum. I can't help to think of Edward, the physical therapy intern from two years ago. Doc called him Indy because of his fixation with Indiana Jones.

On the last day of his internship, we did a marathon of the original three Indiana Jones movies, complete with commentary between each film by Edward. His enthusiasm reminds me so much of Davis's during our date. Only Davis's enthusiasm was less about me and more about…

"Pickleball," he says, humor dancing in his features. "Did I fixate on it?"

"Just a bit." I offer a sassy smile. "You even suggested playing a game for our second date."

"Smooth." His head tips back as laughter rumbles in his chest.

"Why didn't you say anything?" I nibble on the corner of my mouth.

He shrugs. "Probably the same reason you don't tell first dates you have celiacs."

I point at him. "How do you know about…" I release an annoyed breath. "Jackson."

"He wanted to make sure I knew, so I didn't accidentally put you at risk. He mentioned something about a date a few years ago at a pizza parlor that ended with you having a bad reaction."

Overprotective men. My heart both swells at my brother's sweetness and pricks with annoyance. What happened at the pizza parlor could happen to anyone. No matter how hyper-vigilant I am, things can still happen. Eating outside of my home is always risky. But it's a calculated risk that I choose to take.

"We probably both want to wait for those conversations until date two," he says, a wry grin kicking across his face.

"Yeah. These conversations are best for the pickleball court," I tease.

"Yeah." Smirking, he steps closer, the heat of his body laps against me. "I promise that I *did* want to be there. I am sorry that I made you think otherwise."

His warm gaze is fixed on me, reminiscent of hands caressing my skin. An earnest plea fills his expression, loosening my resolve to be angry. I now know that he didn't ignore me. At least not deliberately. What I understand about stimming is that it helps self-regulate emotions and is often done unconsciously. Like when one is nervous on a first date.

But that doesn't explain why he insulted my writing. Bristling, I purse my lips. "You insulted me."

His mouth ticks down. "Georgia, I—"

"Honey, I told you that you didn't need to come."

Both our gazes snap to Estelle, who moves down the corridor toward us.

"Like I'd listen to that." He greets her, wrapping his arms around her in a tight hug. "How are you, Nan? How's Pop?"

Nan? Pop? I blink.

Estelle pulls back, her head tipped up and a big grin on her face. "You're such a good boy, Kenny."

Kenny? Mouth slack, my heart beats like stampeding horses. None of this makes sense. His name is Davis, not Kenny.

"I'm doing better now. The doctor just came out to let me know he got through surgery fine and is in recovery."

Despite the Davis/Kenny confusion, I let out a relieved breath at that. Doc's okay. Well, at least on his way to okay. There are still months of recovery ahead of him, but he's out of surgery.

"When can I see him?" Davis asks.

Should I call him Kenny, like Estelle and Doc do? I'm not sure what to call him. For a weekend that has involved three fictional men poofing into existence, this may be the more jarring fact. Somehow, Davis is Kenny, and Kenny is Davis.

"Tomorrow. They'll move him to a room in a bit. I'll hang around until he's settled." She steps back, her attention drops to me. "Oh, Peach, thank you so much for everything."

"Peach?" Davis spins, his brows nearly reaching his hairline. "You're Peach?"

"Georgia… But your grandparents call me Peach," I admit bashfully.

Clearly, Davis had no idea who I was, but the realization that wrinkles his features telegraphs that he knows who Peach is. No doubt Doc's cupid antics were done to both of us.

"Georgia Peach." His chuckle is warm.

Estelle's head cocks to the right. "You two know each other?"

"Georgia's brother Jackson works with me at No Boundaries," he offers.

"Works with you?" She bats the air. "Such modesty for the CEO and founder."

My right eyebrow may be fused into an arched position at

this point. In the course of a few minutes, everything I thought I knew about Davis was turned upside down. He's Kenny. Doc and Estelle's grandson. Also, he's not just a finance bro, but as No Boundaries' founder and CEO, he is their king.

"I can wait with you while they get Pop admitted," he says.

She shakes her head. "Not needed. Plus, someone needs to take Peach home. She rode in the ambulance, so her car is at SPN."

"It's not—"

"Hush." Estelle dismisses my protest with a flick of her wrist. "It's the least we can do. You've taken such good care of us." She peers up at her grandson. "Peach never left our sides."

"Thank you." His grateful gaze lands on me, causing something to swoop low in my belly.

Stop it! We don't like him. My body is at odds with everything. My brain is unable to reconcile Davis the asshole with Kenny, the sweet grandson of two of my favorite humans. How can he be the same person?

Davis looks between me and his grandmother. "Nan, how will you get home?"

"I drove myself here. I can drive myself home." Resolve glints in her eyes.

His mouth curves into a boyish grin. "I won't argue with you."

The exchange squeezes something in my chest. It's sweet how he worries but doesn't push. If this were me and my brothers, there'd be an entire lecture about how they should drive me home.

"Are those for me?" Estelle points to the food containers still in my hand.

"Yeah." I hand them to her. I pull out one of the water bottles from my purse. "And this."

"Such a thoughtful woman. Not to mention quite fetching." She nudges her grandson.

"You're relentless." With a laugh, he bends to place a tender kiss on her cheek. "Call me once he's settled and when you get home."

"See how thoughtful my handsome grandson is," she coos, winking at me.

"Relentless." My eyeroll is lighthearted.

With a wry grin, she turns and heads down the hall. "Oh, Kenny—" she looks over her shoulder. "Take Peach to grab a bite before you take her to her car. The poor thing hasn't eaten since breakfast."

We both shake our heads as Estelle disappears down the hall.

I clear my throat. "I have so many questions."

"I'm sure you do."

Brows lowered, I motion at him. "Why do they call you Kenny?"

He twists to face me, determination sparks in his eyes. "I'll answer all your questions at the restaurant."

Curiosity bubbles over inside me like a pot of water left on the burner too long. I want to know everything. How did Davis the ass turn out to be Kenny the thoughtful grandson? Despite his proclamation that he wanted to be on our date and never meant to make me feel otherwise, he is the same man who insulted me. The same man who belittled the idea of a happy ending.

"We don't need—"

"Please," he says, a soft plea punctuates that single word.

"Alright," I say, not knowing if it's due to hunger pangs or the pull of curiosity.

CHAPTER TEN

HAPPY ENDINGS

Davis pulls into the blacktop parking lot and parks his car. My gaze flicks to the neon glow of Fisher's Landing's sign above its main entrance.

"Back to the scene of the crime?" A cheeky smile slants my lips.

He turns off the car, twisting his head to meet my stare. "Maybe this time you won't leave halfway through our first drink."

It's a tease-filled comment, but I bristle nonetheless. As rude as leaving midway through a first date is, let's not forget that Davis's dismissive comments led us there.

"Maybe you won't insult me this time," I say, my tone stern but not curt.

"Georgia…" He leans back.

"Davis…" I narrow my eyes. "Or should I call you Kenny?"

"I'm both. Pop gave me the nickname when I was ten." He sits up and shifts in his seat to face me. "And I never insulted you."

"Not everyone is lucky enough to live in a fairy tale, Georgia," I

repeat his words from our date, pitching my voice low to mimic his deep timbre.

"I..." His indignant expression falls.

"You don't know anything about me," I say as hurt surges in my chest.

The snide remarks about romance aren't what stung. It was annoying, but not hurtful. As a romance reader and author, I hear those misguided characterizations of the genre all the time. *It lacks substance. It's not realistic.* All from folks who haven't read the genre. The twinge in my chest isn't about that, but rather, from Davis's assumptions about me. Assumptions that are far too much like the ones my brothers —*especially Rem*— have about me.

"Just because I believe in happy endings doesn't mean I live in a fantasy world. Contrary to what you think of me, my life hasn't been a fairy tale. People have hurt me. Disappointed me..." A small tremor shakes my voice. "But you wouldn't know that because you weren't present at our date. The stimming with your phone aside, you weren't engaged."

"I was engaged."

I roll my eyes. "Yeah, like one-word answers and very few questions about me scream engagement."

He releases a heavy sigh. "Peopling is hard for me."

"It's not easy for anyone." Despite the certainty in my retort, my squared shoulder slump at the hint of sadness underscoring his confession.

What I know about autism is that it can create barriers to connecting with others. It's different for each person, but there are varying degrees of challenges with social interactions.

"Sorry. I'm being insensitive." I meet his stare.

"It's okay."

"It's not. I shouldn't dismiss your experience like that. I don't know what it's like for you."

"To be fair, I don't know what it's like for you, either." His mouth tugs up into a boyish smile.

"I'd like to know." I rake my top teeth over my bottom lip.

"Okay." Warmth shimmers in his eyes. "Social cues aren't my forte. I can't always read them, making it hard to know when I need to talk more or less, or even if what I said was appropriate. I sometimes tend to say the quiet parts out loud, and that may offend some people." His face twists with self-reproach.

"Like asking if someone self-published because they can't get an agent or publisher?" My tone is teasing.

Groaning, he pinches the bridge of his nose. "God, I can't believe I said that. This is what I'm talking about. I often don't realize what I said is inappropriate until it's too late. There are interactions I think went great, only to find out they did not. Like with us."

"You thought our date was going well?" I guffaw.

"Until you walked out... I thought it was banter." He laughs. "But this is what I'm talking about. There are times, like with us. Then there're interactions that leave me knotted up thinking it was shit, only to find out it wasn't. It doesn't erase the self-loathing and the tendency to avoid that person in the in-between."

My mouth pulls into a reassuring smile. "I'll never know what life's like in your shoes, but I understand the challenges with people. It's difficult for me in a different way."

Social cues aren't an issue for me. Between my training as a social worker and my natural ability to read people, I tend to be tapped into most interactions. Though, maybe too tapped in, at times. I'm prone to spinning a bit. So much of my interactions with others is tied up in managing their emotions or, even, the emotions of those not directly involved in that exchange.

"I have this ever-present need to keep people happy, to

smooth away any potential wrinkles," I say, fiddling with my shirt's hem.

Outside of Hope, it isn't something I talk about with most people. Not my mom. Certainly not my brothers. But for some reason, I'm sharing this with Davis. Maybe it's his openness. Maybe it's this strange comfort that relaxes me in his presence. Even when I was angry with him, I was secure enough to walk out on him, despite knowing how it would upset Jackson. *Normal* Georgia would have just sat through that terrible date, if only to make my brother happy. Somehow, with him, I'm not normal, but strangely right.

"You could have fooled me. When I walked into the bar, you were chatting with other customers like you'd known them for years. You were so relaxed and free. I was immediately in awe of you. To be that self-assured to just be." Admiration and self-doubt glisten in his eyes. "There are few people I'm truly relaxed around to just exist as I am."

"It's easier with strangers. There's nothing to lose. As much as I want them to like me, it's not like how it is with the people in my life. There isn't an insistent tug to make them happy."

He nods. "No wonder you're a social worker. It fits."

"Thanks." My brow creases. "No wonder you do so many sports. Do the rules make it easier for you to be around people without having to actually people?"

He huffs a breathy laugh. "Look at you, Counselor Troi. Is someone psychoanalyzing me?"

A large grin curls my lips at the *Star Trek: The Next Generation* reference. I'd noticed the *TNG* phone case during our first date and will admit it ignited some of those initial butterflies about Davis. Butterflies that seem to be waking up again.

Smiling, he goes on. "Pop got me into athletics to help me have structured ways to engage with others. It also helps me exercise the anxiety that often twists inside me. It's still my comfort zone."

"How very Commander Riker of you," I coo.

His entire expression brightens with the comparison. "God, I wish I were as smooth as Will Riker." He leans his head against the headrest, a lopsided grin kicking across his face. "Jackson had mentioned our mutual love of the show."

"Yeah?"

He grins.

"Is *Star Trek: The Next Generation* one of those topics you get a little fixated on?" For some reason, the question comes out breathy.

"Perhaps." A seductive quality oozes from the slow way he pronounces the word, sparking a tingle low in my belly.

"Yeah?" Twirling a tendril of my hair, I bat my eyes.

The notion of Davis the jerk dissolves with every moment we spend together. Our flirty exchange doesn't erase what he'd said, but somehow the memory gets a little fuzzier. The desire to know more about him pulses within me, demolishing any lingering annoyance.

"I have a Captain Picard bobblehead on my nightstand," I breathe.

"God," he groans. "That may be the sexiest thing a woman has ever said."

"If you think that's sexy—" I lean across the console, my mouth scant inches from his, and murmur, "I still have a DVD player, so I can watch the complete series with the special cast and crew commentary."

In the inches between us, the air crackles with a dare. His minty breath caresses against my lips, teasing with the promise of how he'd taste.

"I'm sorry." His gaze melds with mine.

Breath ragged, I blink. "For what?"

"That I hurt your feelings on our bad date. That I insulted your writing and implied your life is a fairy tale. I didn't take the time to get to know you… I'd like to get to know you, if it's not too late."

I pull back, taking both him and his words in. The earnest plea in his voice extinguishes the lone remaining embers of frustration with this man. Davis hurt my feelings, but he's adult enough to own that. To listen to me. To apologize. He doesn't offer excuses. He doesn't twist this into being my fault.

It's so different from Will. *Georgia, you pushed me to make a commitment when I wasn't ready yet.* Will's words from the day he'd picked up the last of his things from my place prick inside me. It would take another six months to learn the truth, that it wasn't my fault. But Will had no problem with me taking on *his* actions as my sins.

"It's not too late," I say, meeting his gaze.

"Okay." A hopeful smile curls his lips. "How about a grilled cheese? I think we've both earned one after the day we've had. The GF Finder App ranks Fisher's Landing as the number two gluten free grilled cheese in the US."

"You know about GF Finder?" I gape.

It's not a well-known App outside of the gluten free community. It's like Yelp, but focused on rating the safety of and menu offerings for gluten free individuals like me. The App has both user-generated ratings and those by dieticians. Up until it came out around five years ago, a lot of my knowledge about how GF-friendly places truly were came from what limited info was often available on restaurants' websites. Even if a place lists things as gluten free, it still may not be safe based on how food is prepared and, even, how it's stored.

"Yeah." He chuckles. "I designed it."

"*You* designed it!"

"All your questions will be answered—" he tips his head toward the brewery's front door "—inside over grilled cheese and a basket of fries with *two* sides of ketchup." He winks.

Clusters of customers occupy the various high and low top tables throughout the brewery. It's busier than I thought it would be on a Sunday night, but several teams linger after the restaurant's Trivia Night Showdown. With a hand nestled against my lower back, Davis escorts me toward two empty stools at the bar. I try to ignore the way my body sinks into the warmth of his palm. Try, but fail miserably.

Up until thirty minutes ago, he was Davis the ass. Now he's Davis something else entirely. Not quite Kenny, Doc and Estelle's thoughtful grandson, but something in-between the sexy blind date that sparked an interest in me before he quelled it with his unintentional jerkery and the too-good-to-be-true grandson.

"Why Kenny?" I ask, picking up the iced tea I'd ordered.

"It's short for *Mackenzie*." He emphasizes the ken in Mackenzie. "Mac is the typical nickname for Mackenzie, and Pop said that I was too special to go with something so mundane. Plus, he had a best friend in school named Kenny whom he said I reminded him of. I was pretty proud to wear the nickname, even now. As you know, *Peach*, getting a nickname from Pop is the gold star of approval." He bumps my shoulder with his.

"Why would you need approval from your grandfather?"

"Because at the time he gave me the nickname, I wasn't his grandson… At least not yet." He taps his fingers against his glass of iced tea.

"What does that mean?" I spin on the stool, my knees pressing into his right thigh.

"Deanna and Mimi didn't become my foster parents until I was ten."

"You were in foster care?"

"Yeah." He turns, his large legs bracketing mine, our gazes tethering.

The action linked us together. Despite the murmured conversations and quiet hum of music, the intimacy of this moment isolates us.

"I was in-and-out of different homes since I was seven," he says in a matter-of-fact way, but something sad darkens his expression.

I reach out, placing my hand on his. "You don't have to tell me about it if—"

"I want to." He squeezes my hand. "Both my parents struggled with drugs. Dad still does—" his forehead wrinkles "—at least I think he does. I went no-contact with him ten years ago. I just couldn't continue to leave myself open to him and his false promises."

An ache twinges in my throat. Nolan Lane isn't fatherly, but I can't imagine him being out of my life. He'll never be the type of dad I imagine Rem wants to be, or that I know Doc is from the stories Estelle shares, but he's there in different ways. I also have my mom, always have.

"What about your mom?" I skate my thumb against his hand, and the gray clouds in his eyes dissolve with each tender stroke.

"She died of an overdose when I was seven. Hence, foster care." He heaves a long breath. "Dad couldn't deal and fell into his habit hard. He got arrested buying meth and the officers found me in the car waiting for him outside his dealer's apartment. A string of arrests and rehab stints left me bouncing between my dad and foster homes."

"I'm so sorry."

"No, I'm sorry. I shouldn't have told you all that. I'm talking too much about my sad history…" His stare drops to his lap, where my fingers are threaded with his.

"I asked." I drag his attention back to me with a gentle

squeeze of his hand. "If you don't want to talk about it, it's okay… But I do want to know."

"You like my sad story?" The corners of his mouth flex into an earnest grin that spreads gooey warmth inside me.

"It helps that I know it has a happy ending."

A chuckle rumbles in his throat. "I'm starting to understand your fondness for the romance genre." He nods, his smile getting a little bigger. "It did end happily. Deanna and Mimi became my foster moms when I was ten, and even though my dad never lost or relinquished his parental rights, they are my moms, and Pop and Nan are my grandparents. At eighteen, I aged out of foster care, but they never let go of me."

"They're your family in all the ways that matter."

Despite the love that envelopes Davis, I know he's haunted by the relationship with his dad. The comment about people failing you that he'd made during our first date in this very brewery whispers inside me. My heart may be melting for this man, but the warning bells that sounded that night about skeptical men still caution me to stay away.

He clears his throat. "I bought a romance novel."

The abrupt topic change causes my eyebrows to shoot up. "You didn't?" I guffaw.

"I did." His thumb massages the top of my hand. "Three to be exact."

"You didn't?" Gaping, I repeat my question, knowing exactly *which* three he'd bought.

"You were so passionate in your defense of the genre that I thought if I was going to start my education, it should start with yours."

"And?"

"I'm halfway through *Twice Baked Love* but—"

"No!" I laughingly whine. "Of all the ones to start with, that is not the one. It's my worst! You should have started with *The Duke's Darling*. It's probably my best."

"I'm enjoying Owen and Selena's story."

I rub the center of my forehead with my free hand. "But it's like a saccharine-sweet Hallmark movie."

"I don't recall icing play in any of the Hallmark movies my Nan watches at the holidays," he teases, bumping his knee against mine. "It is a little cheesy, but it's also heartfelt and layered. How Owen thinks of everyone but himself, and how that even gets in the way of his relationship with Selena. You're really talented."

"You're just saying that."

"Take the compliment, Peach." His mouth quirks.

An unexpected clench tightens my core at the way Peach sounds on his lips. It's playful but loaded with seductive intent. As if he plans to bite into me, then lick up every drop.

Good lord, Georgia. I squeeze my legs together. My legs that are still caged by his.

"Why happy endings?" He juts his chin toward me.

"Besides the obvious ooey-gooey feeling?"

He smirks.

"As a kid, I was sick a lot. Stomach issues. Migraines. It was all related to my celiacs but we didn't know it until I was twelve. My parents also fought a lot until they got divorced when I was eleven. My dad fancies himself the next Andy Warhol. It caused a lot of tension between my parents. He was always leaving to do art shows or teach at a different art institute."

"Jackson? Georgia? Don't you have an older brother called Rembrandt? You're all named after artists?" he says, his nose crinkled.

"Yep." I shrug. "Nolan Lane lives and breathes art. Hence the divorce. My mother never stood a chance against his one true love. After the divorce, he left to chase his dream."

"And I thought I got fixated." His laugh-filled expression sobers. "What about you and your brothers? It's hard to have your dad choose something else over you."

Wouldn't he know this better than anyone? An ache radiates in my chest at Davis losing both his parents to substance abuse. I have empathy for whatever demons his parents face, but it doesn't erase the impact on their son.

I haven't experienced the same pain as this man, but I won't pretend that there isn't a little hurt related to my dad. As a kid, a blend of grief and sadness over the loss of my dad often knotted inside me. But that was more about the loss of the dream of what a father should be versus who Nolan Lane was. Once I let go of that and just accepted my dad and the relationship as is, that sadness got easier to deal with.

"He loves us, and, in his own way, he's been there for me. I'm probably the closest to him out of the three of us. Hope, my bestie and Rem's wife, sends holiday and birthday cards, but Dad and my older brother don't have a relationship. Jackson texts Dad, and they talk a couple of times a year. Dad and I talk a few times a month. Mostly about what books I'm reading, his art, and my writing. He might be the most supportive about my writing."

"The rest of your family isn't supportive?"

"My mom and Jackson are *ish*"—I make air quotes with my fingers—"but they worry that I'm making too much of a financial investment. Hope is one hundred percent Team Georgia, thanks to the beauty of a two-decade-plus long friendship. Rem…not-so-much. He thinks I'm wasting my time and money."

Something unspools inside me with the laying of all my truths on the table. Hope hears some of this, but I try to pick and choose how often I complain about my brother, AKA the love of her life. It's a delicate dance between us at times.

"But you love it."

Smiling, I nod. "I always have. With my health issues and the turmoil between my parents, I lost myself in stories, especially those with happy endings. When I was home sick, I'd scribble stories in notebooks where dad became a famous artist and it smoothed over the issues between him and my mom, or about me finding a magical flower that cured whatever made me sick all the time."

"Focusing on things turning out made it all more bearable for you."

"Yeah." Cringing, I close my eyes. "God, I sound like such an indulgent ninny compared to everything you went through."

"Peach…" His fingers swipe along my jawline, causing my eyes to open and meet his stare. His other hand remains wrapped tightly around mine.

Every bit of his large frame holds me in an intimate little bubble. The heat of his body. The caress of his gaze locked with mine. The sensation of his touch on my skin.

"Suffering is suffering. You were sick and, at the time, you didn't know why. That's scary enough, but then adding your parents' instability, it's a lot. It's not indulgent to want everything to turn out."

"Thank you," I say, my breath catching.

"You're welcome." His hand caresses my cheek before dropping to his lap. "Can we talk about your use of the word ninny?"

Head tipped back, a loud chortle belts out of me. "I didn't."

"That you did."

I point at him. "Before we discuss my use of the word ninny, which you'll find is an excellent word after you read *The Duke's Darling*, you still need to explain how you turned out to be the app designer for GF Finder. I thought you were a business guy like Jackson."

He lifts one eyebrow. "What do you think No Boundaries is?"

"Isn't it some sort of hedge fund or something equally finance bro-ey," I tease.

"Finance bro-ey?" His forehead scrunches. "Now who's judgy?"

Turns out I am. Much of Jackson's early career out of business school was with tech companies that all had a financial slant. Cash apps or banking software companies, so I assumed No Boundaries is just like the rest.

"You design apps for the disabled and chronically ill?" I'm sure my expression teeters between impressed and bewildered.

Turns out Davis isn't a finance bro, but a tech genius. At twenty-four, he designed a verification app heavily used in banking. Using the earnings from that, and a few others he designed that are widely used within the financial world, he created GF Finder and then a social media-like app to help individuals with autism connect with resources and socializing opportunities.

"No Boundaries creates apps that help the disabled and chronically ill live full lives. Between the money I've invested and several other investors, we're able to focus on that mission," he explains.

"I had no idea."

He tilts his head. "Jackson didn't tell you?"

"Nope. Frankly, I'm shocked he didn't use it to crown himself King Do-Gooder. He's not known for his discretion."

"That he isn't." His chuckle is warm. "For months, he's been going on and on about the sister I need to meet. What are the odds she turns out to be the famous Peach my grandparents have gone on and on about for the last few years?"

"What are the odds?" I hum, my fingers gliding over his hand, which remained joined with mine.

It *should* be awkward to just sit here holding this man's hand. What is this? A second chance for a first date? Just a grandson doing what his grandma asked? Whatever was happening here, emotions stretch inside me like an intense game of tug-of-war. The rope pulls me between melting into whatever is happening with Davis and the three men currently corralled by my brother. The men I'm supposed to date.

You're a mess, Georgia. I bite the inside of my cheek, hoping the pain yanks me out of the spell I'm under with Davis.

"Two grilled cheeses, an order of steak fries, and two sides of ketchup," the bartender announces as he places our food on the bar in front of us.

"Thanks," Davis addresses the bartender, but his stare remains tethered with mine.

"We should eat." Releasing his hand, I spin the chair and pick up my sandwich.

He follows the action. "Here's to stories with happy endings," he says, lifting up his grilled cheese in an almost toasting fashion.

"To stories with happy endings." I mirror his action, fighting against the quiet voice inside me that reminds me that there are three men whose happy endings I stole. Whatever this is with Davis, it's not fair to Owen, Lord James, and Lars. Something I need to remember.

CHAPTER ELEVEN

YOUR INTENDED?

My heels click against the long corridor leading from my office toward SPN's courtyard. The sound teases at the dull ache in my head, the result of a night with too little sleep. After leaving Davis, I went into research mode to figure out how my book boyfriends ended up here. The selfie Jackson sent this morning of him and the guys eating a stack of pancakes Owen made, confirmed that this was not a dream.

This is real, and I need to know why it's happening. How often have I tossed a spare coin into a fountain? Or made a wish as I blew out a birthday candle? Yet, none of those came true. Why this one? I can't help but think it's something to do with SPN's fountain.

My phone pings, halting my steps as I reach the courtyard doors. Jackson's name flashes on the screen.

"Probably another selfie of something delicious Owen baked that I can't eat," I grumble, bringing up the messaging app.

Jackson: I'll be by tonight to discuss Just Write.
Me: Just Write?

Jackson: That's what I'm calling this real-life bachelorette thing you've got going on. I have so many ideas.

Me: *Eyeroll Emoji.* Knowing you, this will be an American Gladiator-style competition.

Jackson: Not a bad idea. I need to make sure whoever wins my sister is as much of a specimen of masculinity as I am. Someone to take care of you.

Me: First, BARF. Second, I can take care of myself. Third, let's not subscribe to archaic gender roles.

Jackson: Fine, we could just put their names in a hat and have you pick. Leave it to fate.

Me: Don't be ridiculous.

Jackson: Says the woman who accidentally wished three fictional men into existence. *Tongue-Out Emoji.*

Rolling my eyes, I slip my phone into my blazer pocket and head into the courtyard. Nodding a smile to the only other occupants, I move to the fountain in the courtyard's center. It's not large and fancy like the Trevi Fountain in Italy. My research found limited information about SPN's fountain. Outside of some pictures from events, there appears to be no local lore or myths about this fountain or SPN. The only fact about the fountain is that the building's original owner, Miguel Carlos Domingus, had it constructed for his Scottish wife, Mary. It was built in Plockton, Scotland, and shipped here in 1908.

It's a simple fountain with an oval-shaped base. The brick-like pattern around the base is made up of gray stone with uninterrupted thin white lines that almost glow in the mid-afternoon sun. A small statue of a woman stands in the middle. She's reaching for something, droplets of water trickling from her outstretched hands. The water falls int the pool, where its ripples almost obscure the bottom. Almost, but not quite. Leaning over the edge, I squint at the empty basin.

"Where is it?" I whisper to myself. The lucky penny Doc gave me that I threw in is nowhere to be found. In fact, there are no coins. "There were coins here," I mutter, scanning the courtyard as if it could confirm that fact.

The glittery stone drags my attention back to the fountain's base. Crouching, I trace my fingers across its smooth surface. The thin white lines appear to be embedded in the stone, rather than something painted on or layered into each brick. Brick may not be the right word. I know so little about fountain construction.

"What are you doing?"

"Eeep!" I startle, tumbling back on my ass.

"You okay?" Pilar stands above me, her dark brows ticking up with curiosity, a to-go cup in one hand and a small paper bag in the other.

"Awesome." I offer a flimsy thumbs-up.

"This courtyard isn't faring well this week." She shakes her head.

I rise, swiping at my backside. "At least, nobody is hurt this time."

"And thankfully that pencil skirt is stitched on you or else you may have given Mr. O'Donelly a show." She winks, tipping her head to the two men sitting in the courtyard.

"Not complaining." One of the men offers a salute before returning to his card game.

"Don't be pervy, Mr. O'Donnelly, or I'll make sure you get Judith for PT." Shaking her head at the older man, Pilar turns her focus back on me. "What were you doing?"

"Checking out the fountain." I smooth down my skirt, suddenly questioning its tightness over my shapely figure.

"Why?"

"Uh…." I flick my gaze between her bemused expression and the fountain. "I was curious about the stone. I don't think I've seen stone like this."

"It's called wishing stone."

"It's what?" I say, my voice high-pitched.

"Wishing stone." She juts her chin toward the fountain.

"The uninterrupted line in the stone is calcite. Amateur geologists identify it as a wishing stone. The stones are supposed to grant wishes."

"How do you know this?"

She shrugs. "One of the OG nurses from when this place first became a rehab/hospice facility told me. She was here as a patient the first year I took over for Doc. She had lots of crystals and stones."

"It's made out of wishing stone," I say out loud, but it's more to myself than to Pilar. Slipping my phone out of my blazer pocket, I immediately pull up my new best friend, Google. "Did she know anything else about the fountain? Like—"

"Like does it actually grant wishes?" she almost snorts.

I look up, the dismissive smile slanting Pilar's lips cautions me to not proceed. As close as we are, Pilar isn't my "this could happen" friend. Ever the doctor, she's about what she knows to be true, not what *could* be true.

With a shrug, I push my phone back into my pocket. "I was just curious about the stone. It's...pretty." The word comes out like a question.

"Pretty?" A silent laugh smooths her features. "How about we focus less on the fountain's rock and more on the *very* attractive man with a rock-hard body who dropped this off for you." She hands me the to-go cup and bag.

"Now who's being pervy?" Mr. O'Donnelly snarks.

"Judith," she threatens playfully, causing him to grimace and turn back to his game.

"What man..." The *Peach* scrawled along the to-go cup teases with an answer to my not-fully-asked question.

Belly swooping, I place the cup on the fountain's edge and open the bag. Tucked inside is a small envelope on top of a plastic-wrapped muffin. Pulling out the envelope, I open it and read the card.

Peach,

This is such a small thing for all you did yesterday. Thank you for taking care of Pop and Nan. Captain Picard would approve.

Best,

Davis/Kenny/Whatever you want to call me

p.s. The muffin is from Meghan's Munchies and is rated the number five GF pumpkin muffin in the US.

An obnoxiously large grin kicks across my face. Meghan's Munchies is one of my favorite GF bakeries, which I mentioned to him last night at the brewery. Lifting the cup to my nose, I inhale the distinct aroma of Earl Grey tea.

"Just like Captain Picard." I beam, thinking of our favorite Starship Enterprise Captain ordering it through the ship's replicator.

"What's with this starry-eyed look?" Pilar snaps her fingers, yanking my attention back to her. "Is there an actual contender for your heart? Someone to take you to your cousin's wedding?"

"Uh…. No," I say, my tone unsure.

Despite the flutter in my chest the gift caused, and Pilar's suggestion of Davis being a contender, I have three actual contenders to deal with. Three men who are here specifically to date me. Three men who I owe happy endings to. Either one with me, or to help them get back to theirs. Whatever that looks like or how I'm going to do that, I have no clue.

"Sure," she says, unconvinced. "Can you at least tell me *who* this man is that *you* say isn't a contender, but who makes you look like Pedro Pascal just strolled into the courtyard?"

"It's Kenny," I say slowly. "Who also happens to be Davis."

"What!" Her amber eyes are saucer-sized.

I hold up the bakery bag. "I'll tell you over this."

The afternoon heat still lingers, making me loathe the short walk from my car to the carriage house. Jackson's car is parked behind Hope's in the driveway, which will, no doubt, annoy Rem. Though I'm sure that's why he does it. Precocious is how we described juvenile Jackson, but at twenty-nine he leans into loveable asshole territory. He's the brother that is always there for us when we make a mistake, but he's also the first to give us shit about said mistake.

"Rabbit!" Lars's gruff voice greets me as I walk into the backyard, causing me to halt.

Jackson and Lars sit beneath the large patio umbrella... *Arm-wrestling?* Brow pinched, my jaw nearly hits the cobblestone path that loops through the backyard.

"Hey, sis!" Jackson waves with his free hand and then juts his chin at Lars. "You're going down, Twilight."

"Dream on, pretty boy."

"At least you admit I'm prettier than you." Jackson's mouth slants into a lopsided grin.

What the actual fuck, I mouth. The last message from Jackson that came in before I left SPN said he'd see me at the house. I assumed that meant just him. Not Lars. *Wait... Where are the other two?*

"My lady!" Lord James drawls, causing me to turn.

"Good gravy." My murmur is breathless.

Lord James saunters from my carriage house, his green eyes fixed on me. His typical Mr. Darcy outfit has been replaced by a suit. The way the navy fabric molds over his sculpted physique may be illegal in several states. No indication of the balmy air mars his face, whereas sweat kisses my hairline and pools in unsexy places.

"The only thing more stunning than this day is you." Reaching me, he takes my right hand, and lifts it to his mouth and presses a gentle kiss to my knuckles.

"Th...th...thank you," I stammer. Shaking away the temporary dazed sensation caused by my sexy duke looking like the archetype for a billionaire romance male love interest, I spin. "Jackson, what are they doing here?"

"Not happy to see us, rabbit?" Lars says through gritted teeth, his face scrunched in the battle with my brother.

"No!"

"Wounded," Lars teases, pushing my brother's arm closer to the tabletop.

"I'm sorry." Sighing, I peer between him and Lord James, a half-stoic, half-indignant expression fills the duke's features. "I'm happy to see you both. I'm sorry for my rudeness. It's just… The whole reason Jackson took you is to hide this from Hope and Rem." I rub my temples.

"My lady, would you care to lie down? You look unwell." Lord James tucks a loose strand of my hair behind my ear. "I could carry you upstairs and put you to bed," he says, his voice dripping with sinful intentions.

"Oh…." My mouth goes dry.

"No, you don't." Jackson slams Lars's arm to the table and jumps up. "We talked about this, Lord No Boundaries. There will be none of your Mr. Darcy seductiveness outside of your official date time."

"Official date time?" I ask.

"Each bachelor will have an official date over the next six days."

"Six days?" Face scrunched, I tilt my head. Fogginess creeps in, nipping at my ability to follow the thread.

"Should give you enough time to decide which man to take to the wedding and who you'd like to pursue something with."

Lars steps beside Jackson, patting his shoulder. "Jacky boy worked it out. Each of us will take you on a date; a meal and an activity. The activity we plan, to woo you. You know, romance and all that shit."

"Smooth, K-9 Club." Jackson shakes his head. "And because we don't subscribe to archaic gender roles, the meal portion of the date *you* plan… You know, romance and all that shit."

I laugh at his repetition of my little tut from earlier. Despite the ridiculousness of this entire situation, Jackson treats this like it's normal. As if we're not talking about people's lives—even if three of those people are fictional. Still, it's sweetly reassuring. Although what isn't reassuring is that they are here and….

"Where's Owen?" I look around.

"You're so right about cinnamon. It really is the perfect addition to banana bread," Hope coos, shuffling from inside the house.

"It definitely gives it that extra something." Owen grins, following her with a tray laden with food.

"I repeat, what are they doing here? We were hiding them from Hope and Rem," I hiss through clenched teeth to Jackson.

"Like you were going to keep this from Hope very long —" he *tsks* "—and if one of these men is our future brother-in-law, we need to integrate them into the family," he whispers back, his tight smile fixed on Hope, who moves toward the table where Lars pulls out the chair for her. "Aw, the wolf has manners." His tight smile softens to a real one.

I arch a brow.

"Georgia!" Hope waves me over. "Have you met Jackson's friends from pickleball?"

"Uh, yeah." I move to the table.

"She may know them better than anyone." Smirking, he plops onto a chair beside Lars, their snickered expressions in silent conversation with each other.

Again, my eyebrow arches at him. Well, not just him, but *them*. They are like two sides of the same snarky coin. One, the polished suit-wearing version, the other in ripped jeans and flannel.

"Owen helped me put together some tidbits. He's amazing. Better than any sous chef I've ever had," Hope says, taking a small stack of plates from the tray and handing them to Owen.

Of course, he is. All of Owen's culinary expertise comes from Hope. So much of her passion for food is infused into my small-town baker character. Though that was intentional versus my accidental infusion of aspects of Jackson into my werewolf alpha. I can't help but wonder what real life person may linger inside my handsome duke, who sits spine straight beside me.

"I'm grateful for Baker, because LJ over there is useless in the kitchen." Lars chuckles, grabbing a plate and piling food on it.

"Baker? LJ?" Hope's brows kiss.

"Owen Baker. Lars has this thing about not calling people by their actual names, so he calls me by my last name," Owen explains, pouring water into a glass from the pitcher on the table.

She nods, her brown eyes sparking with interest. "And who's LJ?"

"Lord James." Lars says, handing the now full plate to Jackson, who accepts, an "Oh shit" expression blooming on both of their faces just as…

"Lord James?" Hope's gaze narrows on my duke. "I thought your name was Jim?"

"It certainly is not," he scoffs and then looks to me, his face aghast. "I mean… Yes… Jim is my name." His lips pinch.

Every muscle in my body tightens. None of my book boyfriends are good liars. It's core to their literary DNA, so whatever ruse Jackson cooked up is coming undone. Not to mention, Hope is perceptive.

She wags a carrot stick at Lars. "And what was your name again?"

"Lars…" He wrinkles his nose. "I mean Larsy?"

"Larry." Jackson coughs.

"Why didn't Owen get a new name?" I lean over to Jackson and whisper.

"Every good lie has some truth," he whispers back.

"*Good* is the important word in that sentence," I hiss.

"Owen Baker? Lord James? Lars?" Her fierce stare jumps between me and Jackson. "Who are these men?"

I cover my face with my hands, a twinge thuds behind my closed eyes. Lying to my best friend is a shitty thing to do, even if the plan was for it to be temporary to not stress her out during her pregnancy. It's not the stress of this situation's impact on her that I worry about, but the favor I'll need from her.

"They're Owen Baker, Lars the alpha werewolf pack leader, and Lord James the sexual harassy duke… And they're here to date Georgia," Jackson says.

"They're what!" Hope shrills.

"Sorry, sis." He lets out a long breath. "I thought this would work."

"I, for one, never thought this charade would work. *Jim?* As if a duke is named Jim? How ludicrous," Lord James drawls.

"This would work? Duke? Dating Georgia? What in the H E double-hockey-sticks is going on?" Hope's high-pitched questions cause me to lower my hands and face her. "Kitchen, now."

Nodding, I rise, lightly swat the back of Jackson's head, and follow her into the house. That dull ache behind my eyes has grown to a steady throb. This is all so messy. It's like I'm Hurricane Georgia. Thanks to the toss of a "lucky" penny into a fountain, I'm leaving a path of destruction everywhere. At this moment, I wonder how lucky that stupid penny is.

"Georgia Angelica Lane!" Hope whirls to me the moment we enter the kitchen. "What's happening? Who are those men? Did Jackson hire three men to pretend to be fictional characters and date you?"

"No!" I step back, my butt coming into contact with the small breakfast table. "Jackson didn't hire escorts to date me and pretend to be fictional characters."

"Georgia, *did you*?" Brow scrunched, she cocks her head. "Wait, how did you find escorts that resemble your book characters? Is there an app for that? Please tell me you did your research to vet them."

"They're not escorts." I rub at my temples.

"What's happening? Who are these men?" Her eyes widen. "Oh my god, are you okay? Are they stalker fanboys who think they are your characters? Are you and Jackson being held hostage? Blink twice if you need me to—"

Laughter bubbles out of me, its intensity racking through me. Leave it to Hope to go from my trio being hired escorts to stalking fanboys in two point five seconds.

"Should I call Rem?"

"No!" My laughter dies. "Don't call Rem, please."

"If you're in trouble—"

"I'm not in trouble… Well, not that kind of trouble." I rub the center of my forehead, the throb intensifying.

My adherence to a gluten free diet combats my celiacs, but too much stress causes migraine flare-ups. The seeds of one sprouting with the pulsating ache, the queasy sensation swirling in my belly, and fuzziness, which wasn't just my reaction to Lord James in his suit.

I look up, meeting her perplexed gaze. "What I'm about to tell you is ridiculous and unbelievable, but it's true, and you can't tell Rem. Please."

"Are you sure you're not in trouble *trouble*?"

I nod, that action causing a twinge behind my eyes.

She looks between her wedding ring and me. "Okay."

"You better sit down." I pull out one of the chairs from the table.

This is the second time this story has spilled out of me. Like Jackson, Hope believes me. Even if her face scrunches with disbelief, and her "Oh my word's" fill the kitchen. Only the story I share with Hope contains the tidbits about Davis/Kenny. I'm not sure why I include him in the tale, because he's not part of this. Even if there's still a flutter in my chest at his thoughtful gift. Despite the pull to him, I need to stay away. No good will come from further interaction with him.

"Why go on a date with these three guys when you just had a do-over date with Davis?"

"It wasn't a do-over date. It was just a grandson showing appreciation," I say, my flimsy protest doesn't convince even me.

Swatting at the air, she goes on, "Whatever it was, it's clear there are sparks. Why not pursue that?"

"Because Davis wasn't poofed into my life by a possibly magic fountain at the facility where I work. Lars, Lord James, and Owen were, and I owe them. Whether it's with me or not, I owe them happy endings."

"You don't owe anybody anything. You didn't wish for them to be transported here. You wished to know what your happy ending is and how to find it."

"That doesn't matter. They're still here. I stole the happy endings I wrote for them."

That knowledge aches within me. I know all too well the pain of losing the tomorrow you hoped for. Even if the guys were ripped away from their stories during their third-act breakup, I know what they stand to lose. I can't take that from them.

She motions at me. "What if Doc's accident was the fountain's way of bringing Davis back into your life? A second chance for a happy ending? One with Davis?"

"You're reaching, woman," I groan. "If that was true, then why are Lord James, Lars, and Owen still here?"

"I don't know." Her expression falls. "Are you attracted to them? I mean, they're all gorgeous, but do you feel the spark?

Even when you hated Davis, you still mentioned his sexy nerd aesthetic."

"I *never* hated him."

A 'gotcha' smile lights her face. No doubt, she threw that line in to poke just a little more at the Davis bear. The bear that roams inside me with the tiniest of crushes on someone I shouldn't desire.

"Let's focus on my three actual suitors." I clear my throat. "I'll admit that Owen is sweet, but there's nothing there… But that may come—" I say quickly, causing her to close her mouth, the *see* comment almost visible on her red-painted lips. "Lars is too much like Jackson. Lord James, though, there's a pull to him."

"Okay," she draws out the word with a thoughtful nod. "So, I guess we're doing this."

"Yep."

"And we're keeping this from Rem?"

"Yep."

"At least their names won't raise any suspicion with him."

It's the one time I'm grateful for my older brother's lack of support. Unlike the rest of the Lane family, Rem hasn't read my books, and I don't anticipate that he'll read them anytime soon. Even if he didn't disapprove of my indie publishing, he's more of a historical fiction or true crime reader.

"I'm sorry to ask this of you." I reach over and squeeze her hand. "I know you hate lying to him, but I'm not ready for him to know about this. It will just add to his idea of me as the screwup."

"You're not a screwup. He doesn't think that." Her mouth purses.

I scoff. "Just tell the three men outside whose entire lives were ripped away from them because of me."

"None of this is your fault."

If only I could believe Hope. To see this situation, my brother and myself, through her eyes. In my eyes, this is one giant mess of my doing, which will likely not shock Rem. His *"Really, Georgia"* reaction already scolds inside me.

Sighing, she rubs her belly. "Alright, let's head back out there to your book boyfriends. Rem will be home soon, and we'll need to introduce him to *Jackson's pickleball friends,*" she says with air quotes before rising.

"Thank you." I thread my arm in hers, guiding her outside.

"Just name your next fabulous female main character after me and make sure it's a steamy hockey romance." She waggles her eyebrows. "Emphasis on the steamy."

"My lady." Lord James rises and crosses the patio toward me as we exit the house.

"My lady?" Rem asks, his bewildered voice pulling all our gazes toward the backyard entrance where he stands, his face scrunched and a bouquet of flowers in one hand.

"Baby, have you met Jackson's pickleball friends?" She gestures to each man. "Lars, Owen, and… *Jim,*" she almost laughs the name.

Lord James blanches.

"Hi. I'm Rem, Jackson and Georgia's older brother." Nodding, he moves toward the patio, his gaze fixed on Lord James.

Lars and Owen both offer quick waves. Jackson just smirks.

Spine straight, Lord James steps toward my brother. "I am"—he grimaces—"Jim. I'm your sister's soon-to-be intended," he says with a short bow.

"Her what?"

Damn you, unlucky penny! Squinting against the still bright early evening sun, a painful fuzziness blurs my vision.

"Ha!" Hope barks with laughter, slapping Lord James's shoulder. "Jim here is a real joker. You'll love his quirky English sense of humor." She bats her long lashes. "Are those flowers for me?"

"Yeah." Rem leans in, presses a kiss to her cheek, and hands her the bouquet. "Georgia, are you okay?" Pulling back, he tips his head toward me, concern furrows his brow.

"I'm…" I flick my wrist as if that will answer his question.

"You don't look good. Are you having a reaction? Did you have something you shouldn't?"

"No… I didn't… It's just a migraine," I bite out. "I'm going to go lie down. Sorry." Hand on my forehead, I start toward the carriage house.

"I can escort you," Lord James murmurs, moving beside me and taking my arm.

"Jim… How about you grab a seat?" Jackson hops up, his tone full of warning, and moves to my side. "I've got Georgia."

"I don't—"

"That way I can grab Wentworth and watch him for the night, so you can sleep this off," Jackson cuts in, his tone warm even if it reeks of the same placation one would give a child.

At this moment, I can't fight him. Not when the migraine sinks into me with gnarled claws, squeezing away my ability to process. And I need to be focused to figure this all out. After all, in the next six days I'm dating the potential Mr. Georgia Lane, as Jackson would say. Only, while my brother has me doing my own version of *The Bachelorette*, I'm going to try to figure out how to get all three back to their stories. If I don't, I'll need to choose one of them in hopes that the other two will be transported back to their realities. And if that doesn't work…

Don't do that, Georgia. It will all be okay… I hope.

CHAPTER TWELVE

TWICE BAKED LOVE

I'm going on a date with Owen Baker. Standing in front of my mirror, my hair pulled into a flirty high ponytail, the thought plays on repeat inside me. How many times had I daydreamed about Captain Wentworth whisking me into his arms and carrying me off from one of my bad dates? No doubt several of my readers fantasized about the cinnamon roll small-town baker doing the same. Only Owen Baker isn't who I am fantasizing about.

"Bad Georgia," I mutter to myself. Tonight, my focus should be on my book boyfriends.

Instead of my typical Wednesday night curled up with a book and Wentworth, I'm off for the first of my *Just Write* dates. Over the next six days, I'll go on a date with each book boyfriend. Between each date, we'll interact only as a group. Jackson believes the strategy keeps this whole thing fair, not tipping the "contest" to any one man's favor. Despite what my brother teases, this isn't a contest; this is our lives.

Smoothing down my dress's skirt, I suck in one last breath and take in my reflection in the mirror. I am the picture of the female main character in a small-town romance. The sapphire blue fabric hugs my breasts and flows out in an A-line silhouette. Ballet flats in the same color as my dress and tiny teacup-shaped dangle earrings top off my outfit. With a swipe of glossy pink lipstick, I smack my lips and offer a "guess this is happening" smile.

"Time to go on a date with a fictional man." I chuckle as the knock rattles my front door.

Slipping my lipstick into my purse, I grab it and head to the door. Jackson insisted that each man pick me up rather than meeting me at the location. He thinks it adds to the romance. All I'm thinking about is where are we going, and how we're going to get there. None of my book boyfriends have real licenses, identification cards, or anything that ties them to this world. No job. No family. Nothing in this reality, outside of a connection to me and a hope of a possible future.

"Hi!" Opening the door, I infuse as much pep into my greeting as possible.

"Hi," Owen says, his eyes skim down my body and back up to my face. "You look lovely."

I should swoon. Flames should arc through me from the heat of his attention on me. *Nothing.*

"Thanks!" I force my smile just a little bigger, channeling Hope's cheerleading persona from high school.

"You're...welcome?" One blond brow arching, Owen offers an unsure grin.

Maybe not so much pep. It's freaking him out. I clear my throat. "Ready?"

"Yeah." He nods, holding out his arm for me to take.

One of the benefits of the neighborhood I live in is that it's a short ten-minute walk to Old Tustin. Shops, cafes, restaurants, and even an improv theatre fill the mix of Spanish, Victorian, and Mid-Century buildings that make up downtown. The conversation, mostly about my workday and the homemade chicken pot pie he'd made for Jackson and my other suitors to have for dinner, flows easily between us.

Owen is sweet. With artic-blue eyes, short-cropped blond

hair, and a warm, open smile contrasted against a strong jawline, he's the stereotypical rom-com lead. But the moment he rests his palm on my lower back to guide me toward our destination, my body has no reaction. No butterflies. No hitched breath. None of the cliches I write about in my books are present.

We stop in front of a white brick building, a decadent aroma drifting from inside. *The Secret Ingredient* is embossed in gold script at the center of a large picture window. Inside, several couples stand chatting at one of the six mini kitchen islands throughout the space.

"A cooking class?" I guffaw.

His mouth flexes into a lopsided grin. "It's a baking class, actually. Biscuits to be exact. It's not an original date idea for a baker, but I thought you'd enjoy *actually* baking with me, instead of just writing about it."

"I thought Lars was the snarky one," I tease.

"Between him and Jackson, I think their Jedi Master-level snark is rubbing off on me."

"We're baking biscuits?" My gaze jumps between him and the ingredients visible through the window.

"Gluten free," he adds, seeming to track what I was checking. "The whole class. I double checked before I made the reservation."

"Very sweet."

His thoughtfulness should wobble my knees. My brain communicates this, but my heart and vagina aren't listening.

Grabbing our aprons, we wash our hands and claim our assigned kitchen counter. Five other pairs; three couples, and two sets of besties, make up the class. The instructor guides us through the art of baking biscuits. It's part baking class and part sage life lessons.

"Sometimes we make mistakes in the recipe that can be fixed with other ingredients, saving what we've made. Sometimes those mistakes require improvisation to find a new path forward, creating something not expected, but just as good," the instructor says, sprinkling GF flour onto the counter in front of him to roll out his dough. "Sometimes, we can't fix an error and must start again. The beauty of that is we learn, so we don't make that same mistake. Just like in life."

Nodding, I soak in his words while shaping the dough. The tacky, pliable coolness in my palms allows me to shape it into a ball. It's not a perfect ball, not like the one Owen molds in his hands. Of course, his would be perfect. The nimble and automatic ways his hands work as we prepare our biscuits demonstrate that he's a man who knows what he's doing. A man who knows the destination and how to get there, even if, at this moment, it's just to ensure the perfect biscuit.

With a long sigh, I crush my doughball to start again.

"It doesn't have to be perfect, Georgia." Warmth radiates from Owen's expression.

"I know—" I frown, rolling the dough in my palms. "But it does have to be right."

"Right is rarely perfect." He sprinkles flour on a rolling pin and begins to roll out his dough, his mouth quirked into a teasing grin.

"Like Selena and you." I smile.

Owen and Selena's romance is one of second chances. In many ways, their story leans into the stereotypical small-town romance cliches. The high school valedictorian turned big city businesswoman returns home to run into the boy she still pines for. With eyes only for his former high school girlfriend, Owen never noticed the type-A personality president of the debate team, Selena—at least not in *that* way. Not until she slipped in a mud puddle in front of his bakery after returning for her brother's wedding.

"Yeah." He wipes flour off his hands before grabbing a biscuit cutter, the spark of wistfulness glinting in his eyes. "Not at first. I believe she threatened to sue me for the slickness of the sidewalk in front of my bakery."

A scoff pops out of me. "It was such a silly meet-cute. She could have just taken that conference call on her phone from her brother's florist shop rather than run to her car in her heels in the middle of a downpour to take it."

"Nah." Amusement teases at the corners of his mouth. "It was perfect. Selena all focused, making a mistake, and then blaming someone else… Only to apologize ten minutes later. She's quick to frazzle, but even quicker to apologize for it. It was part of her journey. To not just learn that she makes mistakes, but to forgive herself for them."

"Huh." I cock my head to the right. "Most people think her story arc is about her embracing her softer side. At least, that's what reviewers think."

"They're wrong. The softness comes with it, but Selena carried so much responsibility for managing her fragile mother, who broke down after her dad's death and, even for her siblings, who had their own reactions. Your book is about forgiveness. Not just Selena's forgiveness of her mother for the emotional abandonment, but for herself."

Realization revs up my pulse. "You read your book."

"Jackson has copies on his bookshelf. I read mine and I'm halfway through Lord James's now."

After Owen found the copies of their stories on my bookshelf at my apartment, I took them back from him. It's not a secret. All three know that they have endings already written. They just don't know the details. Not about Owen showing up in front of Selena's office building just as she walks out, her things in a box after quitting her job. His big romantic gesture mere minutes after she'd decided to go back to Sugarville.

It may be cruel to keep their endings from them – at least the details – but my reasoning at the time seemed sound. *What if I can't get them back to their stories? What if I do, and somehow knowing their ending messes it up?*

"Do you think it's a good idea to read them?"

"Who knows?" He shrugs. "What I do know is you're talented. You tell a good story."

"But it's not just a story." A knot tightens in my stomach with the knowledge that these aren't just stories, but lives; Owen, Lars, and Lord James' lives, with three very real hearts that love three women.

"Not just stories," he breathes.

"I'm sorry I took you from her. From your happy ending." Emotions make my words come out in a shaky, almost gargled quality.

"I'm not."

My questioning stare snaps to his.

"I love Selena. That will never change, but I don't know if I'm meant to be part of her story or a portion of it." His declaration is as soft as it is certain.

"What does that mean?"

"It means that sometimes we're just a supporting character in someone's journey, and not their counterpart to go on that journey with them. Until I read your book, all I knew was my heart and only parts of Selena that she shared with me. After reading Selena's point of view, I got to truly know her heart. As much as I know she loves me and Sugarville, I don't think she'd have quit her job and moved back. It felt more like what was expected versus what was right for her."

"But she loves you." My brows rise.

"Her keeping her career and staying in the city doesn't change that."

"Do you think I should have had you move to the city? But the bakery? Your family?" My eyes widen. "Do you think you two should stay broken up?"

Romance novels have rules. The couple can break up a million times and experience all sorts of relationship dysfunction throughout the narrative, but by the time the reader reaches *The End*, they need to be together. It's a hard rule; no ifs, ands, or buts about it. Guilt churns at the idea that I somehow wrote a story where the ending isn't happy.

"Sorry..." He frowns. "I may be overstepping. You're the author. It's your story."

My gaze melds with his. "It's not. Not anymore... Or maybe it never was. It's your life. Selena and your lives. Just as it's the others' lives. I guess you're given a chance most people aren't. You know what's going to happen, and if you're not happy with that, how would you want to change it?"

"*If* I could get back, you mean?"

"Yeah," I breathe, hoping that I can find a way.

He sets the last biscuit on the baking sheet. "I'd still go to her, but sooner. Before she quits her job, so we could figure out a path forward, one where she doesn't give up everything that she's worked for."

I cringe. "I really did lose my feminist card with that book."

He chuckles. "It was a tough choice. I'd never want Selena to give up her passion, and she'd never let me desert my responsibilities in Sugarville. That's why we had our third-act breakup. She believed it was what was best for me and her, even if it wasn't what was best for *us*. A solution without each giving up what's important to us must exist. If I had the chance to do it again, I'd like to find that solution with her. For us to discover a way together."

"And if not?"

A pensive expression shimmers in his features. "Then it was a beautiful love story about two people who were a portion of each other's story. Not all couples are meant to be forever... Doesn't mean it's not romantic or unhappy. Some relationships are just meant to play *a* part."

"And you're okay with that?"

"I accept that may be the outcome, but I still hope for an ending with me a part of Selena's story and her in mine. If we're not, I'm still grateful for the time we had and wouldn't change it." He hands me the cookie sheet and then gestures for me to take it to the oven.

"You're way more Zen than me." Shaking my head, I move to the oven while he begins to cut out biscuits from my dough.

"It's to be expected after what happened with Will."

"Yeah." The word comes out strangled.

No doubt my bigmouth younger brother has filled in the blanks with his CliffsNotes version of my last relationship. While I bristle at the idea that Will's fingerprints are all over my dismal romantic life since our breakup, I know it's true. Despite my brothers' insinuation, I still put myself out there, though. Bad date after worst date, I still try, because I believe in and hope for love.

I want love like in my books. Although I wonder how great the love in my books is, if the male main character questions whether he and the female lead are meant to be together. Maybe my heart is too broken to even write love, let alone find it.

"Will and I are in a different situation than you and Selena. You two only have geography and fears about making mistakes to get over. Will loved someone else." I point to him, trying to keep the hurt out of my voice. I'm not entirely sure if the twinge is about Will or my possibly failed book happy ending.

"To quote Lord James, 'He's a fool.' You're utterly loveable, Georgia. If I wasn't—"

"In love with someone else." My tease is laced with remorse. "Story of my life."

"I'm sorry."

"Me too." A ragged sigh heaves out of me. "For everything, but above all for—"

"Me not being *him*."

"Whomever *him* is," I whisper, not saying the quiet part

out loud. That ember of fear I try to snuff out: that *he* may not exist.

"For what it's worth, I wish I were him for you."

"Me too," I murmur.

Falling for these men isn't the plan. Still, a sense of loss hollows out inside me, as if I'm a jigsaw puzzle missing the final piece. Without it, the picture isn't quite right. It's not the idea that Owen isn't the person I want to share my story with, but that it's one more person who isn't. In the ebb and flow of how I feel about a life alone, at this moment it aches.

My smile is more for show, but I offer it, nonetheless. "It would be nice to have a boyfriend who bakes."

He wipes his hands, grabs the second cookie sheet, and slides it into the oven with the one I just put in there. "In the meantime, you have a friend who bakes. In ten to fifteen minutes, we'll have biscuits to celebrate the start *of* our friendship."

"To friendship." I put out my hand.

He takes it. "To friendship."

Over two biscuits, each side smothered with homemade jam, we again toast to our new friendship. Owen's admission that, despite how much he loves Selena, he accepts that he may not end up with her, solidifies my resolve to get him back to her. The depth of his love is evident in his willingness to sacrifice being with her for her sake. It's like how Selena sacrificed being with him to not take him away from his life in Sugarville. They may not be perfect, but they are right for each other, and I want to get them back together.

I'll go on my next two dates to decide between Lars and Lord James. Both men appear less emotionally attached to their love interests than Owen, but, then again, they don't wear their emotions on their faces like he does. They'll need to be unpeeled just a bit to discover which one will be less hurt to remain with me—if it comes to that.

I hope it doesn't come to *that*. My goal is to get them all back. To give them a chance to write their own happy endings. But if I have to choose one to get the other two back, I'll do it. Even if the idea of stealing what should be someone else's happy ending makes me queasy.

"I know we just gorged on biscuits, but what are your thoughts on dessert for dinner?" I ask, the leftover biscuits in a box in my hands, as I follow Owen towards Special Ingredient's entrance.

He holds the door for me. "Dessert for dinner? You're speaking my love language." He smirks. "Friendship language rather."

Laughing, I shuffle out. The lukewarm evening air kisses my skin. This time of year, Southern California teeters between summer and coming fall, with hot days and nights that are both coolish and warmish.

"There's this amazing ice cream place around the block—"

"Peach?" A low timbre steals my words. The almost lush deepness thrums through me.

CHAPTER THIRTEEN

I'M HER DAVIS

"Davis," I breathe, spinning to face him.

Every clichéd body reaction roars awake. Clenched belly. Wobbly knees. Stuttered breath. There may even be a few I've never experienced before.

Davis's handsome features spark beneath the glow of the streetlamp, making that boyish grin pop bright. The one he wore throughout our second chance date, or whatever it was, at Fisher's Landing. The one I imagined stretched across his face after I texted him *Thank You* for the muffin and tea. The same smile that I imagine he wears each time we exchange quick texts about Doc's recovery.

"You're going with Davis?" he says with a cheeky lilt.

"It's your name." *Good god, am I batting my eyes?*

"I did say you could call me whatever you wanted."

"Yeah, and I choose Davis." Dragon-size wings flutter in my abdomen.

"You choose Davis." Winking, he holds up a shopping bag with *Arvida Books* printed on the front. "I picked up those other books you recommended."

It's clear our texts go beyond just checking on Doc. They also include Davis's romance reading education. We agree that for him to have a well-developed opinion, he should sample the genre.

"I just suggested those this afternoon." Head tipped back, I let out a soft chuckle that sounds a little too much like a giggle.

"Well, *Peach*, I'm a good student. I learn quickly." It's somehow a little dirty the way it slips from his smirking mouth.

The possibilities of that eagerness crackles between us. My body's temperature rises with the fantasy of Davis, his mouth close to my ear, whispering, "Tell me how you want to be touched." His hands roaming just where I tell him.

"Yeah?" I bite my lower lip, tamping down the breathiness in my voice.

A throat clears. "Hi. I'm Owen."

Oh crap! I'm on a date... Sort of. Blinking away the sex-charged headiness, I look between Owen, who stands just a step behind me, one eyebrow quirked with accusation, and Davis, who shifts foot-to-foot.

"Owen?" A furrow notches Davis's brow "Like in your books?"

"It's a common name." I swat the air.

One dark eyebrow cocked, Davis studies Owen.

"I'm...*Peach's* friend." A question mark is almost visible in the wrinkle of Owen's brow at me being called Peach. "*Just* friends," he adds, reaching out his hand to Davis.

"I'm Davis... Her Davis." Taking Owen's hand, he clicks his tongue twice. "I mean Peach's...Georgia's *friend...*" He clicks his tongue again. "I work with her brother Jackson."

"I know Jackson. We're pickleball friends."

Davis's head tilts. "I've never seen you at the court before."

"New pickleball friends," I blurt.

"Okay." Davis juts his chin to Owen. "You should come with him on Saturday. It was just going to be Jackson and me, since the rest of the regulars all have plans." He clicks his tongue. "Though that makes the teams uneven. You can do one-on-ones or doubles. Maybe we can round robin a few matches or—"

"I'll bring my friend Lars. He's very competitive." Owen tosses me a wink. "Maybe Peach will come to cheer us on."

"It's an indoor court," Davis teases.

A silent laugh lights my face. "I am an indoorsy girl."

"So, you've read Peach's books?" Tipping his head toward Davis, Owen pushes his hands into his pockets.

"*Twice Baked Love* and I'm halfway through *The Duke's Darling*." His gaze meets mine. "I hear it's her best one."

Swoon! Someone get my smelling salts. With a bite of the inside of my cheek, I attempt to quell the heated tipsiness fogging my brain from making good choices. Friendship may be the nature of my relationship with Owen, but there are still two other potential suitors to deal with. Until I can discover a way to send them back to their stories, I shouldn't indulge in this gooey sensation inside me about Davis. I should say goodbye and leave with Owen.

"You're halfway through it?" I ask. *Really, Georgia? You're the literal worst.*

"Yeah."

"Me too!" Owen grins. "Isn't our Peach a talented writer?" He nudges me with his elbow.

It's not subtle, and it's one hundred percent something Hope would do. *No wonder there's no chemistry with Owen.*

"She's very talented. I've been up late the last few nights because of her." A seductive grin flexes the corners of his mouth, causing a clench in my core. "I'll admit that I'm not sure how I feel about Lord James. He's a bit of a smug bastard."

"He grows on you." Owen chuckles. "Wait, are you at the part in Lady Cecily's father's study?"

"Yeah." Davis's ears turn bright pink.

That scene may be one of my steamiest. Lady Cecily, her cries of passion muffled after she lets Lord James ball up his cravat and shove it into her mouth, sits on the edge of her father's desk, her legs wide. On his knees before her, Lord James, almost a little feral, fucks her with his mouth, her father just down the hall unaware of his rival's ravishment of his daughter.

"Oh… *That* scene." I swallow thickly, imagining myself on that desk and Davis between my legs. *Stop it, Georgia!*

"Yeah," he says, his darkening gaze falls to my lips.

It may be my own attraction speaking, but the lust-filled thoughts are almost visible in his pupils. Like a picture window, showing me the filthy things he imagines, all of which involve us reenacting the spicier parts of my books.

"Yeah," I repeat, desire swelling between my thighs.

"It was *well* written." Owen's cough extinguishes the charge in the air.

In its place, awkwardness hangs. It's clear we should all depart. Owen and I are off to continue our non-date, and Davis to whatever plans he has for tonight. Still, we all remain on the sidewalk.

"Ice cream!" Owen claps his hands together. "We were just about to get some ice cream, want to join?"

"I…" Davis rubs his nape and clicks his tongue a few times. "I wouldn't want to interfere with your plans."

"Nah." Owen makes a dismissive gesture. "You're not interfering at all."

"Are you sure?" He looks between me and Owen.

The smart thing is to tell him goodbye. To not drag him along. It's clear there is something between us. Something I shouldn't pursue until I resolve the issue of my book boyfriends.

"You should come with us." My vision locks with his.

What am I doing? It's like my brain is speaking a different language than the rest of my body. Inviting Davis is a bad idea. Texting Davis is a bad idea. Yet here I am, the queen of bad ideas.

"If you're sure," he murmurs.

"I am."

"Excellent!" Owen grins. "Lead the way, Georgia Peach."

It's a short walk to Gemma's Creamery. Just enough time for Owen to nudge my shoulder and whisper, "He calls you Peach?" and for me to poke him back and mutter, "It's not like *that*."

The small parlor is quiet, which isn't surprising on a weekday evening. With its bubble gum pink interior and new selections weekly, Gemma's is one of my favorite ice cream places. It also takes food allergies and preferences seriously with peanut-free, vegan, and GF-safe sections with dedicated scoopers. Owen gets two scoops of cinnamon roll ice cream from the non-GF section, while Davis and I get single scoops from the GF section; his chocolate, while I choose peanut butter.

Davis isn't gluten free. It's just one of the many topics we discussed the other night. I don't expect the people around me to have the same diet as me. The only time it's an issue is with shared meals or intimacy. Will would get frustrated when I pulled away from him if he tried to kiss me after he'd been drinking or eating something that could cause a reaction. "It's a little overkill, Georgia," he'd scold each time, but he wasn't the one dealing with a reaction. I was.

"Why two?" I point at the two spoons stabbed into Davis's ice cream.

"The second one is for you, in case you want to try. I know how you feel about double dipping"—he winks—"but peanut butter and chocolate go great together. Thought this may be a fair compromise in case you want to try some?"

"That they do." I spin and grab a second spoon from the little dispenser beside the register. "In case you want to try some." Flashing a sassy smile, I hold up the second spoon and sashay toward the small booth in the corner that Owen has claimed for us.

My steps halt at Owen's expression. From the little booth in the corner, his eyes sparkle with playful accusation reminiscent of catching a child with their hand in the cookie jar. Though my hand isn't in anyone's cookie jar, even if the idea of Davis's in mine prickles heat up my spine.

Eyes narrowed, I mouth, *What?*

You like him, he mouths back.

"Not happening," I mutter under my breath and take the seat across from Owen.

He looks to where Davis is paying for our ice cream. "Why not?" he whispers back.

"Lars and Lord James, remember?"

"They're not your *him*."

"What makes you say that?" I whisper-hiss.

"Neither of them makes you look like that." He aims his spoon at me.

I release an annoyed breath. "My focus is on the three men I accidentally wished for, not the one that I may or may not—"

"Liiiiike?" He waggles his eyebrows.

"Should I grab us some water too?" Davis approaches and places his dish on the table.

"I'm okay. Thank you." I smile, ignoring Owen's assessing gaze.

"Oh no, I have to go," Owen says, his tone robotic.

I shoot him a *what are you doing* look.

His answering smirk is so much like Lars or my brother's, I wonder if they *are* rubbing off on him.

"Is everything okay?" Davis asks.

"Yep. Just an early morning. Those muffins don't bake themselves, you know?"

"Muffins?" Forehead pinched, Davis looks between me and Owen. "You're a baker like Owen in the book?"

"What are the odds?" A nervous laugh punctuates his retort.

"Do you need to go too?" Davis looks at me.

"No!" Owen's protest is high-pitched. "I mean"—he offers an apologetic smile—"don't end your fun because of me. You two, stay. Enjoy your ice cream." He scoops up the leftover biscuits and his ice cream. "Can you walk Georgia home? It's not far and I know she doesn't need anyone, but I'd feel better."

"Of course."

"Sorry, Georgia." The twitch of his lips telegraphs that he's only sorry-ish.

It's clear he's playing matchmaker. *Seriously, how much of my bestie did I use to inspire his character?*

Shaking his head, Davis watches as Owen leaves. "You have a friend named Owen who is a baker?" It's more accusation than question.

"Yep."

"The resemblance is uncanny." He nibbles on the corner of his mouth.

"Yep." Shifting in my seat, I spoon up some ice cream.

"Did you base the character on him?" he asks, sliding onto the bench across from me.

"On my best friend Hope."

"He's so much like the character." He clicks his tongue twice.

"You want to try this?" I hold up my dish as a distraction.

As much as I tell fictional stories in my books, lying isn't my forte. Each time I do, the knot in my stomach coils tight, causing a queasy ache. Avoiding the topic is preferable. Though it's just a form of a lie. It's more like lying lite. Like diet soda, it leaves the same artificial taste in my mouth, but without the unwanted calories.

He spoons up some of my ice cream and some of his own on the same spoon. "So good," he moans after his first lick.

"Yeah?" I do the same with his and mine. "Oh god! Why haven't I done this before? Next time a scoop of each."

"Agreed." He spoons up another bite.

Next time? Those two words thrum through me with the promise of something I shouldn't have, but I crave anyway. Five days ago, I sat across from Davis at Fisher's Landing, scoffing at the idea of a next time with him, but here I am daydreaming about it.

"Hope is the inspiration for Owen Baker?" he asks.

"Yeah." Chuckling, I scoop up another bite. "I didn't realize how much of an inspiration until recently."

"Do you pull a lot from your life?"

"Bits and pieces. Most writers cannibalize their lives just a bit. But at the end of the day, it's fiction."

"Will *our* not-so-meet/cute make it into one of your books?" he teases.

"Maybe." With a bat of my lashes, I offer a cheeky smile.

He leans back and his boyish grin erupts, every feature bright with playfulness. "It would be the perfect start for the female main character to be rescued from Mr. Foot-in-His-Mouth by her *Mr. Right*. The perfect meet-cute."

"Yeah…" I sigh, causing him to arch one brow. "I already had that meet/cute in real life." I rake my teeth against my bottom lip, weighing how much to tell him.

The two half-eaten ice cream dishes that we're sharing teeter us between friendship and something more. Opening my emotional baggage from past relationships would cannonball us into date territory, but the earnest expression covering his face coaxes me on.

"My ex, Will. That's how we met," I say, dragging my spoon through my ice cream. "Lena, my cousin, Hope, and I were inseparable growing up and that extended into our twenties. The three of us were at a bar. I went to get us more drinks, and this guy who had been hitting on me most of the night got extra pushy—"

"How?"

"He grabbed my ass."

My attention moves to Davis, his fingers curled around the table's edge, and an equally sharp tic tightens his jaw. Anger shadows his bright expression.

"He didn't hurt me." I reach over and squeeze his forearm, glad when his rigid muscles relax. "I slapped his hand away. Just as I spun to tell him to fuck off, Will stepped in. After he and his friends escorted Mr. Handsy out, Will sent over a round of drinks for us to make up for the failing of his sex." I roll my eyes. "At twenty-two, I thought it was about the swooniest thing."

"How long did you date?"

"Five years."

"That's a long time. Were you in love?"

"*I* was," I say.

"Just you?" His brow puckers.

"Just me."

He nods. "What happened?"

"The CliffsNotes version?"

He threads our fingers. "Whatever version you want to share."

His palm's warmth eases the tension within me about telling this story. I'm not someone who doesn't share myself with others. I'm just selective with whom I open up fully. Most people just get pieces of what I want to share with them. For a moment, I think of Owen talking about being a portion or a part of someone's life, and I get it. With portions, you only share some things, with someone who is part of your life, you share everything.

It's a dangerous game I'm playing, and I know it. Still, I want to share these things. With Davis, I don't sense the need to hide portions of myself. To only worry about his feelings, his wants. It's a little addicting and terrifying to be comfortable enough to just exist without worrying about managing.

"From the moment I met Will I thought he was it… I thought we were so happy. Five years ago, we even planned to move in together. Three days before that, he broke up with me in a text message." Eyes closed, that last text exchange flashes in my memory.

"A fucking text message?" Davis seethes.

I squeeze his hand in mine. "*He* thought that not doing it in person would save me from the embarrassment of my reaction in front of him. Turns out he'd been hooking up with my cousin Lena on-and-off for the last three years of our relationship. Of course, she claims they were only drunken kisses. Nothing more. But the moment Lena broke up with her boyfriend, Will showed up at her place to console her. She says one thing led to another, and he admitted he'd been in love with her for most of our relationship. That—" my voice wobbles. "It had been her he'd noticed at the bar that night, but she'd had a boyfriend at the time."

"You were inseparable since you were girls," he almost parrots my words.

"I haven't spoken to her since she came to my apartment a month after Will dumped me to confess everything." I blink, damming up the threatening tears.

Despite the far too many tears already shed, their betrayal always coaxes more. Two people I loved lied to me. They broke my trust, making me question if they ever loved me. Making me question myself.

"Next Saturday will be the first time in five years that I'll be in the same room with Lena and Will." I swallow down the emotions tangled in my throat.

"Why will you be in a room with them?"

"They're getting married," I say quietly. An acidic taste burns my throat.

"Why put yourself through that?" He clicks his tongue.

"For my mom."

"She shouldn't ask that of you." The dark clouds in his expression contrast with the soft, steady timbre of his voice.

"She hasn't."

"Then why?"

"Because my mom is the only mother Lena has ever known, and Lena is the last remaining tie to my mom's sister. My aunt died when Lena was a toddler, and my mom stepped in to help my uncle raise her."

Mouth dragging into a frown, the storminess in his eyes dulls, and his shoulders slump. His demeanor mirrors the resignation that sighs within me over this situation.

It may hurt. It may not make sense to anyone else. But there are times we just have to do things for the sake of others, even if they don't ask us to do it.

"It will be fine."

"For everyone else, but what about you?" His gaze links with mine, causing an unsteady *thump-thump* in my chest.

"It will be fine," I repeat, ignoring the twinge in my heart.

"They sell pints here."

"What?" A nervous laugh falls out of me with his abrupt topic change.

He tips his head toward the glass door freezers along the parlor's wall. "I'll get an assortment of pints, and we can do a *TNG* marathon after the wedding."

"You don't have to." I pull my hand from his and pick up my spoon.

"I want to."

I clear my throat. "Sorry for just emotionally dumping on you."

He picks up his spoon. "I did it last time, so it was your turn."

"Perhaps, we should switch to something more fun." I tap my fingernails against the tabletop. "Favorite *TNG* episode?"

"Easy—" A lopsided grin slants his mouth. "*Rascals.*"

"The one where Picard, Guinan, and others are transformed back into children after the transporter malfunctions?"

He nods.

"That's my favorite, too!" I bounce in my seat.

"Favorite movie?" He grins.

We continue like that throughout the remainder of our ice cream and our walk home. Taking turns asking questions, trading answers. Some silly, like what our favorite board games are; mine, *Scrabble*, and his, *Monopoly*. Others more serious, like who our favorite person is; mine, Hope, and his, Doc.

We get so lost in our little game that I walk past my house. Four blocks. Embarrassment flushes my cheeks when the realization hits me, but he says nothing. He just falls into step once I turn us back toward my place.

"Favorite ice cream?" I ask, walking up the sidewalk to the house's back gate, the crickets' melody humming in the night air.

"Cookies and cream," he says.

Face scrunched, I twist to face him. "Why'd you get chocolate?"

"I like chocolate."

"But it's not your favorite." I arch a brow.

"Cookies and cream isn't in the GF section."

I fiddle with my dress. "You don't have to only eat GF around me. It's not necessary. I can be around it. I just can't have it."

"I know." Clicking his tongue, he shuffles his feet, the shopping bag in his hand rustling. "You can be around it, but you can't have it. You also can't be kissed by someone who has just had it. It wouldn't be safe."

"And you want to kiss me." My simple declaration is breathless.

"So much." He steps close, a charge ignites in the

narrowing space between us. "And I think you want to kiss me, too."

"You do?" The question is less taunt and more panted submission to his accusation.

The heat that cascades within me reiterates how very right he is. I want Davis to kiss me, but not as much as I want to kiss him. To run my fingers through his raven hair and muss it up as I revel in the taste of him.

"Tell me I'm wrong." Dropping the shopping bag to the sidewalk, he prowls closer, my back meeting the gate, its metal cool against my heated body.

"You're not wrong," I breathe.

His hands come to either side of my body, caging me in. The furnace of his form licks against my skin, scorching every inch. "Tell me what you want." He nuzzles his nose along my jawline. "I'm yours to command."

I place my palm on his chest. "Did you just quote me to me?"

"Yep. God, you smell good." He swipes his nose down my neck and inhales deeply. "It's a good line."

It is a good line. It's the line Lord James says to Lady Cecily just after she murmurs, "You declare me a goddess, then get on your knees and worship me, my dear acolyte." But that's Lord James's line meant for another woman.

"Davis—" I cup his face, guiding his stare to meet mine. "I may write fictional men, but I don't want lines. Especially those meant for someone else. I don't want you to say to me what you think I want to hear, just what you mean."

"I do mean it." He raises his hand, cradling my cheek. "We both know you're better at words than me. I'm just borrowing them to express how I feel. I have thought about nothing but kissing you, about making you smile, since we met. Please don't doubt what I want... And what I want is to kiss *you*."

The way every inch of me melts into his words and his

touch washes away lingering doubt. Every red light is green. I will pass Go. I will collect this man's kisses.

"You have the right words," I whisper, my pulse roaring. "Kiss me, please."

His mouth is on mine before I finish my request. It's soft at first. Each press tests and plays to find the right rhythm. Though the fire that crackles inside me telegraphs that everything he does is just right. With gentle nibbles, he coaxes me open, swiping his tongue over mine, the sweetness of our blended tastes is almost too decadent.

"Davis," I moan, his mouth dragging down my neck, sucking on the sensitive flesh along my throat.

"Mm hmm." His fingers knead the soft flesh of my waist. "You like that?"

"Yes." I rub myself against his growing erection, the friction zings promised pleasure through me.

"Fuck," he groans.

"You like that?" Rubbing myself against him, I thread my fingers into his hair and tug, just a bit.

"Yes," he almost growls, lifting me into his arms.

My legs wrap around his waist, and he presses me tight against the gate. The coil at my center winds tighter with the move of his hips against me. His hands glide up my thighs, pushing my skirt up, coming into contact with my....

"Spanx..." Wincing, I bury my face in his neck. "I didn't plan on this. On you touching... Oh god."

Please lord, do your girl a solid and send a sinkhole right now! Shapewear may keep things tight and prevent the chaffing that sometimes comes with my thicker thighs, but it is a mood killer. When I'm intimate, I nix them. I'll excuse myself to the bathroom to remove them and hide them in my purse, or just not wear a dress if I suspect sexy things will happen. I never get caught up like this.

"I told you Christmas was my favorite holiday, remember?" He traces the barrier between the shorts and my skin. "You know why?"

"Cause Santa Claus doesn't wear Spanx?" I groan.

He shakes his head, his eyes reminiscent of a smoldering wildfire. "Because I like unwrapping gifts. The anticipation with each rip of the barrier between me and my present." He slides his finger beneath the restricting shorts, caressing the sensitive skin.

"Oh, god," I squeak.

"Do you want to be unwrapped?" He grinds against me.

"Yes," I whimper.

"Right there?" He presses a little harder, the delicious rasp of the layers of clothes between us winds the tension tighter. "Look at you, cheeks flushed and eyes glossy, writhing against me like a pussycat in heat." He nips at my ear. "With no thought of us being discovered."

A vine-covered wall to our right and a shady maple tree kitty-corner to that provide the illusion of privacy. My neighbors, any car that moves down the quiet street, or a passerby coming this way may not notice us, but if someone came from the left and looked just long enough, they may see. Writhing my hips against him leaves nothing to the imagination if we are caught. That likelihood of exposure sends an unexpected thrill through me.

He thrusts against me, the tension building at my center. "Do you like the threat of getting caught doing something you're not supposed to?"

"Maybe I just want you so much that I don't care," I pant, moving against him, the coming orgasm teasing awake.

"*Fuck...*" Fingers grip tighter on my thighs, he captures my moans with his hungry kisses.

A violent shudder rips through me with my climax's quick intensity. Blinking away the headiness, I can't remember the last time I came so fast and only from dry humping. Not to mention, I've never let someone bring me to orgasm in public.

"Are you alright?" He caresses my cheeks, his dark eyes soft and searching.

"Very alright," I say a little breathless, a goofy grin slinking across my face.

"Good—" he nuzzles my nose with his "—because I *really* want to make you do that again."

"I think I would enjoy that." I trace the outline of his smile with my fingers. Satiation jellies every bit of me. Even my protesting brain is quiet. All the reasons I shouldn't be doing this are silent. I'd not listen anyway, not when I'm snug against Davis's hard angles.

"That's not who you left with." A disapproving voice snaps me out of my lust-filled haze.

CHAPTER FOURTEEN

I CAN'T DO THIS

My life is a bad rom-com! Cringing, I twist my head and find Rem, his face pinched, standing at the walkway's start, a leash connected to Wentworth dangles from my brother's hand. Beside him, a shit-eating grin spreads across Hope's face.

Davis lowers me to my feet. Fixing my skirt, I step in front of him to help cover the not-so-little situation I helped create in his jeans.

"Rem. Hope. What are you doing here?" I purse my lips.

"We live here," he deadpans.

"Your niece is active tonight, so we went for a walk to settle her." She rubs her belly. "We thought Wentworth may want to join, so you didn't need to walk him after—"

"Your date." Rem hands me the leash, his gaze flicking between me and Davis. "As I said, he's not who you left with."

"I thought Owen and you were just friends," Davis mumbles.

"We are," I murmur.

Lips pursed, Rem quirks one blond brow.

Hope shoots him a sharp look and then turns her bright smile on Davis. "Hi. I'm Hope, the best friend."

"I'm Davis." He rubs his nape

"Davis?" Her brows waggle. "*The* Davis."

And I thought the Spanx situation was bad, but this... Eyes closed, I suck in a steadying breath.

"Davis? The guy from the other night? The one Jackson set you up with? The one you walked out on?" Rem *tsks*.

"I think they got past that, honey." Hope pats his shoulder.

Davis clears his throat. "*The* Davis?"

God, please, sinkhole, now! I rub my temples.

"We should go inside." Hope nudges Rem along. "I'll see you in the morning. Stop by for breakfast. We have lots to discuss. Just let me know if I should make breakfast for four." She winks, tugging Rem past us and through the gate.

"That's your best friend and older brother?"

"Yup." I nod, watching them shuffle down the cobblestone walkway toward the back of the house.

"And they just caught me dry humping you against their back gate?"

I cringe. "Technically we were post-dry humping, but *yeah*."

For a beat, we just look at each other, both our faces crinkled with embarrassment. Then a loud laugh erupts out of him, causing me to follow. The situation is ridiculous, but this is my life.

"I'm so messy." I wave at myself. "You should run, very fast and very far."

He places his hands on my hips and shakes his head. "I'd rather run *with* you."

"Davis, my life is a mess. I can't make any promises, not now, and that's not fair to you. I've already been such a selfish ass."

Am I like Will? Realization aches in my chest. Here, I am stringing Davis along, taking these little moments of happiness and pleasure from him, all while I'm entangled with my book boyfriends. One of whom I may have to choose to be with for the sake of the other two.

"Why do you think you're being selfish?" His brows knit. "If it's because you came and I didn't? Trust me, if your brother and Hope hadn't interrupted us, I was about thirty seconds away from losing all control, but even if I didn't—" he squeezes my waist "—the satisfaction I got from this body shuddering against me makes me greedy for more. In fact, do you have other surfaces I can press you up against?"

I laugh. "I'm being serious."

"Me too." He smirks.

The mix of sweetness and steady strength oozing from Davis is too appealing. I could just lose myself in him, throwing away any sense of doing what's right. Right for my book boyfriends. They deserve their happy endings, as does Davis. It's not fair to toy with him like this, when I may have to be with someone else.

"I can't be with you or anyone else, not right now. Not until I figure my messy life out."

"How long will that take?"

I shake my head. "I don't expect you to wait around."

"What if I wanted to wait?" he murmurs.

"It's not fair for you."

He steps back, his hands still on my waist, and studies me. "Is this really *for* me or is it *because* of me?"

"What?"

He nods, his throat bobbing. "Is this to protect me from your messy life or is it because you don't like—"

"No! I like you… a lot." My protest is swift. So swift that I don't register the words sprinting out of my mouth until they are nestled in the space between us. Those words are like a truth bomb ready to explode. I like Davis Makenzie. I *really* like him.

"You like me, but you can't be with me right now." Hurt hardens his features.

I close my eyes, imagining how many times Davis heard this from his dad. Someone saying they want you but can't be with you doesn't make you feel less unwanted. I know this, even if I know how much I want him, it doesn't change how he may feel right now.

Opening my eyes, I swallow thickly. "Or anyone else." *That is anyone but one of my book boyfriends.* "I'm so sorry…"

"I should go." He releases me and steps back.

Nodding, I push back the threatening tears. The ones that I know will come once he walks away.

"Goodbye, Peach." He offers me one last look, picks up his bag, and walks away.

"Goodbye, Davis," I whisper. Wentworth nuzzles his cool nose against my calf, offering comfort I don't deserve.

Wiping my eyes, Wentworth and I head to my carriage house. The pained expression covering Davis's face haunts me. The story about his dad making promises to him, to be a family, radiates an ache in my chest. How often had younger Davis, and even adult Davis, been tugged along by someone who couldn't be with him? I can't do that to him, although I already have.

Unleashing Wentworth, I hang the leash on the hook by the door and lean against the wall. Queasiness sloshes in my stomach, reminding me that I should have listened to myself. I should have thought of Davis and not just about being with him.

"But I want tc be with him," I mumble, my gaze dragging to the laptop I discarded on the coffee table.

In the past, writing provided refuge for moments like this. When things were too overwhelming, I could escape into my words. I could write an ending where everything works out. Everyone is happy, even me. But those words aren't there.

"I'm so messy." Pushing away from the door, I head toward my room but then stop.

The laptop's siren song pulls me back to it. Not to write, though. To research. To find a way to fix this. To help everyone I've hurt since I'd made that stupid wish.

CHAPTER FIFTEEN

DO YOU KNOW ANY WITCHES?

The alarm on my cell phone jolts me awake. Six a.m. is too early after only two hours of sleep. Research had claimed the hours I should have spent slumbering. I'd looked into theories and legends, taking me down various rabbit holes that all led to one constant universal truth: wishes have consequences, both intended and unintended.

The unintended stack up. Ripping my three book boyfriends from the only lives they know. Doc's accident. The hurt on Davis's face last night. Even if I believe that the first two aren't *exactly* my fault, the last one is. I led him on. I hurt him. There's no other way of looking at it.

"What have you done, Georgia?" I sigh over a sharp twinge in my chest.

Wentworth rises from the end of the bed and lumbers to me. He cuddles into me, and I lean into his squishy body. For just a moment, I lose myself in the comfort of his silken coat.

Scooting out of bed, I brush my teeth and take Wentworth out for a short walk before feeding him. The single text from Hope this morning says *Don't even think of NOT coming over for breakfast*, which means I won't spend the morning wallowing, hate-spiraling, or following that *Reddit* thread about the theory on fountains before I head to SPN. Instead, I shower and get ready. Tossing my hair into a messy bun, I tug on black pants, a jewel tone blouse, a blazer, and slip some gold hoops into my earlobes. It's my go-to 'I appear put together, but I'm not' look.

"You're a mess, but at least you're a hot mess," I offer a half-hearted smile and swipe pink lipstick on.

A forceful knock on my front door startles me. It can't be Hope, because I'd just texted her *the teapot emoji*. It's our sign to put the kettle on because I will be spilling the tea, so she knows I'm on my way.

"What if it's Davis?" Longing flutters in my chest.

I haven't heard from him since he walked away last night. Although that's to be expected when five minutes after I use him as a scratching post, I tell him I can't see him.

It's almost too much to hope. That somewhere between his goodbye last night and this morning's sunrise, that he… I'm not sure what, but I spin on my heels and run toward the door anyway, an excited Wentworth trotting behind me.

I fling open the front door, and my expression falls. Even Wentworth huffs a disappointed breath and turns back to claim his bed in the corner.

Lord James, a rakish smile anchoring his face, stands on the small porch outside my front door. A charcoal suit hugs his defined physique, and a single red rose, which looks suspiciously like the ones from Mr. Rios's yard down the street, is in his hand.

"My lady," he drawls, offering a small bow.

"Lord James." Disappointment ripples through me.

"Are you displeased to see me?"

"Yes… No… I mean, no, I am. I'm just…" I gnaw on my bottom lip. "I'm surprised. Our date isn't until Sunday night."

Jackson's *Just Write* dating schedule has me going on a date with each man and making a decision by Tuesday. That leaves enough time to prepare the lucky bachelor to attend the wedding with me. While a date for the wedding may be Jackson's goal for me, mine is to be done with this. By Tuesday, I will either get all three of these men back to their stories or I'll choose one of them. The internet research that kept me up most of the night didn't offer a lot of hope, but I have a potential resolution.

"I took advantage of an empty townhouse to steal over to your abode."

Head tilted, I raise one eyebrow. "You're under strict orders not to leave the townhouse nor see me outside of our official date unless with the group."

"What kind of hero would I be if I listened to someone else, rather than my heart?" He reaches out, handing me the flower, his buttery timbre is flirtatious.

"One who listens." Smirking, I take the flower.

"My capacity to listen is boundless." He steps closer, and his large body towers over me. Those emerald eyes almost bore into me. Hand raised, he fiddles with my earring before dragging one finger along my jawline and down the long column of my throat. "Soon you shall discover my limitless potential, my lady."

"Lord James."

"Call me James," he murmurs, tracing slow circles along my skin.

"James…" My breath whooshes from me.

I'm not unimpacted by him, but the reaction is reminiscent of shoving a jigsaw piece into the wrong puzzle. It doesn't fit, not completely, and the image isn't correct, but it's there, nonetheless.

He leans close, his breath rasps against my lips, the sensation akin to the caress of rough palms. "I am but yours to command."

"What?" Palm on his chest, I push him back, putting distance between us. "That's for Lady Cecily, not me."

"My lady?"

"It's Georgia, not 'my lady'!" Hands on my hips, I mimic his accent.

A fire burns within me. It's the second time in an eight-hour period that a man has used a line on me meant for another woman, but something about how James calls me "my lady" stokes that anger. It's like a placeholder endearment for whatever lady is there.

He places his hand on his chest. "Pardon me?"

"Don't recycle lines *I* wrote for *you* to say to someone else" —I point to him and then myself—"I deserve better."

"My la… Georgia, you deserve everything, and that's what I plan to give you." He crosses the threshold, causing me to step back. "All I have to give—"

Shoulders slumping, I finish his line. "Is yours. All you need to do is ask."

It's not just the recycled line for another woman being spewed to me, but annoyance at my own stupid expectations. James is just acting as I wrote him to be. Owen may have surprised me last night, but I can't forget that these three men are creations from my imagination.

Not to mention, I have a flimsy foundation to be upset that he's using lines meant for someone else. We're not in a relationship, and I don't want to be. Attraction aside, James isn't the man who consumes my thoughts. None of my book boyfriends are. Worry nips at me that even if I don't have to choose one of them, I may have already lost the man I want to give my heart to.

"It's okay," I say, my voice small.

"Georgia…" He steps forward, stops, and heaves a long breath. "I mean no offense. I thought I was being romantic. This world is utterly different than mine. I am not sure how things work or how I work here."

"I'm so sorry. This may be harder for you than for Lars or Owen. Their books are at least modern-day, even if Lars's has supernatural beings. His world still has internet and cars."

He nods, his throat bobbing, and takes a careful step closer. "Please know that my feelings for you are real. My ways may not be what you're accustomed to, but do not doubt my sincerity."

"You don't even know me."

"But I do." He grips my shoulders. "You're beautiful, kind, talented, brilliant, strong, and a million other things I have yet to discover about you. From the moment I clamped eyes on you, my heart knew it was you. You may believe that you wrote me to fall in love with Lady Cecily, but I think I was written for you." He cups my face and leans in.

My pulse roars.

It's almost like watching a car wreck. Everything is in slow motion.

"No." Blinking out of the little trance, I pull out of his hold. "This isn't a good idea."

"Is this not the point?" He gestures, his tone curt. "For you to pick one of us?"

This all feels wrong. If I say, "Yes", this all could end. Lars and Owen may be sent back. It's the easy solution, but since when do I do things the easy way? Just like with publishing, I took the harder path. *My path.*

They don't belong here. I need to try to get all three of them back where they truly belong. That needs to be my focus. James may be the sure thing, but he himself says he doesn't understand this world. That he doesn't fit. Even if he doesn't love Lady Cecily, how happy would he be in a place where he doesn't belong?

I square my shoulders. "Stick to the plan. Outside of Sunday, do not see me unless with the group."

"As you command." His reply is hard-edged. "We'll play your game, my lady."

"This isn't a game."

"I know that." He cocks an eyebrow. "Do you?"

"What does that mean?" I glare.

"Georgia, is everything okay?"

I twist toward the door where Rem stands, his narrowed gaze jumps between me and James. "Yes. *Jim* was just leaving."

"As you command," he says again, a sardonic smile sketched across his face. With a curt bow, James turns and strides out of the apartment.

"Owen, then Davis, and now Jim. Shall I expect any other men to appear?" Rem asks, his tone teeters between playful and judgmental.

"I hope not." Sighing, I cross my arms over my chest. "Is there something you need, Rem?"

"Hope sent me to check on you. You were supposed to be down ten minutes ago, and you weren't responding to your texts."

I look at the kitchen table where my cell phone sits beside my purse. "Sorry. I'm coming now."

Grabbing my things, I give Wentworth a goodbye pet and then follow Rem out. Shaking his head, he turns, pulls out his keys, and locks my door. I blanch at the action, thinking of how Jackson says Rem checks my door most days because I sometimes forget to lock it.

"Georgia," he calls as we reach the bottom of the stairs.

Sucking in a breath, I turn to face him.

He rakes his fingers through his short blond hair. "I know I gave you a hard time about your first date with Davis and needing to move on from Will, but…"

"But what?" My mouth flattens.

"This"—he waves his hand at me—"what are you doing? You go on a date with one guy, only for me to find you pressed up against the back gate by another man, and now I find a third man in your apartment before the sun is barely up."

"You said for me to move on," I snark.

"Don't be cute." A crease dips his forehead.

"It's not a big deal."

"It *is* a big deal. This isn't you. You were with Will for five years. When he broke up with you, you were devastated. You didn't get out of bed for a week, then Lena..." His mouth pulls down. "For two years, the only people you socialized with was us, outside of a few happy hours with your colleagues. You didn't start dating until the last three years, and every single date was a one-time-only event. Now, you're with three men in a ten-hour period."

"First, way to slut shame, Mr. Future Girl Dad."

He flinches.

"Second, I wasn't *with* three men. One is a friend. One is... well *Jim*... And Davis may have been something, but not anymore." My voice quakes.

"May have been?"

I massage between my eyes, a dull ache forming there. "Don't worry, I've lived up to your expectations and screwed that up."

"Georgia—"

I hold my palm up. "No. I don't want to fight with you. I don't want to cry. I don't want to hear all the ways that I disappoint you. For Hope's sake, who's expecting me for breakfast, let's just agree that I am a fuck up, and go about our day."

"Georgia," he says, his features pinched.

"Please." The twinge in my throat causes my voice to come out as a creak.

Mouth tight, he nods. "Fine. Tell Hope, I headed to the office."

He turns and starts down the path toward the gate, my attention follows each slow step. Hand on the knob, his shoulders slump, and he spins.

"I don't think you're a screwup. It kills me that you believe that's my opinion of you."

"Then why do you act like it?" I ask, my mouth dry. But I forge on, "Like every decision I make is the wrong one."

"I'm the eldest. It's in our DNA."

"You don't *worry* about Jackson the way you worry about me," I scoff, making air quotes.

He opens and then closes his mouth.

"Even when I do what you want, it's still not the right thing. *'Don't study English. Get a real degree, Georgia',*" I mock his deep baritone. "So, I did. I got my bachelor's and master's in social work to make you happy."

"You love what you do."

"It doesn't change the fact that it wasn't my first choice. You make underhanded comments about how much I make. You refuse to see that, despite your concerns about writing being a dead-end, I'm making it work. Yes, I don't make a lot from it, but I make enough to pay for it. Jackson spends just as much on his recreational activities, but that isn't an issue. At least I make money from something you call my hobby." I toss up my hands. "It's just some sexist bullshit and you know it."

"It has nothing to do with you being a girl."

"Then why?" I hiss through clenched teeth.

"Because Jackson wasn't the sick one. The one I stayed up at night worrying about. The person I was terrified I was going to lose."

My ire deflates just a bit, but not completely. Seven years older, Rem has always taken on a lot. He's our family's protector. It had to be so scary for him. The turmoil of our parents' relationship was exacerbated by a sick sister. Each time a reaction landed in the ER or kept me home from school, he'd held my hand.

It took a string of doctor visits to arrive at my diagnosis. Once we knew what was happening, it became easier to prevent the flare-ups. Everyone was careful once we knew, especially Rem.

"I'm not that sick kid anymore. Haven't been for a long time." I meet his gaze. "I just hope one day you can see that." Turning, I walk away.

The showdown with my brother frazzles my nerves, but I suck in a deep breath. The cool morning air fills my lungs and quells the anxiety that prickles under the surface of my skin. Leaving the argument outside, I open the patio door and step into the kitchen. Hope sits at the Queen Anne-style table, a mini breakfast smorgasbord of pastries, fruit, eggs, potatoes, and meats covers its surface.

Plopping onto a chair, I release a long breath. "I like Davis."

"Tell me something I don't know." Elbows on the table's edge, she leans forward, her chin resting on her hands, and playfulness dancing in her brown eyes.

"I may have figured out a way to get my book boyfriends back to their stories."

"You have?" Owen exclaims, causing me to spin in my chair. He stands, head twisted our way and teakettle mid-pour, at the stovetop.

I point. "What are you doing here... Jackson has *one* job, and he can't even do that... And Rem thinks he's the responsible one." I shake my head.

"Jackson dropped me off before he and Lars went for a morning run," he says, pouring hot water into the humming-bird-themed teapot.

"Advantage of an empty townhouse," I mutter James's words to myself. "Why are you here?"

Hope rubs her belly. "With this little biscuit coming in six weeks, my doctor wants me to slow down a bit, so Owen's going to help me out."

"As long as you need me," he says, placing the ceramic pot in the center of the table. He takes the seat beside her.

Side-by-side, in their matching lavender Good Girl's Grub T-shirts, it hits me how much my bestie and the cinnamon roll baker are alike. Both helpers. Both patient but willing to push when needed.

"You'll be a dynamic duo in the kitchen together." I accept the cup of tea Owen poured for me.

"That we will. I'm happy to have Owen as part of the Good Girl's Grub team for as long as he's here." Affection shines in her features. "But you said you have an idea? What is it? How can we help?"

"I do…" I tap my fingers against the side of the porcelain cup. The action soothes the jitteriness inside me. "I have a plan, but I'd like to keep it between us because I don't want to give Lars and James false hope. Sorry to ask you to keep this secret, Owen, but…"

He makes a *locking-the-door* and *tossing-away-the-key* motion against his mouth. It's a little silly, but the sweetness draws a thankful smile to my mouth.

"A lot of the research I've found online is about wishing wells and not fountains made out of wishing stones. But there seems to be a theory that if you shout the wish into the well and then open your mouth to swallow the echo, that will take it back…"

"So, you're going to shout your wish into the SPN fountain and swallow it?" The skepticism is evident in Hope's tone, despite her pasted on *sure this could totally work* smile.

"No—" I wave my hand at the ridiculousness of her suggestion. "But my theory is if I can get back the not-so-lucky penny I used to make the wish, then maybe I can somehow reverse engineer this and get Owen and the rest of the guys back. You know, if I take back my payment for the wish, then the fountain will take back my wish."

"How are you going to know it's your penny?"

"The date," I say smugly, sipping my tea.

Before I tossed that penny in, I'd sat on the fountain's edge studying it. It was just your average penny. No distinguishable traits outside of its date. If I close my eyes tight enough, I can picture my thumb swiping along those tiny numbers.

"It had the same date as the year my first book was published. All I need to do is find the penny with that date, and I'll know it's my wish. Then I can unwish, and *poof*, everything is fixed. My book boyfriends are back to their stories." Bouncing in my seat, I toss my hands in the air like a magician.

"Didn't you say the fountain was empty when you checked it out on Monday? How are you supposed to find that penny?"

"What if there are multiple pennies with that date?" Owen adds, his face wrinkled. "You wouldn't want to accidentally undo someone else's wish."

"We're not saying this is a bad idea," Hope says, her tone sugary sweet. "We're just asking questions. We're just..."

"Wondering if you have a Plan B?" Owen's indulgent grin mirrors one you'd give a child.

"Ugh!" Whining, I rest my head on the table. While farfetched in my brain, now spoken aloud, I deflate with the knowledge that this plan is terrible. I can't just return a wish, like an ill-fitting sweater.

Hope pats the top of my head. "There, there. It will be okay."

"Says you. I may have to marry a roguish duke or a snarky werewolf."

"Outside of the occasional shedding, Lars isn't that bad... And Lord James...he *grows* on you," Owen says, the word "grows" coming out more question than fact.

"Why do you think you have to marry one of them? I thought you said you just needed to pick one of them to send the others back," Hope muses.

Head raised, I meet her questioning gaze. "I wished for my happy ending. In my books, all my happy endings come with marriage, or at least a proposal. It stands to reason that if my happy ending is one of these three men, then it needs to be a complete one. Like in my books. It's all connected to my *stupid* heteronormative books. The penny. Them"—I point at Owen, who frowns. "If we can't resolve this, it may be the only way to get any of them back."

"You can't marry someone you don't love," Owen protests.

"It may be the only way to get you back to Selena. For you to have a chance to rewrite your own happy ending."

"But what about you?"

"I'll be okay." I sit up, smoothing my hands against my thighs, and meeting his worry-filled stare.

"You can't sacrifice your happiness for others," he murmurs.

"It's not a sacrifice when I'm responsible," I say, my throat working. "My happiness can't come at your expense."

"Georgia…" He sighs. "It doesn't need to be like this."

"Agreed." Hope squeezes his forearm. "Why don't we make marriage plan C. Let's not completely scratch the coin theory, but let's identify another solution for plan B. We can work both angles together. Georgia, did your research say anything else?"

Raking my teeth against my lower lip, I nod. "Do you know any witches?"

CHAPTER SIXTEEN

FRIENDS?

Turns out finding a witch isn't that difficult. With one quick Google search, Hope finds three witchcraft shops. Three clicks later, we set up an appointment to meet with a witchy consultant at Four Corners Spiritual Healing and Witchcraft Center.

Several online articles and a lively *Reddit* thread regarding wishes suggest an undoing spell. It's the magical equivalent of "backsies" for a wish granted or still in progress. Outside of playing light as a feather, stiff as a board as a teenager, I'm ill-qualified to attempt spell casting.

Unable to get an appointment until Sunday, I'll balance my efforts between locating the coin and my upcoming dates to figure out which of the two will be least impacted if they have to remain. Approaching SPN's front desk, my stomach twists with the hope that I'll not have to go on either date.

"Hey, Kerry." I smile, leaning on the front of the reception desk.

"Georgia." She peers up from her paperback.

The knot in my stomach spools tighter when I spy the green-eyed, bearded man on the cover of her copy of *The Duke's Darling*. This morning's interaction with James still grates. In mere minutes, he flipped from seductive to indignant to apologetic and then to something else entirely with his insinuation that I thought this was all a game. The entire exchange pulls me in different directions. Empathy for how this must all be for him. Annoyance with his persistence. Above all, I'm resolved to get him back where he belongs.

"I'm happy to see Lord James survives the duel, but did Lady Cecily really agree to marry the marquis?" She tosses her head back in a dramatic whine, her fat blonde curls bouncing. "God, if a man said the things he says to Lady Cecily, I'd swoon."

"You'd be surprised," I mutter, remembering that *very* man saying those words to me this morning.

Both he and Davis had used my own words on me in their seduction, with vastly different effects. With James, it churned revulsion in me, but with Davis, just a desire for his own words. Words he spoke freely and the truth of them were more enticing than anything in my books. Because they're from a man with *real* feelings for me.

Feelings I took advantage of. An acidic burn crawls up my throat, and I push it back down with the rest of my boondoggle of emotions. Guilt. Anger. Fear. All the perfect ingredients for the self-loathing stew blending inside me.

I smooth down my blazer, hoping the action soothes the torrent of emotions. "I was wondering if you could help me. You're in the know with just about everything here."

"That I am." She waggles her sculpted eyebrows. "Is this about the new speech therapist? I hear he's single and ready to mingle."

Laughing, I roll my eyes. "I'll let you do the mingling."

Kerry is as single as me, but gets less romantic intervention from fellow staff or Doc. It may be because she radiates "the mingle" vibe, where I give off sad, lonely romance author. Kerry revels in her singlehood. Maybe if I had a little more Kerry in me, I wouldn't have gotten myself into this situation.

"Do you know what happens to the coins in the fountain? I asked the head of maintenance, and they had no idea, but I know they are gone."

"Uh..." Crimson shades her complexion.

"You won't be in trouble. I just need to know what happens to them," I say, keeping my voice low and quiet.

Kerry shifts in her seat, her fingers curling tightly around the book. "I collect them early Sunday mornings."

"What do you do with them?"

She looks behind her and then whispers, "They're wishes, so I use them to help wishes come true. Each week, I collect the change, and then monthly, I add them to my own personal donation to the Make-A-Wish Foundation."

"You what?" My eyes widen.

Her mouth slides into a deep frown. "I didn't think it would be an issue since the coins were just there and nobody did anything with them. Doesn't it make more sense for the money to be doing good rather than just sitting there?"

I can't fault her logic. It is a waste to just leave the money where it does nothing for anyone. Even if those are someone's wishes, wouldn't whoever grants them want the money to be used for good? Unless it breaks some sort of wishing rule. *Note to self, ask my witchcraft consultant.* Though I'm sure Kerry's collection of the coins, even if for a good cause, breaks some SPN regulation.

"Nobody knows you're doing this?" I ask the question we both already know the answer to.

"I mentioned it to Velma three years ago, and she went on and on about paperwork and that it would need to align with our annual charitable gifts campaign or be approved by the board." Her fingers twitch while dog-earing and un-dog-earing a page in the book.

"It's okay, Kerry," I assure her, grabbing the book from her.

It's partly to help calm her and mostly to stop her from ruining the pages. I'm not anti-dog-earing one's pages, but a sour sensation burns my throat at it happening to one of my books. I may be annoyed with James, but I don't want his story's pages treated with a lack of care.

"Are you going to tell her? Am I in trouble?" She gnaws on her lip, her big brown eyes a little glossy.

The fear about Velma Hendersen, SPN's Director, is no joke. She's formidable. Even Doc sometimes avoids her. Despite her pixie-size and youth—she's only two years older than me—the 'rules first, questions later' head administrator is a little tough at times. In any rom-com, she's the villain ready to close the small-town bookshop and turn it into a high-end office supply store that outlaws rainbow-colored sticky note packets and gel pens.

"No. This stays between us. It's sweet what you're doing." I squeeze her hand, a small smile tugs at her lips.

It is sweet. Even if it means plan A—the long shot—is completely demolished. Unless…

"Kerry, have you donated the money you collected on Sunday already?"

She nods.

Demolished. I sigh. *Guess, it's witch or bust.*

Giftbag in hand, I stride down the long hospital corridor toward Doc's room, my kitten heels click against the vinyl floor. Tomorrow, Doc will transfer to SPN for a few days of inpatient rehab before he heads home to complete the remainder of his recovery via outpatient services. Even if I get to see him tomorrow after he's admitted, Estelle gave the all-clear for visitors, and I jumped at the chance.

Despite the updates from both Davis and Estelle, the prick of anxiety about Doc won't be subdued until I see him. Of course, no text came from Davis today about his grandfather. I wouldn't expect one, or any other future messages from Davis, after last night. Seeing Doc today may smooth down my guilt about his accident, but my actions over the last six days ensure an ample supply to go around.

"Hey." Smiling, I enter Doc's room.

Late afternoon sunshine streams in from the open blinds, bathing the room in a soft glow. In a not hospital-issued blue checkered robe, Doc sits bolstered up in the bed by several pillows, his face crinkled in annoyance.

"Peach!" His big smile smooths down his features. "Thank god, you're here. Estelle left on some terrible reality show, and I can't get this remote to work to turn it off."

Placing the gift bag on the bedside table, I grab the remote from him. I click the little *TV* button. "Should work now. It's a universal remote and somehow it was on satellite," I explain and hand him the remote.

"A decorated doctor for over forty years, and I'm nearly bested by a remote." Taking the controller, he almost scowls at it.

"Where's Estelle?"

"She's grabbing dinner for us."

"They don't feed you in this joint?" I tease

"Hospital food will kill you, and as I told her, I have no plans to meet my maker anytime soon." He chuckles.

"Not to mention, she'd kill you if you did." I wink.

"Yes, she would."

Laughter curls my lips. Just five days ago, Estelle made that same joke in this very hospital, while waiting for news about Doc. So much has happened between then and now that it almost seems a lifetime ago.

I take in the sparkle in his eyes and the upward curve of his mouth. The stiffness of his movement and small wince as he places the remote down on the bedside table is the only indication that he's not one hundred percent.

"Is that for me?" He points at the gift bag.

"It's just a little something to keep you busy until you come back to SPN."

"You mean as a volunteer and not a patient?" he teases, picking up the bag and pulling out the orange tissue paper.

"Yeah—" I swallow hard "—I am so sorry, Doc."

"Just as we thought..." he says, his face twinkling.

"Thought what?"

"That you'd be *Peach* about this." He motions at me. "We knew you'd blame yourself. It's why Estelle didn't clear you to visit for a few days in hopes your guilt would deplete just a bit. She mentioned that you stayed by her side the entire time I was in surgery, and how you apologized throughout. Your capacity for empathy makes you one of the best social workers I've ever worked with, and an even better writer, but it's also a curse."

"I'm sorry." I wince. "Sorry for saying sorry, I mean."

Shaking his head, he reaches over and squeezes my hand. "Take it from someone that's been in the caring profession for a long time, sometimes it's not ours to take on or fix."

"What does that mean?"

"Things happen. Accidents—" he waves at himself. "Illnesses. Breakups. Disappointed people. Life. We can't always control what happens, and we don't need to take responsibility for the things that we didn't actually do."

"We can still be sorry they happen."

"If *that* sorry serves you, rather than you serving it." His warm gaze meets mine.

Doc's words roam inside me, not quite nestling in and finding a place to call home. They're just there wandering around. Logically, I understand the gist of what he's saying.

One shouldn't take responsibility for other people's actions, but I don't see the correlation. Doc's injury was an accident. I know that, but it doesn't change my regret that it occurred.

"I sound like an inspirational poster." Laughing, he taps my hand. "Enough life philosophy, let's see what you brought me?" He pulls out a paperback from the gift bag. "*Dating Dr. Dill* by Nisha Sharma," he reads the title out loud.

"It's a modern retelling of Shakespeare's *The Taming of the Shrew*," I say, taking the chair by his bedside, hanging my purse on its arm.

"Is it steamy?" He waggles his eyebrows.

"Just a bit." With a cheeky expression, I squeeze together my index finger and thumb.

"Guess Estelle and I can't do this one for our weekly dramatic readings."

"Perhaps just a buddy read for you two." I laugh. "There are two other books in the series that I've already ordered from Heartbound Book Shop. They'll be delivered on Monday. They should keep you busy while recovering."

He sits the book on the bedside table. "I'd rather use my downtime to read *your* next book."

"Ah..." I tap my foot against the chair leg.

"Still blocked?"

"How?" I gesture at him.

"Each time I ask you about it, you get all dodgy like you owe me money. Once you committed to the idea for your first book, it only took you four months before you had the initial draft complete. The same for the other two. It's been at least six months since you started this book. With the others, you brainstormed and discussed ideas. You were almost like a kid the night before Christmas, all full of anticipation about your story."

I slump into the chair's cushioned back. "I don't think I'm that kid anymore."

My passion for storytelling is braided into my DNA.

Whether I'm reading or writing them, stories offer comfort. Each celiac flare up. My parents' turbulent marriage and, later, divorce. Will and Lena. Through every big and little heartbreak, my stories were there.

"They're not talking to me." I blink back the sting of looming tears.

It's silly to cry over this, but pain radiates in my chest with the idea that I'll have no more stories to tell. It almost hollows me out, leaving nothing behind but me.

"Are they not speaking, or are you just not listening?" Thoughtfulness shimmers in his gaze. "Anytime you have a story idea, you start with how it turns out. It's hard to start a story at the end and even harder to write it, if that ending isn't the right one."

Blinking, I think of Owen's critique of *Twice Baked Love*. It's his and Selena's story, and even he believes the ending may be the wrong one.

"If we only have a single notion of how things are supposed to turn out, we'll never hear the rest of the story. We're too focused on trying to force things to fit that ending, and when they don't, we toss them."

"But if you know how it should be, why wouldn't you work to make that happen?"

"Does the end serve the story, or does the story serve the ending?" His mouth quirks. "Peach, you're one of my favorite writers, but you get so bogged down by making things turn out the way you picture that you aren't open to anything else."

The comfort I find in my stories is the endings. That no matter what happens, everything turns out as it should. *Well, as I believe it should.* That singular focus on not just the ending, but that things would end how I want them has steadied me in choppy waters, but it's also kept me from seeing the here and now.

Both my brothers' voices echo inside me. Jackson's warnings about Will that I ignored, and Rem's concerns about my inability to commit after a single date. So many of those dates were terrible, but some of them weren't… *Until I found a reason for them to be.*

"And not just in my books." I dash away the few tears that escape.

It's strange how my little security blanket now seems to smother, rather than snuggle around me. The stories may not be talking to me, but the fixation on happy endings guides me like a wayward compass. I have no idea how things will turn out. My book boyfriends. My writing. Davis. All were impacted by my fixation.

"I hate to see you cry, but sometimes we need to just let it out." Doc holds up the tissue box from the bedside table.

I take a few and dab at my eyes. "I'm supposed to be here comforting you. You're the one busted up and in the hospital." I wipe away my remaining tears and toss the tissue in the waste basket near the bed.

He *tsks*. "I broke my hip, but my noggin is still at one hundred percent."

"And so is your heart." I lean over and take his hand.

"Not to mention this helps me as much as you, especially after the last few days of everyone fussing over me. This reminds me that I still got it. That no matter what, I have ways to do the things that give me passion—like encouraging my favorite author to write a swoony medical romance inspired by Estelle and me." He winks, causing me to laugh.

"Ha!" A laugh barks out of me. "Thank you for believing in me even when I don't always believe in myself."

"Always." He squeezes my hand, his palm's warmth surges through me, unwinding my tension. "Now, don't forget about my good heart when I grill you about my grandson." His mouth twitches into a smirk.

"Excuse me?"

"Estelle said that there were so many sparks between you two on Sunday that she thought you'd set off the fire alarm."

"You're ridiculous." Despite my dismissive laugh, the heat that crawls up my neck and claims my cheeks betrays my attempt to appear unaffected by the mention of Davis.

In no world do I want to talk to Doc about his grandson. Even if I hadn't dry humped Davis like a horny teenager and then told him I couldn't be with him, all in the course of five minutes, talking to *his* grandfather about a possible romantic entanglement is too mortifying.

"He often is ridiculous." A deep voice steals into the room.

That now-familiar rich timbre causes me to twist in the chair to the open door. Davis stands there, a large to-go bag in his arms, and the ghost of a smile lifts at the corners of his mouth.

"Davis," I breathe, ignoring the hope that swoops in my stomach that his almost smile is due to seeing me and not just about his grandfather.

"Georgia," he says.

Georgia? My stomach drops, the sensation akin to falling to the ground.

Those two syllables reiterate who I am to him now. I'm Georgia, not Peach. It's self-indulgent to mourn the loss of a relationship that was barely anything, especially one lost before it started because of me.

"Are you just going to stand there gawking? I'm starving." Estelle tuts, pushing into the room. "Hey, Peach. I'm so glad you're still here. We have plenty, if you want to join."

I stand up. "Thank you, but I should go. Let you all have family time."

"Pish-posh." She flicks her wrist. "How else are we going to meddle with you two if you dash away?"

"Nan," Davis groans.

I offer a small smile. "I really do need to head out. Thank you, though."

With a quick head nod to Estelle and Doc, I turn and head toward the door. Davis remains like a watchdog beside the entryway, the bag of food in his hands, his stare jumping from me to the window. Whether he can't or won't hold my gaze doesn't matter. It's clear that I hurt him, and he wants nothing to do with me.

That truth reverberates with each click of my heels down the hall. The further away I get, the more realization unfurls inside me that I will never be anything but Georgia to Davis. It's not that I'm someone other than who I am with Davis, but in his presence, there was a freedom to just be with someone without fixating on how things would turn out. The ember of hope flickered awake within me at the idea of a possible future with him, but not a story already written.

Reaching the elevator lobby, I press the button. My reflection stares back at me in the shiny metal doors. My eyes, devoid of any sparkle, are puffy. A frown anchors my face, my complexion pale from a night of little sleep. My hair unwashed and swept into a messy bun. The glossy pink lipstick and brightly colored clothes are a flimsy mask.

"Georgia, wait."

I spin to find Davis jogging down the quiet corridor toward the small bank of elevators. With each step closer, my pulse ticks up.

"You left your purse." He holds up my bag.

The roar of my pulse quiets with the realization that he's not here for *me*. No sweeping romantic gesture. No declaration that, despite everything I've done, he still likes me. *Seriously, no more romance novels. Only nonfiction from here on out.*

"Thank you." Nodding, I take it. "Sorry I left it."

He shrugs. "It's alright."

"Is it?" I say, guilt thick in my throat.

His forehead creases.

"I led you on. I hurt you." I gesture between us. "Here you are, all sweet and thoughtful, and I'm all 'Let me stick my tongue down your throat and use you as a human scratching post with no forethought about how it may impact you.' I'm the literal worst. All I was thinking is how much I like you and how adorable you are—"

"You think I'm adorable?"

"Have *you* seen you? Those muscles. That bedhead hair, which I know from last night, is all thick and silky. God, those glasses. You're like the epitome of hot nerd." I swing my purse, sputtering wildly. "Even when you annoyed me on our first date, I was still attracted to you… But then you turn out to be, well, *you*."

His face pinches. "Me?"

"Yes. You!" I toss both my hands up, the purse smacking against the side of my face, but I go on, "You're not who I thought, and I'm so happy to have been wrong. Funny. Sweet. Considerate. Dorky in a sexy way. A little unsure and totally confident about it, which doesn't make sense, but it makes sense to me. But my life is messy and—"

My mini-rant is silenced by Davis's lips pressing against mine. His strong arms band around me, pulling me close. The way I melt into him is akin to ice cream left in the hot sun, and he licks up every last drop of my kisses.

"Did you mean to kiss me?" I pull back, a little breathless.

"Yeah… I hope that's okay. I should have asked, first," he murmurs as his palms rub slow, soothing circles down my spine.

"No… I liked it." I smile. "But why did you kiss me?"

"You think I'm adorable." Playfulness sparks in his ashen eyes. "And as adorable as I think you are, especially when you sputter like that, I thought kissing you would get you to stop spiraling."

"Makes sense." I lick my lips. "I may require more intervention, because I'm about to spiral again."

"Gladly." With an almost wicked grin, he takes my mouth.

Dropping the purse to the floor, my arms encircle his neck.

Pleasure zings along my spine with the press of his body against me. Somehow, he's both the coziest place to land and the sturdiest support all in one.

His kisses make me a little drunk. There's no thought about anything but this moment. No worry about my unfinished book, the wedding, or the three fictional men whose futures are wrapped up in mine. In this moment, I submerge myself into the idea of just being with this very real man with no script of anything beyond right now.

"Yes," I whimper as his hands slide down and curl around my backside.

"God, this ass. It's featured heavily in my daydreams since Friday." He squeezes, eliciting a little giggle from me. "Did you just giggle?"

"Maybe."

He kisses below the shell of my ear. "I like that sound. I want to hear it again," he murmurs, squeezing my backside again.

"Davis." I bury my face against his chest to cover my giggles.

Blinking away the giddiness of this moment, I tip my head up. Our gazes meet in quiet debate. It would be so easy to just remain in his arms, letting go of all the responsibilities I have to my book boyfriends. To only think of my wants and needs with no concern for theirs.

"I am the worst." I close my eyes and slosh a hard breath. "I just did it again."

"In fairness, I think we both did it."

Eyes now open, I straighten and lower my arms. He releases me and steps back.

A shiver jolts through me with the loss of my cozy spot in his arms. It's cold in the shadow of what just happened. True to the queen of bad ideas crown I wear, there's no regret about my impromptu public display of affection with Davis. The only regret I feel is that it can't happen again.

"This isn't fair to you. I shouldn't have kissed you," I say, wringing my hands.

His mouth quirks. "I kissed you first."

"But I shouldn't have kissed back."

"Did you not like the kiss?"

"Quite the opposite."

"And you said you like me. That I'm adorable," he says, his kiss-swollen lips tick up into the boyish grin that makes my heart flutter.

"True." I bite back the smile that wants to creep across my face.

"But you can't be with anyone right now." He sighs.

"I'm so sorry… God, I wish…" I clamp my mouth shut.

Wishing is what got me into this mess. If only I hadn't made that wish, none of this would have happened. Davis just would have been another bad date, and I'd still just be "Georgia" to him. Only *that* Georgia wouldn't have played with his emotions. She also wouldn't know the loveliness of being in his arms or the harmony of his laughter.

But this Georgia has responsibilities. Until those are met, I can't give in to this. I can't steal my book boyfriends' happiness to secure my own.

"I don't want to make you promises that I may not be able to keep," I murmur.

It wouldn't be fair to fall into something with Davis without any guarantee of a future. To do what his dad did to him, or Will did to me, make promises that aren't kept.

"Friends?"

"What?" I arch one brow.

"Just because we can't be together, doesn't mean we can't be friends?" A hopeful expression lights his face.

"I don't know if that's a good idea…" I bite my lower lip.

"Why not? I like you, and you like me. That's pretty evident, but if it's not the right time for more than friends, it's not the right time. And it may never be, but it doesn't mean we have to say goodbye to each other. We could be friends."

"Friends…" I say the word slowly, as if putting on a pair of new shoes. They're not the right fit, but I still want to wear them because a piece of Davis is better than none at all. "Friends, but of the non-kissing kind."

"Good idea." Smirking, he puts out his hand. "Friends."

I take it. "Friends."

"Why don't you stay. Have dinner with us." A coaxing expression fills his features. "We grabbed food from Café Amore. We got the mushroom risotto."

"From their GF menu?" My gaze flicks to where my hand remains enfolded in his long fingers.

"*Yeah*. Nan mentioned you'd be visiting, so I thought… Just in case you wanted to stay, you should have options."

Oh god, trying to just be friends with this man may be the hardest thing I ever do. But picking up my purse, saying goodbye, and getting on this elevator holds no allure for me. Right now, I want to climb into his arms and forget all my promises to everyone, even the one to him that we could just be friends.

He lets go of my hand and bends to pick up my discarded purse. "Unless you need to get home to Wentworth." He smiles, his voice a little quiet.

"Jackson is taking him to the park, so he's good." I take my purse. "I could stay for a little bit. They do have the best risotto," I add, as if Café Amore's food is the only reason I'm staying. Clearly, I've learned nothing and am still choosing to sit next to the flames. My only hope is that I'm the only one who gets burned.

CHAPTER SEVENTEEN

SHIFTED HEART

Jeans. Sneakers. Be ready at seven. These are the only instructions Lars gives for tonight's date, causing me to imagine we're doing something woodsy. I *just* had to write a book about a lumberjack werewolf from the Pacific Northwest. Why hadn't I written a sexy tech genius turned entrepreneur do-gooder who enjoyed sharing mushroom risotto and playing Uno at his grandfather's hospital bedside on a Thursday night?

That's who elicits the flip in my stomach as I stand in front of the mirror and brush my dark tresses up into a high ponytail. *Because that's what you do with your friends.* You toss and turn all night, your skin still on fire, imagining what it would be like to snuggle close to your friend. Those thoughts do no good for anyone. Friendship is all that can happen with Davis. Even if my witchcraft consultant undoes this mess I've created, there's no guarantee that Davis will still want me. Like he said, it may never be the right time.

I'm not foolish enough to think he'll just wait around for me. Between now and when I fix this, a million things could happen. He may realize that I'm too much for him. He may meet someone else.

"Hey," I say as I open the front door.

"Rabbit." Lars leans his massive frame against the door jam, his gruff timbre low and violet eyes seductive.

At least that's what I think he's going for. It comes off more playacting than panty-dropping, causing me to snort.

"That's not the normal reaction I get," he mutters, his face twisted into a pout.

"Sorry." I clear my throat and meet his half-perplexed, half-annoyed gaze with batted eyelashes. "I mean, *hello Larsy.*"

Groaning, he straightens. "God, you never reminded me more of Jackson as you do right now. You're both smartasses."

"We are siblings, after all," I sass, slipping my cell phone into my back pocket and grabbing my keys.

"Don't remind me."

"Why so grumpy, Larsy-poo? Did Jackson give you the whole *hurt her and I'll kill you talk* before you headed this way?" I tease, shutting the door behind us and locking it.

During my date with Owen, he shared that Jackson gave him quite the talk. My younger brother may be playful, but he's just as protective as Rem.

"No." Lars's mouth flattens into a firm line. "He just grumbled for me to have fun before he left for work this morning."

Strange. My head tilts, remembering that the only text exchange with Jackson today was to provide instructions for the date. The day of my date with Owen, Jackson had sent several cheeky messages about sexy cinnamon rolls.

"I see you got my message about appropriate attire for tonight." He gestures at me.

If I'm going to do something woodsy, I'm going to look cute doing it. I've paired hip-hugging, dark wash jeans with white Skechers. My swept-up hair allows me to show off the silver teapot stud earrings that Hope got me last Christmas. A flannel, in shades of purple in a plaid design, is tied at my waist over a pink tank top that both accentuates my shapely figure and covers my snack pouch. One can love their body as it is, but still want to cover their jiggly bits.

"Just tell me we're not killing anything. Blood stains are a pain to get out," I say, taking the stairs.

"I don't intend for us to kill anything, but I make no promises about blood." His low chuckle teases.

The waivers we sign at Andersen's, a local pub that specializes in axe throwing, make no promises about blood. In fact, they aren't liable for any injury. After a quick tutorial from the bar's axe consultant, we square off in front of the targets. The bar has a one drink maximum for any axe throwers, so we opt to take our turn and then imbibe after.

It's more fun than I expected. The bar has customers compete against each other, and then puts the scores on their leader board. At the end of the night, the top scorer wins a *Kiss My Big Axe* T-shirt and a free beer.

"This isn't what I expected, but it tracks with something you'd do for a date night." I laugh, tossing my axe, which smacks into the board just on the edge of the target.

"What did you expect?" He aims his axe, releases, and we watch it sail right to the bullseye.

"I thought you'd chase me through the woods or something."

He leans close, his grin inches from mine. "The night's still young, rabbit."

With a laugh, I tut, "Back in your designated box or I'll tell our axe consultant you're breaking the rules."

Lars's flirtation is harmless. It's more the playful banter between friends than anything akin to romance. We have zero sexual tension, like what I have with Davis. Also, Lars doesn't exhibit any *intentions* like James. I'm not sure what James's intentions are. His swift mood swings back and forth yesterday morning gave me pause.

"Nice job, rabbit." Lars lets out a loud whistle after my axe makes contact with the target instead of the plywood surrounding it.

"Thanks." I high-five him and step back to snap a quick photo of my target, so I can show Hope later.

It's not surprising Lars is destroying me, but I'm pleased with my performance. Pride surges in my chest at how well I'm doing. It's only my third toss, and I've already hit the target. *Maybe I am an athletic girl, after all.*

That thought causes my mouth to curl up at the memory of my not-so-cute first date with Davis. What I perceived as a snide dig about my weight is just his matter-of-fact way of speaking. He says what he thinks. There's no underhandedness or hidden meaning to suss out.

"Pumpkin cider," Lars says, placing my pint in front of me. "I'll never understand the Lanes' obsession with pumpkin. Jackson has three different types of pumpkin ale in his fridge."

He takes the chair across from me at the two-person hightop we've claimed. The table offers a perfect view of the designated axe throwing zones on the other side of the bar.

A smirk slants my mouth. It's the fifth time Lars has brought up Jackson. The different running trails they hit each morning before Jackson has to get ready for work. Their game of fetch with Wentworth last night at the park which turned more into them playing catch while my dog slept under a tree. How Jackson puts ketchup on his eggs, which Lars insists is an abomination. "And they say werewolves are monsters," he'd grumbled as we walked from my place to Andersen's. Throughout our date, he's woven my brother into the fabric of our conversation.

"I hope living with Jackson hasn't been too tough." I sip my drink.

"Not at all. I enjoy being with Jackson—" face scrunched, he shifts in his seat "—I mean, he's fine. It's fine."

Interesting. I arch one brow. "Do you miss home?"

I know Owen and James do. Both have admitted it in their own ways. Owen misses Selena but accepts that he may not get back to her. James mourns being part of a world he understands. At least, that's what he shared yesterday morning. I may think this is hardest on him, because the world he inhabits is so different than this one, but all three are far away from everyone they know and love.

For a woman who's never lived away from her childhood home, outside of college dorms, I can't imagine what this might be like for them. *Oh god, I'm thirty-two and still technically live at home.* Rem is right, I may need to move. *One life crisis at a time, Georgia.*

"At times," he admits quietly.

My head tilts. "At times?"

He scrubs his hands down his face. "At home, I'm alpha. I'm responsible for my entire pack. Their safety. Their needs. Everything. Here, I just get to think about myself. What I want. What I need. Not what I'm supposed to do."

It's how I wrote Lars. He has such big, broad shoulders because he carries the weight of everything on them. My werewolf may be snarky and flirtatious, but he's also deeply grounded in caring for others. Until now, I had no idea the toll that burden has on him.

"I never thought of how hard all that responsibility would be on you." My apologetic gaze meets his.

Lars's story arc is about letting go of that responsibility. The push and pull between Ivy and him is about his reluctance to step away out of fear of what would happen to his pack. The idea of that responsibility's pressure on him never bled into my narrative, nor is it in my character study for him.

"I'd imagine you can relate to the pressure." He juts his chin toward me.

"Hardly, I'm not the alpha. I'm just me."

He huffs a dismissive laugh. "Just a woman who takes responsibility for ensuring everyone is happy but herself."

"Excuse me?" I scoff.

"I know you plan to pick whichever one of us you think would be least impacted, so the others can hopefully get back." He picks up his bottle of beer and takes a long pull.

"How?" Eyes narrowed, I point at him. "Owen."

"The baker can't keep a secret to save his life."

"Does James know?"

"Just me." He places his hand on his chest. "And as honest as I am, I can keep secrets. I assume you don't want your brother to know that you're willing to sacrifice your happiness for us. To let him believe this little charade that one of us is meant for you."

"He worries enough."

"I know." His mouth curves down. "You both have such big hearts. It's why he's so invested in you finding someone. Not just for the wedding, but for the long haul. He's hopeful that if you're always going to focus on everyone else's happiness, there will be one person that focuses on *yours*."

"Ugh," I groan, tossing my head back. "To take care of me? How did my feminist mother raise two sexist men?"

"Jackson isn't sexist. He's just a little protective of you, but not for the reason you think." His fingers balance the beer bottle, rolling it against the table's surface. "It's more about protecting that big heart of yours, rabbit. He worries that you give so much to others, that you don't leave enough for yourself. That, with the right person, they'd help you with either holding onto some of that or give you some of theirs to replenish you."

Tapping my fingers against the table's surface in rhythm with the slam of axes, I mentally flip through my life's big and little decisions. My plan to attend Lena and Will's wedding. My decision not to study English. One may argue—at least I know Jackson would—most of my relationship with Will found me sacrificing my wants and needs for his.

"A friend of mine recently said I'm a little too fixated on endings," I say.

"Of course you are. Call it people pleasing or an overwhelming sense of duty, we're both obsessed with how things turn out. We do what's needed to ensure everyone else's happiness, and the best way to keep them that way is to know it's their happy ending. It's not right or wrong, it's just who we are."

"And which one am I? People pleaser or just uber-responsible?"

He studies me. "Based on what Jackson has shared, and my own observation, you're a little of column A and B."

I open my mouth to protest, but close it without speaking. He's not wrong, but he's not entirely right.

"Which are you?" I ask.

"Definitely column B." Chuckling, he curls his fingers around the bottle, lifts it to his mouth, but stops. "Though, it doesn't matter because whatever the reason, it costs us the things we truly want, because we're so focused on everyone else."

"And what about you?"

For the first time, Lars can focus on what he wants rather than what's best for his pack. Jackson may want me to find someone who replenishes me, but what if I'm meant to be that for Lars? Not in a romantic way, but as a friend.

"You already wrote my happy ending." He leans back, taking another swig.

"But if you could rewrite it, what would you want? Not what you think is best for the pack or anyone else. What do *you* want?"

"I could ask you the same thing." He places his beer down, his violet eyes studying me.

So many wants tangle inside me, each fighting for dominance. Like a greedy child in a candy store, I want it all. My book boyfriends' happiness. Break my writer's block. Davis.

They may not be mutually exclusive, my lady. James's statement about our individual happy endings echoes inside me. In this, he's right. Without their happiness, I cannot secure my own. No matter how I slice it, I could never be happy if those I'm responsible for aren't. It's just not how I'm programmed.

"It's hard, isn't it?" A laugh rumbles in his chest.

"So hard!" I whine, lowering my forehead to the table.

"For the record, I don't think you should choose any of us to marry. But, if you're going to be all self-sacrificing about this, you should pick… *Jackson*?"

"Jackson?" Nose wrinkled, I jolt up. "I'm not marrying my brother. Eww! What kind of werewolf did I write?"

"No." He pulls a sour face and then motions toward the entrance.

Spinning in my seat, I shake my head. Jackson and two other random men stroll through the front door. His attention fixed on the phone in his hand, Davis walks in behind them. A statuesque woman with chestnut curls is beside him. They don't seem to notice us as they claim a large table near the axe ring.

"That sneaky bastard is totally checking in on us." I roll my eyes.

It's the classic "I'm not paying attention, but I'm totally paying attention" stance. Jackson's focus appears to be on the axe consultant going over the waivers, but the quick flick of his eyes toward our table betrays him. Davis, on the other hand, is enthralled with something on his phone. Each time the attractive woman beside him speaks, he nods and mumbles something I can't quite make out.

To others, it may appear that he's not paying attention to

her, but I know otherwise. He's likely stimming. He may even be looking up something she's asked about. She may have his complete attention, even if it doesn't appear so. *Or, he could be ignoring her.* Which I am hoping for.

She places her hand on his bicep, drawing his focus to her. Her red-painted lips lift in a large grin as he looks up.

We're just friends. He can do whatever he wants. I grip the table's edge,

Loud snapping fingers cause me to twist back in my seat to face Lars. "Oh, rabbit," he sniffs the air, accusation lighting his features.

I glower. "You're not supposed to smell me, remember."

"I'm not smelling you." He tips his head toward where Davis sits, his back to us. "You're all over him." He inhales deeply. "Mates."

"I… We're…. *not* mated." I gesture wildly.

He leans forward, resting his elbows on the table, a lopsided grin flexing. "Maybe, *but* there's been some mating-like activities between you two."

"Just kissing. We kissed once…well twice—" my face twists "—well, technically it was more than twice, but it was only two instances of very short make-out sessions. But that's it. We're *just* friends."

"*Uh-huh*… Because friends look at each other like that." Eyebrows raised, he makes a "turn around" motion with his index finger.

Spinning in my seat, my gaze slams into Davis's. He's twisted and now sits facing our table. Those beautiful eyes are locked on me, and the questions 'what are you doing here?' and 'who is he?' are almost audible in the wrinkles on his forehead. Though I'm sure the jump of my gaze between Davis and the leggy brunette making bedroom eyes at him telegraphs the same exact questions.

Jealousy is absurd in this situation, and so is this awkward charge between us. Davis and I are friends. Lars and I are friends. Everybody is friends here.

Releasing a long breath, I offer a smile and wave at Davis. With a nod, he waves back.

Twisting, I face Lars. "You said you miss home at times. What do you miss?"

"So, we're just going to ignore Glasses over there pining from across the room?"

"His name is Davis, not Glasses."

"The guy from your date with Owen?"

"He really doesn't keep anything to himself," I grumble, leaning my arms on the table and rubbing at my temples.

"Yeah, but he bakes." He huffs a laugh. "Well, as I said before, I don't think you should pick any of us, especially when there is someone who looks at you like that."

"Like how?" I keep my eyes on his, fighting the urge to turn around and see the *like that* look he alludes to shining back at me in Davis's gaze. Even without turning around, the heat of his stare burns into me. I know he's looking.

"Like a man in pain because he sees what he wants, but he can't have it."

"It's not the right time for us," I say, an ache quiets my voice.

"From what Jackson says, it hasn't been the *right* time for a while."

"Sounds like Jackson is as chatty as Owen," I mutter, taking a gulp of my cider.

"It comes from a good place." He leans back. "He worries that your dickhead ex and cousin hurt you so badly that you find any reason to hide from any chance you'd be hurt again."

"I date." I lean forward, my tone indignant, "I made out with and dry humped Davis."

"I knew it was more than kissing." He quirks one eyebrow. "But you're still finding every excuse to not go for Davis."

"I have you three to worry about."

"Excuses." Challenge glints in his eyes.

"I won't take your happy endings away. I know what that's like, and I won't do it," I say, a gentle tremor chokes me.

"That may be true, but I also think you're more terrified to risk your heart again."

"You've known me for barely a week," I hiss.

He juts his chin toward me. "True, but I'm a hunter. I know when animals are scared and hurt. I know the ways they burrow into the ground or skitter through the forest to protect themselves."

My silence and his words hang between us. *They're not all Will. You'll find any excuse.* Pilar, my brothers, and even, at times, Hope's cautions over the last few years echo inside me.

"I don't want to be a cliché." My admission is quiet.

He reaches over, resting his large palm on my forearm. "You're not. You're just someone who got hurt."

"I don't recall writing a psychoanalyzing werewolf." My snarky comment is half-hearted.

Just like Owen, my werewolf isn't what I thought. Beneath the protective snark is an unexpected perceptiveness. Maybe it's part of his wolfy traits that I didn't realize I'd embedded into his character, or maybe he's more than the words on the page.

"Sorry to disappoint." He picks up his beer.

"You don't." I smile. "I like that even though I technically wrote you all, there are still things I don't know."

"Like your question from earlier about what I miss about home?" His wry expression seems to offer mercy, moving us away from unwrapping my issues. "Running in the woods. But Jackson has taken me on a few trails. They aren't quite like Silver Falls but still allow the wolf in me to run free."

The wolves in *Shifted Heart* change at will. The moon heightens their wolfy tendencies, but they control the shift.

Still, that wolf sometimes needs to be exercised a bit. Hence, the frequent competition. It's probably good Jackson has custody of my book boyfriends, because Lars isn't the nap around the house all day kind of wolf.

"How about friends? Ivy? Victor?" I sip my cider.

"If this is to deduce if I'm as mopey as Owen about Selena, sorry to disappoint. Ivy is like no woman I've met"—his mouth quirks—"though, she's a vampire, so I guess that tracks. She's gorgeous, fierce, and has this dry wit... but I don't think I really love her. Not in the way you're supposed to love someone."

"How's that?"

"Like they haunt you in a good way. No matter where you are, they're with you. Your heart isn't just consumed by, but beats for them. Outside of when you've mentioned her, or Owen asks me about something in my book, she's not here." He places his hand on his heart.

A dull ache pricks in my throat at the idea of a romance I wrote where the two people aren't in love. It's almost too much to know that two of my books didn't actually have happy endings. At least, not the endings their main male characters want. Owen thought the ending was wrong, and Lars isn't in love with his leading lady.

"Did you ever love her?" I croak.

He reaches over and squeezes my forearm. "I did. I do, in my own way. It's not the HEA that's promised on the front of your books. And at least I know that at the point I left the story, Ivy was doing what she truly loves."

With each man snatched away from their story right after the third act breakup, the ladies are living out that portion of the story. At least, that's what I believe. Selena is back in the big city at her corporate job. Lady Cecily prepares to marry the marquis, who is a kind—if not a little boring—man. Ivy is working with the human/supernatural alliance.

"What is he doing?" Lars mutters, his stare focused across the room.

I follow his gaze. A laughing Jackson wiggles his hips and does jazz fingers with one hand while holding up the axe for a video one of the men in their group is taking.

"He needs to be careful, or he could hurt himself," he almost growls.

My right eyebrow ticks up. "What about Victor?" I ask, thinking of Kerry's belief about the sexual undercurrent between Lars and Victor as they wrestled in the pond.

"What about Victor?" he asks, but doesn't look away from my brother.

"Did you look at him with pining intentions?"

"No," he says quickly. "But I did look at him."

"How did you look at him?"

"If you're asking if I looked at him the same way I looked at Ivy, the answer is yes. I like both."

"But you didn't *pine* for either?"

"No." His mouth pursed, he motions frantically toward Jackson. "He is going to hurt himself if he tosses like that. Not to mention he'll completely miss."

"So, you didn't look at them like you look at Jackson."

"Yes... Wait. What?" Wide-eyed and jaw slack, his focus snaps back to me.

I smile. "You like Jackson."

"I do not. He's a pain in the ass."

"I can smell it on you." With a cheeky expression, I sniff the air.

"You really are his sister," he grumbles.

"If it makes you feel better, I think he's *totally* into you, too."

Scoffing, he waves his hands in the air as if this is the silliest thing in the world. Even if Lars isn't owning up to it, it's clear they both like each other. Hell, the sparks kindled awake at their first meeting, and those embers have strengthened over the last few days.

A furrow forms at the center of his forehead. "Not that you're right, but I'll indulge you. What makes you say that he's into me?"

I lean on the table and meet his skeptical gaze. "He didn't lecture you before our date. He's also been radio-silent most of the day, which is classic sulking younger brother behavior. He just *happens* to show up at the same place where we're having our date. Plus, no matter how he may be pretending, his gaze drifts over here every few minutes, and he isn't looking at me, wolfy."

Lars turns his head. Jackson faces us, an axe in one hand, a big smile on his face as someone takes a picture with their phone. As if on cue, his vision moves to Lars. In that moment, it's like everything dissolves. The loud voices, the slam of axes, and the hard rock music that booms throughout the bar all quiet as Lars and my brother's gazes link. Each man's face is a little serene, a little scared, and a lot pining.

"You should go over there." I nudge his knee with mine. "Show him the correct stance. You know… so he doesn't hurt himself."

"I should?" His tone is unsure.

I don't know if Lars and Jackson are each other's happy endings. What I do know is the way they look at each other deserves a chance to see what may happen.

"Yeah. You should."

CHAPTER EIGHTEEN

HOSPITAL

"Okay," Lars says, nodding but not making a move. His violet eyes are fixed on my brother, but his massive frame remains glued to the chair.

From across the bar, Jackson stands motionless, his brow wrinkled, and his mouth stretched into a confused smile. No doubt, he's perplexed by his sister and her date sitting across the bar, staring at him.

"Move it, wolfy"—I kick his shin—"or that guy in the corner checking Jackson out will make his move."

Eyes narrowed, his head snaps to a tall, ginger-haired man smiling Jackson's way. There's little concern that my brother will reciprocate the redhead's attention with how his focus is locked on *his* werewolf, but I'll use it as motivation, nonetheless.

"The hell he will," he grits. Attention zeroed in on Jackson, Lars prowls toward the axe ring.

My smile falters with Jackson's at first shocked, and then annoyed expression. The two of them go back and forth about something; Lars scrubbing his palm down his face and Jackson wagging a finger at him. Features pinched, Jackson aims his free hand from across the room toward me. It's clear their argument isn't about Jackson's axe-throwing position. It's about me.

Jackson may like Lars, but he'll never go for it. As brash as my brother is, his moral compass is due north. In no world would he go for anyone that he thought I was interested in. Even if he and Hope hadn't sat beside me soothing away my tears after the truth about Lena and Will came out, my brother isn't built to not think of others. He's a protector.

"Jackson!" Arms flailing in the air, I scream over the crowd.

Several people turn to stare at me, including my brother. Confusion twists his features.

"Let Lars show you!" I cup my hands around my mouth to boost my shout.

A silent conversation plays between our expressions. His is confused. Mine is coaxing.

He likes you. Go for it, I mouth.

He just gapes until I give him a thumbs up.

Still a little unsure, he peers between Lars and me and then nods. A tentative smile blooming, he then utters something to Lars. With a hesitant, but hopeful expression covering his face, Lars places his big hands on Jackson's waist. Aiming him toward the target, he towers over my brother. His careful movement paints the picture of what's happening. Lars's mouth is inches from Jackson's ear, his gruff voice instructing him. His strong hands coasting from Jackson's hips to his arm, guiding him in the proper axe-throwing technique.

"Someone's getting laid tonight," I laughingly mutter to myself before twisting back in my seat.

As happy as I am for my brother and Lars, this does complicate things. Something I hadn't thought of until just now. What if this isn't just a little flirtation but something real between them? If I undo the wish, what happens to Lars? To my brother? And if I'm unable to undo it, do I pick

Lars? Will I have to marry him? How will my brother feel about that?

Stop spiraling! With a long breath, I pick up my cider. Things are already a mess, and I just keep making them messier. At least this will offer a little happiness to both Lars and Jackson, even if it may only be temporary.

"Did your date just leave you for your brother?"

Looking up, I find Davis, a furrow notching his brow, peering between me and my brother. Lars stands a few feet off to the side, his complete focus on Jackson as he throws his axe.

"Yeah." I take a long pull of my drink. "But Lars is just a friend. One who's clearly into my brother," I chuckle, watching Lars lift Jackson into a swinging hug after he hits the bullseye.

"Clearly." Laughter vibrates in Davis's chest. "May I?" He taps the top of the chair Lars had vacated.

"Of course."

He takes the seat. "So, Lars? Like in your book?"

"Yeah." I take another quick pull from my drink.

Davis's dedication to his romance education means he's making his way through my books. Last night, while Estelle kicked our asses at Uno, he'd shared that he was almost done with *The Duke's Darling*. Which means he may have started reading Lars's book and may be able to clock the similarities between the books and the two men he's met.

I don't want to lie to him, but how does one explain that they made a wish with a lucky penny that accidentally brought three fictional men to life? Even I have trouble at times believing this, and I'm living it.

"You really do cannibalize your life for your books." His chuckle is warm.

"You have no idea." I huff a laugh.

"Was Lord James based on anyone?"

"He wasn't, but now I'm not so sure." Waving my right

hand in the air, I blow out a breath that sounds like helicopter blades whooshing through the air. "Recently, I've discovered that I've pulled from people in my life without knowing."

"Here's hoping he was just a figment of your imagination because I'm not sure I'd care for him in real life."

One eyebrow raised, my head tilts. "He didn't grow on you after all?"

"No." He crinkles his nose.

Somehow, even his look of distaste is adorable, eliciting a flutter in my chest. It may be the effect of that boyish grin. Davis has this mix of sweet nerdiness and virile manliness. Like someone who can do your taxes, change your tire, and press you up against a back gate, his masculinity rubbing against you until you see stars.

"So, you didn't like the book?" I ask, slamming the rest of my drink, the liquid cooling my heated bloodstream from my *more than-friendly* thoughts about Davis.

"I didn't say that." His face scrunches. "The book was great. Your prose is vivid. It transports you into the story and keeps you turning the page. The characters are layered and rich. I just didn't like Lord James. His sole focus is on destroying Lady Cecily's father, and he doesn't hesitate to manipulate her... to play with her heart to get what he wants."

"Huh... Most readers find him dashing. They loved seeing his arc of letting go of his thirst for vengeance to be with Lady Cecily."

"I want to believe that, but even in his pseudo-redemption arc, he still gets what he ultimately wants. Sure, he grovels and renounces the vendetta with her father, but he still gets everything in the end; his vengeance and the lady. A lady I don't think he deserves." He clicks his tongue twice. "Is Lady Cecily based on you? She has some peachy qualities to her."

"Peachy?" An obnoxious chortle bursts from me.

"Yeah, peachy." He doubles down with a smirk.

"What are these peachy qualities?"

"Are we fishing for compliments?" He leans forward on his elbows and mischief sparks in his features.

"Just character research to see if I accidentally imprinted on Lady Cecily." I bat my lashes like a brazen flirt, instead of being the un-batting-eye friend I *should* be.

"Feisty. Sweet. Witty. Beautiful," he says, his low voice a little husky. "Loyal. Supportive. Sometimes a little too focused on everyone else's happiness, instead of her own."

Et tu, Davis? There's no disguising the frown that replaces my flirtatious smile. He's not wrong, but annoyance still festers inside me with the second mention of this particular proclivity of mine by two different men in a ten-minute period.

"Did I say something wrong?" He leans back, concern dipping his smile.

"No…" I sigh. "Not you. I've had a few people lecture me about that little character flaw. That my fixation on other people's happiness is getting in the way of my own."

"As far as flaws, it could be worse. There are already enough people focused on their own happiness with no regard for how it impacts others," he says, sadness coats his words.

A twinge surges in my chest with the memory of Davis's comment about most people disappointing you during our first date. Not just his dad who made promises that he never kept –because something was always more important than his son – but the many other adults along the way.

"And you've had a lot of *that* character flaw already. I can't imagine what it must have been like," I say, my expression soft.

"Yeah. Lots of people focused on getting a check for a foster kid until they found one with autism too challenging. Until my moms came along. They aren't as self-sacrificing as Lady Cecily, but they care about others… They care about me.

Until them and my grandparents, I'd never felt like what I wanted mattered. That I mattered."

"You matter." Reaching across the table, I thread our fingers. The action was partly meant to comfort him, but mostly to soothe my own emotions. It physically hurts to think about this man in any pain.

"It's okay—" He squeezes our joined hands. "I know. My sad story has a happy ending, remember?"

"I know, but it doesn't mean that I'm not sad for what you went through. No matter how things were with my parents' marriage as a kid, I knew they were there. That I was important. It hurts to think that you didn't have that, and not just because you're wonderful, but because every kid deserves that."

"You think I'm wonderful?" He strokes his thumb over the top of my hand, the skin hums under the caress of his rough pads.

"Now, who's fishing for compliments?" I tease, biting my lower lip. "But, yes, you're wonderful."

"For the record, I think you're wonderful too." His throat bobs. "Which is why I'll be obnoxious and say while your preoccupation with other people's happiness may not hurt anyone but yourself, I don't like the idea of you being hurt."

His words caress me almost as sweetly as his fingers. They aren't chiding like those of my brothers but pained. It's as if somehow my hurt is *his*.

"Like with you going to your cousin and ex's wedding for your mom's sake. I know you say it's what you do for people you love. I just hope you don't forget to give yourself some of those peachy qualities that I like so much."

The frenzied rise of my pulse drowns out the bar's soundtrack of laughter, rock music, and the *thwack* of axes. Lars's words about my brother's hope for someone who will either help me keep a little bit of myself for me, or help replenish me, sing inside me.

"You have a big heart. If I didn't have years of stories from my grandparents, the last few days of getting to know you have shown me that. Who else would give a man who insulted her a second chance, after all?" he says, humor sparking in his features. "I may be overstepping, but like you said, sometimes we do things for the people we care…uh, like. And I like you, Peach."

A gentle current zips between us. The charge ripples through my entire body, sparking every cell awake with want. A want I shouldn't have, but at this moment, it's the only thing I can think of. To throw caution to the wind, closing the inches between us and sealing my lips against his. To just fall into this moment with no thought of tomorrow.

A tomorrow that may leave him hurt and left behind. That thought dims the electric pulse urging me closer to Davis. How many people have already used and discarded him because of their wants? Lars may tut that I'm just trying to guard my heart, but it's also about Davis. Right now, there's no guarantee for us, and I don't want to string him along.

"It's not overstepping, you're being a good friend," I murmur, releasing his hand.

His mouth lifts into a wry smile. "A good friend."

"Speaking of friends, I'm keeping you from yours." I lean against the chair's hard back, its sturdiness bolstering my resolve to stay in place, to keep distance between us. Clearly, I can't be trusted to make good decisions around this man.

"Just some of the department heads from No Boundaries. Jackson wrangled us into a happy hour." He tips his head toward the table where Jackson sits, Lars beside him, his tree-trunk-sized arm wrapped around my brother's shoulders.

"Of course, he did." I shake my head.

It's no surprise this run-in is Jackson-orchestrated. Even if my younger brother would never make a move on Lars without my literal thumbs up, he pines with the best of them. No doubt the green-eyed monster took control of his good senses, leading him to come spy on our date under the guise of a happy hour.

"You should get back to them. You're the boss and all that." I motion to him.

"Why don't you come with me?"

"I… I shouldn't." Hesitation thickens in my throat causing the words to come out strangled. "I should head home. I've been out a lot this week and need to spend some time with Wentworth."

"Okay." He stands up. "Let's go."

"Excuse me?" I cough out.

"I hate happy hours. Making small talk with people I just spent nine hours with, at a loud bar that doesn't even serve french fries, is my idea of a nightmare."

"Why did you come then?"

"Jackson asked."

"You don't have to do something just because someone asks."

"Okay, Lady Cecily," he teases.

"Ha…ha," I mock laugh with an exaggerated eye roll. "It's totally different. Jackson won't be hurt if you don't come out with him. Why come?"

"I like your brother. He knows I hate happy hours, so when he asks me to join, I know it's something important to him."

"Like agreeing to go on a happy hour date with his sister?" It comes out more sarcastic than I intend.

"Yes." He clicks his tongue. "Full disclosure… I'd seen pictures of you on your brother's social media, so it was easy to say yes."

Oh. It's so fucking cliché, but heat flushes my cheeks, nonetheless. It's not that I don't know that Davis is attracted to me, but the unexpected sense of validation makes me question my feminist ethics.

"You'd be doing your *friend* a solid by letting me escape

this ritualistic torture masquerading as social bonding." Smirking, he looks toward Jackson. "Plus, I'm sure your brother or his friend wouldn't let you go home by yourself."

Ugh. Stupid overprotective brother and his werewolf. My brow dips with frustration. While whatever is happening with Jackson and Lars complicates things, I don't want to preempt their time together. It may be short enough as it is.

"By letting me take you home, you'd be helping out me and your brother. You live for that stuff," he says, a soft chuckle curls his lips.

Thwarted by my peachiness. Laughing, I stand up. "You can take me home."

Davis parks his car in front of the house, right behind my vehicle. I peer between the house and him. Outside of Hope's SUV and my car in the driveway, and a light on downstairs, it's quiet. Just like the last time he brought me home. A zing travels along my nerves with the memory of him pressing me against the back gate.

"Do you need to walk Wentworth?" he asks.

"Yeah. Why?"

"Umm…" Tongue clicking, he clutches and unclutches his hands around the steering wheel. "Maybe I could walk with you. Through the neighborhood or there's a park a few blocks away that your brother has mentioned. It has a nice dog run and play area."

"I…"

"Or Gemma's. They have that outdoor patio and serve puppy-friendly ice cream," he forges ahead, taking advantage of my hesitation.

This isn't a good idea. None of this. Not letting him drive me home. Definitely not going out for ice cream with him and my dog. The last time we had ice cream together it ended with me pinned up against the back gate.

"They do have the pumpkin pup bowl, which is Wentworth's favorite." I smile.

Bad Georgia! As much as I lie to myself that friends do things like this, the feelings surging inside me about Davis aren't merely friendly. Not at all. I like him. I *really* like him.

With every new interaction, our initial meeting fades away, offering a clear picture of who he is. It's addicting. Like a good book... with each page, I want to just keep reading.

Davis and I stroll down the sidewalk. The little cleared throat noise he makes once we reach the gate signals that the memory of our last time here is, no doubt, playing inside him.

"Oh," Hope gasps as we open the gate. Face pinched and hand on her belly, she stands on the other side.

"Hope, is everything okay?" I blink, taking in the pained expression tightening her features.

"I think I'm in labor," she grits out, wincing.

"What!" I rush to her side. "It's too early. You're only seven and a half months along."

"Tell your overachieving niece that." She envelops my hand in a vise-like grip. "I thought it was just Braxton Hicks, but it's been the last hour... And there's been some vaginal discharge that I'm not sure isn't my water breaking."

"You don't know?" My question is high-pitched.

"No, Georgia, I don't know. I've never had a baby before, remember? Books and online videos can only tell you so much." Her tone is sweetly sarcastic.

"Should we call someone? Your doctor? Rem?" Davis asks, coming to Hope's other side.

"Thanks, Davis, but I've already made calls. Rem is in San Diego for work. He's on his way. My doctor will meet me at the hospital." Eyes wide, she looks between Davis and me. "Oh god, did I mention vaginal discharge in front of Davis?"

Shrugging his shoulders, he offers a lopsided grin. "With

two moms, you'd be surprised how used to the mention of lady business I am."

"Lady business?" I snort.

"Oh, he's sweet." She makes a motion with her free hand, her keys jangling.

"Hope, were you about to drive yourself to the hospital?" I gape. "Why didn't you call?"

"You were on that da… *out* with Lars. I didn't want to bug you," she says, the words coming out like a question.

I don't know whether to laugh or cry. Even in the middle of possible labor, my bestie is still shipping me and Davis.

"We should get you to the hospital." Patting her hand, I start to guide her through the gate.

"I'll take you," Davis says, following.

"No, it's—"

He shakes his head. "This way, you can sit with her in the backseat and hold her hand. You focus on Hope, and I'll focus on you…uh…getting you there safe."

"I like his plan," Hope breathes, as her hand tightens harshly around mine and she bends at the waist.

"Okay." I nod. "You're the boss."

"If only your niece knew that and wasn't deciding to come early. Let's go to the hospital and Davis, I'll try not to have this baby in your backseat—" her face creases "—Although, she was conceived in one."

CHAPTER NINETEEN

THE LAST NIGHT AS FRIENDS

"She's got a strong heartbeat," Della, the midwife, reports with a warm smile.

"She does." Hope beams, her hand folded tight around mine, her gaze locked on the emergency room monitor hooked to her belly.

The best part of possible labor, there is no long wait to be seen. Upon arrival at the hospital, a nurse spotted Davis and me helping Hope out of the vehicle. He grabbed a wheelchair from inside and escorted us in. With a quick thank you to Davis, I followed Hope inside as they wheeled her to triage.

"It is strong." I wipe my eyes.

The sonogram video of my niece's heartbeat doesn't compare to hearing it in person. Inside my bestie's round belly is who I know will soon be one of my favorite people. Somehow, experiencing this in real life rather than a recorded video makes this all real.

"There's like a *real* little human in there." My laugh is watery.

"What did you think? That I'd just swallowed a watermelon?" she quips.

"You do like fruit."

The nurse chuckles. "Keep that sense of humor. As parents, you'll need it."

"If only she were my co-parent instead of my very tardy husband." Frowning, she looks to the clock on the wall above a counter lined with medical supplies. "He should be here by now. He was only thirty minutes out when I spoke to him, and it's been an hour."

I squeeze her hand. "Probably just hit traffic."

"We're going to do a physical exam to confirm labor. Do you want bestie to stay for that?"

"Oh yeah, she's used to *lady business,*" she winks, repeating Davis's words from earlier.

The moment we'd parted from him, she'd tugged me close and whispered, "Davis?" The almost obscene way his name rolled from her lips telegraphed so much. *What happened to Lars? Why is Davis here? Please tell me you're climbing him like a sexy ladder.* Those questions, and I'm sure way more, lurked behind her gaze. It's only a matter of time before she pounces on me.

Della finishes the exam, including a swab of Hope's lady business. The baby's heartbeat is strong with no apparent distress, and all signs are that this is a false alarm, but they are confirming a few things and consulting with Hope's OB-GYN before giving the all-clear. With a quick smile, Della ducks out of the room, leaving us alone.

"So embarrassing," Hope mutters, rubbing the center of her forehead.

"Now, now"—I pat her hand—"it could still be labor."

Head tossed back, a whiny laugh whooshes out of her. "I just freaked."

"Like you said earlier, you've never had a baby. Anyone would have done the same thing. It's better to know than to give birth to my niece in your kitchen, while in the middle of making pastries."

"I panicked. The contractions kept coming, and the

discharge… And your brother was gone. This is all *his* fault," she grumbles.

"Pretty sure it was both of you in that backseat making my niece."

"Now isn't the time to be 'Quippy' Georgia, Now's the time to be 'Blame Rem for knocking up your bestie and not being here' Georgia."

"That is a mouthful." I chuckle, squeezing her hand. "I'll be whatever Georgia you want."

"I know you will." She sighs. "And I love you for that, but…"

"But you want Rem."

"He just makes everything better." A wistful expression dances in her features. "No matter how scary any situation is, I know he's got me."

"It helps that the man *always* has a plan." The tiniest note of sarcasm punctuates my statement.

"It's not *just* that. Although I do love that about him. He's dependable and sturdy. Even if he doesn't have a plan, I know that he'll still be there. That we can handle anything together."

"He's your person."

This is the love that I write about… that I want. To have someone whose mere presence is a balm for any of life's weariness and a cherry on top of its sundaes.

"You'll always be my bestie, you know that."

"Yeah, but I also know that in these moments hubby trumps bestie." A soft smile curls my lips.

"Where is he?" She tosses her free hand up.

This isn't like Rem. It's been almost an hour since he told Hope he was only thirty minutes away. With my focus on Hope's triage by the midwife and the little *No Cell Phone* signs on the wall, I've not checked my mobile.

"Maybe he's in the waiting room. They only let one loved one in at a time."

"Can you check?" Her smile is apologetic.

"Of course." With a quick nod, I slip out.

I step through the mechanical sliding doors into the ER's waiting room. The quiet hum of a TV underscores muffled conversations of waiting patients and loved ones. Scanning the room, I find exactly who I'm looking for.

In the corner sits Rem. His body hunched forward and elbows on his knees, he scrubs his hands down his face. Even from across the room, the worry that radiates off him is palpable.

I approach him. "Hey."

He shoots up. "Is she okay? The baby? Are they—"

"They're both okay. It looks like a false alarm. They did an exam and are confirming a few things with the doctor."

"They're okay." He lets out a hard breath.

"Other than a little bit of embarrassment, she's okay. You should head back there."

"Thank god." He closes his eyes. "She can't come yet. Hope isn't due for six weeks. We haven't finalized our birth plan or the nursery. I still need to put together the crib. We're still interviewing nannies."

"Looks like my niece is already a handful." A silent laugh curls my mouth into a devilish grin at the idea of baby girl Lane messing up all his plans. "Hope's in bay three. Why don't you go back, and I'll wait here."

Eyes open and hands on his hips, he peers between me and the mechanical doors that lead into the ER. He just stands there, his face scrunched, and feet sealed to the scuffed vinyl floor.

"Both your girls are okay. It will all be okay." My tone is coaxing.

"Will it?" he rasps. "The entire way here, every scenario ran through my head. What if I lost her? The baby? Both?"

"But you didn't... It was just a false alarm." Reaching out, I place my palm on his upper arm.

His eyes, the same color as mine, are glossy with worry. "But there's no guarantee that something may not happen. No matter how much I plan, I can't protect them. I can't…"

"No one can guarantee a happy ending, no matter how much planning is done." I motion to him.

"Things don't just happen. You need a plan, Georgia," he says. A muscle ticks in his jaw.

"I know, but we also can't control everything. We can't ensure that nothing bad ever happens."

He rakes his fingers into his hair. "I feel so helpless."

"You're not, though." I squeeze his arm. "You can hold her hand, and you two can face all of life's uncertainties together. Just like you did for me as a kid."

Each celiac flare-up or anytime our parents argued, he never fixed it. He never had a plan. He just sat beside me.

"It may annoy me at times that you always have suggestions"—I make air quotes—"for how I should live my life—"

"At times?" he huffs a hoarse laugh.

"*But*—" Batting the air, I go on, "I know it's part of you. It's how you manage your anxiety about things, and it's also something I'll admit I begrudgingly love about you… But what I love the most is how you'd sit next to me and rub my back, telling me you were there for me. Sometimes that's all you need to do."

"I never knew what to do," he says, his throat bobbing. "I couldn't make you healthy. I couldn't make Mom and Dad stop arguing. I don't want to feel that *helpless* again. To not be able to take care of the people I love."

"At least you try." Realization slinks through me. "You deal with the anxiety of what might happen by trying to plan for every foreseeable outcome to prevent the negative. I just find excuses to not even risk it."

Fear is a formidable adversary. My brother and I fight that

fear in different ways. He plans his counterattack, while I hide. I'm sure Lars's werewolf analysis would agree.

"We're more alike than I realize sometimes," I say, a small smile tugs my mouth up. "We're both terrified things won't turn out."

Things happen. Accidents. Illnesses. Breakups. Disappointed people. Life. We can't always control what happens, and we don't need to take responsibility for the things that we didn't actually do. Doc's words from last night whisper inside me. Their truth unspools my own.

"Let the plan serve you, not you serve the plan." I take Rem's hands, folding them into my smaller ones. "I'm not going to tell you that everything will be okay, because it may not. Any number of terrible things may happen, but so will many wonderful things and just everyday things... And it's okay to have plans, but it's also okay to just sit beside your wife and hold her hand when she's a little scared and a lot embarrassed, or just listen to Jackson when he complains about something, instead of trying to fix it—"

"*Or* just support your sister in her decisions, rather than trying to plan out her life for her," he says, his shoulders slumping.

"Yeah." I nibble on the corner of my lip. "But you might be right about my self-sabotaging any potential Mr. Right."

"Did it hurt to admit I was right?" His chuckle is soft.

"So much," I whine.

"Even if I was right about that, I know I need to back off at times. I don't want you to ever think that I don't love you or see how amazing you are. As much as I worry about you and want to protect you, I am also in awe of you. I haven't said it enough..." He clears his throat at my '*enough*' expression. "*Or* at all, but I'm proud of you. Your work at SPN. Your books. How you've come back after Will and Lena. What an amazing aunt you already are to little Georgia."

"Georgia?" A too-full sensation blooms in my chest.

"Hope wants to name her after you, and after tonight, I think it's fitting."

"Because she's already not listening and messing with her daddy?" I dash away escaping tears.

"That, and I'm hoping she's as tenacious and big-hearted as you… I'm sorry for being, well…me." His mouth tips into a crooked smile.

"And I'm sorry for being, well, me."

We are who we are. In so many ways, Rem and I are as different as night and day, but we're part of the same coin. You can't have one without the other.

"I love you." He pulls me into a hug.

"I love you, too." I squeeze him just a little tighter.

"For the record, I don't want you to move out." He rests his chin atop my head.

"It might be time, though."

"If that's what you want, but know that it's not what I want, and you always have a home with me."

"I know." I step out of my brother's embrace. "But I think it will be good for me. Outside of the dorms, I've never lived on my own. As much as I push back with you about making my own decisions, I've never not had a safety net."

"Just because you move out doesn't mean I won't still be there. That you don't still have us." Affection shimmers in his expression. "But if it's what you feel is best, I'll support you."

"Thank you." I grin, knowing that these are baby steps.

Rem may have suggested that I move out on Saturday, but, no doubt, its actuality spiderwebs inside him. My living somewhere else loosens his ability to protect me. To be there in the minute it takes to cross the backyard.

"I doubt Hope will be as understanding as I am about you deserting her." Palm rested on his chest, his expression is wry.

"Hush." I make a shoo motion. "Now, get in there before Hope kicks both our asses. She may be a Care Bear ninety-nine percent of the time, but bears have teeth."

Laughter vibrates in his chest. "God, I love that woman." He starts to move to the door before stopping. "Hope has her keys, right?"

"Yeah, why?"

"Perfect. My spare car key is on her ring. Just grab my keys from Davis after he gets back. If you want to head home, he can take you, and I'll call you to let you know how she's doing. That way, you can get some rest."

"Davis?" My mouth drops open.

"I found him in the waiting room when I got here. He volunteered to take my keys to walk Wentworth. I think he was looking for some way to help."

Warmth fizzes within me as if expensive champagne flows through my veins. After I'd thanked him, I thought he'd just left. I had zero expectations that he'd stay.

"I'm not sure what Davis is to you, but—"

"He's a friend," I jump in, the word "friend" leaving a bitter taste in my mouth.

"Not to be all *me* about this, but maybe rethink that designation. While you were in there taking care of Hope, he was looking for ways to take care of you. I like him."

"Me too," I murmur.

That truth lights up every cell. It's not reminiscent of fireworks bursting in the sky, their radiance intense but brief. It's akin to streetlamps flickering awake, their steady glow lighting the way.

"Go for it." Determination glints in his eyes. "We know I use plans to manage my anxiety, but your plans sometimes hold you back. You hoped for a future with Will that I think—even if Lena hadn't happened—wouldn't have come true."

"I thought you liked Will."

"I tolerated him for your sake. He was fine enough, but his focus was always on himself. I want the men with my siblings to think of *their* needs from time to time. Will barely did that. Everything was always about or in service to him."

"You never said anything."

"Maybe, sometimes, I do just sit by and support you after all." A furrow mars his brow. "For that one, I wish I'd been more my textbook self."

"I probably wouldn't have listened." My short huff of laughter is laced with self-deprecation.

"You would have been torn between making *him* happy or me. You may push back against me and chart your own course, but your ship always steers back toward what's best for others. Not as much, but Jackson is like that, too. It's why I want both of you with partners who won't take advantage of that. That will support you when you're taking care of everyone else."

"We get that trait from our big brother."

It's not just our names that bind the three of us. Each of us our cemented in a foundation of caring for others. That foundation guides us in almost all our decisions. Jackson may be the most balanced out of the three of us, but all our compasses point north.

A cheeky smile invades my features. "Speaking of Jackson, you're going to like his new guy. He's a real golden retriever type."

"Well, I know I like your new guy or, at least, I hope you'll let him be your new guy." Palms raised, he walks backward. "I know, I know. Let you live *your* life. Just don't let the fear of what could happen or it not being what you planned stop you from living it."

Rem disappears through the automatic doors to check on Hope, and I take a seat in the waiting room in the identical position I found him. Leaned forward, elbows on my knees, I scrub my hands down my face. Is it the fear of getting hurt that holds me back from being with Davis? Are my book boyfriends just an excuse to not get hurt again? Is my pushing him away less about not breaking his heart, but protecting my own?

"I am such a cliché," I mutter to myself.

"Is everything okay? How's Hope? Is the baby alright?"

Raising my head, I meet Davis's gaze, a mix of warmth and worry shines in the dark pupils. Worry for and about me.

"Yeah. It looks like a false alarm." I sit up. "Rem said you went to walk Wentworth."

"Yeah." His smile is bashful. "I also picked up a grilled cheese and fries from Fisher's Landing, since I know you haven't eaten." He hands me a paper sack emblazoned with the restaurant's logo.

"Thank you." I accept the bag. "You didn't need to do all that."

"I wanted to."

The earnestness that brightens his features illuminates his truth. Davis wants to take care of me, and I want to take care of him. That fact roars inside me, drowning out all the reasons this is a bad idea. I may hurt him. He may hurt me. All those things could happen. All the best stories come with that angst of not knowing how things will turn out, and I want to write a story with Davis.

"Wanna share?" Slipping the to-go box out of the bag, I hold it up. "We can even double-dip our fries."

"Sure." His mouth twitches into a big grin.

Before I can start the next chapter in my story with Davis, I need to take care of my book boyfriends. Until then, I can share a meal with my friend. That's what friends do, after all. Even if I hope, tonight is the last night I call him just a friend.

CHAPTER TWENTY

BUT I NEVER GOT MY CHANCE

A cup of tea in hand and my closed laptop beside me on my couch, the early morning sun breaks through my open window. The minty aroma of the tea fills my nostrils, sparking memories of Davis. The press of his strong shoulder against mine while we sat in the ER waiting room. The way his entire being lit as he told me about a new app his company is developing to assist disabled folks with dating.

"Dating is difficult for anyone, but for people with disabilities, there are unique challenges," he says, dipping a fry in our shared ketchup in the open food container balanced on my lap.

"Like dates that misconstrue aspects of someone's neurodivergence as them being rude." My expression is somehow both cheeky and sheepish.

"Exactly." His smile is large. *"Although that someone may have also been rude."*

Sinking into the memory, I settle against the plush couch cushions. Since last night, my thoughts haven't drifted far from Davis. For the first time, I'm allowing myself to want this. Not just want him, but to focus on *my* wants and needs rather than others.

I'm not tossing my book boyfriends aside with no thought

of what happens to them. I still have a responsibility to help them, but it doesn't mean I need to tie myself to someone I don't love out of obligation.

Step one, talk to them. Forehead scrunched, I cluck my tongue.

Lars and Owen aren't a concern, but James... I'm not entirely sure how he'll react to this. He's insistent that he feels something, so I want to handle this with care. Even if I don't *care* for him, I don't want to hurt him. But not wanting to hurt someone isn't a reason to be with them. I just need to talk to him, but first... pastries.

It's Saturday, i.e., it's brunch with Hope day. Though this week's date with my bestie will look a little different.

"Morning!" I almost sing, striding into the house, Wentworth trots behind me, and I carry a tray of fresh fruit and a pastry box in my hands.

"Thank god, you brought food." Rem exhales, closing the fridge and bending to give Wentworth ear scratches. "I thought I was going to have to cook."

Placing the food on the kitchen island, I jest, "And your fragile male ego can't handle your chef wife's critique."

"I was scared she'd try to help." He pulls down some plates.

"I heard that!" Hope bellows from the living room.

It turns out that last night's false alarm was a combo of thrush, the cause of the discharge that had concerned Hope, Braxton Hicks contractions, and a healthy dose of first pregnancy anxiety. Hope's not on bed rest, but her OB-GYN prescribed medication for the yeast infection and recommended she slow down a bit and take more breaks to combat the Braxton Hicks. Of course, Rem wants to Bubble Wrap her.

"And will her warden let her have breakfast at the table or should I serve her couch-side," I tease, opening the food containers.

"I'm not bedridden." Lips pursed, Hope shuffles into the

room. "This is sweet, but you didn't need to do this. *Oooh,* you got breakfast bars from Meghan's Munchies." She inspects the contents of the pastry box.

"It's Saturday. We always brunch on Saturdays."

"Yeah, but aren't you supposed to go to pickleball?"

With Hope's false alarm, I'd almost forgotten the pickleball date I agreed to on Wednesday night with Owen and Davis. Thanks to Davis's, "Do you think you'll want to learn to play or just watch?" comment last night, I'd remembered our plans. Only, while they play, I'll spectate between bites of a pecan breakfast bar.

"I'm still going, but thought I'd bring sustenance for you to snack on, since I'm ditching you to go—"

"Cheer on *Davis.*" She shimmies her body just a bit.

"I'll be there to cheer on *all* the guys, but *especially* Davis," I purr. Pickleball isn't a panty dropper for me, but the idea of seeing Davis all sweaty in athletic competition sets a tingle pulsing low in my belly.

"Yes!" Hope whoops. "As soon as I saw you in your booty-popping yoga pants, I knew you'd finally come to your good senses." Eyebrows waggling, Hope slaps my behind.

It's my sexiest leisure-wear ensemble. A pair of curve-hugging black yoga pants and a teal V-neck tank top. Despite the casual vibe, I washed, dried, and straightened my hair. The outfit says, "Oh, this old thing?" while my loose strands almost purr, "Hey, big fella."

"Not to mention, do I detect some mascara and—" she clutches her chest and mock gasps. "And lipstick?"

"Hush!" I toss a napkin at her.

"Leave her alone, Hope," Rem chides softly.

"Thanks." I grin.

"Though, I'm also happy she listened to me about Davis."

Laughing, I roll my eyes.

Last night's conversation melted away that undercurrent of tension between Rem and me. One conversation doesn't fix things, but it's a start. Our newfound lightness relaxes us to just be with each other. Him not telling me what to do, me not being tied up in knots about making him happy, because no matter what I know he loves me.

"Baby, the doctor said to be mindful of your sugar intake," Rem cautions as Hope plucks up a pecan bar from the pastry box.

"Don't worry, warden. I grabbed keto bars, so she can have it with some berries to ensure no negative impact to her glucose levels." I bump his hip with mine. A big smile belts across his face.

"You're teaming up on me." Pouting, she tips her head down to her belly. "Little Georgia, you best be on your mama's side when you get here."

The surge of emotion in my chest causes my mouth to lift in the biggest smile. Every single inch of my being radiates the happiness that overflows inside me.

Last night, emerging from the ER, the moment Hope saw me, she squealed, "We're naming her Georgia!" Even though I knew it was going to happen, tear-filled laughter fell out of me, causing Davis to loop his arm around me.

"I still can't believe you're naming her after me." I wipe at my eyes.

"Not if you make me cry in my own kitchen." She sniffles.

"Do not make my wife cry." Rem comes up behind Hope and wraps his arms around her, nuzzling her neck.

"My wife." Head tipped back, her sigh his contented. "Will I ever get tired of hearing you call me that?"

He places his palm on her round belly. "I hope never, because I plan on calling you it for a very long time."

"Get a room!"

"Don't be hateful." Hope wiggles her finger playfully.

"Yeah, or I'll have to grill your new guy," he teases.

"You're going to do that anyway." I bat at the air.

"True."

"I need details, woman. When's this happening or did it happen last night?" Hope tilts her head.

"Today, I hope… I just need to talk to my book boyfriends first, and then I'll talk to Davis. Hopefully, he still wants me."

Even if last night offers the certainty that Davis still likes me, despite my less-than-stellar behavior, there's no guarantee that he'll want to start something. My life is still messy. We both have our own past hurts that may impact things. There are a number of things that could lead him to say no. All that matters is that I'm letting myself say yes, and if I get my heart broken, I know I can come back from it. I've done it before, but I hope I don't have to again.

"Not want you?" Hope scoffs. "Oh, that man will be on his knees by the end of the night, especially with you in *those* yoga pants."

"I'd prefer not to have that mental image—" Rem crinkles his nose. "Also, *book boyfriends*?"

"I'm going to let you handle that one, Hope," I tease, pulling my buzzing phone from my bag. "Jackson is out front, so I'm off to pickleball. Should I drop Wentworth off at my place?"

"Nah." Hope bends and pats his head. "He's going to be my snuggle buddy while I watch food porn on TV and then my excuse to get rid of your brother after he hovers too much and I make him take Wentworth to the park."

"Again, book boyfriends?" Rem wildly waves his hands.

Hope pats his cheek. "Wait until I tell you about the witchcraft consultant."

With a quick hug to a smugly pleased Hope and a confused Rem, I pet Wentworth, grab a pastry, and head out. Opening the back gate, I smack into a hard body, strong hands coming up and gripping my arms to steady me.

"James…" I almost gasp, my breath whooshing out of me from the impact.

"Georgia," he drawls.

"I didn't know you were coming over." I step out of his hold, my gaze dragging down his lean physique clad in a muscle-hugging T-shirt and shorts. "Are you coming with us? I thought it was just going to be Owen and Lars playing with Jackson and Davis."

"Owen sends his apologies. He was called away to work."

Shoot, I forgot. Good Girl's Grub is catering a local fundraising event this afternoon. With Hope slowing down, Owen must be covering for her today.

"I shall take his place in today's tourney." James places his hand on his chest and offers a quick bow. "I am here to collect you. Lars and Jackson are in the carriage…uh…vehicle."

We just stand there and stare at each other. The charge that used to electrify the air between us is missing. Whether that's due to his pushiness, snide comment about me not knowing that this isn't a game, or my feelings for Davis, that hum in my bloodstream from our first meeting is quiet.

Certainty courses through me, straightening my spine. I am not this duke's darling, and he is definitely not mine.

"Are you displeased to see me?" His mouth drags down. "Of course, you are. *Perhaps*, I acted the callous brute the last time we met."

"You insinuated that I think this is all a game." My gaze narrows, and I cross my arms over my chest.

"Apologies… It may not be your intention, but there is a bit of a game in this with each of us vying for your heart."

The protest dies on my lips. His accusation is nothing but the truth. In my attempt to help these men, I allowed it to become a game. The unrealistic nature of this entire thing is blinding me. As "game" as Owen, Lars, and James have been, what choice did they have from the moment they'd poofed from their worlds to mine, they haven't had any real choice in this. As worried as I was about leading Davis on, didn't I just do that to them?

Shoulders slumped, my arms fall to my sides. "It appears

I'm the callous one. I didn't mean to… I am so sorry for all this. You all deserve so much better."

"I know it was not your intention. Perhaps you were a bit carried away with this whole thing." He reaches out, his palms soothing along my arms. "It's understandable. Please know that I bear no ill will. In fact, I think Jackson may be the true culprit."

"Jackson is just trying to help."

"I know," he says quickly. "This situation is hard for me. I am not entirely sure who I am and what I am supposed to be here. I think it brings out the worst parts of myself."

"I am sorry for all of this," I repeat again, regret shaking my voice.

"I know you are, dear Georgia." His mouth curves up. "I believe we both were carried away. I know I do get that way when I truly want something. Though, from what I gather from Owen, it's how *you* wrote me."

He's right. It's how I wrote Lord James, after all. His character is single-minded about everything. First, his thirst for vengeance, and then, about Lady Cecily. As much as Lars and Owen's real life selves surprise me, James appears most true to his on-page persona.

"I should amend that statement. It's not *a* something that I want, it's *a someone*. Please know that has not changed. As unsure as this entire situation is, the one thing I am certain of is how I feel about you. I want you, Georgia," he murmurs, his green eyes crackle with desire.

"James, I am so sorry for everything. For my wish. For all of it… But I don't want to be with you." I step back.

"Pardon?" His brow puckers.

"I am so—"

"No," he snaps, causing me to flinch. "Are you choosing Lars, because I will warn you that he and your brother are… *friendly*."

"I know about them," I say, softening my tone and body

language to help calm him. It's a technique I use with upset patients or their loved ones at SPN. I'm not scared that he'll hurt me, but the storminess shadowing his features gives me pause.

"It can't be Owen." Hands on his hips, he puffs out a hard breath.

"What's wrong with Owen?" Indignation fuels my glower.

"He's fine enough, but he's not me." He pats his chest for emphasis. "A woman like you needs more than Owen can offer. Perhaps it is why you wrote him first, you needed to work your way up to a man like me. A man who would match your passion, not be drowned by it." He steps closer and I move backwards. His forward movement halts.

"Just because a man is quiet and thoughtful, doesn't mean he lacks passion. Don't underestimate Owen, I would be lucky to be with him." My glare slams into him.

"It is him, then?" James cocks one eyebrow.

"It's not Owen." I shake my head. "It's none of you... I don't have those feelings for any of you."

"None of us?" he scoffs.

"Correct."

"I have not had *my* chance, yet." He gestures between us.

"It wouldn't make a difference."

"Is this due to our last exchange? We just discussed this situation's difficulty on me and how much I want you," he says, his softer tone in direct contrast to the hardness in his gaze.

"I'm sorry."

He studies me, the dark edge of his features seeming to relax. "I am, too. I had hoped it was me. It is why I assumed I was brought here. Perhaps, it was not for you, but *because* of you after all."

A queasy sensation rolls in my stomach. No matter how I

feel about James, he's still here because of me. They all are. This doesn't change that.

"I am *really* sorry." I swallow the hard lump in my throat.

"No apologies needed, my lady." Posture relaxing, he puts out his hand. "Although, may I still call you Georgia? That is if you are amenable to a friendship with me. If we cannot be more, I would like to be friends with you."

Something akin to whiplash seizes me with his quick turn-around. It's just like Thursday morning. He blinks between emotions, causing a dizzy sensation. But this may just be his single-minded nature at play. Once James decides something…whether indignation or forgiveness, that's it for him.

"Are you sure?"

His lips quirk. "As determined as you have penned me to be, Georgia, you have crafted a man with honor. I would never force my affections."

"Friends."

Despite apprehension coiling my muscles tight at his quick rebound, I take his hand. This is who he is. James does nothing with restraint. Friendship. Love. His affair with Lady Cecily is proof of this. Once he fell, it was hard. Still, the moment she chose the marquis, he stepped aside until he learns her choice was made to protect him from her father who planned to have him killed, rather than be with his daughter.

The difference is that my rebuke of his advances isn't to save his life. The only thing I want is to help him.

"I will figure out a way to get you back," I say.

"And if you don't succeed?"

"I don't know," I whisper, realization thick in my throat that I have no idea how any of this will end.

And as scary as that is, I'll proceed.

CHAPTER TWENTY-ONE

THE DUEL... PICKLEBALL-STYLE

The remaining tension with James dissolves in the twenty-minute ride to the Fairbanks Tennis Club. Between his repeated nudges as if to say *I told you they were friendly* each time Lars reached across the console to squeeze Jackson's knee, or James's musings about the similarities of pickleball and the yard tennis he'd played as a child, I relax.

"I don't recall writing that." I wrinkle my nose.

"I have the memory of playing with my cousin Reginald as children," he says, sliding out of the backseat of the SUV once we're parked at the complex.

The sprawling compound nestled beside a local park offers both indoor and outdoor courts for tennis and pickleball. Jackson and Davis play on Saturdays with two other people from No Boundaries. This week. it will just be them against Lars and James. However, I seriously doubt Lars will want to be on James's team.

I'm thankful we'll be indoors. The notorious Southern California September heat is already climbing skyward, and I don't sweat sexy. A pink hue doesn't kiss my skin. I just get blotchy and glisten like a live pig that wandered into a BBQ.

"Hey, Larsy-poo." Smirking, Jackson juts his chin toward

Lars. "Can you take my gym bag in. We're at court three. I just need a moment with Georgia."

Lars flashes a lopsided grin. "I got you Jacky Bear… Come on, Lord Short Breeches, let's head in." He hoists the gym bag onto his shoulder.

I know what this is about. Outside of a "Are you sure?" last night when I said I was heading out with Davis, we've not talked about the werewolf in the room. I may have given a thumbs up, but knowing Jackson, he still worries about how his new relationship impacts me.

His focus jumps to where Lars and James disappear through the entrance and then back to me. "I wanted to check in about—"

"About you stealing my would-be suitor," I tease.

"I didn't mean for Lars and me to happen."

"It's totally fine." I reach out and squeeze his forearm. "Lars and I were never going to be anything. It's clear there's something between you two."

A furrow mars his brow. "All morning, I just kept thinking, am I like Lena? Did Lars and I do to you what she and Will did to you?"

I huff a short laugh. "This is completely different. Lars and I were never in a relationship. Not to mention, you didn't sneak around. I'm assuming outside of the longing stares and lingering hand touches, nothing happened until after I gave you the all-clear sign."

"Outside of some vivid dreams… nothing." A sigh rolls through him, relaxing his posture. "You're really okay with all this?"

"Yes." I lightly punch his bicep. "Don't be melodramatic."

"Good, because I really like him."

"You *really* like him?" My right eyebrow lifts. "So, this is like a *real* thing and not just a little hormone-filled dalliance."

"Dalliance?" He guffaws. "Maybe it's time to cut down on

your historical romance reading… But yes, I think this could be something real with him."

"But what if he…" I motion with my hand as if that fills in the words that I'm hesitant to speak out of fear of what the reality of those unsaid words may do to my brother.

"Doesn't stay?" Nodding, a thoughtful but sad expression covers his face.

So much about this situation is uncharted. If the witchcraft consultant helps me undo my wish, will all three of my book boyfriends return to their original stories? Will Lars want to, and if so, what happens to my brother?

"It's worth the risk. I may only have a short time with Lars, but that fear isn't holding me back. Whatever happens, happens. In the meantime, I'm going to enjoy the time we have together and hope that fate or, maybe, the author of this story writes one with us together."

"This story?" My laugh is breathy.

He shrugs. "Who knows, maybe we're just characters in someone's story, just like Lars, Owen, and James."

"Maybe… Or maybe this is just our lives."

"Whether a story or just my life, I hope it gets spicier." He winks. "I'd like to take advantage of having a sexy werewolf boyfriend."

"Maybe he'll chase you through the woods on your next jog." I waggle my brows.

"*God*, I hope so."

"You may be the most well-adjusted of the three Lane siblings, you know that." I bump his shoulder with mine.

Looping his arm around me, he tucks me into his side. "I've learned a lot from my big brother and sister."

"Mostly what not to do."

"And, also, what to do," he says, admiration shines bright in his eyes.

"And we've learned a lot from you. It appears that I'm

taking a page out of your book. I'm withdrawing myself from this pseudo-Bachelorette competition."

"Because not one of these men is the costar of your story."

"Correct."

"And you like Davis." He squeezes me.

"And I like Davis."

"I figured it out last night at the bar, but then Lars filled in the blanks."

"And he says Owen has a big mouth," I quip. "But this isn't just about my feelings for Davis, it's about me. It's about me pushing past my fears to put my wants and needs first."

He twists to face me. "Does that include putting your wants and needs first about the wedding?"

"Yeah." I brush my hair behind my ears, the action settles the anxious knot in my stomach. "I spoke to Mom this morning."

Before picking up the food for Hope and Rem earlier, I stopped by her place to tell her I'm not going to go to the wedding because it would be too hard to sit there, forcing a smile of happiness for two people who'd hurt me so badly. I don't love Will anymore. My not wanting to be there isn't about me wishing it was me, but about the knowledge that two people who supposedly loved me had no care for my heart.

Even if Will and I weren't meant to be, he once claimed to love me, and Lena claims she still does. If you truly love someone, you don't treat their heart like a flimsy napkin so easily tossed away.

"I'm proud of you for making this decision."

"Mom said the same thing." I smile. "I told her that she should still go. Lena hurt me, but I don't want to take her family away from her."

"Even though she took Will away from you," he grumbles.

"She didn't, though... Will and I were never going to be a

forever thing. No matter how much I thought that was going to happen, it never was."

Rem's comment about Will accompanied me most of the night while mulling over this decision. Time allows us hindsight to see what we were once blind to. The future I envisioned with Will seemed so real... until it wasn't. In the aftermath of that heartbreak, I see the little clues that I'd missed that it...that *we* would never be. Will's hesitation to take our relationship to the next step. Every step of the way, he'd pull back just a bit. How everything was always about him. Even our dates. He never went to Fisher's Landing with me, let alone show up at the ER with a to-go box from there for me.

"As much as I love this Zen Georgia, I wish I could see his face when he finds out you're not coming. That guy hates losing."

"*That* he does." I loop my arm with Jackson's and stroll toward the entrance.

The memory of how grumbly Will would get if Jackson beat him at basketball, or he lost to Rem at cards, is a sharp contrast to Davis's pretend aghast expression each time Estelle squealed *Uno* the other night. Will would never happily lose to anyone, willingly or not.

"As devastatingly good as I look in my tux, I'm happy to stay home with you next weekend. We can—"

"Not necessary." I pat his forearm. "You go. As understanding as Mom is, she and Uncle Hans will be disappointed if you're not there."

"Will you tell Lena before or just not show up?" Jackson opens the door and holds it for me. "I kind of hope it's option B, so I can see Will's annoyed face that not only did you not show up, but he'd already paid for your meal. Which, out of principle, I will not eat, no matter how good the steak is... I'll just let it sit there to mock him."

"As delightful as that sounds, I'm still me." I laugh. "Plus,

Uncle Hans is paying for the wedding, so that dulls any perverse pleasure. I'm going to email Lena today, and I'll offer to cover the cost of my meal to Uncle Hans."

"Georgia," he groans.

"Baby steps, little bro," I coo, moving down the long walkway toward the pickleball courts.

Jackson reserved one of the four indoor courts. A mural depicting a park scene covers the walls dividing the four courts. The vibrant colors simulate spectators watching from checkered blankets laid atop lush green grass.

Above the courts, a balcony allows spectators to peer down on the matches. For the next hour, that's where I'll be. Despite my athletic wear, I slipped on a pair of black flip flops, so there's no confusion that I will not be participating in this sporty escapade outside of spectatorship. Perched at the edge of the balcony, I nibble my pecan bar and watch Jackson, Lars, and James hit practice balls while waiting for Davis. The mix of the tasty pastry and relief about the decisions I've made relaxes every muscle into contentment.

My chill demeanor is short-lived with the slam of a door, drawing my attention to the court's entrance. Davis strides in. A red muscle shirt molds over his sculpted torso, and a pair of black mesh shorts hang just right on his hips.

"Oh, my," I almost whimper, my core clenches with the many illicit thoughts fuzzing my focus.

With a wave to the guys, he tosses his bag on the side. Bending, he unzips his duffle and pulls out an eyeglass case. Straightening, he looks around,

"I thought Georgia was coming?" he shouts to Jackson, who volleys the ball back to Lars.

"Her highness is watching from above," Jackson drawls.

"Like the angel she is," Lars quips, making me roll my eyes at his playful but friendly flirtation.

Head tipped up, a big smile kicking across his face, Davis waves at me. "Hey."

"Hey." I wave back, my timbre breathy.

For just a moment, our stares tether with one another. The resultant heat sends a tingle across my body. That big smile still beaming, he slips his glasses off, and the image of him taking those off before tugging off his shirt, pushing me onto a bed, and prowling up my body causes me to let out a quiet moan.

"Shit," he groans, his face twisting with surprise, as one of the balls slams into his stomach.

"Dreadfully sorry," James says, pressing the paddle against his chest. "I must be more out of practice than I thought."

Was that on purpose?

James's quick shrug before returning to his practice with Jackson and Lars telegraphs that it may have been just an accident. Not to mention my perceptive brother or his werewolf's continued volley of the ball shows no indication of concern.

After changing into a pair of goggles, which somehow only heighten his hot nerd aesthetic, Davis is introduced to James. While he's met Owen and Lars, this feels different. With Owen and Lars, the concern swimming in my belly with their meeting had more to do with how to explain their mere existence.

With James, it's less that, and more an uneasiness for these two to meet. Davis shared that he doesn't like James's character in my book. While we weren't a couple, I pretty much just broke up with James for Davis. Although, I wasn't with James, nor am I technically with Davis.

Girl, you're a mess. I shove the rest of the breakfast bar into my mouth to hide my cringe.

The four of them split into teams. Lars partners with Davis. Between the sounds of the games from the other three courts visible from my vantage point, I only hear their grunts as they hit the ball, James's *bloody hells* with missed shots, and Jackson and Lars's playful taunts.

As much as pickleball may not excite me, watching Davis play skyrockets my internal temperature. Despite the cool air from the above vent blowing down on me, heat crisscrosses along my spine with his cat-like grace and periodic grunts while in play. If this thing with Davis happens, Hope and I may need to move our regular brunch date to Sundays because I plan on spending a lot of time at the pickleball court.

"Yes!" I hoot and whistle after Davis scores, tying the match.

Peering up at me, he hoists his paddle in the air. "Thanks, Peach," he shouts, his sweat-dampened face lights up like the Fourth of July.

"Does *our* lady have a preferred champion?" Annoyance bolsters James's tease.

Guilt and mortification flushes my cheeks. While I have been honest with James, I still shouldn't be so obvious in front of him. As much as I believe his feelings for me may just be misplaced or a projection, it's not fair to him for me to gush openly over Davis.

I clear my throat and holler down with an apologetic smile. "You're all my champions."

"Don't worry about making Lord Short Breeches feel better. This isn't a 'Everyone Gets a Trophy' game, so go ahead and cheer loudly for me and Goggles. We're dominating Pretty Boy and Lord Sour Puss," Lars snarks, slapping Davis's back.

"Dominating?" Jackson straightens. "You *just* tied it."

"You should know better than anyone that I enjoy the chase."

"That *I* do."

"Enough flirting! Get back to the match," James shouts, gesturing at Jackson with his paddle.

They continue to play. While James and Lars are new to pickleball, their athletic prowess matches Davis and Jackson. In fact, at times James and Davis appear to go head-to-head. Each time Davis hits, James seems to hit back. Even jumping in front of my brother from time-to-time. Grunted curse words accompany each thwack of the ball against a paddle and the squeak of sneakers on the court's floor.

I may be new to the rules of pickleball, but I'm pretty sure it's supposed to be more of a team sport. As the game goes on, Lars and Jackson almost fade into the background. With Davis, it appears more involuntary. No matter his movement, the ball is always aimed his way by James's relentless play. He jumps after the ball, cutting my brother off each time, and smacks it towards Davis.

My pulse kicks up with each hit. This isn't just James's fierce competitive spirit. He's gunning for Davis, just as he'd done with the marquis during the horse race in his book.

"Got it!" James calls out, lunging in front of my brother.

Jackson lurches back just as James's paddle comes into contact with the ball. He's hit it with so much anger that the whiffleball whizzes towards Davis with the intensity of a missile. Face scrunched into a steely expression, he volleys it back toward Jackson.

James jumps in front of him. His wild swing sends the ball out of bounds. Leaning forward, he lets out a growl.

"What the fuck, man? We're supposed to be a team!" Jackson yells, his hands on his hips.

James tips his head up and mutters something to my brother that I cannot make out. His face is sweat-kissed as he looks up at me, a scowl twisting his features.

"Shit," I mutter to myself.

He's pissed. It's something I forgot about James's character. He hates to lose. I could offer false comfort that the game he's angry about losing is what he plays on this court, but I know that's only a lie I'm telling myself. Somehow in the brief interaction with Davis—even from up here—James clocked my feelings.

"One more and we win," Lars shouts, plucking up the ball and tossing it toward Davis.

"Okay," he says, catching it.

"Do not be too quick to count me out. I never lose." James's glare flicks between me and Davis.

Again, my understanding of the rules is minimal, but I know to win, you need to score eleven points and be up by two. Right now, Davis and Lars are one point away. Curling my fingers around the metal rail between the balcony and the court below, I suck in a deep breath. The initial excited crackle within me about the game sours with the anger radiating from James.

I just want this to be over. The game. My book boyfriends. All of it. I especially want the little voice hissing inside me that this is all my fault to shut up. *Though, isn't it?*

"Shit!" Davis grunts, swinging and missing.

"Our serve," James shouts, his tone taunt-filled, and rushes to scoop up the ball.

Jackson's head shake communicates that what he's muttering is, no doubt, a sarcastic "Our?" Over the last fifteen minutes of this game, he's spent more time just standing there than playing. It's not like my ultra-competitive brother to just stand by. As competitive as Jackson is, he never pushes out a teammate. He's more the type to push them along.

A queasy familiarity envelopes me. As if I've somehow experienced this scenario before.

They volley the ball back and forth until we return to the match point or whatever it's called in pickleball. Only this time, it's James and Jackson's team. At this point, I should just refer to it as James's team.

James bounces the ball and tosses it into the air. With one smooth swing, he sends the ball sailing towards Davis. Lars lets out a growl while his teammate hits the ball back. It ping-pongs back and forth until…

"Damn!" Davis skids to a stop. The ball, still in bounds, slams to the ground at his feet.

My stomach drops with his visible disappointment. Shoulders hunched and paddle by his side, he shakes his head.

I want to shout, "You did so good" or some equally stupid form of comfort. But what I really want to do is run down there and wrap my arms around him.

Instead, I clap and cheer, "Nice job, guys. You all played awesomely."

James stands tall, his chest a little puffed out. "Some of us played better than others."

"You're a terrible winner, Lord Smug Bastard," Lars grumbles.

"Apologies. I just get a little carried away in competition." He huffs a laugh and strides towards Lars with his hand extended. "No hard feelings, old chap."

Carried away? I bristle.

Those four syllables trigger a memory of excuses from Will.

I just got carried away by your excitement about moving in together.

We just got carried away, and one thing led to another.

Lars begrudgingly shakes James's hand before he saunters to Jackson. The two men shake hands but then embrace, their laugh-filled conversation drowning out the exchange between James and Davis. Taking Davis's outstretched hand, James says something and then peers up at me, an expression I can't read covering his face.

Davis's head tips my way and then back to James. Shaking his head, he lets go of James's hand and steps back. Ripping off his goggles, he looks back up at me, his face twisted with pain.

I shake my head. I don't know what James told him, but

whatever it is, it's not good because the way Davis peers up at me guts me.

"I…I gotta go." he says loudly, spinning.

"What?" Jackson turns to face him.

"Something came up," he shouts, scooping up his bag.

"Davis, wait!" I call.

He looks up at me, his typically boyish smile replaced by a firm line. With a slow shake of his head, he hoists his bag over his shoulder and walks out the door.

I spin on my flip flops, cursing that I didn't wear sneakers, and run toward the stairs. My heart races with each slap of the sandals against the steps to the first floor, hoping I don't fall.

"Davis!" My shout is breathless, as I push through the doors that spill out into the corridor that runs along the courts and locker rooms.

He stops, his back towards me. Shoulders squared, he faces me. "Is *he* why your life is messy?"

CHAPTER TWENTY-TWO

I DON'T WANT TO BE YOUR FRIEND

"Yes," I say, my voice small.

It's the truth. No matter how much I wish it wasn't. No matter what feelings I don't have for James, he's part of my messy life.

"Then you *are* seeing him," he says, a hard edge coats the accusation.

"No, I'm not."

"But *he* says you are."

"He's lying. I'm not seeing him."

"But were you?"

"I…" I release a hard breath. "Sort of. But not really. We never dated, but we had a plan to go on a date. A plan I ended because I don't want to be with him. I want to be with you. I choose you." I step closer, taking his hands.

"Choose me?" he scoffs, yanking his hands away. "So, it is what he said it was. That this is just a game with you as the bachelorette and us as the besotted suitors."

"It wasn't a game!" My voice cracks. "At least, I never meant for it to be."

"You didn't mean to? But you did. Were we just options so you weren't alone?" he demands.

"No!" I grab his hands again, forcing his eyes to meet mine. "I would never do that to you. To them. It wasn't like that."

"Then how was it?" His stare is cold, but he hasn't pulled his hands from mine, which emboldens me to continue.

"I'm messy. It's messy. They appeared. Then Jackson thought of this Just Write competition, and I went with it. I shouldn't have. It wasn't a game, but I see how this looks… how this must feel for you. You're right to be angry. I am sorry. I, of all people, know better," I say, realization thickens my throat.

"Just Write? Jackson?" His face pinches.

"Oh god, don't blame him. Don't fire him. This is all my fault. I made the wish. I should have stopped this. Jackson was just trying to help."

"Wish?"

"Your grandpa gave me a lucky penny—although I question its luckiness—and I made an ill-advised wish and tossed it into the fountain at SPN. Next thing I knew, Lars, Owen, and James appeared, and they were all, 'We're here for you, Georgia.' And I'm like, *What?*" —Releasing our joined hands, I gesture wildly—"The whole thing is farcical and unrealistic, but it's real. It's my messy life. The messy life I wanted to keep you from… But here it is, all over you because, according to Lars, I'm all over you."

"Lars? What?" The furrow deepens on his brow.

"His werewolf super smell power detects my scent all over you because of our mating-adjacent activities and my inability to stay away from you like I should. I should leave you alone, but I don't want to, not in the least. I don't want to be friends with you. I want more. To let myself go after what I want, rather than letting the fear that it may not work out hold me back."

I vomit out all the sordid details. Everything that has happened in the last week spills from my lips. How our not-so-cute first date led me to make a wish. The appearance of my book boyfriends and their belief that one of them may be my happy ending. My willingness to choose one of them. My failed attempt to stay away from him. My ultimate decision to choose my own wants. How much I want him, despite knowing that I'm no good for him. I even blather on about my choice not to attend the wedding. Davis just stands there, his eyebrows almost reaching his hairline, and his mouth slack.

When I finish, I rub my temples. "God, this all sounds unreal."

"You think Lars, Owen, and James are book characters?" His question is hesitant, as if approaching a wild animal.

Perhaps, I am. Between my rapid speech and wild gestures, I'm the opposite of cool, calm, and collected.

"It's all unbelievable. At times, even I have trouble believing it, but they are real," I implore.

I'm not entirely sure what I'm asking for. For him to believe me? For him to forgive me? For him to still want me despite everything I've done? *All of the above.*

Even I know that's too much to hope for. This all may be over with Davis. That knowledge snarls inside me. Despite the ache, I don't regret telling him. I may regret my actions, but not my honesty with him.

"I should have told you sooner. You deserved to know this before I started something with you," I murmur.

"But we didn't start anything. Not really." He slumps with a long breath. "We're just friends. You didn't owe me anything, and I shouldn't be angry. Like you said, I wasn't technically part of your little dating competition."

"I'm still sorry. For my actions. For hurting you."

His brows link, seeming to mull over something. "You pumped the brakes. Even if you didn't tell me all this, you were honest that your life is messy and that you couldn't do anything."

I blink. "You believe me?"

He motions between us. "None of this makes sense. Not how this happened. Not that this happened at all. Above all, the fact that I believe you makes no sense. I don't believe that you *believe*, but that *I* believe this is all real. It may be early, but I know you. You may love happy endings, but you're not prone to fantastical thinking. Somehow, you wished characters in your books into real life... Characters I've had ice cream with and played pickleball with. God..." He wrinkles his nose. "This really is happening."

I let out a strangled laugh. "It's so ridiculous, and I should have told you sooner. I just worried that you'd think I was a few chapters short of a novel or making up the worst excuse for not wanting to be with you." I take his hand. "Because I do want to be with you... If you'll have me."

He releases it. "I can't. Like you said, your life is messy. I can't do messy, not again. I've already had someone tug me along with promises of wanting me, only to have them prioritize other things over me."

I bristle. "I wouldn't—"

"But you already did," he cuts in, his tone somber but hard. "You may choose me now, but who says you will make that same choice tomorrow? Who says that tomorrow you won't wake up and decide that whatever responsibility you have to someone else is more important than me? I won't let my heart be played like that. It took too long to put myself back together."

Every protest dies in my throat. He's right. His heart deserves better.

"I understand," I whisper.

"I am sorry, Georgia," he says, curling his fingers around the strap of his bag. "It may be best if we don't see each other anymore... even as friends."

Even though it feels like my heart is shattering, I nod. If I try to speak, I know tears will come.

Turning, Davis moves down the long corridor. The quiet squeak of his sneakers against the tile mocks the painful throb in my chest.

"It is for the best, Georgia." James's smooth English accent causes me to whirl. He stands there, his smug grin casting a sardonic expression on his face.

"Why did you do that?" I glare.

"It needed to be done."

"Why?" Teeth gritted, I stalk closer. "Because you hate to lose, so you ensured you could fix the game. That you could win at any cost, no matter whose heart gets hurt. Even though this isn't a game. It's real life. *My* real life. My heart."

"I play to win, and if Davis truly cared for you, he would too. Instead, he sulks away like a petulant child. If he were worthy, he would fight."

"He is," I hiss. *He is, but I'm not.*

"And yet he walks away."

I say nothing.

"If he were worthy, he would be here. He would do every underhanded thing to get what he wants. That's what a man does when he loves someone."

"And I assume you're *that* man." Fire rages in my veins.

"You have no idea what lengths I would go to"—he prowls closer, causing me to move backward—"in order to get back to the woman I love."

"Back?" I breathe as my back hits the wall.

"Yes, back," he snarls. "I would walk through fire, face any foe, and even pretend to care for *you*, if it got me back to Cecily."

"But you—"

"Pretended." Smirking, he lets out a dark laugh. "Silly Georgia, so desperate to be loved. You are but a means to an end. I would do anything to break this curse. In no world—either mine or this one—do you compare with *her*."

The venom in his confession stirs memories of Will, his caramel smooth voice dripping with pity the last time I spoke to him after Lena's confession. *No matter how much I tried, I couldn't get Lena out of my system. She's not just in my blood-stream, but who causes my heart to pump.* The memory of whimpering, "What was I?" and his indifferent, "Not her" hits like a knife plunged into my heart alongside James's admission.

James towers over me, his hand lifted to my cheek. His soft strokes contrast with his icy stare. It's coolness causing me to shrink inward.

"You are pretty enough, pet, but you don't compare to any of the women we were forced to leave behind because of your wish. Not Selena. Not Ivy. And certainly not Cecily."

"You read the books." My voice is shaky.

"In hopes they would help me find a way to break this curse. They were rather educational." He mindlessly twirls a lock of my hair around his finger. "Owen believes there are pieces of you in each heroine, and he is not wrong. Though I believe each woman is more aspirational than reflective of you. You pale in comparison to each."

You're not her. Will's words and James's insult play together like playground bullies taunting me. That somehow all of this is my fault, because I'm not who they want.

But this isn't about what they want, it's about what I want.

I swat his hand away. "If that's true, then why go for me. Even if you're pretending, none of this makes sense. How would making me fall for you—which I didn't because you disgust me—how does this help you? How does what you did to Davis help you?"

"First, he is a distraction. You need to pick one of us or figure out how to keep your promise, not get caught up in a romance with a man unwilling to fight for you. Second, if one of my compatriots was meant for you, my hope was that my flirtation would spur them to act. Jealousy can be quite the motivator. Though it appears that was for not. Neither of them wanted you either." A serpentine grin tugs at his lips. "Third, I hate to lose."

Will. Acidic bile crawls up my throat, choking my ability to speak. Charming. Competitive. Manipulative. It's all Will, wrapped up in my duke. Just like Will, I had no idea who James truly was.

Green eyes locked on me, his arms bracket me, caging me in. "Fourth, I had hoped that while I was trapped here, we could have a little fun. You may never be Cecily, but there is nothing that says you would not be an enjoyable substitute."

"I am nobody's fucking substitute." I slam my hands against his chest and push him away.

"Now, now, my lady, do not be crass." He *tsks*.

"She's not *your* lady!"

We both spin to find Davis striding down the hall. His gaze is stormy, and his hands are balled into tight fists at his sides.

"You came back." Blinking, I swallow thickly.

"Yeah." Reaching me, he pulls me against him and glowers at James. "And I heard what you said and you're fucking wrong about her. She doesn't pale in comparison to anyone, she's the goddamn sun."

Palms up, James steps back, a dismissive expression etched on his features. "Perhaps, I misjudged you, after all."

"Not as much as Lady Cecily misjudged you." Letting go of me, he steps up to James, his face inches from his. "You're not the misunderstood rake, but a selfish bastard. You don't deserve Lady Cecily, and you certainly do not deserve a woman like Georgia, who assessed your unworthiness and didn't choose you. In fact, I doubt you deserve anyone, you wannabe Mr. Darcy chucklefuck. You *used* Lady Cecily, and you tried to use Georgia, but she saw through your bullshit."

"I never used Cecily."

"You did. Let's not pretend otherwise." He jabs his index finger into James's chest. "You claim to love her, but you used her for your revenge and didn't even have the kindness to allow her to marry someone who actually cared for her. Who doesn't just see her as a means to an end, but their actual endgame. Women like Cecily and Georgia deserve men who know that. Who think of them first."

"I..." Mouth dragged down, James's indignant expression falls.

"Davis," I say softly, placing my hand on his arm.

With a slow rod, he steps back. His arm comes around me and tucks me against him. "Are you okay?" he whispers, placing a soft kiss on my temple.

"Yeah."

"Georgia, I am—"

"Don't speak to her," Davis snarls.

Closing his mouth, James steps back.

"What's going on?" Jackson asks as he and Lars emerge from the court entrance down the hall, confusion contorting their expressions.

"I'm going to take Georgia home, if you could ensure that Discount Darcy stays away from her." Davis takes my hand.

"What the fuck did you do?" Jackson's forward movement is halted by Lars's paw gripping his shoulder.

"Easy." Lars juts his chin toward me. "Should I let your brother at him or..."

"Don't hurt him, please." I face James. "As much as I'd enjoy Jackson and Lars ripping you limb from limb, you don't deserve that. Just as you don't deserve Lady Cecily. You call this a curse, but maybe it's a blessing for Lady Cecily. I should know because I once loved a man who cared more about someone else than he did me... himself." I huff a dismissive laugh. "And it appears I based you on that man."

James opens and then closes his mouth. Emotion dulls his

expression. Whether it's remorse, regret, or self-pity, I don't care. At this moment, his feelings aren't mine to care for.

"Fuck, he is Will." Jackson's mouth drops open. "No wonder I didn't trust him with you."

"Don't worry, rabbit. I'll make sure my bruiser doesn't kill Lord Dickwad. You two, head out." Lars gestures at me and Davis.

"Let's go." I squeeze Davis's hand.

Attention forward, we move down the hall. Well, at least mine is forward. Davis looks behind us from time to time. I suspect it's less about checking if James is following us and more about shooting him death glares. Once outside, Davis leads me behind the building where his vehicle is parked beside some shady maple trees.

"Why did you come back?" I ask, once we're in his car.

"Because I don't want to be your friend." He shifts in the driver's seat to face me.

"I don't understand."

"I want to be more," he rasps, lifting his hands and bracketing my face.

"But you said—"

"I know what I said, and I'm sorry. I'm sorry I said it. I'm sorry I doubted you. Doubted us."

"There's no guarantee," I whisper.

"I know. You may wake up tomorrow and decide you don't want me. I could decide I don't want you, though, that seems very unlikely. Any number of things could happen. You could break my heart in a million ways, and I could break yours..." He clicks his tongue twice. "But we could also make each other's hearts in a million ways. I don't know what the future has in store, but the further I walked away from you, the more I knew I was making a mistake. You said you choose me, well, I choose you... I choose us."

"Davis, you need to kiss me or I'm going to start crying."

A boyish grin curls his lips before he leans in, taking my

mouth with his. My entire body melts into this moment. The press of his lips. The nibble of mine until I open fully for him.

"This is for real, right?" My question is breathless.

"Very much so." He traces the outline of my lips.

"Just checking." I grin. "More kissing, please."

Laughing, he leans in, his smile meeting mine. The gentle current of our kisses turns desperate and hungrier as if we're both starving for one another. Fingers threading into my hair, he kisses along my jawline. His mouth coasts down my neck in languid nips and sucks.

A pleased, greedy sound falls from him.

Back arched, I gasp with the gentle scrape of his teeth along my collarbone. He trails his mouth down to the not-so-subtle hint of cleavage in my tank top. The heat of his kisses cause wildfire to explode within me.

"Davis," I moan.

His hands slip beneath my top, and his rough palms skate up my spine.

"Peach," he murmurs against my skin, his hot mouth dragging back up to meet mine. "We should stop."

"Yeah… Totally…" I pant between our deepening kisses.

"Fuck," he groans with my gentle tug of his hair. "We need to stop."

"Do we?" I breathe.

"Yes." He nips at my ear, "Because the first time I fuck you can't be in my car."

"Oh god." My vagina clenches at the idea of sinking fully onto Davis in his front seat, his hands gripped tight around my ass, urging me on with playful slaps of each globe. "That doesn't sound that bad."

Chuckling, he pulls back. "Oh, I plan to fuck you in this car and a number of other places I've fantasized about since meeting you, but I want our first time to be someplace I can take my time with you. Not something frenzied where someone—including your brother who may or may not still be here—could observe."

"Good call." I scrunch my nose. "You know I have an apartment with a bedroom and a door?"

"Do you now?" He nuzzles my nose with his.

"Does my *not* friend want to come over for a playdate?"

CHAPTER TWENTY-THREE

TRUTH AND PROMISES

Davis doesn't come over. Instead, he wants to go on a date. Since our first date didn't end well and the subsequent interactions weren't dates, per se, he wants to take me out.

"Up or down?" I hold my hair up and then release it, the silky strands falling past my shoulders.

While I trust my own opinion, for tonight I'm tapping into reinforcements. Hope is propped up in her bed amidst a rainbow of the outfits I brought.

Since we're doing dinner and a movie, I went with a pair of hip-hugging black pants—minus the Spanx because I have intentions. The gravity-defying power of my pushup bra, putting the *girls* on full display in my red V-neck flowy blouse, reiterates my hope to indulge in my very unfriendly desires about Davis.

"Since you're wearing the denim jacket with your blouse, I vote for your hair up with some gold hoops." Hope pets Wentworth, who rests his head on her thighs. "Should we anticipate a sleepover with this love nugget tonight?"

"Maybe." I shimmy my hips.

She squeals and claps her hands, causing Wentworth to let

out an annoyed huff. "Sorry, buddy, but your mom is dusting off her vagina. That calls for cheers."

"It hasn't been that long…" I crinkle my nose. Outside of a terrible one-night stand two years ago, my vagina's only visitor has been my vibrator. "God, I hope I still have moves."

"It's like riding a bike." She bats the air.

"Only it's a dick," I quip.

"Language! We have impressionable ears in the room." She tosses a pillow at me. "I swear little Georgia's first words may be a four-letter one thanks to Jackson and you."

"But those are all the best words," I crow, brushing my hair up into a high ponytail.

"Ha!" She mock laughs. "Your dusty vag, aside, how are you doing with all this?"

"You mean knowing that I based James on Will?" I sigh.

It's probably the most disturbing thing about this entire day. Finding out the truth about James's nature isn't as traumatic as knowing who he's based on. Worry nips at me about what it says that the archetype for the dashing duke was the man who so thoroughly broke my heart.

"It's just strange. Until the guys showed up, I hadn't realized how much of my characters I based on real people. You and Owen. Jackson and Lars," I say, motioning with the hairbrush.

"There are a lot of similarities, but they're not carbon copies of us. Lars is like the unpolished version of Jackson… And Owen lacks my sass." She taps her fingers on her thigh. "Though, it makes sense why you'd base those characters on us. We are the two people you're closest to. Especially when you started writing the books. Until the last three years, when you've expanded your social network a bit."

"Yeah, but *why* did I write a Will character?" I grimace. "Oh god, does my subconscious still want him?"

"No!" she laughingly protests.

"Then why?" I toss the hairbrush onto the bed. "Because I

don't want him. If this situation has taught me anything, it's that, as painful as what happened was, I'm grateful for it. Will was a terrible boyfriend. That relationship wasn't at all what I thought it was. I deserved better."

"You deserve everything." Her mouth lifts into a sweet smile. "Maybe you wrote *The Duke's Darling* to say goodbye."

My face scrunches. "We'd already said goodbye."

"Yeah, but I think writing the book allowed you to finally let go of that relationship and the expectations you'd had for your life. You may not have finalized, edited, and published the book until a year ago, but it was three years ago when you finished your initial draft. Three years ago, when you started to get back out there again. To live your life again."

Blinking, I sit on the edge of the bed. The writing and publication table flips in my mind's eye like a picture book telling the story. While indie publishing my books gives me a faster pace than traditional publishing's glacial speed, I take time with each book. Drafting may only take three to four months—*well, until my current work in progress*—but the revision, editing, and other stages of publication may take up to a year or more.

"If the book was about saying goodbye, then why did I have James end up with Lady Cecily?"

"You mean the Georgia-in-Regency-Costume character?" She smirks.

"Yikes! Am I a narcissist as well?" Cringing, I cover my face.

"One character flaw at a time," she teases, tapping her bare foot against my hip. "You did it because you're obsessed with the expected happy ending. You'd never write a romance where the rakish duke remains unreformed and the heroine ends up with the quiet, and a little boring, but sweet marquis."

"She should have ended up with the marquis." I shake my head.

"At least real-life Lady Georgia may end up with the marquis."

"No dukes for me, reformed or otherwise. Never again." Laughing, I stand up and move to stand in front of the mirror hanging on the closet door to slip on my earrings.

"Not to mention, *your* marquis doesn't sound boring. Not in the least."

Happiness fizzes inside me. Davis is nothing like I thought, and somehow, everything I want all in one handsome package. Just like Lady Cecily with the birdwatching Simon Davenport, the Marquis of Hampton, I could have missed out on a sweet man.

"I almost missed my chance with Davis, not just because our first date went so poorly, but because of my own preconceived notions. He could have done everything right, and our time together may still have ended with just that date. When I play back that first date, I see the little ways in which I'd gone into it with the idea that he'd not be *it*. That he wasn't like—"

"The boyfriends from your books."

"God!" I laughingly groan. "Such a cliché."

"We're all a little clichéd at times. I was the girl who pined for her best friend's older brother." She pats her belly. "And look how that turned out. My money is on a happy ending for you."

"Whether things turn out with Davis or not," I add. My gaze meets hers, and certainty curves my lips.

For the first time in my life, I have no idea how things will turn out, or even a sense that they will. If they don't, it doesn't mean my story won't be happy. Every story ends. But how it ends isn't certain. What is certain is that if I only focus on the endings, I miss all the pages in between.

"More importantly, it doesn't matter how it ends. What matters is that I just live it."

"Good girl," she purrs, making us both laugh. "Now, important question, do you have condoms in your purse?

Because I know you're wearing your sexy, barely-there black lace panties and I'm sure they won't be on long."

"Eww…gross," Rem groans, appearing at the door. "I did not need that thought in my head. I may have to give Davis *the talk*."

"You certainly will not." Eyes narrowed, I place my hands on my hips.

"Why do you have your keys?" Hope points at him.

"I'm trying to decide if I want to stay here and be the intimidating older brother when Davis picks her up *or* head over to Jackson's and be the enraged older brother there with Jim or whatever the Duke of Dickery is called."

Per my younger brother, James is currently brooding in his guest room. Needless to say, it's been awkward at Jackson's, but where else is James supposed to go. As much as I'd like to knee him in the balls, I still have a responsibility for his safety. Even if he's been careless with me, I won't be with him. Jackson and Lars are on strict orders not to kill him, nor let him out of their sight. At least until after I meet with the witchcraft consultant tomorrow. Thankfully, Owen will be back from the catering gig soon. If anyone can ensure the peace, it's him and his baked goods.

"I'm leaning toward brotherly intimidation of Georgia's gentleman caller," he teases.

"Why don't you crawl into this bed to snuggle with me and Wentworth instead?" Hope bats her lashes.

"Are you using your feminine wiles to entice me to get in that bed with you, ignoring my brotherly duties?" He arches one blond eyebrow.

She holds up the remote control. "We can watch *Law & Order*."

"Temptress." Laughing, he tosses his keys down on the bedstand and turns to leave. "I'll make some popcorn."

"How quickly he's gone from being pined for to being *the* besotted one," I snark with a playful lilt.

"I assure you, I'm equally besotted." She sighs with contentment. "That was ten percent distraction and one hundred percent me wanting to snuggle with my hubby."

"One hundred and ten percent… Overachiever." I wink.

Saying goodbye to Hope, I grab my purse—which does have an ample supply of condoms—and head down to meet Davis. He's going to pick me up at Hope and Rem's front door.

"Davis," I greet, opening the front door.

"Peach," he murmurs, his gaze sweeps down my body, its heat rouging my cheeks. "You look so pretty."

"Thank you."

"God, calling a woman pretty sounds so cheesy." He rubs his nape. "But it feels right with you. You're probably the prettiest woman I've ever seen."

"I like cheesy." I don't try to hide my giant grin and flushed cheeks.

"Good, because I may be your own personal cheese factory." Mouth tugged up, he holds up a small gift bag. "I brought you this."

"You didn't need to…" I take the bag and a swoop flutters in my abdomen.

"I know, but when I was at the bookstore the other night, I saw them and thought of you."

"You had this with you the *other* night?" The flush on my cheeks deepens, thinking of his shopping bag bearing witness to what transpired against the back gate.

"Yeah." His expression is unrepentant.

Digging into the bag, I pull out a small box. Inside are a pair of dangly earrings in the shape of bookcases. Giddiness invades every inch of my being at how adorable this is.

"I love them," I say, taking out my gold hoops and putting in the earrings. "Thank you." I rise to my tiptoes and plant a grateful kiss on his cheek.

"You brought my sister bookish earrings," Rem drawls,

coming up behind me. "Damn, I want to put the fear in you, but that might be the sweetest thing I've seen a boyfriend do for her. Keep it up."

Shaking my head, I look behind my shoulder. "He's not my boyfriend."

"Not yet." Rem pops a piece of popcorn in his mouth from the bowl in his hand. "The night's still young."

"It's too early for labels." I turn back to Davis.

"Yeah, I agree. It's too early for labels." Davis takes my hand. "It's only five o'clock. Let's see what happens by ten."

"Oh yeah, I'm going to like him," Rem says through a mouth full of popcorn.

It's a short drive from Tustin to Irvine, where we're going for dinner and a movie. It's also where Davis lives and his company is located. He pulls up to a four-story red brick building that appears more residential than commercial.

"Where are we?"

"My place," he says, easing the car into a subterrain garage beneath the building.

I arch one eyebrow. "I thought we were going *out* for dinner and a movie."

"We are." Mischief gleams in his expression.

The car parked, he takes my hand and guides me towards the elevators. He swipes a keycard and pushes the *roof* on the row of floor options. My hand remains in his during the short ride up. The elevator opens to a small glass enclosed lobby that overlooks a rooftop garden. Swiping his keycard again, he unlocks the glass door and leads me onto the roof.

Succulents, bright orange flowers bursting from their vibrant green stalks, and leafy trees in red clay pots create a romantic garden oasis. Ivy twines around a six-foot fence flanking each side of the building, serving as a barrier between the roof and the street below.

In the center of a cluster of bistro tables sits one draped in a white linen tablecloth. A bouquet of pink roses rests at the center of the snowy white covering. In the distance, several outdoor couches and chairs face a large projection screen.

"Rooftop dinner and a movie?" Smiling, I wave towards the little setup.

"Yeah. It's outside, so we're technically out."

"That we are."

He squeezes my hand, still gripped in his. "Sometimes too much peopling takes a lot, out of me and today was *a lot*."

"I'm sorry." I wince. "We could have done this a different night."

"No way." He pulls me close, his free hand coming to my cheek. "I asked you out, remember? This lets me keep my promise for a night out with dinner and a movie."

"And promises are important to you."

"Yes." He caresses my cheek, his gaze open and adoring.

"I like that about you, but if you ever need a break or need something from me, even if it's only space, just say. It's okay to put your needs first, at times. As long as you communicate them… Even if it means breaking a promise."

"If you promise to do the same. Even if you think it may hurt my feelings." He moves his hands to my waist, pulling me flush with him.

I wrap my arms around his neck. "Deal."

"Deal." He bends, nuzzling my nose with his. "I may be peopled out a bit today, but please know that I want to be here with you. I want to enjoy dinner and a movie with you. I took some time after I dropped you off, before I got all this ready, to recharge my social battery."

"At least it's just us, so I'm the only people you need to people with." I peer around the rooftop. "I can't believe you reserved the roof for our date." My face scrunches. "Oh god, I hope you didn't have to pay a huge fee."

"No fee. I just closed it for the night."

"*You* just closed it?"

"Yeah," he draws out the word. "I own this building."

"You own an entire building?" My jaw goes slack.

It's not unknown to me that Davis has money. He's a tech god and CEO, after all. Apps he'd invented are widely used across the financial industry. The revenue from that, and his investors, fund his company. I just didn't think he had "owns a building" money.

He clears his throat. "Um…three."

"You own *three* buildings?"

"Nan did real estate before she retired. She drilled it into me that property is a good investment."

"Thirty-six and you own three buildings *and* are a sexy tech genius turned CEO."

"You think I'm sexy?"

I make a "have you seen you" face and go on, "Am I in a billionaire romance? Oh my god, are you Christian Gray? Do you have a red room with whips and chains?" I waggle my eyebrows.

"No, but I do have a guest room full of *Star Trek* memorabilia, including bobbleheads of each captain." Smirking, he guides me to the table and pulls out my chair.

"Swoon!" I fan myself and take my seat.

"Wait until you see the collection of Enterprise models." He presses a slow kiss to my lips, one that makes me grateful that I'm already seated, thanks to its knee-wobbling impact, before he takes his chair across from me.

We settle at the table. Two place settings sit opposite the flowers. He moves the vase to the side, saying it obstructs his preferred view. and my stomach flips. With Davis, it's the little things that pull me deeper *in like* with this man. Somehow, each small gesture feels huge with him.

Below the table sits a small cooler and an insulated to-go food carrier. He pulls out champagne from the cooler. Popping the bubbly, he pours us each a glass.

"This is very impressive." I clink my glass against his and take a sip, the dry sweetness buzzes on my taste buds.

"Full disclosure, my assistant set this up," he says, his expression is bashful.

"Your assistant." I laugh. "I really am in a billionaire romance."

"Nah. More like 'a guy who's comfortable and lucky enough to have amazing people work with him and are willing to help him out' romance." He opens the food containers and begins to plate our food.

"Not as catchy as billionaire romance." I grin. "This looks amazing." My stomach almost dances with anticipation at the mouth-watering steak, fries, and broccoli covering my plate.

"They're rated number eight for sirloin on GF Finder," he says, unfolding his napkin and placing it on his lap.

"Only number eight," I mock gasp.

"But number two for steak fries."

"Better than Fisher's Landing? How dare you, sir." I pick up a fry and dip it into the ketchup. "Let me be the judge of that."

I don't need to verbalize the results of my assessment. The happy moan that falls out of me with my first bite confirms it.

The only thing tastier than this meal is just being with Davis. Conversation flows easily from topic to topic. Our favorite places to travel. Our current streaming obsession.

We occasionally lapse into snatches of quiet, but even those are not awkward or uncomfortable. It's more like taking a breath. For me, I just sink into those moments, suspecting that he needs them to just let his brain be. He'd once said that his brain is always going in social interactions, trying to decipher cues. I won't pretend I haven't done a bit of googling and followed a few autistic creators on social media to help educate myself, but I know that autism is different for everyone.

"So, today was your first pickleball experience?" He breaks the silence. "Outside of dukes behaving badly, what did you think?"

"If this is your ploy to try to get me to play, I'll warn you I don't sweat sexy."

He chuckles. "I doubt that."

"This is not false modesty. I resemble a strawberry sundae left on the sidewalk on a ninety-degree day." I aim my fork at him. "But I could be persuaded to come watch you play again."

"Minus the duke."

"Minus the duke." My mouth pulls down. "You should never have been put in that situation. I should have been honest with you from the start. I'm sorry I lied."

"We've already gone over this, you didn't lie. You just didn't tell me."

"Which is a lie in a different outfit." I lean back, placing the fork on the table. "As important as promises are to you, the truth is to me. I trusted and loved two people who kept something big from me. Even if they never lied outright to me, because I never asked them what was going on—either because I trusted them or was too scared to see what was happening right in front of me—a lie is a lie no matter how you package it."

"You not telling me about your book men, and what your ex and cousin did are two different situations, but I get it. It's kind of like how even little promises eat away at me to not break—" His face scrunches. "It's funny how we both deal with the aftermath of others hurting us by trying not to emulate their behavior."

"Yeah."

As much as I love stories, I've never had anything but a tight relationship with the truth. After Will and Lena, anxiety twisted in my stomach anytime I lied or withheld something. This is, perhaps, what has been the hardest part of this entire situation.

"I don't want to be like them and somehow…" The hard lump in my throat steals away my ability to finish my confession.

"You're nothing like them." Reaching over, he takes my hand. "Just like I'm not like my dad. Saying that doesn't erase that fear. But, as you told me to be okay with sometimes breaking promises, you do the same. This whole situation is strange, and you made decisions that you thought would cause the least amount of damage. Continuing to beat yourself up about it, especially after I've accepted your completely unnecessary apology, hurts us both."

My head tilts. "How?"

"When someone accepts your apology and you continue to apologize, you're saying you don't believe them. That you think I'm lying."

"I don't think you're lying."

"Good." His mouth quirks. "Then we agree. You're not a liar and neither am I, so no more apologizing for Owen, Lars, and the Duke of Chucklefuck."

"Deal." My mouth ticks up in a grateful smile.

"Deal." He releases my hand and picks up his fork. "So, back to pickleball. You said you may be willing to come again?"

"Yeah." I pick up my fork. "It's amazing to watch you play. You have this catlike grace on the court. You're so sure in all your movements and this relaxed joy radiates off you. Well, when some asshole isn't gunning for you, that is."

He dabs his mouth with the napkin. "It's why I love it. All the sports Pop encouraged me to play as a kid were all team-based. I love them, but there's a lot of managing myself and everyone else. I must anticipate what my opponents want and what my teammates need. As much as athletics gives me a structure to interact with people where I know the rules, for the most part, there's still a level of anticipating necessary."

"But don't you have to do that in pickleball, too?"

"Not completely. When I play head-to-head, it's just me and my opponent. When I play doubles, it's just my teammate and our opponents. It may not make sense to anyone else, but fewer people equals less pressure. It's more manageable."

"It must take a lot out of you to run an entire company," I say, taking a sip of my bubbly.

"I almost didn't start my company because of fear. I worried about what that pressure might do. As a kid, I'd get overstimulated, resulting in meltdowns and such, making foster parents see me as too much trouble. I just wanted to be like everyone else, but I wasn't. So, I used to mask a lot."

Several of the autistic influencers I follow talk about masking. It's something many of them do either consciously or unconsciously to tamp down their natural autistic tendencies. From what they shared online, while it may offer temporary relief in a world that doesn't embrace neurodiversity, it can have a severe impact on the autistic person. That knowledge causes me to worry about the pressure of running a company like No Boundaries might have on Davis.

"I'd force myself past my limitations, causing burnout. Things would be foggy, impacting my ability to focus or be present. I'd have trouble speaking. Sometimes, I'd be so exhausted that I couldn't get out of bed for days," he says.

Reaching across the table, I thread our fingers. "Does this still happen?"

"I still do some masking, but not as much. Still, the burnout does happen from time to time. It was a major issue in high school and my first few years of college. My moms found me a therapist who has helped me establish coping strategies."

"Such as?" I soothe my thumb in slow strokes against his hand.

"A good support system. People who know me and understand me, or at least, try to. Doing what I need to do daily to take care of myself. Like taking breaks after I've peopled too much." He squeezes our joined hands. "Also, knowing the signs and what I need to do to take care of myself. I imagine it's similar with your celiacs?"

"Yeah," I murmur. "And those strategies have been helping?"

He nods. "There are days I'm wiped out. But I know if I had to do it all over again, I'd still make the same decision."

"What you're doing with No Boundaries is amazing," I say, worry nipping at me. "Please don't take this the wrong way, but you said you worried it would be too much. Do you still have that worry?"

"Yes."

"And you still carry on? You could probably fade into the background and let someone else run things."

"I could and, maybe, one day I will. But not now." Leaning toward me, he lifts our joined hands to his lips and presses a gentle kiss on my knuckles. "I like that you worry about me."

"It's kind of my thing, remember?" My mouth slants into a teasing smirk.

"As long as you leave a little of that for yourself."

"I'm working on that."

"In the meantime, I can worry for you." He sits back, his hand still linked with mine.

"I'd like that."

CHAPTER TWENTY-FOUR

AN OUTDOORSY GIRL?

After dinner, Davis cleaned up and then appeared with popcorn, gluten free Oreos, and two diet sodas. Despite being full from our meal, there's something about movies that brings out the snacker in both of us. Snuggled close on the outdoor sofa, we munch on the popcorn from the shared bowl in my lap and watch *Star Trek: Generations*.

"Do you ever think you'll write a Sci-Fi romance?" he asks as the credits roll on the screen.

"I'm not sure what I'll write next... *or* if I will," I say, my voice quiet.

Even after the talk with Doc this week, I'm still stuck. This morning, before everything, I sat on my couch with my laptop, and nothing came. Each idea I considered just wandered in my mind, without forming sentences or paragraphs, let alone an entire chapter. I thought that by letting go of the expectations for what I believed I needed to do, that it would free the stories within me. But they remain locked away.

"Maybe my stories really are gone," I whisper my confession.

"That can't be true." His mouth purses. "The force is too

strong with you. Even if you hadn't been the Yoda to my romance education, your passion and talent oozes from every page of your books." Forehead creased, he sits up. "Is it because of this situation? Because of Lord Fuckwad?"

"First, blasphemy. You do not make *Star Wars* references while we're watching *Star Trek*." My tap on his chest is playful. "No, this we can't blame on James. I've been blocked for months. Every time I start something, it just doesn't work."

"What doesn't work?"

"The ending." Sighing, I lean against the sofa cushion. "When I write a book, it's like watching a movie in reverse. The ending comes first, and then I reverse engineer the story to get there."

"And that's not working?"

"No," I whine. "I've started four different manuscripts in the last six months with no progress beyond the first twenty thousand words."

His brow dips. "Do all writers start with the ending?"

"Every writer does things a little differently. Your grandpa thinks that my intense focus on the ending is what's blocking me. That I should let the story just breathe and listen to what it has to say to me." I scoff a laugh. "It's silly, but I hoped letting go of the expectations in my actual life about how things should end might free the words. Like they were blocked because I was blocked in my own life by the concept of endings. Like going to Lena and Will's wedding to show that I'm over what happened and complete that heartbreak to badass arc..." I motion between us, "...or by pausing my life to figure out how to fulfill an accidental wish."

Nodding, he seems to consider something before speaking, "I don't write books, but I do write code, so I get it. With apps, we start with what we want it to do and work backwards."

"And what happens if you get stuck?"

"We try to figure it out, but if we can't, we tweak the final product. If the coding isn't there yet, it doesn't mean the app won't work. We just adjust what it will look like."

"The app serves the code, not the code serving the app," I mutter.

"Huh?" He tilts his head.

"It's something your grandfather said about the ending serving the story versus the story serving the ending."

"Pop and his sage advice." He smirks. "For what it's worth, I don't think starting with the end is the issue, but not being open to tweaking that ending may be. Let that ending inspire you to start the story, and then let that story reveal itself to you. It may surprise you and be far more than what you'd originally thought."

I can't help but think of my book boyfriends at this moment. All three men are different from what I wrote for them. Both Lars and Owen express a desire for a happy ending different than what I wrote. The stories I wrote aren't bad, they're just not their stories.

Neither is the story I wrote about Davis. After I walked out on him at Fisher's Landing, I thought he'd just be a footnoted bad date.

"I have a recent appreciation of stories turning out differently than I thought," I say, my voice is breathy.

"Yeah." He leans close, and playful wickedness flashes in his beautiful eyes.

"Yeah," I say, every drop of tension dissolves into the ooey gooeyness inside me. This man.

Something about the way Davis looks at me feels like a warm embrace, as if his strong arms had already enveloped me. This man is quickly becoming my comfort food. His presence is both nourishing and decadent.

"It may not seem like it now, but I believe you have many stories still in there, and I know you'll be able to hear them... when you're ready." He nuzzles his nose along my jawline. "Just don't write anymore dukes."

Laughter bubbles out of me. "Deal."

"Deal." He presses a string of gentle kisses from my chin to the corners of my mouth until he captures my lips in a slow embrace.

The buzz in my bloodstream grows with each kiss. Davis's languid kisses are like savoring sips of an expensive wine; both restrained to not consume too quickly but greedy for every drop.

"Davis, wait," I say breathless, scooting from him, his head tilting.

Placing the popcorn bowl down on the wicker coffee table in front of us, I unwrap the little moist towelettes he'd brought with the snacks and clean off my hands. "Would you mind cleaning your hands?" I grab a second towelette and hand it to him.

His right eyebrow quirks. "Why?"

"Because you likely have salt and butter on it from the popcorn, and I'd prefer not getting it all over me." I flash a sultry expression.

In one of my books, I wouldn't write my characters stopping to clean their hands. Their passionate kisses would just lead to a sexy romp with no thought of what fingers slathered in butter and salt may do to one's lady bits. But this isn't a book, this is my life, and as messy as it is, I'd prefer my vagina be unsalted and unbuttered.

Nodding, his mouth forms an *O*. He opens the packet and cleans his hands.

"Do you want to go down to my apartment?"

I crawl onto his lap. "Nope."

"Here?"

I slip my jacket off and drop it on the sofa beside us. "Is that okay?"

"Very okay." His hands coast down my body, cupping my backside. "The back gate, almost the car, and now the roof... Perhaps, you are an outdoorsy girl."

"Perhaps... Or maybe you just bring a more adventurous side out of me?" Clasping his face, I lean in and take him in a deep kiss.

There's no sweet preamble or tease. I want him, and I'm not holding back, not anymore. He opens fully for my demanding kisses. A pleased moan rumbles in his throat as my tongue slides over his.

His fingers curl tight around my ass, settling me on his growing erection. I move against him. The friction fans the wantonness crackling inside me. Tugging my blouse off, I toss it on top of my jacket and then remove my bra. Goosebumps erupt across my heated skin with the lick of cool air over my naked upper half.

Davis's gaze meanders down my body, his eyes dark with need.

"I like the way you look at me," I murmur.

"How do you think I look at you?" He trails one finger in a slow glide from the top of my belly button up my torso.

"Like you want to savor and gobble me up," I say with a tiny hitch of breath.

"Mm hmm." He leans in and flicks his tongue against my right nipple. "Perhaps, I'll do both."

"Oh god," I whimper.

"God? I'll have to do better, so it's my name you're moaning," he hums against my skin before taking the hard bud into his mouth.

Back bowing, my fingers thread into his hair, keeping him in place. The combination of his animalistic noises, the loveliness of his mouth on me, and the friction of our middles coming together cranks the tension tight at my center. With nipping kisses, he moves to my other breast.

"Yes." I move against him, chasing relief.

"Does my greedy girl want more?" he rasps and then bites on my nipple before soothing the tip with gentle strokes of his tongue.

"Yes!"

He kisses upward, sucking along my neck. "Do you know how sweet you taste?"

"And you haven't had all of me yet."

"Is that an invitation?"

I grind myself against him. "Yes."

"Fuck," he groans, flipping me off him and onto the sofa.

Before I'm able to get my bearings, he slips off my shoes and drops them in front of the coffee table. Standing between my legs, he bends, his arms coming to either side of me, and takes my mouth in a ravenous kiss. With slow kisses down my body, he lowers to his knees before me, his hands stroking along my thighs. His sinful smirk teases with the unbuttoning of my pants.

My pulse thuds as he slowly drags my pants down my legs. My barely-there black lacy panties soon follow. Tossing my clothes aside, he spreads my legs wide. His fingertip glides up my inner left thigh, across the small triangle of hair along my pussy, and down the inside of my right leg.

"Look at you," he says, his voice hoarse and dark. "I wish you could see how fucking beautiful you are."

"Tell me," I murmur.

He makes a pleased noise in his throat. "This soft, flushed skin. These thick thighs that I've dreamed about burying myself between since I walked into that bar and saw you in that short black dress."

"Thick thighs?" I laugh.

"Yep." He grips them tighter, causing a soft moan to fall out of me. "Maybe it's the wrong thing to say, but I love your thick thighs. I fucking *love* your body. It's soft, strong, and sexy."

The way he looks at me is thrilling, like he's both a starved wolf ready to devour and a devoted acolyte on his knees in worship. He doesn't just appreciate my body, but revels in it.

He rises, his mouth coasting down my neck, sucking and

nipping the flesh. "This long throat. Your silky skin. These pink nipples and lovely tits of yours."

My laugh is cut off by his hard suck of each peak.

"And this pussy…" He slides his finger along my wet center licking his lips. "Look at how pretty it is, all wet for me already. I already know I'll never have my fill of you."

"Why don't you…find out," I barely get the command out due to his unhurried caresses against my clit.

"Gladly." Straightening, he takes off his glasses and sets them on the coffee table and then rips off his shirt.

The *ready to work* expression on his face and the sight of his sculpted torso twines the crank in my core just a little more. The only thing I want more than this man's mouth on every inch of me is to lick along the cut planes of his stomach before I fall to my knees.

"I want to see you." Breathless, I sit up, grabbing him by the belt and tugging him closer.

"Wait your turn." He uncurls my hand from his belt and shakes his finger playfully. "Now, spread your legs."

The command in his tone zings pleasure through me. Doing as he asks, I sit back and open wide for him. He lowers to his knees in front of me. Gripping my hips, he coasts his tongue in a slow lick down my seam. I almost want to cry with the sensation of his tongue against me. My entire body pulses between sweet relief and begging for more. Each lick and suck both satisfies and teases out more want in me.

The feral noises he makes during his focused ministrations leave me feeling that I am both his meal and his queen. He worships and devours. My sex-fogged brain is unable to discern which, and my body just rejoices in it.

"Davis!" I cry as a violent tremor shakes my thighs with my release.

"I could do this all night." He soothes his fingers in gentle strokes against my shaking thighs.

"I may not last," I pant out my laugh.

"Oh, you'll last."

I pull him up and take him in a deep kiss, his arms banding around my back, and our naked torsos finding each other. "I do taste sweet." I smirk.

He laughs.

Biting my lower lip, I undo his belt. "My turn to find out how you taste."

"Fuck," he groans with pleasure as I slip my hand inside his jeans and cup him over his underwear.

"Someone is eager." Batting my eyes, I massage him over the fabric, his cock jerking with my touch.

"Peach…"

Eyes locked with his, I drag down his jeans and his boxers. Giggles burst from me at his trying to kick them off his sneakered feet. He plops beside me on the sofa, laughter raking through him.

"This never happens in your books," he grumbles, kicking off his shoes and then removing the rest of his clothes.

"It sure doesn't," I tease, crawling onto his lap, his hardness rubs against my still-sensitive pussy sending a shiver through both of us. "That may not happen in my books, but this does." Slipping off his lap, I drag my mouth down his body until I fall to my knees in front of him.

"Wait," he says, pulling me back up. "To protect your knees." He moves his clothes in front of him, providing a cushion.

'Oh god." My breath catches. "I am in very real danger of falling so fucking hard for you."

"Ditto." He reaches out and tucks me close for a sweet kiss.

Pushing him back, I rest my thighs on my heels in front of him. Skating my fingers along his muscular legs, I take him in. The ridges of his stomach. The dusting of dark hair along his chest, the silky fur marching down to his thick length.

Licking my lips, I skate my fingers along the veiny shaft to the tip coated in beads of pre-cum.

"This may be more of a meal than I anticipated," I say, my voice husky and teasing. "But I like a challenge."

He groans with my slow pumps of his length. Leaning forward, I lick the tip and let out an appreciative moan at its salty taste. I swirl my tongue around his tip, massaging the crown. Inch by glorious inch, I take him more fully into my mouth. His controlled hip thrusts, and gentle tugs on my hair telegraphs his battle for restraint. It's clear he wants more but holds himself back.

I'm almost drunk with power at the fact that this man's desire for me is only tamped down by *his* want to take care of me. That knowledge surges need within me. Need to give him what he wants. Need to take what *I* want… And what I want is to feel him coming apart.

Releasing him, I look up through hooded lashes. "Do you want to come in my mouth or inside me?"

"There's a condom in my jeans' pocket," he breathes.

I grab it and hand it to him. He unwraps it and rolls it on.

"Get on my lap," he growls.

"I do like bossy you," I sass, rising and straddling him.

A pleasure-filled whimper escapes with the sensation of him sliding into me. The fullness is almost too decadent. It's like a buffet of sweets. One knows they've had enough but still goes back for more.

I rock my hips in gentle movement against him, testing out taking just a little bit more. With each rock, my body relaxes.

Hands on my waist, he urges me further until I'm fully seated on him, causing him to let out a grunted "Fuck."

"You like?" My playful coo is breathless.

"So fucking much."

I move up and down on him. The movement both teases

him and hits different spots within me, surging that twinge of pleasure.

"That's my girl," he whispers in my ear. "Take what you need." With a soft slap of my ass, he urges me on.

"Yes," I whine, my nails digging into his shoulders.

"You like that?"

"Yes." I moan with his second slap.

Our panting breaths and moans meld with the soundtrack of the world below us: car honks, people laughing, and dogs barking in the distance. Somehow, we're both utterly secluded from it, but aware of it. That idea heightens my chase.

His hips meet mine in indulgent, hard thrusts. Despite the deliciously rough brush of our bodies, the tenderness of his gaze locked on me is like a soft caress. His body may demand, but that stare gives.

"I'm so close," I moan.

"Tell me what you need." He strokes my cheek.

Taking his hand, I move it to where we're joined.

"You need both." His rough callouses against my clit sparks more sensation.

"Yes!"

His mouth covers mine, drinking up my cries. Fingers biting into my hips, he thrusts into me. The action prolongs the waves of orgasm raking through me and heralding his own.

"Peach!" he calls out, his body's shudder rolls through both of us.

Our breaths ragged, we remain tethered together. My head on his shoulder, and his arms banding around me. Despite the kiss of cool air against my skin, now clammy from sweat, I have no desire to move away from this man.

"You were wrong," he murmurs.

Brows knitted, I lift my head. "About what?"

He traces along my sweat-dotted hairline. "You definitely sweat sexy."

CHAPTER TWENTY-FIVE

FOLDED PANTIES AND GLUTEN FREE BREAD

Davis Makenzie is a lather, rinse, and repeat type of snuggler. After we got into bed last night, post-shower, he pulled me into his nook. His hand slid under the T-shirt he'd lent me and he rubbed soothing strokes on my flesh while we talked until I fell asleep. Later, I woke up to find him, face down in his pillow, beside me before I dozed off again. Now, I lie on my side while Davis is pressed tight to my back, his arm slung over my middle.

Contentment sighs through me at another learned factoid about this man. Since last night, I've collected facts like seashells, documenting my first visit to Davisland. Like, how despite the beige walls and neutral brown furniture, he has an assortment of *Star Trek* novelty glasses in his kitchen. Or how he organizes his bookshelves by genre, one shelf now dedicated to the romance books he's bought. I was also pleased to find that his shelves were not reserved for just books by white, heterosexual, non-disabled cis male authors. His preferred genres appear to be nonfiction, fantasy, and Sci-Fi.

I also got a tour of his *Star Trek* Museum, which is what I dubbed his guest room last night. Each item reveals more and more about this man as he pointed out his various treasures.

Stories about how or where he got them. How his moms took him to a *Star Trek* convention for his sixteenth birthday. The show's importance to him.

"It's not that Star Fleet was perfect, but the Enterprise welcomed almost everyone. Everyone had a place," Davis said as he ran his fingers along the display case of miniature Enterprise models.

"Even androids." I tease.

"I think Data was who I related to the most. He appeared human, but wasn't. Still, he belonged to their…"

"Family," I finish for him. I wrap my arms around his middle and squeeze tight.

"So much of my life, I felt like I didn't fit."

"I get it." I tip my head up to look at him. "I was always sick as a kid, which led to me missing a lot of school and fun things. While my celiac diagnosis helped, a lot of parents didn't want to deal with the food allergy kid. I was healthy, but still missed out… And even when I was invited. I still couldn't fully participate. No cakes. No pizza. All the things."

"You'll always have cake with me." He leans in, pressing a sweet kiss.

"And you fit with me," I murmur, our gazes tethering.

The memory makes my insides all gooey. With each moment spent with this man, I like him even more. Right now, the need to pee is stronger than the feeling raging inside me than my like of Davis. Wiggling from beneath his arm, I slip out of bed without waking him. As I take one last glance at him, the blanket bunched at his middle exposing his naked torso, a gentle snore buzzes from him. A smile on my face, I tiptoe to the bathroom.

There, I take care of my business, use the spare toothbrush Davis gave me last night, and splash some cold water on my face. My freshly laundered clothes sit in a neat, folded pile atop the counter. Post last night's rooftop romp, he'd offered to wash my clothes, so I had something clean for today after he'd asked me to sleep over.

"This man." I chuckle, staring at my perfectly folded clothes.

Davis's thoughtfulness is like an unexpected rainstorm on a hot day. It alleviates and nourishes all at the same time. Each time I think I know what to anticipate, he does something romantic, like folding my underwear. Even I don't do that. I just toss it in my drawer.

Smiling, I pad to the living room. As much as my body craves to crawl back in beside Davis, I don't want to risk waking him. It's only seven, and he may not be an early riser like me. Most weekends, I wake early to walk Wentworth and then write, so my internal clock is preset. Whether he is a morning person or not will just be one more factoid I learn about him.

At least the quiet will give me time to mull over a few ideas. Last night, lying in bed, I shared some of the stories I've started and stopped over the last six months. The current work in progress is a soccer romance about the team's publicist and the star player. I have this whole *Never Been Kissed* moment where he proclaims his love for her minutes before the game starts and just as it appears she won't show, the publicist emerges onto the field. The ending is so clear that I can almost touch it. But I'm stuck. I just keep rewriting a scene with the team's goofy mascot and the female main character, where he teases her about liking the star player.

Curled up on Davis's couch, I pull up the manuscript's backup file on my online drive through my mobile. The phone isn't my preferred way to work on manuscripts, but from time to time, I'll jot notes or draft things on it if I don't have my laptop with me.

"Patrick," I mutter the mascot's name and tap a finger against my chin.

This is supposed to be just a comedic relief scene after

Elsie, the female main character, has a negative interaction with a sexist sports reporter. But it keeps turning into more. Too much banter. Too much bonding.

"Too much chemistry." My eyes grow wide.

Is this why I can't move forward? Eyes closed, I play the scene in my head. Their tease-filled exchange leading Patrick to help the romantically challenged Elsie woo her soccer player. That's where I stop every time, because this isn't supposed to be a *Cyrano de Bergerac* retelling.

"But what if it is?" Mischief lifts the corners of my mouth into a large grin.

That's exactly what I'm doing, being mischievous. The ending could still work, but what if it's not Logan, the team's star, but Patrick, the goofy but adorable mascot?

My eyes snap open. As if they have a mind of their own, my fingers fly over the little keyboard on my phone. The stream of consciousness flows out of me. Later, once I have time to sit on my laptop, I'll fix the many, many grammar, spelling, and word flow issues. Right now, I'm just listening to the story. For the first time in months, giddy excitement pulses through me as I write. Though I know I'll regret this tiny screen when a migraine comes, but this is too good to let go.

"God, you're beautiful." Davis's hoarse voice pulls my attention.

He leans against the entry to the living room. His hair is sleep-mussed, and a lazy smile flexes at the corners of his mouth.

"Thank you." I bite my lower lip.

His brow dips. "Did I say that out loud?"

"Yup… And I'm not complaining."

"Good." He saunters over to me. "I plan to say it a lot." He nestles beside me and tucks me into his chest.

"Excellent plan." I relax into him. "As long as you're okay with me telling you how dreamy you are."

"Not dreamy enough to keep you in bed with me." Nuzzling his nose in my hair, he loops his arms around my middle.

"I didn't wake you, did I?"

"Nah. I usually get up at eight on the weekends to work out."

"Eight?" I blink. "I didn't realize I've been working that long."

"Are you writing on your phone?"

"Yeah. I pulled up the soccer romance idea I told you about last night and have been allowing the story to speak to me. I must have lost track of time."

"That's great, Peach." He squeezes me. "I'm sorry I interrupted your flow."

"This is the best interruption." I tip my head up and offer a sweet smile.

He smiles back. "Proposal."

I arch one eyebrow. "Last night was fantastic sex, but not 'run off to Vegas after our second date' good."

"Snarky comments like that remind me that you and Jackson are related." He chuckles with an eye roll. "Since I know you write most weekend mornings and it's been a while since you've had the flow, why don't you borrow my computer. I'll hit the gym downstairs for an hour, and then after, we can do breakfast before I take you home."

"I wouldn't want to—"

"Let me work out, keeping my weekend regimen, while you write and keep yours? If these sleepovers become a regular thing, which, frankly, I hope they do, we need to integrate each other into our lives. Might as well start now."

Yet another factoid about Davis for my collection. Not the part about waking up by eight on the weekends to work out, but that he wants more of this. More of me.

Sitting up, I shift to face him. "Show me your computer."

An hour later, I lean back in his desk chair, my arms high overhead in a long stretch, and soak in the happiness washing over me with the thousand words added to my manuscript this morning. With a pleased, self-satisfied smile, I save my work on my online drive and send a backup to my email. Too many horror stories of authors losing ninety-thousand-word manuscripts reinforce the need to back up my backups of my writing. Pushing away from his desk, I shuffle down from the little alcove between the bedrooms toward the kitchen. Both the grumble in my stomach and the knowledge that Davis will be back soon, has me in search of food.

He'd said we'd have breakfast after our morning routines were wrapped up. Not sure if he meant to go out or eat here. No doubt, he'll be hungry after his workout, so it would be nice to surprise him with food.

Opening the fridge, I peruse the contents, locating veggies, cheese, and eggs for omelets and some raspberries and blueberries for a side. My mouth drags down with his already unsealed butter container, indicating it's been used. Since I can't verify that it hasn't come into contact with gluten, I may just make Davis an omelet and snack on some of the chopped veggies and the berries.

As I'm closing the fridge, an unopened container of butter, next to a still-sealed jar of jam, on the fridge's door shelf snags my attention. Both are marked with a large *P* in black Sharpie.

Looks like I do get to have an omelet after all! Wiggling my hips, I grab the unopened butter and place it on the counter with the rest of the ingredients.

After three misses, I find the pans in the cabinet below the countertop stove. Placing a large skillet on a burner, I notice a loaf of gluten free bread beside a toaster still in the box. Blinking, I scan the kitchen. On the other side of the stove sits whole wheat bread and a second toaster. One still plugged into the wall.

"No." Head shaking, I run back to the fridge and swing it open.

On the top shelf, I find sealed containers marked with a *P*, including yogurt, cream cheese, salsa, and sour cream. Their identical matches, only unsealed and without a *P*, are located on the shelf below. Laughter wooshes out of me as I find another thing of jam, again not labeled, which is unsealed, on the bottom rack in the fridge's door. In almost a possessed state, I rifle through his cabinets finding an assortment of gluten free snacks: chips, pretzels, popcorn, cereal, crackers, and cookies. Some of which are my favorites that I've mentioned

You'll always have cake with me. His words from last night are the reason my cheeks are lifted with a large grin.

"Why a P?" My breath catches. "P for Peach."

Shutting the cabinets, I lean against the kitchen island, my gaze locked on the unopened butter beside the pile of ingredients next to the stove. *All of this is for me.* To make sure that I'm comfortable. That, here, I belong.

"Were you going to cook? That's sweet. But I planned to cook for you. You're the guest, after all," he says, striding into the kitchen, shirt damp with sweat and face glistening.

"Did you buy new butter and jam for me?" I peer at him, my pulse kicking up.

"Yeah."

"And bread?" I point to the counter.

"Yeah." His face wrinkles.

"And a *toaster*?"

"Yeah."

"Not to mention my own versions of things *and* so many gluten-free snacks?"

"Yeah… Did I do something wrong?" He rubs the back of his head.

Pushing off the counter, I rush to him and fling myself into his arms. "So right." I press my smile against his.

This is the opposite of being cool about this. I should flash a coy smile and say, "Oh, that's sweet." Instead, I choose to tackle him in his own kitchen with fevered kisses. With how his lips meet each press and the tightness of his arms banded around me, it's clear he's onboard with my lack of aloof coolness.

"You are about the sweetest man," I pant between kisses.

"Did you see the gluten-free French fries in the freezer?" he murmurs, his low timbre humming through me.

"You didn't?" I whimper.

"Yup." He lifts me onto the counter, his large body coming between my legs.

"I was so wrong."

"About what?" His hands still on my bare thighs.

"I'm not in danger of falling for you, I'm already falling."

"Ditto." He smiles.

"Do you want to fuck me on this counter or take me back to your bed?" I slide my hand beneath his T-shirt, skating my fingers across the muscular cuts.

"Not beating around the bush, eh?" A loud bark of laughter sprints out of him.

"I have other things I'd prefer you do with my bush." I skate my finger along his happy trail, my voice dripping with sultriness.

"My sweet, silly Peach." He nuzzles along my chin. "But I'm all sweaty and gross."

"Make me all sweaty and gross, then we're even," I coo.

"You do sweat sexy… Hold on." Gripping me tight, he lifts me into his arms.

"I'm too heavy." I giggle my protest.

"Nope," he grunts, his face pinched.

I cling to him like a horny, but slightly terrified koala. While having a man carry me into the bedroom to ravage me is a fantasy many romance readers have, I don't want to be dropped on the floor. Davis's muscular physique and broad shoulders indicate regular weightlifting in his workout regime but I fear I may be too hefty for him.

With several quick strides, he deposits me on the top of the dining room table. The surface is cool against my bare ass. Despite being awake for over two hours, I've not changed from the *Real Men Drink Earl Gray* T-shirt with Captain Picard's likeness that Davis had lent me. A shirt I plan to steal.

"See, I am too heavy for you," I tut playfully.

"Hardly. I'm just hungry."

"And I'm your meal." I offer a nipped kiss.

"Yep." With a rakish grin, he yanks off my T-shirt and then his, tossing both aside.

I trail my finger down his chest. "Someone's ready to work for his meal."

Winking, he takes off his glasses and places them on the table. "No work... this is all play."

"Oh," I gasp, his mouth coming to my left breast, sucking and licking the nipple.

Back bowed, heat surges between my legs with his focused work on my breasts. His rough hands massage my outer thighs. The rasp of the mesh fabric of his shorts against my naked core teases pleasure. Need bounds within me when he drags his mouth down my body. Hand placed on my stomach, he eases me back until I'm prone on the table. Gripping my thighs, he lifts me to meet his mouth.

"God," I whine with the first slow lick.

The slide of his tongue against me is akin to the first taste of ice cream on a winter's day. It's unhurried because there's no fear that it will melt away. There is plenty of time to relish every last drop. Despite the grind of my hips and little whimpered pleas, he keeps his pace. The slow march will be my undoing.

"Davis, please." Rising to my elbows, I look at him, my breath ragged.

He lifts his gaze, his pupils as wicked as a starless night. "Be patient. I'll make sure you're taken care of. Just let me enjoy this. I've worked up an appetite and your pussy is too good not to savor." He takes my clit in his mouth in a hard suck, rolling it with his tongue.

"Oh go...go...go...god," I stammer, lying back, my chest heaving.

His eyes may be as black as night, but this man has me seeing stars. The orgasm that rips loose with his final suck has fireworks exploding in my vision. Body still shaking, he lifts me and moves me to bend over the table. His hand and mouth soothe along my trembling form. Kissing down my spine, he caresses the globes of my ass.

"You're so pretty like this. Sated but still hungry for more." He slides one hand between my legs and pushes a finger inside me.

"Ooh. More?" I moan.

"I told you I was going to take care of you." He pats my ass with his free hand. "Legs wide like a good girl."

A strangled whimper of unintelligible words tumbles out of my mouth. My body clenches around his finger.

He bends close, nipping at my earlobe. "Does someone like being called 'good girl?"

"I guess I do," I pant out.

Right now, my lust-filled brain isn't ready to process this newly-realized praise kink. Apparently, it's not just my female main characters who enjoy a man doing depraved things to them while calling them a good girl.

Legs wide, I jut my backside out, moving against his working finger. Promised pleasure twines tight. My taut muscles are begging for relief.

"This is how you like it, isn't it?" he rasps. "You like it slow at first." He plays with my clit, while his other finger glides in-and-out of me, making me whimper. "Then a little more."

I cry out as he inserts a second finger inside me.

"That's my sweet Peach." He crooks his fingers.

Like a coming storm, sex with Davis starts slow with languid strokes and kisses but gains momentum until it's a steady downpour. The building tension makes my legs wobble, but I don't need to worry. Davis has me. His left arm loops around my middle, steadying me, while he works me.

"I'm gonna... Davis!" I scream, my nails dig into the table's surface with the force of my release.

He lifts my shaking form into his arms like I weigh nothing. Self-satisfaction sparks in his features as he carries me into his room.

"Light as a feather," he teases, tossing me onto the bed and crawling atop me.

"Stiff as a board." I run my hand over the tented fabric of his shorts.

Laughing, he takes my mouth. The hard kiss bruises in the best way. The way that tells me that this man is on fire for me. His dark eyes, demanding kisses, and the press of his hardness against me inflame my desire for more.

"Pants off. Condom, now," I command between kisses.

He rolls off me. Discarding his clothes, he opens the bedstand drawer and grabs a condom.

"Care to try a new angle?" I coo, getting on all fours, and tossing a saucy expression over my shoulder.

"This ass," he praises with a little tap causing me to let out a soft moan.

"No butt stuff yet."

"I like that you said *yet*." He grips my hips, his hard cock rubbing against me.

My answering laugh is cut off by his slow push into me. Hips high, I bury my face in the pillow with his indulgent drives. It doesn't take me long to be at the brink again. Not with his deepening pumps, filthy praises, and stroke of my clit. Like a stealthy orgasm cat burglar, this man somehow knows the combination to unlock every ounce of pleasure from me.

"Davis!" My cry is muffled by the pillow.

Fingers biting, he slams harder into me. The force prolongs the waves of release.

"God," he groans, his body jerking with climax.

After a few panted moments, he kisses the top of my head and slides out of me. Still breathless, I lay atop his comforter while he goes to take care of the condom. Returning, he scoops me into his arms, pressing me against his chest. Our bodies sated and sweaty, we just lay there.

"If these sleepovers become a regular thing, I may have to start doing cardio to keep up with you." Smirking, I trace the outline of his boyish grin with my fingertip.

"If all my trips to the gym end with that, I'll happily write you a seven-day-a-week cardio regimen to follow."

"My poor vagina."

"Oh, I'll take care of her." His grin is devilish.

"I have no doubts." I sit up in bed. "Now, let me take you to the shower to get cleaned off. Time for me to pamper you, Mr. Sweet Man."

He just lies there with his arms up. "Fine. If I must be pampered, I'll let you carry me into the shower."

"I may be equal opportunity in pampering one another, but carrying people will forever be your jurisdiction."

"Fine." He jumps off the bed and then hoists me into his arms. "I shall carry you off to my shower and you shall bathe me, woman."

Laughing, I let him carry me away. Though he's not carrying me far because I know I'm already gone for this man.

CHAPTER TWENTY-SIX

THIRD ACT BREAKUP

Contentment thrums through me with my full belly from our breakfast this morning and the delicious ache between my legs after our rigorous sex. The only thing more rigorous than our sex was how Davis cleaned his table while I made our breakfast. The lopsided grin on his face as he wiped down the wooden surface telegraphed zero regrets.

With my appointment with the witchcraft consultant later today, Davis is dropping me home so I can change. The clothes I'm wearing are clean, thanks to his extreme thoughtfulness, but I prefer not to walk around in last night's outfit.

Also, I want to spend time with Wentworth. The guilt about my bad puppy parenting this week is eating away at me. I never spend this much time away from him. My remorse waned a bit thanks to the picture Hope sent of Rem spooning my good boy in bed this morning.

As much as I know, it's time for me to move out, I'll miss things like that. It's nice having an entire team to help me parent Wentworth. But as Rem says, he'll still be there. It might just be be a drive versus a short walk.

"Not to be *that* guy…" Davis blows out a breath. "But would you and Wentworth want company at the park?"

"Don't you need some alone time to recharge?" I shift in the passenger seat to face him.

"I'm good." A crease furrows his brow. "Unless *you* need space. Am I being too much? Like… is this too clingy?"

"No!" I reach over and take his hand, laughter laces my protest. "Not at all. I like spending time with you. I just don't want you to think that you're expected to be with me all the time or anything like that. If you need your time, that's fine."

"I don't expect that or, rather, I don't think you expect that." He squeezes my hand. "I also enjoy spending time with you. Maybe I'm a little greedy because I got so much of you in the last nineteen hours that I'm not ready to let go. Plus, this week won't offer any opportunity to see you."

Over breakfast, Davis shared that he'll attend a tech conference and some meetings in the Bay Area on Tuesday, not returning until late Saturday. The conference is only until Thursday, but the meetings he'd canceled to fly home after his grandfather's accident were rescheduled for Friday and Saturday morning. His assistant finalized the details yesterday. This may be our last chance to hang out until then. While he worries that asking to hang with me and my dog may make him appear clingy, the icky sensation sloshing inside me comes from the fact that I may not see him for seven days, teasing that maybe I'm the clingy one.

Not to mention, Davis says this is what he wants. If he needed time alone, he'd ask for it. We made each other that promise last night, and as I already know, promises are important to him.

"Let's get Wentworth." I grin.

"Awesomesauce." He beams, reaching for the door handle.

"Did you just say awesomesauce?" I chortle, opening my door.

"The woman who cried out good gravy after I went down

on her in the shower this morning has no room to judge my use of awesomesauce," he teases.

Heat blooms in my cheeks. Okay, so maybe my pampering of him wasn't *that* altruistic. In my vagina's defense, he did say he'd take care of her… and take care of her he did.

Laughing, we walk hand-in-hand toward the back gate. We both snicker like teenagers as our gazes jump from the gate to one another. It shall be a very long time before I look at this gate with anything but heated memories.

"Georgia."

We spin at the sound of James's smooth English accent. Standing at the start of the walkway leading to the gate, his mouth is drawn into a firm line, and his bloodshot eyes are locked on me.

"I told you to stay away from her," Davis snarls. His arm loops around my middle and pulls me close to him in a protective, possessive gesture that I like far too much.

Bad feminist.

"What are you doing here, James?" Spine straight, I glare at him, surprised to see a plea swimming in his green pupils.

"I came to apologize," he says, his voice thick. "I am ashamed of my behavior. How I treated you."

"How you manipulated her, you mean?" Davis snipes. He takes a step forward, but I halt his movement with a hand on his arm.

"Yes. I did that. Georgia, I used your initial attraction to me and the uncertainty of this entire situation to manipulate you. You deserved better than a cad using you to get what he wants."

I cross my arms over my chest. "Is this more of your manipulation? Are you hopeful that I'll forgive you and you can try to, *what*… Worm your way back in and figure out some way to use me or—"

"No." His protest is quick. "It is understandable that you would doubt me. I toyed with your emotions from the beginning. Even my last visit here had been a game. I had over-heard Owen tell Lars about him." He gestures at Davis.

"That's why you came to my apartment Thursday morning?" I scoff. "Why tell me this?"

"To be honest about who I am. About the type of man that I am..." Teeth gritted, he shakes his head. "Though, my actions are not the trademark of a man. At least, not a good one."

"That's for sure," Davis mutters.

"What I did was inexcusable. I'm not here for forgiveness."

"Then why are you here?" I narrow my eyes.

"To own my actions and assure you that I was wrong. You are not a poor imitation. You are your own woman. Just as Lady Cecily is. It was not only cruel for me to say so, but misguided. The idea that even for a moment you would think that you are somehow less than because of my words gutted me."

"*You* should be gutted," Davis hisses. "Not only did you play mind games with her heart, but after she realized you aren't worthy, you insulted her. I know men like you; you can't have something for whatever reason, so you ensure nobody else has it. But Georgia isn't a fucking toy for you to play with."

Jaw clenched, Davis's icy stare locks on James. Something a little predatory drifts between the two men. Not from James, but more from Davis, who appears like a wolf protecting his pack. Dangerous doesn't waft off Davis. However, if I unleashed him, I don't doubt he'd strike on my behalf. *And again, I like that way too much.*

"It's okay, baby," I murmur, stroking his arm.

His posture eases.

"You are correct about me, Davis." James nods, his throat bobbing.

I assess him. The dark circles under his eyes. The slump of

his shoulders. The downward curl of his lips. James is the picture of remorse. Not to mention his confession calls out his actions. He doesn't just offer apologies but acknowledges what he did and how sorry he is for it. Not because *his actions* hurt me, but because *he* hurt me.

Every argument with Will flashes in my memory. This honest contrition is so opposite of Will's blanket "Sorry for that's" or "Sorry you feel that way." Those were rare, however. An apology from Will always twisted into everything being my fault. *This wouldn't have happened if you hadn't pushed me to move in. She gave me what I was looking for, what was missing with you.*

"Why this sudden change of heart?" I ask, gesturing at him.

"As you can imagine, your brother gave me quite the tongue lashing after my deplorable behavior yesterday. As did Lars and Owen," he says.

"So, you're only apologizing because of them?" Anger coats my accusation.

"No!" Frowning, he pulls out a copy of *The Duke's Darling* from his suit pocket and holds it up. "Because of this."

My face pinches. "What does my book have to do with this?"

"After the tongue lashing, I brooded in the guest room—"

"You mean sulked," Davis grumbles.

"Brooded." James glowers. "The copies of your books were there. I reread Lady Cecily and my story... And your gentleman"—he gestures to Davis—"was spot on. I engaged in the same manipulation of Cecily as I did to you. Good men do not toy with a young lady's heart for their own gain. I love Cecily, but she deserves better, as do you."

"Yes, *I* do. We both do."

Lady Cecily ending up with the wrong man is my doing. The last twenty-four hours has me questioning the story I wrote.

The book follows the typical historical romance pattern of a rakish duke's redemption. My obsession with a story, where the rake chooses the plump bookworm, blinded me to any alternative. It doesn't take my Master's in Social Work to assess that *The Duke's Darling* may be less about *his* redemption and more about my own. A redemption where not only am I chosen, but the power is in my hands to decide if I'll take him back.

"While you're responsible for your actions here, you may not be in the book. I wrote the story," I offer, my shoulders slump with a long sigh.

His expression turns sorrowful as he shakes his head. "I'm not entirely sure how any of this works, but even if you are the author, it is still my story, *my* actions."

Davis squeezes my middle. "Like you said, the story spoke to you."

Chewing on the corner of my mouth, I take in both their words. So much of what I know about my stories is topsy-turvy now. I talk about them speaking to me. Didn't I just spend two hours this morning listening to Patrick and Elsie's characters? How much of the stories I write is me, and how much is them?

"I don't know how any of this works either," I confess.

"What I do know is that it appears that this time, at least, the better man won the lady." James juts his chin toward Davis.

"This isn't a game, and Georgia isn't some prize to win. She's so much more than that." Davis glares.

I press into him. "It's okay. I know that."

He kisses my temple.

Gaze cast down, James shakes his head. "She should never have ended up with me."

"I didn't," I say, my head tilts.

"Cecily. She should have married Simon Davenport, not me. The third act breakup, as Owen calls it, should have been our end. I do not deserve the happy ending the book offers. Simon should have been *her* Davis, not me."

I blink. "But you claim to love her. You said you did all of this because of her. To get back to her."

"I do love Cecily… And I did do all this for her, but now, I wonder how much of it is love for her, or my need to win. To beat my fellow fictional brotherhood of would-be suitors and Davis, here, for your affection. Even the book's happy ending is tarnished by the fact that it still gives me what I want, while taking away everything from her. In marrying me, she loses her family. Her father may be a bastard, but he is good to her and was all she's had since her mother passed as a girl. I may want the ending promised in the book, with her carrying my name and my child, but I do not deserve it. Not at her expense. Nor at yours." He meets my gaze, his eyes shimmering with regret. "I was willing to take everything from you to get what I want. Men like that, like me, do not deserve happy endings."

The raw emotion in his voice stills my breath. I believe him. James may be inspired by Will, but he's not him. Just as Owen isn't Hope, and Lars isn't Jackson. Nor am I any of the women I wrote about. The seeds of who each of my book boyfriends is may have been planted by me, but they have grown into their own people.

"I won't take her, nor anyone else's happiness to ensure mine. I don't want to be *that* man anymore," he says, his voice quiet.

"You *truly* mean that," I murmur, certainty coursing through me.

"I do."

"I accept your apology," I step forward, holding out my hand.

"Georgia, I do not deserve—"

"It's not about what you deserve, but what I want." I look between Davis's cautious expression and then back to James.

"I don't know what the future looks like for us, but what I know is that I accept your apology."

"Thank you." A phantom smile flexing, he takes my hand. "You truly are spectacular, Georgia Lane."

"You really are remarkable," Davis whispers, his watchful gaze locked on James, who strides away. "I don't know if I can forgive him."

"You don't have to." I turn to face him and wrap my arms around his middle. "Acceptance of someone's apology doesn't equate forgiveness. It just means that I accept they are sorry. Forgiveness is a longer journey, and I'm not sure if that's one I will walk with James or not, but I do believe he is remorseful."

"Again, you are remarkable." He leans in, pressing his forehead to mine.

"I think you're pretty remarkable, too."

"Shall we go get Wentworth from Hope and Rem?"

"Let's make a quick stop at my apartment first." I scrape my teeth along my lower lip.

"Someone's insatiable." He quirks his right brow.

"It's your fault, you went all primal, protective caveman for a moment. And I'm choosing not to examine it through a feminist lens and just go with what it does to my lady bits."

"Well—" he squeezes my ass, pressing me flush with him. "You calling me baby did cause a stirring in my *man bits*," he says, his timbre low and playful.

"Someone best get to carrying me to my apartment."

He hoists me over his shoulder. A barrage of obnoxious giggles belting from me earns me a playful swat on my butt.

"To your lady cave!"

CHAPTER TWENTY-SEVEN

THE WITCHCRAFT CONSULTANT

"**G**ood thing Davis is leaving for a few days, or else you'd have trouble walking," Hope teases from the passenger's seat.

Not only did Hope schedule the appointment with the witchcraft consultant, but she insisted on coming. I'm not sure I'd visit a witch without her. In our two-decade-plus long friendship, there are very few moments—big or small—we haven't shared. That includes my second date escapades with Davis.

"Thank goodness Rem and I were having lunch on the back patio or else your vagina would need life support." She waggles her eyebrows.

Thanks to my brother and bestie catching us on our way to my apartment, me giggling about being hoisted over Davis's shoulder, no sex was had. Within moments, Hope dragged me away to dish, leaving our fellas to play with Wentworth in the backyard.

Our fellas. Giddiness flutters in my chest with that.

"Before we left, Rem told me that he likes Davis. Like, he really likes him." Hope grins, her dimples popping.

"Rem and I share that feeling," I say, turning onto the

street where Four Corners Spiritual and Witchcraft Center is located.

"In fact, he mentioned he's going to meet Davis for pickleball next Sunday."

"I know." My cheeks lift with a giant grin.

Not that I need either of my brothers' approval, but it's nice that they both like him. As much as the brotherly judgment frustrates me, contentment relaxes through me. Not to use a *Star Wars* reference, but all's right in the force now. Even if I still have this pesky 'fictional men come to life' situation to deal with, things seem right.

Hope clears her throat. "Have you heard from Lena since you emailed?"

"Yeah," I draw out the word.

"And?"

I shrug my shoulders. "Okay."

"Okay?" She gestures wildly.

"That's all she said."

"You email *your* cousin—a woman that was like a sister to you until *she* cheated with *your* boyfriend, then scooped him up, and is now marrying the jerk—to tell her you're not attending their wedding *a* week before their nuptials and her response is… okay," she says, her tone is high-pitched.

"Those are the facts," I say, pulling into the parking lot.

"How are you so chill about this? Is this a delayed reaction, emotional bomb situation like the time Trent Ott broke up with you two days before senior prom?"

"I really have had the worst dating history." Lip pursed, I shake my head. "No, this isn't like that. I'm *really* okay with it."

The truth is, I am. This isn't a brave front. Even Lena's name in my inbox didn't trigger dread. Pulling up her message, I just shrugged. Perhaps the reason I didn't rush to tell Hope is that it doesn't matter anymore.

"You don't think she owes you more? I mean, at least, an 'I

totally understand and I'm the scum of the earth and beg your forgiveness' in her email would be nice." Hope's face puckers into an annoyed pout.

Laughter vibrates in my chest. Hope is the queen of sweet, but she also goes scorched earth for the people she loves. After the invites came, she refused to attend with Rem until I told her I was going. She said yes, but bought a white dress to *stick it to that B-word,* as she cooed with a devious curl of her mouth at the boutique where we bought our dresses for the wedding. It's something I adore about my bestie. She loves fiercely, which is why my brother's heart and all future Lane offspring are in good hands.

"I love you." Smiling, I park and then turn off the car and lean back in the seat.

"Love you, too." She reaches over and takes my hand. "Are you sure you're okay with her response?"

"There was a time I wanted her to show contrition or beg for forgiveness or... I don't know..." I sigh. "But all I felt when her response came was nothing, and I think that means that I'm finally past all this. My choice not to go to the wedding is truly about me and not about getting revenge. The fact that I had no expectations of any sort of response and am indifferent to the one I got is a good thing. They hurt me, but I'm not hurt anymore."

"Wow, Davis must have some powerful peen."

A chortle erupts out of me. "This isn't about getting dicked down. As much as I'm enjoying Davis and whatever this will turn into, this isn't about him. It's about me finally getting myself unstuck from everything that held me back."

The hurt. The expectations. The disappointment. Each emotion had been a shackle holding me back from moving forward over the last five years.

"For the first time in, probably forever, I'm free to just live my life."

"I'm so proud of you." She squeezes my hand. "But I'm

still wearing that white satin dress with the crown on Saturday."

"Scorched earth," I chuckle.

We hop out and head toward Four Corners. The idea of a witchcraft consultant conjures images of a spooky Victorian mansion with a black cat on the front porch, not a storefront in a commercial strip mall. Four Corners Spiritual Healing and Witchcraft Center is between a frozen yogurt shop and a tuxedo rental place.

"Oh, fro-yo." Hope points to the Yu-Go Gurl Yogurt Shoppe sign next to Four Corners. "Do you think they have sugar-free vanilla?"

"After." I laugh, redirecting her to Four Corners' front door.

"Awesome." She claps her hands together. "No trip to ye ol' local witch is complete without fro-yo."

Head shaking, I open the door for her. The bell above the door chimes as we enter. The sweet scent of lavender fills my nostrils, and soft Celtic instrumental music drifts around the space. Books about magic and metaphysical practice, tarot card decks, crystals, essential oil products, and a hodgepodge of trinkets fill the shelves. Mini faux birch trees, piled high with gemstone, bead, and Celtic jewelry, bookend the register – almost eclipsing a young female employee in an *I'm That Witch* tank top.

"How can I help you?" she greets, her bright smile warm.

"We have an appointment under Georgia Lane with Glinda," Hope says.

"Let me go check that she's ready," she says, rounding the counter and skipping toward a purple curtain separating the store from the back.

"Seriously? Glinda?" I gape.

"It was either her or Ursula. At least we know she'll be a good witch." Hope nudges my side with her elbow.

"These are unfortunate names to have to go into the witchcraft profession with," I deadpan.

The staff member returns and leads us back to Glinda. An elderly woman rises to greet us. Her bluish gray hair is swept up in a top knot, and tiny spectacles connected to a chain dangle from her neck. The consultation room is painted in a lovely shade of desert rose, the pinkish walls making the small space cozy and inviting. A plush white sofa sits opposite a matching chair and a glass coffee table between both has a small tea service on it.

Glinda O'Brien introduces herself, explaining that she is a tenth-generation Cailleach, or wise woman. Her family, which immigrated to the US from Ireland in the early twentieth century, has a long history as healers, midwives, and women with other "special skills".

"I come from a long line of women who knew how to get shit done, dear," she says in a thick southern twang, mischief twinkles in her blue eyes.

After pouring each of us a cup of herbal tea, Glinda goes over the intake form with a series of questions. Her mix of sassiness and grandmotherly vibes eases me into sharing everything. The fountain. The wish. My book boyfriends. Even Davis.

"You have some visitors," she muses, clapping her hands. "My nan once had a woman time travel from the Bronze Age, desperate to get back to the man she left behind, but this is the first time I've heard of people coming from other realms."

"Other realms?"

"Now, dear, let's not be self-centered and think we're the only realm out there. There are infinite realms or realities, however you put it. This isn't the only plane of existence."

"But there from stories that *I* wrote. That I made up." I gesture to myself.

"They could just be that or more." Mouth slanted into a nonchalant grin, she shrugs. "Though, that's not the issue.

Where the stories come from are not what brings you here. It's your wish and how to possibly get these three men back to their worlds, correct?"

"Yes." I nod, my fingers wrapped tight around the teacup.

"Finish your tea, dear, and we'll proceed." She smirks over her teacup.

Hope and I have a silent conversation over our cups. My comfort with Glinda aside, the way she says, "Drink your tea, dear," is suss.

"It's not a potion." Glinda rolls her eyes, seeming to sense our hesitation. "It's loose leaf. I'm going to read the leaves to help me in my assessment of your issue. I swear there is more propaganda against witches. I blame Disney. They've done more harm to the witch community than the Puritans."

"They did have *The Witches of Waverly Place*. That was good rep," Hope offers with a smile before sipping her tea.

Only Hope. With a snort, I drink my tea.

Placing the now drained teacup in front of Glinda, she brings the cup close to her face and examines it.

"Just as I thought—" She frowns. "The wish has been granted. Once given, it cannot be taken back."

I scoot to the edge of the couch. "What about a wish undoing spell? I read about them online."

"They're more complicated than the internet would have you believe. This wish wasn't from a spell, so the magic is different. Harder to undo and, sometimes, comes at great cost."

"Great cost?" Hope clutches my hand.

"Yes. It also may require a witch far stronger than me. One with a proclivity for blood or dark magic," Glinda says.

"Oh, I don't like the sound of that."

"Me either." I rub my temples. "Is there anything else that could undo it?"

"If the wish hadn't yet been completed, you might be able to take it back. Some believe that if you speak the wish into the well or fountain and swallow the echo, you take it back. But your wish is granted."

"What do you mean it's completed?" I huff, confusion contorting my face.

"Oh my god, does that mean Davis is her happy ending?" Hope squeals, wiggling as much as her very pregnant body will allow.

I shoot her a *Really?* expression.

"But you didn't wish for your happy ending to happen. You wished to know what it was and for help to get it." Glinda cautions.

Eyes closed, I slump against the sofa's back. My mind wanders back to when I was perched at the edge of the SPN fountain. Knowledge and help is what I asked for. In all the chaos, I almost forgot.

"You're right," I murmur, my eyes fluttering open.

"Do you know what your happy ending is, then?" Hope asks, her brown eyes meeting mine. "Wait, I thought you said you weren't going to focus on endings anymore."

"I'm not." Laughter lifts my mouth into what I imagine may appear like an unhinged smile. "That's it."

"What's it?"

I motion between Hope and me. "No ending."

"No ending? That makes no sense. Are you, like, immortal now?"

"No." I sit up, gripping her hands. "My obsession with happy endings impacted my ability to just live. It affected my love life, my writing, and I'm sure a million other things. My worry about things not turning out stunted me. Don't you see? This whole thing has been about that. About me just living in the here and now rather than tied up with what may or may not happen."

"Focusing so much on the end, blinds us from the gift that is the in-between. That's when the good stuff happens. It's like in a book, the middle is when it gets interesting," Glinda says, her expression warm.

As ending-obsessed as I am, I love the middle of any story. It's when we get to really know the characters and try to guess what's about to happen. Once the end comes, no matter how satisfying it is, there's some grief because the story is done. The middle, though, is where the good stuff is. We don't know what's going to happen, but we're along for the ride. We're open to what may or may not happen.

Like plot twists where a bad date turns out to be the man who makes your heart race. If I had held onto the expectations about the ending with Davis I foresaw on our first date, I would have missed out on someone I am falling so hard for. No doubt, there are a million other things I missed out on because of my fixation with how they were *supposed* to turn out.

Glinda's explanation isn't telling me anything new, rather, it validates what I've learned through this experience. It also reiterates the role Owen, Lars, and even James play in guiding me to this newfound outlook. Each man has helped me to understand this lesson in their own way.

"What happens to them? My wish is complete. Are they just stuck here?" I ask, guilt spools tight in my stomach.

"Wishes don't always work the way we think they're going to work. The Fates have their own workings. Your wish may not just be for you, but then again it may. I'm not sure what happens to your three young men and—I'm sorry—I don't know how to get them back."

"What about the time-traveling lady your grandma helped?" Hope asks.

"She was unable to help Clidna get back." She frowns. "Whatever brought her to our time wanted her here."

"What happened to her?" I ask, my throat thick with regret.

"She passed a few years ago, but had a good life. She was a midwife for her village and became a nurse here. My grandfather had uh…*connections*… to get her some documents to start her life here. She helped a lot of people, though. Her great-granddaughter, Iris, is the young lady who greeted you and is pre-med. I like to think that's why she was brought here, but who knows."

"There's no way to help them get back?" I deflate.

It's less a question and more confirmation of what she'd already told us. These three men are here because of me, with no way to get them back. James's apology whispers inside me about not wanting his happiness if it cost someone else's theirs. Even if I didn't intend to do so, haven't I done just that?

Yup.

"I'll consult some of my books and if I find an answer, I'll reach out," she offers. The downward curve of her mouth communicates her disbelief that any answers exist.

"Thank you." With a soft smile, I rise.

"Georgia, you didn't come here for it, but I saw more in your cup. About love. Career. Family. Would you like to know? No extra charge." She holds up the cup.

The cup shines with so much temptation. To know if the things I hope will happen, or if things I haven't yet even hoped for happen instead. To know what won't come true to prevent any heartbreak. All I have to do is say yes.

"No. I just want to live it."

"Excellent." Her warm stare moves to Hope, who looks between her cup and me.

"Go on." I bump her shoulder with mine.

CHAPTER TWENTY-EIGHT

LUCKY FRO-YO

Even the sweetness of the fifteenth-best peanut butter frozen yogurt in the country, per the GF Finder app, isn't enough to quell the guilt swirling inside me. Hope and I sit at a table outside Yo-Go Gurl Yogurt. She spoons up her sugar-free vanilla, piled high with strawberries, raspberries, and almonds, while I drag my spoon through my peanut butter yogurt, sans toppings.

Lars, Owen, and James are stuck here with no way to get them back. While I did not wish for them, they are here because of me. Each may say they are alright with it, but it's all wrong. None of them were given a say in this.

"When are you going to tell them?" Hope asks, raking her teeth along her bottom lip.

My shoulders slump. "Today. Once I drop you off, I'll head over to Jackson's to give them the news."

"What are you going to say?"

"I don't know…" I motion with my spoon, my tone flippant. "Hey, guys, thanks for being magically transported against your will to help me figure out my life. Good news, I figured out my life. Bad news, you're stuck here."

"Considering everything, they've adjusted to life here.

Owen is killing it at Good Girl's Grub, Lars is shacking up with Jackson, and James is…a work in progress."

"I guess," I say, my speech hesitant.

It's true. James's duke-ish dickery aside, the three of them are adjusting to life in this realm. The time away from the stories already written for them seems to offer each the respite to soul search. Over the last eight days, each man has shared with me new insights into themselves, the women left behind, and their stories.

Smiling, she goes on, "Also, it wasn't exactly against their will. Owen says that there was a call to come, and they simply answered."

"I wonder how much choice they had," I grumble, thinking of me holding that stupid, unlucky, but maybe also lucky, penny before tossing it into the SPN fountain.

"About as much choice as you." She aims her fierce expression at me. "Let's not go backward. Even if you wished for help, you didn't wish for this. Not to mention your misplaced guilt does nothing for anyone, especially Lars, Owen, and the duke."

"You're right." With a sigh, I rest my elbows on the table and lean forward.

A guilt-laden temper tantrum does nothing for the guys. My contrition offers them no solace or solutions. They're stuck here, and we need to figure out what that looks like in the long term. Their adjustment may appear promising, but it could just be temporary. Like going on vacation. It also could be some strange Stockholm Syndrome-coping mechanism from being whisked from their reality to ours.

"I had hoped the witchcraft consultant would have had a solution. That this all would have—"

"A happy ending," she interjects, her face twinkling.

"Ugh!" Whining, I push my dish away and rest my head on the table.

Guess I'm not as Zen as I thought. After a lifetime hooked

on happy endings, it's going to take more than one week to get me off them.

"At least we know that your thought that selecting one of them would send the other two back was wrong."

"How do we know that?" I raise my head.

"Your wish is complete, and they are all here. If you selected one of them, they'd still be here anyway. So, at least we dodge the 'you marrying the duke' bullet."

"I would have *never* picked James." I make a sour expression.

"I worried about it for a hot minute, but you figured him out far quicker than with your last Lord of Jerkery."

"Don't remind me." My head tilts. "Anyway, picking one of them wouldn't have completed the wish either. They were always supposed to be my guides, not the solution."

"Then why did they think that their happy ending may be wrapped up in yours?"

I blink. "What?"

"You said that James told you that your happy endings may not be mutually exclusive."

I bat at the air. "It was just a line he used to manipulate me."

"But Owen said something similar."

My brow scrunches. "What? When?"

"The day we made the witchcraft consultant appointment. After you left for work, Owen said his happy ending brought him here, as much as yours, but he'd be sad to see you sacrifice your happiness for him or any of the guys."

Leaning back, I tap my fingers on the table. Was Owen speaking of his book's happy ending or something else? If they felt a call to come help me, what does that have to do with their happy ending?

"None of this makes sense." I toss my right arm up, accidentally slapping my purse which dangled on the chair's back, causing it to slam to the cement walkway.

Loose change, lip gloss, a pen, a tampon—because *of course* it does—and my wallet tumble out of the open purse. The pen rolls until it comes into contact with a passerby's sneakers. Cringing, I lunge out of my seat to scoop up the items, mumbling an apology.

"It's alright."

The familiar baritone causes me to look up, my heart thudding. "Will?"

Crouched on the ground, a tampon in my hand, I see my ex. *Kill me now!* Shoving my things into my purse, I rise, my bag clutched tight to my chest.

"Georgia…" Eyes wide. Mouth ajar. Breath ragged. He just stares at me as if I'm a ghost who's come back from the dead.

It's been five years since we last saw each other. Outside of that last phone call after Lena's confession, the only interaction with him was my RSVP for the wedding, and that was done via their wedding website. Nothing like saying, "I'll have the steak meal" to your ex's wedding with a slideshow of their happy pictures on the screen set to an instrumental version of "Hopelessly Devoted to You".

"Hi, jerkface," Hope calls out, causing me to turn, her warm expression now stern.

"Hope, nice to see you." He coughs.

"The feeling is not mutual." She takes a demure bite of yogurt.

He makes a huffed sound and then clears his throat. "You dropped this, Georgia."

Facing him, I hold out my hand and he deposits the loose change in it. "Thank you… What are you doing here?" I ask, closing my fingers around the coins.

He tips his head towards the tuxedo shop next to Four Corners. "Picking up my tux."

The only thing worse than running into your ex is doing it

in front of the shop where he's about to pick up his suit for his wedding to *your* cousin. *Oh, my messy life.*

"I didn't realize it was you when I saw the purse fall. I swear." Happy crinkles kiss the edges of his gray eyes, the pupils the same shade as a stormy sky. "But I am happy to see you… You look good."

"Too good for you, but not for her new CEO boyfriend that properly D's her down like no man ever has and worships her like the queen she is." Hope's snark drips with a saccharin-sweet venom.

I look over my shoulder and mouth, *Subtle* followed by *D's me down.* My bestie just grins.

Davis isn't my boyfriend—not yet—but I'm not correcting her. While I'm over Will, there's still a piece of me that enjoys what Hope's little comment is no doubt doing to him. He'll act all aloof on the outside at the dig, but he'll find some way to reassert himself. Will may not want me, but my successful CEO boyfriend's sexual prowess likely threatens his middle management sometimes orgasm-giving self-confidence.

Again, Davis is not my boyfriend, yet. Keyword, yet.

"Glad you found someone." Mouth drawn into a firm line, he raises one hand, raking it into his chestnut strands, his bicep flexing with the movement.

So predictable. I bite the inside of my cheek, tamping down the blooming snicker.

"I'm happy for you." His mouth lifts into a small smile. "I know we didn't end well—"

"Because you led her on, cheated on her, dumped her, and then ran off with her cousin," Hope jumps in helpfully.

Lips pursed, he continues, "Anyway, I know that we didn't end well, and that's on me."

The way he utters the phrase is akin to just forgetting the towels before a beach trip. It minimizes both his actions and their aftermath. This is textbook Will.

"On you?" I say, my jaw clenched. "This isn't like the

time you accidentally brought me the wrong type of cupcake for my birthday, and I got sick. Or the time you forgot to tell me your boss's wedding was black tie and I showed up dressed for a garden party. You and Lena hurt me."

"And now you're hurting Lena back," he hisses.

"I'm doing nothing of the sort."

"A week before our wedding you email her to say you're not coming." His eyes narrow.

"I'm sorry she's upset, but—"

"She's been crying since your email came. She'd hoped that your RSVP might be a second chance for the two of you."

My RSVP had always been about keeping the peace. About my mother, uncle, and brothers. This situation is hard enough without forcing anyone to choose sides. Even my decision not to go came with a long conversation with my mother and an email exchange with my uncle, reassuring them that this changes nothing with how I feel about them. Even Uncle Hans responded with an, *I love you* before he told me, *Don't be silly, you're not paying for anything.*

"She's so hurt. She misses you," he says, disappointment lacing his words.

"I didn't mean to hurt Lena."

"Well, you did." His glare tightens that knot in my stomach. "Was that your game all along? Make her think there's a chance? Did you RSVP only to do this?"

"No!"

"You used to be more empathetic than this. You used to think about others. I thought you—" His chide is halted by a yogurt dish smashing into his face.

Eyes wide, I whirl.

Hope, hands on her hips and face pinched, glares at Will. "Don't you dare lecture her about empathy you gaslighting butthead."

"Real mature, Hope," he mutters, swiping at his face.

She picks up my dish and aims it. "I could demonstrate my maturity level. I am doing everything for two these days."

A ghost of a smile belts across my face as I hold my palm up. "It's all good, Hope. I got this," I say, plucking up some napkins from the table and handing them to Will.

"Fine." She sits back down, patting her belly. "Baby girl and I are here for backup when you need us."

With a grateful smile to my bestie, I face Will. "Listen, I'm sorry that Lena is hurting. That was never my intention. Playing games with someone's heart is more your thing, not mine."

He flinches.

"Contrary to what you think, my decisions no longer concern you, nor are they made because of you. I choose not to attend your wedding for my sake. You both hurt me, but I'm not doing this for vengeance. This is about my needs. My wants. About putting myself first. You may have been careless with my heart, but I'm no longer going to be with it."

"I'm sorry." He releases a hard breath. "For everything. For accusing you of doing this deliberately. I should have known better. It's not like you. I just… I love her so much, and I don't want her to pay for my crimes. Things haven't been the same between her and your family since…"

I arch a brow.

He motions at me. "I know. Why would we expect that? What we did was wrong, but she fought it for so long. I was the one who pushed. I was the selfish one. I should have ended things with you before anything happened, but I didn't. Each time something happened, she'd push me away, saying she didn't want to hurt you. That this couldn't happen again. Still, I just…"

"Used me so you weren't alone until you could have her. I was your consolation prize."

"Yes," he says, his gaze downcast.

"I'm nobody's consolation."

That declaration roars through me. I deserve to be some-one's first choice, especially my own.

"You deserved better… For what it's worth, what I did to you is the biggest mistake of my life. It hurt you, and it hurts Lena. I am so sorry," he whispers.

"You may be, but that doesn't matter to me anymore."

It really doesn't. In the initial breakup text exchange, followed by the tearful in-person and then telephone exchanges with him, Will's apologies were nonexistent. Each interaction was just gaslighting bullshit used as weapons to make me believe it was my fault. His apology means nothing to me, because at the end of the day, what I wanted more than his remorse was that this all had never happened. As painful as what happened was, I know it's just part of the twists and turns of my story leading me to my next chapter. One where I don't settle for less than what I deserve—from my partner and, above all, from myself.

Even now, despite the hint of remorse in his features, his apology means nothing. It's not about me or his actions. It's about Lena. He regrets that his actions cause her pain, not that they hurt me. For Will, it's always been about Lena. From the moment he met me, it was her he wanted. This isn't like with James, where he realized the error of his ways.

"I know you can't forgive me, but can you forgive her? She misses you." His stare implores.

"No," I say simply. "I may not be hurt anymore, but I don't trust either of you. You blame yourself for this, but honestly, both of you betrayed me."

"I understand," he says, swallowing thickly.

"I hope you make her happy. That you're good to her… Better than you were to me."

"I am," he says. "At least, I try. I don't deserve her, but she still loves me."

"Well, you clearly have a type." I let out a humorless laugh. "I do wish the best for you both, please know that."

"I wish the best for you, as well."

"Goodbye, Will."

"Goodbye, Georgia." With a quick nod, he turns and walks towards the tuxedo shop.

Hope shuffles over, wrapping her arm around me. "That was a lot."

"Yeah." I sigh.

"How are you?"

"Weirdly okay." I place my head on her shoulder. "Did you really toss your frozen yogurt at him?"

"Yeah, I kind of regret that."

"Because you're still hungry."

"Yeah." She pouts.

"Let's go get you a refresher." I lift my head from her shoulder.

Unclenching my hand, my vision catches on the three pennies resting in my palm. I'd held tight to them throughout the entire exchange. Something swoops in my stomach at the three coins glistening in the late afternoon sun like little beacons leading me home. Examining them closer, my heart stutters.

"Hope, I have an idea."

CHAPTER TWENTY-NINE

HAPPY ENDINGS

*I*t *was right in front of me all along!* The potential solution is as crystal clear as the building in front of me. Parking my car at SPN, I grab my purse and hop out. Hope is back at the house. My bestie may ride shotgun for my big life events, but after a Braxton Hicks contraction as we walked to my car, we opted to drop her at home.

Before dropping Hope off, we called Jackson to bring the guys to SPN. Then I reached out to Kerry, who I knew was working today, for a favor. Reaching the main courtyard entrance, a sign that reads *Closed for Maintenance* is posted on the door, and my mouth lifts into a thankful smile.

"There are signs on all the entrances like you asked. Is everything okay?" Kerry asks as I enter the courtyard.

My steps halt. "Ahh… Yeah, I just need the courtyard for something *author*-related." My tone comes off shiftier than I mean it to.

"O—kay." The dip of her brow telegraphs her disbelief. No doubt Kerry thinks I'm up to something nefarious.

"This is such a lovely spot to shoot some promo videos for my socials, and you know how Velma is about that stuff. You know… beg for forgiveness rather than ask for permission."

My exaggerated wink is conspiratorial, knowing Kerry is likely thinking about her repurposing the tossed coins into weekly donations to the Make-A-Wish Foundation without the SPN's administrator's permission.

The pebble of guilt lodges in my stomach at my manipulation, but I'll deal with it. There isn't enough time to explain this whole thing to Kerry. Though something tells me that she'd believe me. Besides her love of historical romance, she adores anything with magical elements.

"Totally! Want me to help take the video, so—"

"No need. My cameramen are here," I interrupt with a wave to my book boyfriends strolling through the main entrance.

"*Girl*, do you ever have cameramen?" Kerry breathes, her gaze sweeping over the three men striding toward us.

Individually, each is impressive. All three are over six feet, with muscular frames. Owen is the sexy boy next door. James is regal handsomeness. Lars is rugged sexiness. Together, the three ooze enough sexual pheromones to impregnate a woman just by looking at them.

"Georgia." James offers a quick bow and then turns to Kerry, his mouth opens, and nothing comes out. He just stares, his green eyes appearing to be entranced.

"Hi, I'm Kerry," she says, holding out her hand.

After a far too long beat, he blinks, takes her hand, and murmurs, "James."

"Is she the witch?" Lars juts his chin at Kerry, whose left eyebrow quirks.

"No, she's not the witch…for the *promo*." Even my breathy laugh is suss.

"Promo?" Owen's head tilts.

I flash him a *shut it* look.

"She's no witch, but she does cast a spell," James drawls, his large hand still enveloping hers.

"Oh." A dreamy expression shines in Kerry's features.

Owen shakes his head. Lars snickers.

"Kerry, I think we've got this. Would you mind giving us some privacy?" I ask.

"Sure," she says, her hand still in James's, pink staining her cheeks.

No good will come from this!

"Sorry, we're on a tight timeframe. It would be a huge help if you could keep guard... In case Velma comes in. You know how she loves those random drop-ins on the week-ends." In a very un-Georgia-like move, I take hold of Kerry's shoulders and guide her towards the door.

"Goodbye, Kerry," James murmurs, bowing as I push Kerry out the door. "What a delightful creature. Who is this Kerry?"

Shutting the door, I spin, wagging a finger. "Not for you."

He raises his hands. "I wasn't... I know. Sorry."

"Ugh! Enough with the apologies." I toss my hand up as I stride toward them. "Just do better."

Owen places a hand on James's shoulder. "Now might be the time for you to just be single."

"You may be correct, my friend," he sighs.

"Where's Jackson?" I scan the space.

"Outside. He didn't... He thought it would be best," Lars says, clearing his throat. That playful sparkle in his eyes is dull, and his mouth curves downward.

This must be hard for both Jackson and Lars because if this works, then it's goodbye for them. Jackson had them all on speaker phone as I said, "I think I figured out how to get you all back." So, there's no secret to what this all may mean for each of them.

"As we have been summoned, I imagine the witchcraft consultant provided a solution to this situation." James waves his hand between all of us.

"No. She said my wish is complete, and there isn't a way

to solve it. At least, not one she knew about or had the power to fix," I say, my tone soft.

"So, we're here forever?" Lars asks, his expression unreadable.

"But you said that you had a way." James's forehead crinkles.

"I do. At least, I think I do. But I want to give you all the choice." I pull out the three pennies from my pocket.

This all began with a wish. It seems fitting for it to end with one. Only not mine, theirs.

The idea came to me after exchanging well-wishes with Will. In so many ways, this whole thing started with the end of that relationship. A relationship where all my wishes and hopes for the future appeared to be ripped away. Only—as Rem said—it never was my future. It was me forcing myself into what I *thought* was supposed to happen. Who I thought I was supposed to be with.

So many of my failed dates since Will weren't just their fault, but mine. It wasn't the fear of getting hurt by someone else that held me back, but of making the wrong choice again. Some of them were exactly who I pictured, but I didn't trust that.

I didn't trust me.

Thanks to this wish gone right or wrong, however you look at it, I trust myself now. Right now, I trust that this may be the answer we've been looking for.

"I don't know how wishes work or if this will. What I do know is that I want to give you the choice. Something you didn't have from the start. Even if I didn't mean for you to be brought here, you had no choice in that. I want to give it back to you." I hand each man a penny. "For you to wish for your happiness. Whatever that is. It's your choice."

"You want us to wish?" Owen says, his speech hesitant.

"What if it goes sideways like yours did?" Lars asks.

"But my wish didn't actually go sideways," I say.

This entire situation isn't what I wished for. None of this went as planned. Even if I didn't plan for it. It didn't come with a guaranteed happy ending, like one of my books. It just is. My eyes are now open, and my heart is ready to live life knowing that things may not turn out okay. It's both terrifying and freeing.

"Wishes don't work the way we think they should… But they do work. We just have to be open to it. Each of you has helped me know what I want and at great sacrifice to yourselves. Selena. Ivy and your pack. Lady Cecily." I meet each man's stare.

"You want us to leave. To wish to go back." A tight smile anchors Lars's hard expression.

"I want you to do whatever you want to do. To wish for what you want. To do what I'd failed to do, write your own endings… your own stories," I murmur.

Whether their stories are only figments of my imagination or communicated to me telepathically in some strange inter-realm game of telephone, these are their stories, not mine. This morning, as I listened to Elsie and Patrick's story, the words came alive with each tap of my fingers on the keyboard, and that truth nested deep within me.

"Whatever we want," Owen murmurs, holding the coin up.

"Yes." Stepping back, I gesture to the fountain. "Make your wishes."

"And what if we don't want to wish?" Lars asks.

"That's your choice. Whatever you choose, I'm here for you as you've been here for me."

In a different way each, of these men have guided me to reclaim my own story. Even before they magically appeared, they'd been part of the piecing back together my heart. It's now their turn to reclaim their stories.

"Thank you, rabbit." Lars reaches over and squeezes my shoulder.

Coin in hand, each man stands at the edge of the fountain. The stone gleams in the not-quite-evening sunshine.

"I wish whatever is supposed to happen, happens." Owen tosses his coin into the water.

"I wish for those I left behind's happiness, as well as my own." Lars follows suit.

Face wrinkled, James studies the coin before lifting it to his lips and pressing a tender kiss. "I wish for Lady Cecily to get her true happy ending," he murmurs and then tosses it in.

The three just stand, their gazes fixed on the ripples in the fountain's pool. I don't know what I thought would happen. Just as the night I made my wish, it's quiet. Nothing out of the ordinary. No poof of magic or sprinkle of fairy dust.

"What happens now?" Owen turns.

"I don't know, but we can find out together." I step closer to them.

"You're not done with us after all, rabbit," Lars snarks.

"No. I think we're stuck with each other."

Owen takes a step and then stops. Laughter brightens his features. "We may not all be stuck," he says.

"What?"

He tips his head up to the sky and then back to me. "Come back to me, Owen," he says.

"Is Selena calling you home?"

"Yeah. She is or, at least, someone is."

I fling my arms around him. "I'm so happy for you." Stepping back, I beam. "Now, go write your story. Whatever ending *you* want."

"Thank you, Georgia." He leans in and presses a gentle kiss to the center of my forehead. "Goodbye, fellas." Grinning, he steps back. His form becomes transparent until he disappears.

A blend of sad happiness mixes within me. Owen deserves to go back and rewrite his ending. I just know I'll miss him. So will Hope, who may need to look for a new backup chef.

My eyes flick to Lars and James. Each remains fixed to their spots, their stares locked to where their friend used to be.

"Do you hear anything?" My question is cautious.

"No," they both say.

Lars sniffs, and then his head jerks towards the door. A giant grin erupts on his face the moment Jackson emerges into the courtyard.

"You're still here. I'm not too late," he says through panted breaths, rushing towards Lars. "I know I said I didn't want to get in your way, but—"

His muscular arms pull Jackson into a tight embrace, and Lars silences him with a kiss. Their mouths cling in deepening kisses between Jackson muttering "I'm selfish but I don't want you to go," and Lars's "Shut up, pretty boy, I'm right where I want to be."

Hand on my heart, I melt into the gooey sensation enveloping me. Lars's heart's desire is my brother, but he couldn't embrace that completely without knowing the people he left behind would be okay. Jackson's appearance is, no doubt, Lars's own mystical voice calling him home.

"At least this means I will no longer have to share the guest room. Lars snores, so your brother may never sleep again." James makes a huffed laugh.

"I don't think they plan to do a lot of sleeping," I quip, my mouth lifting at Lars hoisting Jackson into his arms, his long legs wrapping around the werewolf's middle.

"We're right here, gentlemen, though that term may not fit," James tuts.

"Hush, Lord Jealous." Lars sets Jackson down.

"Not your best retort, old chap."

My stomach sinks. "So, no messages or voices for you?"

"No, but there wouldn't be, would there? My wish wasn't about me."

With a frown, I turn to him. "You could have wished for anything you wanted."

"But I did wish for what I want. Cecily's happiness is what I desire. Even if it's not with me. She deserves the world and a man who is worthy to give her it... And I'm not him. My entire life has been about my wants, my desires. I don't want to be that man anymore."

"You may not be who I thought you were."

"But I am." He frowns. "Please, don't let me forget that or get comfortable in that idea that I am not. Comfort and delusion shall only blind me to the path ahead. The one to become the man you think I may be, but that I know I am not. At least, not yet."

"If Cecily's happiness is what you want, how do we know she has it?" I ask.

"Georgia!" Arms flailing, Kerry trots into the courtyard, several pieces of paper in her right hand. "Sorry to interrupt, but Velma sighting. I was able to snag the signs before she saw them and came to investigate."

"Thanks, Kerry, but we're done here." I smile.

She stops short in front of me and James, her brown eyes bright. She flashes a flirty smile at James. He clears his throat, nods, and then averts his gaze. It's for the best. Even if I don't appreciate the disappointment puckering Kerry's lips into a pout, she's not for him.

More importantly, James isn't for anyone. At least, right now. Like he says, he's a work in progress. Kerry deserves a man with his shit together. Despite the tailored suit, James is very much not together.

"Which book is this for anyway?" Kerry asks, her pout twists into a curious expression.

"All of them."

"Ooh, I can't wait to see it," she coos.

"When it's all done," I say, that knot in my stomach tightening with this lie and the forthcoming one when I pretend the video footage got erased. I make a mental note to bring Kerry a latte from her favorite coffeeshop every day next week in amends for lying to her.

"Oh fun!" She claps. "I love your books so much. They always have the best twists. Like I never saw Simon Davenport as Lady Cecily's endgame, but that man." She makes a pretend swooning movement.

"Simon Davenport makes you swoon?" James says aghast.

"Oh yeah." She wiggles her hips. "The unexpected dirty mouth of a quiet, well-mannered ornithologist."

"Simon Davenport? The Marquis of Hampton?" I blink.

"Yes! So sexy! He's one of my favorite book boyfriends you've written."

"Figures," James mutters.

She goes on, ignoring him. "I don't normally like love triangles, but the way you did it was so clever. First, I was shipping *that cad* Lord James, but then, like Cecily, I fell hard for Simon. It was such a great analogy for avoiding red flaggy men."

"Cad? I'm… *He's* not that red flaggy," James grumbles to himself.

I bump James's arm with my shoulder. "I'm happy you liked that Lady Cecily found her happiness at the end of the book."

His softened expression telegraphs the realization settling in him. His wish came true. Lady Cecily is with the marquis. She's happy, and even if James's mouth ticks down, I know it's what he wants. Sometimes a little grief and sadness are wrapped up in our heart's desires coming true.

"Yeah. It's one of my favorite HEAs. Even better than Owen and Selena or Victor and Ivy."

"Victor and Ivy? My second?" Lars gapes.

Tucked into Lars's side, Jackson's mouth quirks. "Not that I'm complaining, but what about Lars?"

"Who's Lars?" Confusion contorts her pretty features.

CHAPTER THIRTY

OUR STORY

Who is Lars, indeed? Turns out he's just a footnote in *Shifted Heart*. Instead of it being Ivy and Lars's story, it's hers and Victor's. Lars is simply a brief mention as Victor tells Ivy about the former pack leader who gave up his position for love. Much of the story centers around the pull between Victor and Ivy's own duties. It ends with her still joining the human/supernatural alliance, but making her home base in Victor's territory.

Much like Owen and Selena's story, they don't go to bed every night together, but are happy. Both books depict modern relationships with each couple balancing their personal wants with their deep love for one another. Owen still ends up going to the city, but not in a big romantic gesture. Moments after Selena breaks up with him, saying it's what's best, he rushes after her. "We decide what's best for us together," he says, pulling her into his arms and kissing her with the passion of a man who almost lost the one woman he truly loves. Which he almost did. The rest of the book depicts the complications of a long-distance—sort of—relationship. Sugarville and the city are only ninety minutes away from each other, after all. In the end, Selena still quits her job but instead she leads a mini coup with several other employees leaving with her to start their own consulting firm. She splits her time between the city and Sugarville with her new husband, Owen.

The wishes changed each book's story, but the only ones who notice are the guys and those of us who knew of their true identities. Lady Cecily is happily married to Simon Davenport. Victor enjoys Ivy chasing him through the woods. Owen and Selena got a pair of pugs they named Lars and Duke. Their namesakes are both touched, even if James grumbled, "At least get something that does not snort."

It all ended as it should, and none of it as I planned. Which I'm okay with. Though, it's not truly the end. It's just the middle. For me and for all of us. Lars and James are figuring out their lives here. Just as I am.

Right now, the two of them are helping Rem and Jackson paint the nursery, while Hope and I stretch out on the couch with Wentworth. James's *bloody hells* and Lars's snarky taunts drift downstairs. It's strange how right this all seems. Lars just fits with our little family unit. Jackson took him to meet Mom this week, who adores him. He's also got the stamp of approval from Rem. The duke is slowly growing on my brothers.

"How about a Meghan's Munchies run tomorrow morning while the guys are at pickleball?" Hope taps her bare foot against my calf.

"Excellent suggestion," I muse, a sleepy smile slanting my lips.

"It's too bad Davis won't be home to keep you company tonight. Are you sure you don't want me to stay behind?"

"And let that white dress go to waste. Never." I snuggle into her shoulder.

Tonight is Lena and Will's wedding. I'm insistent that my family still goes. As much as I know I don't want to be there, I want them there for her. Five years don't wash away the first twenty-seven we spent as close as sisters. Part of me will always love Lena and want the best for her. I told her as much in the flowers and the card that I sent this week. That while I can't be there, I want her to know that I truly wish her the best. A path forward with Lena isn't something I'm planning on, but I also don't know. If this thing with my book boyfriends has taught me anything, it's that life has lots of plot twists. Even if I'm not open now, who knows what will happen in my story.

After the guys finish painting, Jackson and Lars head out to get ready for the wedding. I help Hope, who wows in her outfit. With hugs and another round of questioning my certainty, they head out. James remains behind, putting together baby furniture. His figuring out his path of redemption appears to be a lot of manual labor.

Since Sunday, he's done every chore around Jackson's, mine, and Hope and Rem's places. He's even accompanied Hope to work to make himself useful until she hires a replacement for Owen. He's shit at cooking, but is great at heavy lifting and, oddly enough, dealing with the customers with his rakish charm.

Leaving the puttering duke at the house, Wentworth and I trot to my apartment. My plan is a lot of snacks while bingeing *Star Trek: The Next Generation,* or diving into a new book.

Digging out my popcorn popper, I pull down the kernels, butter, and salt. I measure out what I need into the machine and turn it on. I push the start button.

A single knock on the door has me calling out, "Coming."

It may be James checking in on me. Part of me suspects he lingered out of a sense of obligation to watch over me while everyone else is gone.

"Davis!" A large grin belts across my face. "I thought your flight didn't get in until nine."

"I took an earlier flight." He holds up a bag with Gemma's

name printed in fancy script. "I promised someone ice cream and *Star Trek*, remember?"

My stomach swoops. "I remember." Lifting to my tiptoes, I wrap my arms around his neck, my mouth inches from his. "Thank you."

"Thank *you* for wearing these." He pats my butt with his free hand.

"Do you and my butt want to be alone?" I wiggle my ass, knowing how good they look in these yoga pants.

"It is a remarkable ass."

"Men," I scoff playfully.

"Is my girlfriend jealous of her own ass?"

"Girlfriend?"

Outside of Hope dubbing Davis "My CEO Boyfriend" in front of the yogurt shop, there have been no labels. Despite not physically seeing him since Sunday, we've not really been apart. Our sometimes flirty but now deepening text threat is seldom quiet. We even video chatted last night. Still, we haven't set parameters for what's happening beyond both our admissions that we have zero desire to see anyone else.

His forehead creases. "I thought... Is it too soon? I should have asked first. Do you want to be?"

"I don't know if it's too soon..." My mouth tugs up just a little bit more. "But I don't care, because I want to be your girlfriend."

"Awesomesauce." He smirks, causing me to giggle.

"Such a dork," I whisper, capturing his mouth in a slow kiss.

Chuckling, he nuzzles his nose against mine. "Remember on our first date when you said you already knew kissing me would be the worst thing ever?"

"What I said is that I didn't think I'd like it."

"Oh, you like it." Gaze smoldering, he traces his thumb along the outline of my mouth.

"Perhaps." I peer up through my lashes. "I may require

more sampling to be sure. You know… in the name of science."

"Science." He slants his mouth over mine.

I don't know what the future holds. We may have a long story together or a short one. It may be happy or full of sadness. There may be plot twists or just a smooth, steady current. It may be everything I want it to be or not.

What I do know is I am ready to see how our story reveals itself to me… Oh, and I like kissing him. *A lot.*

"Best part of the week," Pilar says, a twinkle plays in her amber eyes.

"Agreed." I grin, settling against the SPN wall with her.

It's Friday night, AKA Doc and Estelle's weekly performance. This will never not be my favorite part of the week. It's up there with Saturday brunch with Hope and my six-month-old niece, whom Lars calls LG for Little Georgia, and James calls Her Majesty, or weekly Sunday family dinners. The new tradition has dinner rotating between my brothers' places. Next month, after I move into my new place, I'll join the hosting rotation.

"I am thinking they're going to do *Much Ado About Nothing*. What's your guess?" Pilar muses, tipping her head towards where Estelle directs two staff members to place the chairs that she and Doc will use.

Doc is more than healed since his hip injury, but Estelle plans to keep "the old goat" safe. For the last several months, the weekly readings have been done fireside-style, with the two of them sitting in chairs. As much as Doc itches to flutter around the courtyard like before, he's listening to Estelle. At least for now. Davis gives it two more months before his grandfather buzzes around during his weekly performances.

"I don't know. I'm thinking *The Merchant of Venice*." I smile, thinking of how Estelle made me and Davis her famous lasagna last Saturday night.

Another favorite night of the week is any night with Davis. One of those nights is always spent with his grandparents. Estelle has become quite the gluten free chef over the last few months. Between bites of whatever delicious meal she's made, Estelle and Doc tease us about how they knew we'd be a perfect fit for each other.

"I'll be right back," Pilar says, patting my arm before shuffling over to chat with a patient's family.

Inhaling the decadent jasmine aroma drifting around the courtyard, I take in the scene. The quiet, babbling fountain and murmured conversations. The way the wishing stone glows in the light from the lanterns and bright moonlight. This place will always be magical to me. Though, I've not heard of any other fantastical things happening here in the last eight months. I'm not sure if what happened to me was a fluke. Like Glinda says… the Fates have their own workings. Whether this fountain grants all wishes or fate just stepped in for mine, I don't know.

"Is this wall taken?"

I look up, and my belly turns in a low swoop.

Hands pushed into the pockets of his jeans, that boyish grin invades every inch of Davis's face.

"It's reserved for my boyfriend," I say cheekily.

"Lucky man."

"Guess so…" I offer a mock-pout. "But he's in Denver for work."

No Boundaries may keep Davis busy, but his family and I remain his priority. No matter the deadline, meeting, or trip, he always makes time for us. He always calls. He always keeps his promises. Even when we assure him it's not a big deal.

"I hope you didn't cut short anything important to rush back." I wrap my arms around him.

"'Cause there's something more important than being with the people I love." He nuzzles his nose against mine.

The ooey-gooey sensation seeps into every bit of me. I don't think I'll ever get used to being loved by Davis Makenzie. In true blue Davis fashion, he didn't hold back. Within two months of dating, he proclaimed his love. I cheered him on in a pickleball tournament he and Jackson competed in to raise money for a local dog rescue. After they won, he'd run over, scooped me up, and said, "God, I love you."

"I never doubt how important I am to you." I press my smile against his.

"Good, because you are very important to me." A sly expression invades his features. "And not just because you're ensuring my childhood dream of a chocolate lab as a pet, when you and Wentworth move in at the end of the month."

"Did you only ask me to move in for my dog?" I arch one eyebrow.

"He is a *really* good dog." He chuckles.

I swat at him. "Guess he'll be your little spoon, then."

"Wentworth is very snuggly, but he's not my little spoon." He bands his arms tight around me.

"I love being your little spoon." I sigh. "I love you, Davis Makenzie."

"I love you, Georgia Lane." He captures my lips in a toe-curling kiss.

Each time this man kisses me, I rejoice in how wrong I was. I do, indeed, love kissing Davis Makenzie. It's better than writing *The End* on my latest manuscript or the grilled cheese from Fisher's Landing.

"If my grandson would stop canoodling with his girlfriend, we could get the show started," Estelle teases from across the courtyard.

"Sorry, Nan." He clears his throat and then smirks.

Cheeks flushed from both my little public display of affection with Davis at my place of employment, and it being pointed out by his grandma, I settle back against the wall. Davis leans beside me, our gazes forward to where his grandparents take their seats. His hand folds around mine, causing every cell to hum with happiness.

"Tonight is a special performance," Doc announces. "We're taking a short break from Shakespeare. For the next month—in honor of our very own Peach's birthday—we're going to be reading Austen."

"What?" Laughter falls out of me. "My birthday isn't until the end of the month."

"It will take us that long to read this." Doc chuckles and holds up a leather-bound book.

"It also gives me a month to spoil you." Davis slides his arm around me, tucking me into him.

Snuggled into Davis, I lose myself in Doc and Estelle's tandem reading from *Pride and Prejudice*. I bite back my tiny laugh at how Lizzie and Darcy's meeting makes me think of me and Davis.

That's where the comparison ends for me because this isn't a book. This is my life—one I hope that I get to live with all my people, especially the sweet man beside me. I don't know what the future has in store for any of us, and that's okay. Right now, the middle is far too good to rush to the next page.

The End.

Thank you for reading *Book Boyfriends*. If you'd like to explore more of my books, turn the page for a sneak peek at the first chapter of

Happy Ever Afterlife

SNEAK PEEK: HAPPY EVER AFTERLIFE

Cane Austen and Me

Pen

"Mommy, what's she doing?" The small chirp of a child's voice draws my attention.

I am not the aforementioned "mommy," but my head tilts toward the tiny human anyway. There's something in the shock and awe in their voice telling me there is a small finger pointing at me.

"It's her stick—"

It's a cane. I don't correct the wrong terminology. Instead, my smile tight and white cane ahead of me, I stroll down the not-yet-fully awake Buffalo-Niagara Airport terminal.

"It helps her see."

Ah, if only it were that magical. It's barely seven a.m. After spending a week with my mother, I lack the temperamental bandwidth to explain to this woman and her child the intricacies of being legally blind. It's a cane. It doesn't help me see, but rather it's a tool to allow me to use nonvisual cues to get from point A to point T. Right now, the point T I'm destined for is the Tim Hortons tucked into the airport's food court.

Aunt Bea always said I was a shining light illuminating the darkness in the world's understanding of what it means to be blind. It's why I've dedicated so much of the last ten years to educate people through my social media page, Cane Austen and Me. To my thirty-thousand followers, I'm the "It" blind girl, documenting my every day and big adventures with Cane Austen, my white cane, helping the non-visually impaired world's knowledge be just a little less obscured about vision loss.

The knowledge that I'm no longer Aunt Bea's little light aches deep in my heart. I can almost feel her soft arms folded around me as she cooed, "Pen, you'll help them understand." No matter how tired I was, she'd have expected me to stop. Explain how the cane works. Tell the child that not all blind people can't see. Set his mommy dearest straight on the blind people facts, helping their little human grow up without misinformation and ensuring that other little humans – ones like me with failing vision – don't repeat the storyline I'd faced as I grew up.

Clear their vision, Aunt Bea's sing-song words dance in my heart.

Sighing, I pivot on my strappy, wedge sandals and head toward the sound of the mother and child. A little boy sits, feet kicking, beside a woman, her long hair gathered into a messy bun, at a half-full gate.

"Hi. I'm Pen." My free hand gathers my long auburn hair, brushing it onto my right shoulder. The action soothes the pulse of anxiety. No matter how many times I do this, it's still awkward as fuck. *Good thing I love you, Aunt Bea.*

The little boy tips his head to his mom, whose forehead puckers in confusion.

Yep, I'm weirding them out. Frankly, I don't blame them. Most people don't have a lot of interactions with the legally blind. Let alone one who walks up to them and introduces themselves. Thanks to Aunt Bea, that is exactly who I am.

Even if there are days – like today – where I wish I wasn't. Where I'd rather fade into the crowd, unseen and forgotten.

"I heard you ask about my cane," I lace just enough sweetness into my words to not send anyone into a sugar-rush. "This is Cane Austen. I'm legally blind, and she helps me stay safe. See how I sweep the cane? It's called constant contact and helps me trail things to guide my path or find things, so I don't trip and fall." With a tight upward curl of my mouth, I demonstrate how I use the cane.

"Are all canes girls?" The little boy's face twists into a pout.

A genuine smile kicks across my face. "Not all, but this one is."

"Why did you name it Cane Austen?" The woman's eyebrows knit.

"So she'll help me find my Mr. Darcy," I quip, making the woman snort with laughter.

It was the same reaction Aunt Bea had. This is my tenth Cane Austen. I've had a new one every year since I was sixteen. While everyone else was getting their first car, I was getting my first cane. The eye condition I have, retinitis pigmentosa, progressed to the point that a cane is necessary to keep me safe. I'd been diagnosed at age six, so I knew my vision was fading to black at a glacial pace…slow but unstoppable. The gradual progression of vision loss didn't lessen the painful realization that, while classmates were getting their licenses and cars, I was facing just another way in which I wasn't like them.

Not allowing me to wallow, Aunt Bea presented me with my first white cane. Blindfolding me – which she found hilarious – she dragged me into the driveway where she gifted me a white cane tied up with a giant red bow. She'd even put a Porsche sticker on it, winking as she affirmed that her niece would travel in style. "You gotta name this bad bitch," she'd crooned, explaining that the cane was my car, and everyone named their vehicles.

The little boy worries his lower lip, as if considering his words. "What does 'legally blind' mean?"

What, indeed? To the world blind means you can't see, but unsuspecting civilians didn't realize that blindness is served on a spectrum. The majority of legally blind people are like me, with some usable vision. There's a whole medical explanation that Trina, my ophthalmologist bestie, would bore people with at parties. I keep it simple, saying I have enough vision to get myself in trouble but not enough to always get myself out of it. Which is why I avoid trouble. As adventurous as Aunt Bea raised me to be, I don't take uncalculated risks.

After finishing my impromptu blindness in-service, I leave the smiling mother/son pair and redirect myself toward Tim Hortons. My flight to LAX doesn't board for another hour, so I have ample time to secure my sought after breakfast sandwich and make it to the gate to lose myself in my steamy romance audiobook. There's something delightful about listening to the swoony and sometimes illicit words of a favorite male narrator, with his hot guy voice, in public places. The idea of exposure makes the risk so much more rewarding. Whoever ends up sitting next to me on my flight home would, no doubt, turn a violent shade of red if they only knew what I was listening to.

Grinning, I stroll toward Tim Hortons. *Bless the airport gods!* I fight the urge to wiggle my hips, spotting only one other person in front of me. The sweet ecstasy of a multigrain breakfast sandwich and apple cinnamon tea is within my grasp. Besides seeing Trina, Tim Hortons was the only thing bringing me joy on this trip back to Buffalo. After moving to Seal Beach, California with Aunt Bea at seventeen, this Western New York staple was the only thing I missed. That includes my mother, who was already on husband number three at that time, and had *no* problem letting her teenaged daughter move cross country without her.

Whenever Aunt Bea and I went home, the first thing we'd do was hit Tim Hortons. Each Christmas, Mom sent us an assortment of teas, coffee, and hot chocolate from the retailer. Even this last Christmas. Though there's no longer a coffee drinker in the house.

I swallow the growing lump in my throat. Adjusting the large weekender bag on my shoulder, I force my focus to the back of the head in front of me. Only, in order for my gaze to actually land on the back of the man's head requires craning my neck. *How tall is he?* I'm five eight, but he's a giant.

"The card machine isn't working," the peppy cashier says to the tall man.

"Oh." His large hand slips to his pocket.

No doubt the action is to grab the wallet bulging from his back pocket and not to call attention to the way the faded jeans hug his firm backside. One that Trina would joke that she could bounce a quarter off. Although, I could think of far more pleasurable things to do with that ass.

Stop checking out his behind! Pushing my red-frame glasses atop my head, I twist my now extra foggy vision away from the tall man's cute butt. I mean, how would I feel if he was ogling me like I'm the last cupcake?

That might be a nice change. It's been a minute since someone looked at me with the same kind of covetous gaze that I'd used when looking at baked goods after that ill-begotten month I tried to give up carbs. Life's too short to not eat a cookie or ten.

"Shit!" he grumbles, closing his wallet. "Is there an ATM around?"

Second-hand embarrassment on his behalf flushes my cheeks. Few people carry cash on them. My always prepared motto means I'm not one of them. No matter what country I'm in, my wallet remains stocked.

The cashier taps the counter. "I think there's one down by gate twelve."

"Thanks. I'll run down and come back," he says, slipping his wallet into his back pocket.

Poor guy. My lips drag into a frown. Traveling is frustrating enough but to toss in an unnecessary trip across the airport terminal is obnoxious.

"No need, I got this," I offer, pulling my glasses back down. "I have cash."

"No, it's–" His words halt as he spins to face me. Beneath the brim of a blue cap, a smile curves at his lips. Its brightness is accentuated by his tidy dark beard.

A sudden swoop seizes my stomach, causing an explosion of butterflies. *That's new. Am I into men with beards?*

A navy Henley molds to his muscular frame. A fresh woodsy scent wafts from him, eliciting scenes of a pre-dawn walk through a dew-kissed forest. His entire aesthetic screams sexy lumberjack. Like someone who would press you against a tree, its rough bark biting into your bare ass, while even rougher hands held you in place.

Good lord, perhaps I need to cut down on my dirty audiobooks.

"That's kind of you, but I have cash. It's just in the bank." A gentle, barely noticeable Irish lilt mingles with his low gruff timbre.

I love the way unique voices tingle along my nerves. Perhaps my dulled vision heightens the way I hear the world, but I revel in the musicality of voices, picking out the unique notes that make each one distinct.

"Those pesky banks holding our cash hostage." My smile lifts, just a little bit more, with his soft chuckle. "It's really no big deal."

"Are you sure?"

"This will give me at least five karma points for the day." Stepping up, I join him at the counter.

"Are you in need of karma points?"

"Well, I did send my mother to voicemail this morning." *Twice.* But he doesn't need to know that.

This trip I lasted three of the five days I'd planned to stay at my mother's house, a new record, before I sought refuge. On day four, I retreated to Trina's, feigning that she had more reliable Wi-Fi for me to work from than the farmhouse my mother lives in with Charlie, her latest husband.

He grins. "I wouldn't want to get in the way of you reaching Nirvana."

"Thanks." I brush my long hair behind my ear, facing the cashier. "Can I get a large apple cinnamon tea and bacon, egg, and cheese breakfast sandwich on a multigrain bagel."

The cashier shakes their head, a big laugh bursting. "That's two apple cinnamon teas and bacon, egg, and cheese breakfast sandwiches on a multigrain bagel."

Twisted toward the man, my eyebrow arches. "Tea?"

He wags a finger. "That judgy eyebrow may cost you some of your karma points."

I gesture at him. "You just don't seem the *tea* type."

"What type do I seem?"

I frown and cock one hip. "Like 'drinks gasoline while eating a burger made out of the grizzly bear he just killed with his bare hands' type."

"That's preposterous," he scoffs. "Everyone knows moose make better burgers."

"I stand corrected." I laugh, pulling out my wallet.

After paying for our food, we slide down the counter. Drinks in hand, we stand waiting for our breakfast sandwiches. Other customers file up to the counter, while we remain in silence. Not uncomfortable or awkward silence, just companionable. Sipping my sweet, spicy tea, my eyes flick between the staff preparing our food and the sexy lumberjack beside me.

I play the game we all play when meeting someone: using the little external clues to put together a picture of who he is.

His clothes are comfortable and well-worn, but clean. One hand grips the to-go cup, while the other brushes the back of his head as if he's nervous.

Do I make him nervous? *No, that can't be.* Men like him make people nervous, not the other way around.

Gnawing on my lower lip, I try to think of the last man I made nervous. Besides Cael, Trina's fiancé who was terrified that her oldest and closest friend wouldn't give him the stamp of approval, the last man with a wisp of nerves around me may have been Alex. *Ugh, Alex.*

"Pen," I blurt.

His head tips to the right. "Pencil?"

Laughter bubbles out of me. "My name is Pen. Well, it's actually Penelope Meadows, but my friends call me Pen."

He grins. "Rowan."

Of course, his name is Rowan. That name radiates big D hot guy energy. Not a Herman or Stanley vibe about him.

"Nice to meet you, Pen." His hand envelops mine, sending a jolt of something zipping along my nerves.

I try not to fixate on that little tingle but have to admit failure. When was the last time my body reacted to someone like this?

"So, are you coming or going?"

Seriously? Coming or going? Who am I? I school my features into a pleasant smile stamping out the blooming wince at my non-stellar verbal skills.

"Excuse me?"

"Are you coming into town or leaving?"

"Both."

"Overachiever," I tease, pivoting towards him, and my arm brushes against his. My senses hum with the quick caress of his muscular body against mine.

He clears his throat. "I drove down from Hamilton, Ontario to catch my flight."

"So, where you heading to?"

"L.A."

"Me too!" I say with far too much pep.

What is wrong with me? I'm like an overexcited puppy. I should be cool and indifferent, not exclaim with the fevered devotion of two ten-year-olds exchanging friendship bracelets on the first day of camp.

"Well, *not* L.A. I live in Seal Beach, but LAX is a direct flight getting me the hell out of here sooner."

Why am I sputtering? *Awkward, party of one.*

"Not a fan of Buffalo?" He shifts, turning to face me.

"I have nothing against Buffalo as a city. People are nice. Love the wings. It's just…"

Stop talking, Pen! Do not emotionally vomit on this poor man. All he wanted was breakfast, not to have you overshare.

"…just prefer being home." I tighten my hold on Cane Austen's handle.

"Buffalo's not home?"

"Not anymore." I shake my head.

Rowan's hat brim shadows the upper half of his face, making it hard to read his expression. Reading facial expressions isn't my forte. Even with the limited vision I do have, it's often difficult to make out the tiny cues that can be found in someone's face. Aunt Bea always talked about the stories in the eyes. Those are stories I'm unable to read. If I'm close enough and the light is just right, I can make out some of the little eyebrow ticks, lip quirks, or forehead wrinkles.

My stories come from the voice and energy. Everyone has a kind of energy they exude. It may make me sound like the lady with a different crystal for each day of the week, but it's something I've learned to trust.

Right now, the energy coming off Rowan telegraphs annoyance, but I don't think it's directed at me. Despite my oversharing, his broad frame remains mere inches away. His obscured gaze fixed on me.

He nods. "I get it. I've only lived in L.A. for three years and it feels more like home than Hamilton where I grew up."

"Canadian boy, eh?"

He snorts at the terrible joke laced in my even worse Canadian accent.

Smirking, I raise my tea to my lips. "So, how did a nice Canadian lad end up in L.A.?"

His hand rubs his neck. "Work."

"What do you do for wo—"

"Christ," he groans, yanking out his cell from his back pocket. "Sorry, this is the fourth call in a row that I've ignored. I need to take this."

"Sure." I smile.

Holding the phone up, he grumbles, "This best be important." Pivoting, he strides away from the counter.

"Ma'am." The cashier holds up two bags with what I suspect are our breakfast sandwiches.

With a nodded "thank you," I take them. In literally five seconds, I've lost Rowan. Scanning the now bustling food court, he's disappeared into the crowd. Do I wait? Do I try to track him down? Do I just take his sandwich in hopes that I run into him again? What if he comes back and thinks I stole his sandwich? Although, I paid for it, so it's not stealing.

"Excuse me, do you see that man I was with?" I ask the cashier.

"He went over there." She points.

"Where? Can you verbally explain?" I hold up Cane Austen in a nonverbal reminder that pointing is not the best way to give direction to the visually impaired.

"Oh, sorry." The blush can be heard in her voice. "Far right corner... My right, not yours."

"Thanks."

Turning, I set off listening for his voice. Moving through the crowd, I make my way toward the far-right corner. Voice recognition is the best way for me to find people in large gatherings. Although, it's not ideal with someone I just met, there's something about Rowan's voice that has imprinted on me, both distinct yet familiar. Like nothing I've heard before but somehow something as well-known to me as my own.

"Damnit, I told you I don't want to do that," Rowan growls.

I halt. Not because I've found him, but due to the frustration underscoring his words. He's pissed.

"This is fucking bullshit."

Really pissed.

With his back to me, he carries on in an annoyed mutter with no idea I'm standing behind him, eavesdropping. It's not intentional, but I'm listening, nonetheless. Granted, my relationship with Rowan is five minutes old, but this anger reads wrong on him. Like an ill-fitting Halloween costume. Also, I'm not going to overthink my use of the word relationship.

Raking my teeth against my lower lip, I clutch the sandwich bag. I should turn, run away, and give the sandwich back to the cashier. Let them give it to the angry man. Not because I'm scared. There's no nip of fear telling me to stay away. Rather, it's more like witnessing someone do something they don't want to do.

"You're being a real motherfucker," he snarls, causing a few onlookers to clear their throats.

Ouch. I don't blame them. His tone is harsh.

Dropping his duffle by his feet, Rowan's rigid stance slumps. His free hand grips the back of his neck. The movement communicates regret.

"I'm sorry. That was uncalled for." Scuffing his sneakers along the floor, he lets out a beleaguered sigh. "I know. You're *my* motherfucker."

Aw. It's almost sweet the way it rolls off his tongue.

"We can discuss this when I get back. My flight gets in…" Pivoting, he comes face-to-face with me, mouth slack. "Pen." It comes out almost pained.

Crap! "I wasn't listening… Well, I was, but not intentionally. I—" I hoist up the Tim Hortons bag. "Breakfast!"

"Thanks," he says, drawing out the word and taking the offered bag.

"Sorry."

The muffled voice of whoever is on the other end of the call crackles between us.

"I should go." Frowning, I turn and hurry away.

So fricking embarrassing. Rowan is clearly having a day and I'm all like "Here I am holding your breakfast sandwich hostage while eavesdropping on your conversation with someone you fondly refer to as motherfucker."

Finding my gate, I fold myself into an uncomfortable plastic chair to devour my breakfast sandwich and fall into my latest audiobook. The sultry timbre of Wesley Williamson – my favorite narrator – helps me escape into the world of thousand-year-old hot vampires with Mr. Darcy vibes. The story being woven in my earbuds helps me leave the last week behind. Leave why I came back to Buffalo, the tension with my mother, and the awkward meet-cute with Rowan.

Rowan. My stomach flip-flops between a sigh and a flutter at the thought of him. I hope everything turns out okay with he and motherfucker. It seemed to have turned the corner before he'd caught me listening in. I scan the boarding area, wondering if he's here. He's not. At least, I don't see him which doesn't mean he's not here. He's bound for L.A. Are we on the same flight? The Buffalo-Niagara Airport is small, but not *that* small. There are several airlines flying direct to Los Angeles in this time window.

"Penelope Meadows, please see the agent at gate eleven's counter." A voice booms over the sound system, interrupting the vampire/awkward girl meet-cute.

Hitting pause, I sling my bag over my shoulder and shuffle with Cane Austen to the counter. "I'm Penelope," I say, reaching the agent.

"Ms. Meadows." The agent beams. "Your seat has been upgraded. I have a new boarding pass for you."

"Upgraded?" I blink.

"You're still in a window seat, but you've been moved to first class. Seat one-A. We'll start pre-boarding in a few minutes for our passengers with disabilities. Would you like assistance going down the jetway?"

First class from Buffalo to Los Angeles? Perhaps I had earned some karma points after all. Thanking the agent and telling them I wouldn't need assistance, I head back to my seat.

Pulling my phone from my pocket, I check my messages. Despite the frown, guilt swirls in my stomach at the four unread messages from my mother. Sighing, I open them and respond.

Me: I'm at my gate.

Mom: Good! Did you click on the links I sent you to those clinical trials?

Eyes closed, I release a hard breath. If it isn't messages about my love life, it's ones about studies to cure my eye condition. *She means well,* Aunt Bea's cautious warning plays on repeat inside me. Opening my eyes, I reply.

Me: I'll look at them when I get home, so I can see them on the larger screen. I'll message when I'm home.

It's a lie, but my energy for this familiar conversation is nonexistent.

I swipe to my message with JoJo, my West Coast bestie. Trina is insistent that I'm allowed two best friends if I designate them by coasts. Trina Lyons, who is two years older than me, was my first bestie due to close proximity. She lived next door until I moved with Aunt Bea to California. I met JoJo Rivers a year later as freshmen in undergrad.

Me: Flight is on time. You still picking me up at the airport?

JoJo: Does a hobby horse have a hickory dick?

Me: A simple yes would do.

JoJo: Then I wouldn't be me. Tongue out emoji.

I snort just a bit. Even with the magnification program on my cell, I have the worst time with GIFs and emojis, so JoJo spells them out for me. It's both sweet and totally self-serving because I'm a hundred percent positive that a majority of the GIFs and emojis that she spells out do not exist.

JoJo: How are you doing, BTW?

God, that's a loaded question. My heart aches just thinking about the many, many responses rattling around in me. How does one respond when their entire world as they know it has been ripped away in a single moment?

Me: Okay.

JoJo: Acceptance smiley face when your friend is pretending they are okay when they're not emoji.

Me: Middle finger emoji.

JoJo: Gasp emoji.

Me: These aren't real emojis emoji.

JoJo: I love you emoji.

Me: I love you too emoji. We'll have all the LAX to Orange County traffic to dig into how I'm doing. I promise.

JoJo: Excited social worker friend emoji.

Hearing them announce pre-boarding, I text goodbye to JoJo and slip my phone into the pocket of my denim jacket. The late June weather is warm, allowing me to sport my favorite pale pink cotton sundress, but the jacket will keep me warm on the plane.

I won't pretend that excitement doesn't crisscross inside me at turning left while boarding the plane. The first-class lifestyle isn't something I've indulged in. Outside of that all-inclusive resort Aunt Bea took me to in celebration of my master's degree. As first-class as I typically get is getting to skip the wait at Bread, my favorite breakfast spot in down-town Seal Beach, because Aunt Bea and I've gone there every Saturday for the last nine years. *Almost every Saturday.*

Ignoring the twinge in my heart, I follow the flight attendant to my seat in the front row, which means more leg room. It also means all my things have to go up top. Pulling out the things I'll want quick access to – bottled water, bag of trail mix, phone, and earbuds – I toss my bag into the overhead bin and plop into my seat.

Head pressed against the window, I lose myself in my audiobook which drowns out the flight's boarding sound-track – murmured apologies, cleared throats, and muttered, "I think that's my seat," and the repeated chastising of a passenger for blocking the aisle.

Someone takes the seat beside me. The furnace of their body laps against my skin. A fresh woodsy scent makes my eyelids flutter open. Straightening, I turn my face toward my seatmate.

"Pen," Rowan drawls.

Want to read the rest of the story?
You can grab the book here

ACKNOWLEDGMENTS

Just as Georgia has three sexy book boyfriends to help her with her story, I had lots of helpers. Only one was a sexy book boyfriend though (at least my sexy book boyfriend).

Book Boyfriends was born during a writers' retreat with Andrea Andersen and Ivy Fairbanks, who—if you paid close attention—I give some nods to in the book. Thank you, ladies for supporting me in so many ways!

This story is what it is because of my amazing editor, Gemma Brocato. Hell, I am the writer I am because of her. Thank you, my literary mama bear!!!

Meghan O'Brien, you are the peanut butter to my jelly. Hands down you are the best friend, alpha reader, and PA in the game. Thank you for your consultation as I crafted a thoughtful/sensitive portrayal of a woman with celiacs disease.

Milo, my pug, thank you for being my personal Wentworth. Every book I've written has had you riding shotgun. I love you, bubba.

My dear readers, I would be NOTHING without you. Without you, these are just words on a page, but you bring them to life. Thank you for letting me share my stories with you.

Thank you to Su from Earthly Charms for this beautiful/fun cover!

Finally, I need to thank my real life book boyfriend—my husband. Liam, there's a little bit of you in every MMC I create, because you've set the bar so high. I am so grateful for your steadfast support. You pushed me to write this book after I told you the idea, and I am so appreciative of that! Even if only your mom (thanks, Marie) buys this book, I am so happy I wrote it and am releasing it into the world.

ALSO BY MELISSA WHITNEY

Available wherever you get e-book, paperback, and audiobooks

All books are available in e-book, paperback, and audio. You can get books at Amazon.com: Melissa Whitney: books, biography, latest update or by requesting at your local library or indie bookstore. Signed copies can be purchased through Heartbound Book Shop: Where Every Page is a Love Story.

The Home Series

Finding Home - Book One

Coming Home - Book Two

Making Home - Book Three (Coming Soon)

The At First Series

At First Smile

Stand Alone Titles

In the Hello and in the Goodbye

Happy Ever Afterlife

ABOUT THE AUTHOR

Melissa Whitney, who hails from Western New York, is a contemporary romance author. As a legally blind woman much of Melissa's work focuses on the exploration of disability, mental health, and trauma through a heartfelt, sexy, and comedic lens.

Melissa's debut novel *In the Hello and in the Goodbye* released in April 2024, with a warm reception from readers for its thoughtful autism and mental health portrayal. Since then, she's released *Finding Home*, a Jane Austen inspired small town romance, *At First Smile*, an own voice hockey romance with blindness rep, and *Coming Home*, a *Little Women* inspired small town romance. Her work has been featured in several publications and on podcasts for its thoughtful, sensitive, and accurate representation of disability and mental health.

Ms. Whitney lives in Southern California with her husband and their rescue pug Milo. When not crafting her swoony stories, she's on the hunt for a pastry, brewing a cup of tea, and diving into her latest swoony romance.

To learn more about Melissa Whitney, you can visit www.melissawhitneywrites.com. Sign up for her newsletter to stay in the know with all things Melissa Whitney. Connect with her on social media (IG: @melissa_whitneyatuhor, Threads @melissa_whitneyauthor or Facebook: Melissa Whitney Author).

www.ingramcontent.com/pod-product-compliance
Lightning Source LLC
Chambersburg PA
CBHW071343300726
48976CB00006B/1753